THE DROP ZONE

SHANDI BOYES

Edited by
SWISH EDITING
Illustrated by
SSB COVERS AND DESIGNS

COPYRIGHT

Written by: Shandi Boyes

Cover: SSB Covers and Design

Beta: Carolyn Wallace

Editing by Nicki at Swish Design & Editing

Proofing by Kay at Swish Design & Editing

DEDICATION

For those suffering.

Remember the sun will always return no matter how strong the storm.

Shandi xx

ALSO BY SHANDI BOYES

Perception Series - New Adult Rock Star Romance

Saving Noah

Fighting Jacob

Taming Nick

Redeeming Slater

Wrapped up with Rise Up

Enigma Series - Steamy Contemporary Romance

Enigma of Life - (Isaac)

Unraveling an Enigma - (Isaac)

Enigma: The Mystery Unmasked - (Isaac)

Enigma: The Final Chapter - (Isaac)

Beneath the Secrets - (Hugo - Part 1)

Beneath the Sheets - (Hugo Conclusion)

Spy Thy Neighbor (Hunter - standalone)

The Opposite Effect - (Brax & Clara)

I Married a Mob Boss - (Rico - Nikolai's Brother)

Second Shot (Hawke's Story)

The Way We Are (Ryan Pt 1)

The Way We Were (Ryan Pt 2)

Sugar and Spice (Cormack)

Bound Series - Steamy Romance & BDSM

Chains (Marcus and Cleo)

Links (Marcus and Cleo)

Bound (Marcus and Cleo)

Restrained (Marcus and Cleo)

Psycho (Dexter)

Russian Mob Chronicles

Nikolai: A Mafia Prince Romance

Nikolai: Taking Back What's Mine

Nikolai: What's Left of Me

Nikolai: Mine to Protect

Asher: My Russian Revenge

Infinite Time Trilogy

Lady In Waiting (Regan)

Man in Queue (Regan)

Couple on Hold (Regan)

Standalones

Just Playin' (Presley and Willow)

COMING SOON:

Skitzo

Colby

BLURB

Look up 'cocky' in the dictionary—overconfident, arrogant, and has an answer for everything. That's Colby McGregor, third in line for the McGregor billionaire dynasty, adventure capitalist, and all-round pain in my backside.

It's my ability to siphon the attitude from his veins that brought us together, but it's the above points keeping me around. He brings out of a side of me no one else sees—*not even my fiancé*. However, our game of tit-for-tat isn't child's play. If we're not careful, more than my upcoming nuptials will be on the line.

The Drop Zone is a heart-warming romantic comedy with a cocky, swoon-worthy hero who'll prove not every story is meant to be read front to back. Sometimes, it's the pages that slip out of a book which are the most rewarding.

PROLOGUE

COLBY

"abian?"

When I slap the cheek of the three hundred pound piece of flesh strapped to the front of me, he doesn't rouse in the slightest. He's out for the count, the gift his family bought him to celebrate his sixtieth birthday not turning out as they had anticipated. He's not distracted by the California coastline we're hovering above like eagles in a near-perfect blue sky. His eyes are rolled into the back of his head, his body slumped in his harness.

This isn't the first time I've had someone pass out while skydiving. I've been pooped, peed, and puked on many times in my past three years of jumping, but this is the first time I've failed to find a pulse on my student's neck. Usually, they're unconscious due to a lack of nutrients. They get themselves so worked up before a jump, they either forget to eat or put the bathrooms at our headquarters to good use.

I didn't get the nervous-shitter vibe from Fabian. He's been a near-perfect student. He followed my instructions to the wire during our debriefing and wasn't the slightest bit fazed when I requested to check the weight he jotted down on the forms we make all first-time jumpers fill in. He looked a little heavier than the two hundred eighty pounds he put down. I was right. Not by much, but enough that some adjustments were required before we got in the air.

Our freefall was near perfect. Fabian screamed like a bitch, but he maintained the arch position as instructed. His head was back, his hips forward, and his legs angled at forty-five degrees. We had a clean deployment of the main parachute and was looking at bringing in a near-perfect landing until he threw a spanner into the works at three thousand feet.

"Come on, Fabian. Now isn't the time to test your ticker."

After executing a swoop, so our parachute crosses the ground at a rate faster than we'd usually descend, I pinch Fabian's flapping lips between my thumb and index finger to check he isn't choking on the puke he nearly succumbed to during our short waddle from our seat to the open airplane door.

I grow desperate when his throat comes up clear. I swoop again. To an inexperienced instructor, swooping at the wrong time can end fatally. Thank fuck for all involved I don't lack skills—neither in the sky or the bedroom.

When my canopy catches the westerly blowing off the scenic coastline, it gives us the push we need to descend our last two thousand feet at a faster rate than the jumpers who followed us out of our aircraft. Fabian isn't getting his money worth with this jump. We've barely been in the air for five minutes.

As the drop zone approaches, I signal to the ground crew that this isn't a standard landing. Thank fuck Tyrone is The

Drop Zone's coordinator today. He knows I don't fool around with shit like this. I'm all for having a good time, but when it comes to my clients, I'd never put their safety at risk.

My third swoop sees Tyrone jumping into action. He gets the safety officer on the ground, and within minutes, ambulance sirens sound in the distance. Now I've just got to land this without the assistance of a man nearly double my size strapped to my front.

A few feet from the drop zone, I pull down on the toggles to flare the chute with the hope it will give us a soft landing. Usually, I'd instruct my student to raise their legs, so my ass lands on the ground and theirs land in my crotch.

That isn't happening today.

I need to change things up. I've got the height advantage needed, so I won't look like a monkey clinging to his back, but I don't know if my ankles are up to the task of stopping over four hundred and seventy pounds of muscle and fat.

"Move, move, move!"

Fabian's family stops recording, suddenly comprehending that the low hang of his head isn't natural. And neither is our landing.

CHAPTER 1

COLBY

Two Years Later…

$\mathcal{W}$hen a persistent vibration on my bedside table disturbs the blonde going to town on my cock, I snatch up my cell phone and peg it across the room. Its crash with the only solid wall in my loft is barely heard over her giggle when I push her head back down, wordlessly demanding she finish what she' started.

It's not often I'm awakened by my balls being sucked into a warm and inviting mouth, so I'm not giving this up for anything. Tyrone can wait. Unwanted meetings with fuckface number crunchers who don't understand what I do can wait. I've got business to take care of, and it has nothing to do with the millions I've amassed the past two years replicating the thrill I experience when the hungry little minx sucking my dick rakes her teeth over the crest of my cock.

Her eagerness to have me coming undone is the best part of my job. With many universities being close to my business, The Drop Zone, we get a lot of college girls passing through our doors. Any buzz a fourteen-thousand-foot jump doesn't take care of, I'm more than willing to take up its slack. My job is to make sure my clients leave thoroughly satisfied. If part of their satisfaction is sucking my cock at ten in the morning, who am I to stop them?

There are no candlelit dinners, movie dates, or corny roller-skating afternoons at Venice Beach required to seal the deal. The adrenaline roaring through their bodies at the end of a terrifying jump already has them mistaking homeless bums as Chris Hemsworth, but my crystal-blue eyes, cut jaw not covered by an inch of scruff, and the appendage they feel digging into their ass when they're harnessed to my front has them looking at me like I'm a god.

And that's precisely what they call me when they shout my name from the rooftops.

That half an inch I'm sure I have on my big brother rams down the blonde's throat when the deep timbre of my business partner roars up the spiral staircase of my loft. "Don't make me come up there, Casper."

He must be pissed. The only time Tyrone calls me Casper is when I bed the girl he's chasing before him, or he's trying to ensure his daddy he didn't partner up with a rich, white kid—he owns him. Tyrone is straight-up African. African lips. African skin. African afro. *African dick.*

I'd rather not know his last trait. Unfortunately, I couldn't ignore it when he swung it around like Tarzan's vine at our annual Christmas giddy-up last year. I couldn't miss the fucker. It was large, long, and hideously emasculating to *any* man within a five-mile radius. It's lucky I'm just as stacked, or I might have crawled into my man cave and cried like a bitch.

Friendly ghost or not, this little white boy is packing heat. I've got the goods and am not ashamed to admit it. Who in their right mind would? Don't go acting like it's only guys who brag about their goods. Those tight white business shirts women are getting around in to spark equality in the workplace weren't invented by men. We wish we were that intelligent. They were designed by women for women, not just to showcase that men lose thirty percent of their brainpower when confronted by a nice pair of titties but as an indicator of our chances before we've even approached our target.

The math is simple—if she's buttoned-up to within a few millimeters of her collarbone, the only chance of you *ever* getting her wet is when you're flicking holy water at her chest while screaming "Hail Mary" at the top of your lungs. The risqué I'll-leave-one-or-two-buttons-undone-as-it's-a-little-hot-today aren't extreme as the preachers' daughters, but you'll have to work your ass off to slide from third base to home plate. That shit takes commitment, matrimony, and all that other whacked-up crap I have no intention of signing up for within the next decade—if ever.

Then you have the women who are confident like me. The ones who know what they have and are happy to flaunt it, but will still make you work for it. They're the three-button girls. Three buttons are the cheese on a Philly steak sandwich—the gooey heart-clogging goodness that holds the world together and makes everything that little bit tastier. They're the girls like Olivia who don't need a heap of false promises to participate in an all-night fuck session before waking you with the holy grain of womanism. She may be sucking my cock right now, but every woman this side of the country knows it is women like Olivia keeping this great country running.

If she has more than three buttons undone, run, mother-fucker, run! Those are the whack job, you'll-forever-sleep-with-one-eye-open girls, the ones who blow up your cell within five minutes of you leaving them alone and track you down when you're having a beer with your mates. I get it, the fourth button is tempting, you'll think what every naïve, horny man has thought before you—that you can handle the madness her fourth unbuttoning brings to the table.

Trust me when I say you'll never be prepared for the shit-storm she'll rain down on you. If forced to pick between One-Button Barbie or Four-Button Betty, you can be assured my money will only *ever* be placed on one thing—a first-class ticket to Ibiza.

"Nu-huh. Don't let his growl fool you. He's really a giant teddy." I push Olivia's lips back onto my cock before straying my eyes to Tyrone, who's just stormed into my loft, demanding I get my ass out of bed before he drags me out of it. "He knew what he'd walk in on *long* before he decided to interrupt us. Now he can suffer the injustice."

My last three words quiver when Olivia swivels her tongue on the underside of my knob. Her excitement about having an audience has me wondering if I miscounted the inches of her cleavage on display late yesterday afternoon. A miscalculation could be easily excused. She wasn't wearing a buttoned-up shirt, so I had to use the old metric scale. I've never been overly good at math, but I'm certain the leather strips on her skin-tight shirt were around the three-button mark.

Panic, that I've crept into the void I swore I'd never tiptoe into again, slips from my mind when Tyrone whacks me up the side of my head with the jeans I left sprawled on the floor last night. Olivia is as kinky as fuck—the thumb she's notching toward my no-go zone while cupping my balls is proof of this—but not enough for me to remove my belt from my jeans, meaning I not only get bitch- slapped with the scent of a hard-working man, the belt buckle I wear to give women an excuse to ogle my crotch adds more color to my pasty white cheeks than Olivia's hearty sucks.

Talk about a mood killer. No guy wants the scent of a man wafting up when he's getting his dick sucked—not even when it's his own scent. Thank fuck Olivia's sucks leave no doubt of her power. I won't even need to come at this rate. She'll just suck the jizz straight out of my sack.

The naughty thoughts in my head take a step back when Tyrone shoves his big ugly mug within an inch of my face. "I said no excuses. This meeting is unavoidable. Without insurance, we'll be shut down by the end of the month."

"Who needs insurance to cover little mishaps? I'm a multi-millionaire. I'm sure I can cover any lawsuits." I scoot up my bed, gaining a few millimeters between my anus and Olivia's exploratory thumb. She got a little eager when I mentioned my wealth. My sphincter nearly undertook a prostate exam twenty-six years too early.

Tyrone looks seconds from completing the exam with more than a thumb when he grumbles, "Your money won't be worth the paper it's printed on if you reschedule this appointment for the fifth time. Without insurance, our pilots can't legally enter the airspace above Cali. Without flights, our customers can't jump. Without jumpers—"

"Yeah, yeah. I get it."

"Clearly, you don't. Our meeting was scheduled for ten this morning on the dot. It's now ten fifteen. Get your ass out of bed and showered before Jamie arrives."

Tyrone doesn't often make fatal errors, but he just did.

"He isn't here yet?"

When he shoots his eyes away like lying is more perverse than watching his best mate get his dick sucked with nothing but a thin sheet for coverage, I nudge my head to the door, giving him his marching orders.

"As you said, our meeting was for ten o'clock sharp. If he can't fulfill his end of our agreement, then why should I?"

"Colby..." There's nothing but pure, I'm-going-to-shred-you-with-my-bare-hands rage in his voice. "Five minutes. That's it." With the growl of a man seconds from going on a rampage, Tyrone exits my loft as quickly as he entered it. His anger is understandable. I've got a trust fund to fall back on. He doesn't. If it weren't for his grammie selling the general store she's owned the past forty years, he would have never amassed the capital needed to get The Drop Zone off the ground.

My surname opens doors not many twenty-two-year-olds fresh out of college have access to, but even the bigwigs in the corporate world know not all trust-fund babies get their inheritance in a lump-sum payment. I'm capped to an annual limit—a limit I could live off without cause for concern until the day I die, but I'm not just a man with a panty-wetting face and a magic leg-opening wand for a schlong. I've got drive and inge-nuity, meaning I won't just emulate my big brother, Cormack's success, I'll trump it. Not only will I have the biggest dick with the McGregor last name, I'll also have the fattest bank balance. Put your money on it, ladies. I have this in the bag.

Just as I would this blowjob if I could get Tyrone out of my fucking head. He's deflating my cock as quickly as two new light aircraft, bonuses for our seventeen staff members, and the massive down payment our four-day adrenaline-hyped getaway drained funds from our business account. We're riding on this meeting more than the influx of clients seeking gift vouchers for the holiday season. Payment is upfront, so even if the gift receiver chickens out, we still get paid. It's a win-win for us *if* my insurance assessor gives me the green light.

Please, God, forgive me for what I am about to do.

After giving the big man a few seconds to hear my prayer, I tug Olivia's head in the opposite direction I've been shoving it all morning. "I'll most likely regret this for the rest of my life, but can I get a rain check?" My dick popping out of her mouth will darken my dreams for eternity.

"You want a raincheck? You're moments from coming. Can't he wait a few more minutes?"

I give her a look, one that reveals I'm letting her hair color give her some leverage. "You've got more than a few minutes to go." *If you can talk, more like thirty.* "But even if I were close to detonation, Tyrone can't wait. I've delayed this meeting for months now. I can't stall it any longer."

"But..." she drops her lip in a cute, I-want-to-fuck-her-face way, "... I wanted to hang out today? I don't have any classes until this afternoon, so I thought we could chill. Maybe download some movies? I could cook for you. You like lasagna, right? What man doesn't? I'll make that for you... from scratch. Then we can cuddle on the couch until I fall asleep in your arms. Aww, it sounds perfect, doesn't it?"

She leaps up to clap her hands together, mercifully lodging enough inches between our naked bodies, so I can slip out of my bed minus the stage-five clinger she's suddenly become. Several alarm bells are ringing in my head. They're all screaming the same thing—*You've stuffed up, motherfucker! She's a stage-five, four-buttons-undone clinger.*

"Betty… ugh, I mean Olivia. That sounds really nice, but I've got a business to run. I don't have time for couch cuddling." She drops her lip again. It does not affect me whatsoever this time around. You only get one chance to divert disaster. I'm not giving it up for anything. "Besides, I'm vegan, remember?"

"What?" She looks seconds from vomiting. She's not the only one. I like my meat when it isn't being served to me by psychopaths. "You ate pepperoni pizza last night."

"No." I laugh while shoving my feet into the jeans Tyrone slapped me up the head with. "That was slices of the tofu roll my momma makes especially for me. She knows how much I love pizza and didn't want me missing out on the food porn that comes with greasy packaging."

Olivia folds her arms in front of her chest—her naked I-really-wish-she-wasn't-a-clinger chest. "Your mom made the pizza we ate last night?"

"Yep." I raise my eyes from her tits to her face. "You couldn't tell the difference, could you? That's how good my momma is. She looks after her little snookie-bear so well, no one will *ever* take her place." If the vegan act doesn't have her running for the hills, I'm sure my momma-boy ruse will.

Alarm bells of a new type blast my eardrums when she murmurs, "Aww, that's *sooo* sweet. I love a man who loves his mother."

After meandering off the bed, she sashays to me standing frozen only a few feet away. I'm truly stunned. I've never had both my vegan and momma-boy ruse shot down before.

After slapping my cheeks with her hands, Olivia lowers her forehead until it braces mine. "Go make your momma proud while I shower. Once I'm no longer smelling like her son, I'll join you downstairs so we can joint-dial her. I'm sure she'll be more than eager to share a veggie-packed lasagna recipe with me. She'd do anything for *our* little snookie-bear."

Missing my bugged eyes, she spins on her heels and makes her way to my bathroom, her head flinging back when she spots my shattered cell just outside the door. "Don't go anywhere. With a broken phone, I'll have no way of tracking you down."

Does anyone know what the weather is like in Ibiza this time of the year?

CHAPTER 2

JAMIE

"*Y*ou piece of shit, ass-hat, pimple-faced virgin who couldn't find a clit if your momma drew you a map."

"Sorry, ma'am, what was that?"

My eyes stray from my clenched fists to the driver of my cab, mortified I expressed my thoughts out loud. I wasn't talking to him. I was cursing the idiotic salesman who sold me a 'supposed' top-of-the-line Lexus. He failed to mention it overheats anytime it goes over forty and that neither the heater nor the tire jack work. Thanks to him, I'm late for a face-to-face meeting I usually hold over the phone. I'm already pissed my boss is bending the rules for a client he should be glad to see the back of, much less the number of dollars racking up on the cab's meter. I have dollars to spend, just not on this.

I'm saved from explaining myself when my cab pulls into the entrance of the business I'm in the process of assessing for insurance. It will be wrapped up with a nice shiny bow the instant The Drop Zone's owners agree to the stipulations we added to their policy. Once that's done, we'll draw the exorbitant monthly premium they need for coverage, and I'll move on to less-demanding clients.

This one is more demanding because people pay them to jump out of perfectly good aircraft. Why is an assessment even needed? That's lunacy right there. We should just deny their request for insurance renewal and move on, but no, for some inane reason, Hugh, my supervisor, isn't seeing the risks I am. Being a skydiver, he often quotes there's more chance of dying from a bee sting than there is from skydiving. Clearly, he hasn't read the recent statistics on how many people in America are allergic to bees.

After handing my driver a bundle of greenbacks to cover my fare, I exit his cab. It's late October, but the weather is ridiculous. My satin blouse is sticking to my skin, and my wavy brown locks have more whitewash fizz than the sandy white beach I smell mingling in the air. The owners of The Drop Zone either spared no expense when they snapped up a prime spot on the California coastline for their business, or they have very impressive connections. The flat land separating the rugged mountain hinterland from the sandy white beach is the equivalent of a pot of gold under a rainbow. If their adventure-capitalist business ever fails, property investors will come knocking the very next day—if they aren't already visiting. Brad is right, this land is the ideal spot for an exclusive adult-only resort complex.

Brad is my fiancé. He works for Markham Properties Corporation. They're a multibillion-dollar investment firm that owns resorts all over the world. When a zoning permit was lodged for The Drop Zone two years ago, they tried to derail their campaign. They've been after this property for years, but the CEO of Attwood Electric had no interest in selling it. Supposedly, this land was purchased with the intention of building a replicate holiday house to the mansion he owns on the East Coast. It went wayward when the founder of Attwood Electric passed away, leaving his entire legacy in the hands of his eldest grandchild. Brad didn't go into much more detail except to say the CEO is a pompous, arrogant prick who needs to learn how democracy works. I'm not sure how politics came into the fight, but nothing stops Brad from going on a Republican rant when he has a few whiskeys in him.

I exhale a big breath before pulling open the door of The Drop Zone. The number of heads in the briefing room watching the safety video reveals they won't have any issues with skyrocketing insurance premiums. There are well over two dozen people in one room, on a Monday, before noon. *Wow.*

"You're late."

My eyes trek a young man I'd guess to be in his mid-twenties when he approaches me from a desk on my right. He has inky black hair, gorgeous dark skin, and sparkling brown eyes.

"You've missed the safety brief, so you'll need to fill in the old-fashioned quiz." He dumps a loaded clipboard onto the counter in front of me. It's a safety disclaimer. "It's a little hard to guess with the getup you've got on, but I'm leaning toward one hundred thirty-two, five-six, B cups... am I right?"

I tug the clipboard in close to my chest during his last comment.

He gives me a flirty smirk. "Don't worry. What you're missing in the front is certainly made up for in the trunk." He nudges his chin to a set of scales on my left. "Jump on. Let's see how accurate I am."

I'm about to tell him I'm here for a meeting when a word-stealing visual enters my sight. A smoking hot blond is galloping down the stairs at the speed of lightning. Since he's paying more attention to his footing than the shirt he's yanking over his head, I'm given a good three-second window to ogle rock-hard abs, glistening pecs, and the quickest peak of a tattoo that should be more amusing than sexy. If you ever accused this man of having tickets on himself, you'd be one hundred percent accurate. He has two lucky number seven raffle tickets tattooed on his right hip—just beside the scrumptious 'V' muscle I shouldn't be drooling over.

When he stops to stand in front of us, the scent of sweat-slicked skin streams into my nose. It's not the same stinky, sweaty pits' smell Brad gets every time he returns from the gym. It's more manly and sweet, which is an odd combination at this time of the day.

"Is she going up?" He nudges his head to me. Not long enough to drink me in as evidently as I did him, but long enough to linger on the three undone buttons of my shirt.

Wanting to put my best foot forward, I fasten my blouse while they talk shop. "Yes, but you're not taking her. I'll call in Drew, then you have no excuse to skip your meeting for the fifth time this month."

"A meeting with a shriveled-dick wannabe who can't arrive at the time he demanded? Let me take her up, then when we land, I'll reschedule."

"They were adamant this time around. Cancel one more time, and our insurance is canceled. He shouldn't be long. Perhaps traffic is heavy?"

When the dark-haired hottie glances past my shoulder, the truth smacks into me. They haven't clicked that I'm Jamie Burgess, supposed shriveled-dick wannabee from Metrics Insurance. People often confuse me for a man since most of my communications are done via email. Every once in a while, I added an 'xx' to the end of my messages with the hope they'd get the hint.

HR shut that down rather quickly. Allegedly, that's more hinting for a sexual harassment claim than disclosing my gender. Bob from Birkham Tires wasn't happy about my supposed proposition for reduced premiums. His tune changed when I was ordered to apologize for my mishap in person. It was too late for him by then. Bridges were burned, and hurtful words were already exchanged. Even if I could get past the fact he's twice my age with a receding hairline that matches my father's, he couldn't come back from that.

Recalling the reason for my trip down memory lane, I try to interrupt the two insanely handsome specimens with the integrity of a woman a few years older than them and light-years ahead in maturity.

I barely get in a word when the blond mutters, "I've got a four-button clinger upstairs."

I have no clue what his comment means, but the dark-skinned hottie certainly does. "A four-button clinger? Are you sure?"

The blond nods. "I did *both* the vegan and the momma-boy ruse. Neither worked."

A grin furls on my mouth when the man who greeted me gasps in surprise. I don't know him, but I'm certain he's acting. He has the whole I'm-a-shit-stirrer vibe going on. "Then, I guess you only have one choice..."

"Move to Ibiza," the blond murmurs at the same time his coworker chuckles, "Marry her."

The blond stops glaring at his friend when I add another option into the mix. "Or you could just tell her you're not interested?"

He stares at me like I'm crazy. Not a simple mind-your-own-business stare. He *stares*—more at my recently buttoned-up shirt than anything, but it's a pulse-quickening stare none-theless.

His stare-down takes an intermission when his coworker steps between us to give me his best customer service friendly face. "We'll be just a minute."

My greeter drags our interrupter out of my line of sight. I don't need to see them to hear their conversation, though. "You're not doing this again, Colby! You're attending your meeting no matter what you say or do."

The ruffling of paper creeps out from their hidey-hole. "I didn't want to do this, Tyrone, but you've left me no choice."

"No..." He sounds like someone just told him his cat died. "That's bullshit. You can't bring that out now."

"Why not? It can be used at any time, for any reason. Four-button clingers included."

I can't hear the words Tyrone mutters next. He's either not speaking or whispering very quietly. Too inquisitive to miss out on any form of gossip, I float toward the corridor where they're camped out. I pretend to peruse some brochures on the way and fix my hair in a mirror on the far wall before flat out sprinting to their side of the office. They didn't move their confrontation to another relocation. They're just not speaking loud enough to project their voices to the other half of their office.

With a roll of his eyes, Tyrone removes a cell phone from his pocket. "Fine. You're a fucking asshole for doing this, but I'll try and reschedule your meeting."

Colby's blond brow shoots up high on his face, his demands unfulfilled. Not needing words to hear his demand, Tyrone mutters, "And I'll make some excuse to get rid of the blonde upstairs, but if the media circulates a story about you having herpes, don't blame me. If she's truly a four-button clinger as claimed, it will take more than an I-love-my-mommy ruse to get rid of her."

I stop grinning at the relieved expression on Colby's face when my cell phone commences ringing. It isn't the standard ringtone you'd expect a thirty-year-old insurance assessor to have. It's a ringtone Athena installed specifically for my clients. It's Ice T's '99 Problems.'

She said I needed a song as nasty as my clients when their premiums jump the national standards, but their profit margin doesn't. I've been accused many times in the past eight years of fucking over my clients as if I'm a pimp, and they're my hookers, so her choice of ringtone is fitting—until Hugh switched my phone consultations to face to face.

Colby and Tyrone don't appear as appreciative of Athena's wit as me. They look as appalled as the sisters from St. Augustine Church hoping a fourteen-thousand-foot jump will bring them closer to God.

If I'm not already going to hell, I am now.

CHAPTER 3

COLBY

*a*s an original gangster tells us how he has ninety-nine problems, but a bitch isn't one, the brunette I was eyeing earlier delves her hand into her soft-leather briefcase. She's got the dorky businesswoman look down pat—silky blouse, tight pencil-pleated skirt, and thick-rimmed glasses balancing on her delicate yet noticeable nose. Her hair is dark, wavy, and out of control, and she has a slim, yet enticing body. If the glare off her glasses didn't veer me in the wrong direction, her eyes are aqua blue. She's pretty if you can look past her fully buttoned-up shirt.

I thought the only nuns I'd be handling today are the ones who come to The Drop Zone to get their rocks off in a way Jesus approves. I had no clue little Ms. Preacher would be visiting me as well.

The chuckle I'm barely containing barrels up my chest when the unnamed brunette's removal of her cell concedes with the loudening of Ice T's deep timbre. The more he tells us about the asses, tits, and whores he has, the more crowded the hallway becomes, but there's no denying the truth. The filthy, badmouth ringtone is coming from Ms. Prim and Proper's cell.

No fucking way.

Just as the brunette's thumb taps her phone, Tyrone drags his from his ear. "No answer. Do you want me to leave a message?"

I don't know if I'm a genius or a moron for trusting my intuition, but something has me demanding for Tyrone to call Jamie back. I've only had this gut-churning feeling once before. It was when I was facing O'Donnell's heart attack six-pound burger from the Irish pub a few blocks from here. My brain was certain I couldn't handle a meal bigger than my stomach. My ego had other ideas.

As usual, my ego won.

I don't know who the winner is this round when the connection of Tyrone's call occurs at the same time Ms. Fancy's cell phone blows up again. She's quick to shut it down, but not quick enough for this little black fox.

Well played, *Ms.* Jamie Burgess. Well played. Believing you were a man had me on the defensive. Now I not only need to switch sides to bring the real game into play—I have to jump ship entirely.

I'd be upset if I weren't looking forward to it.

After snatching my one and only IOU from Tyrone's grasp, I make my way to Jamie. My steps are extra swaggered, the excitement flaring from her eyes not hidden by her hideous glasses adding to my natural boastfulness. The lamb has been spotted by the wolf, and she knows it.

"Ms. Burgess, Colby McGregor, co-owner of The Drop Zone. I believe we have a meeting?"

Shocked by my sudden pleasant nature, she takes a step back before accepting the hand I'm offering. The situation goes from confronting to straight-up awkward when her hand slips into mine. The condensation fogging her glasses confirms her rising body temperature. I didn't need the addition of sweaty palms to seal my theory. My face alone has her heating up everywhere. Imagine the controversy when her body is strapped to mine?

Sometimes the game is just too easy.

Jamie removes her hand from mine before dragging it down her skirt like the sticky situation is coming from my side of our duo. My heart is beating a little bit faster, but that's only because I've got my game face on. It has nothing to do with the jasmine smell vaping off her skin.

Okay, maybe a smidge of my increased pulse is compliments of her scent, but it's only the teeniest tiniest bit. She's too goody two shoes for me. I like my girls with frayed edges. Ones not afraid to express their wickedest desires. You don't have to go down on me in a packed cinema, but I'd rather you not have any qualms about doing it in the back seat of a limo after a movie premiere.

Jamie doesn't just give off vibes that she's not a limo-fucking nympho. Her whole composure reveals she's most likely never sucked a dick in her life, much less any place she'd get busted for it, but it doesn't mean I can't use her naivety to my advantage, though. This is my business. I'll suffer any injustice for it, even wooing a fully buttoned-up brunette out of her no-doubt cotton panties.

"Did they step you through the process okay? Disclaimer? Weight?"

She peers up at me with big, panicked eyes. "I'm not jumping."

I flash her my trademark smirk, cocky dimpled-blemished top lip and all. "Ah, yeah, you are. Metrics Insurance thinks what I do is unsafe. I'm determined to show you it isn't." *And perhaps give you a thrill as you've most likely never been given.*

After removing her leather satchel from her hand and dumping it onto the pamphlets she was pretending to peruse while eavesdropping on my conversation with Tyrone, I guide her into the locker room to our right. She comes willingly, although she's a little heavy-footed.

Her eyes adopt the look of shock when I shrug off my shirt. I could have kept it on, but this is more fun. The tight-ass bumps in my midsection will drop her defenses as well as her jaw which just hit the floor. She's practically eating out of my palm—just as planned.

After putting on a jumpsuit all the instructors wear, I move to the harnesses and rigs in the secure cage of the locker room. She'd be lucky to weigh one twenty, but I bump it up to one thirty for the heaviness of her backed-up orgasms. I didn't realize how much those fuckers weighed until I stopped a blowjob mid-blow. I'm feeling all types of heavy.

"Do you want to jump in that?" I nudge my head to her stick-shoved-up-my-ass outfit. "Might get a little awkward when I harness you up."

I grit my teeth, telling my voice to step the fuck back. It was all hot and virile like I'm strapping her to a St. Andrews Cross to have my way with her, not the harness that will strap her to my body with her clothes still on. Don't misconstrue. Naked skydiving is a thing—just not a side business The Drop Zone hasn't ventured into yet. I never say never, so one day it could possibly steer that way.

Imagine the lawsuits then?

Ms. Prim and Proper pushes her glasses up her nose. "As I stated earlier, I am not jumping. I'm here to discuss a fair and responsible solution for the... w-w-what are you doing?"

The switch-up in our conversation is my fault. Dropping to my knees in front of her to forcefully place her foot into a jumpsuit opening is already stuttering material, not to mention the way my hands flutter along the silky-smooth skin on her thighs when I raise it to her curvaceous hips.

When she glares at me, waiting for an answer, I say, "Getting you ready for our jump... *duh*." I blame a lack of brain cells for my last words. I didn't get much sleep last night, so my mind is still on the head between my legs. The statistics about men having sex on the brain ninety-nine percent of the time is true. I'm living proof of this.

Once I have her zipper in place and the brunette's freshly shampooed hair pulled out of the collar, I grab a harness from the bench at my side, then once again fall to my knees in front of her. I'm not a guy who takes no for an answer.

Don't get your panties in a twist. My statement doesn't include the bedroom. If you say no there, I'll be out the door quicker than I was outrunning the four-button clinger ten minutes ago. I don't have to coerce you between my sheets, just as you sure as hell don't have to tell me no twice, but this is different. The anal pricks sitting in the Ivory Tower at Jamie's firm think The Drop Zone would be better run without me behind its helm. Their pretty darn close, but since they forgot to include Tyrone in their assessment, they're not one hundred percent accurate.

I can't take no for an answer this time around. I have to show Jamie *all* my skills, and since I've just spotted the big-ass diamond on her ring finger, it will need to occur with my clothes on. I don't mow another man's turf—*ever*. Tease them about it, pretend I'm considering it, but if he's spent enough time watering it to put a ring on her finger, you can sure as hell be guaranteed I am not cutting it.

"This isn't necessary. I'm here for a face-to-face consultation, not lessons on being a moron without a *brain*."

Her last word comes out somewhat *purr*-ish which is from me tugging on the straps of her harness right near the band where her lace panties commence. Yeah, I caught sight of the sexy lace combination she's wearing when I forcefully shoved her feet into her jumpsuit. Sue me.

Actually, don't. A lawsuit is the reason for Jamie's visit. I sure as hell don't want another one.

"You good? Not too tight or restrictive?" I stop myself just before asking, *Have you ever been tied up like this before?*

If her inflamed cheeks are anything to go by, I highly doubt it. Ms. Preacher's ringtone doesn't match her mannerisms. She's so stiff, I'm beginning to wonder if her husband-to-be proposed with the *hope* to mow her lawn on their wedding night.

"I'm good. I'm fine." She doesn't sound it. "But I'm still not jumping out of a plane."

She follows me into the cage where I switch out my dual parachute for a single one, my plan altering when I realized it will most likely get me sued. My second proposal isn't any better than my first, but since it doesn't involve the aircraft we're trying not to get grounded, it's more plausible.

"Hugh..." she stops, screwing up her nose. "Mr. Barnett believes it's best for all involved to settle with Mr. Celest out of court. It will increase your premiums, but with the costs spread out over the lifetime of your policy, it will impact your business less, thus allowing it to continue operating at its current capacity, although more stringently than it is now."

While shrugging on my parachute and securing it at the front, I shake my head. "Fabian isn't suing us—"

"You," Jamie corrects.

I give her a look, one that warns I'm about to throw her out of a plane without a parachute. "Fabian isn't suing *me*. It's the insurance company of the holiday club where he purchased his travel insurance. He jumped. He loved it. Then he had a fucking heart attack."

"He had multiple coronary artery failures that resulted in a triple bypass, four weeks in the hospital, and a rehabilitation bill in the millions, all of which Metrics Insurance is footing the bill."

"Because he had one hundred pounds of fat strapped to his midsection. How the fuck is that my fault?" When my raised voice gains me the attention of the nuns milling in the hallway, I lower it. "This isn't about Fabian. It's about the hierarchies so far up *Hugh's* ass..." I say Hugh's name like he's a pedophile, "... they aren't seeing the whole picture. I'm The Drop Zone. This is me." I wave my hand around the locker room. "Without me, it will fail. That's why those *stringent measures*..." I air quote my words like a man without a cock, "... you're attempting to bring in before approving our coverage will *never* happen."

Needing some air before I dig my hole deeper, I make my way outside. It may also place *Ms.* Jamie Burgess into the trap I'm setting. Tyrone is loading the nuns into an aircraft on my right, so I veer to the left. Jamie follows me like she's a tick, and I'm a dog in desperate need of a bath. I am, but we'll save that for another day.

"I understand your frustration, Mr. McGregor, but can you take a moment to see it from our perspective?"

She stops within an inch of my back when I pivot around to face her. She's so close, the angry breaths pumping out of my nose fog her glasses. "Have you always been a number cruncher?"

She pushes her glasses up her nose when its scrunch drops them half an inch before nodding.

"Is it what you've always wanted to do? Did you dream about facts and figures and insurance premiums until your panties got moist?" When her brows furrow, I snicker under my breath, "Figuratively. I get it, Prim, you're untouched and pure. You don't need to spell it out for me."

She's taken aback by my nickname, but she nods all the same.

"Then imagine being told you can't do it anymore. Take off that fitted skirt that showcases your curves in a way your low shoulders are trying to conceal. Remove your silky blouse that can't hide how erect the cool breeze blowing off the coast makes your nipples, then do something else. Something that doesn't make your blood pump and your pussy wet. Go be... meh. Plain. Boring. Unlike you. That's what your company is trying to do to me. They want to muzzle me with bureaucratic tape all because a man got so excited, his heart couldn't keep up with the thrill."

"That's not entirely true, Colby." I'm as shocked by her informal salutation as she was when I mentioned her erect nipples. "You broke your ankles... both of them. That makes you a liability."

"How?" I give her a look that makes it seem as if I said a lot more than I did. "I landed safely, administrated CPR, and brought my jumper back from death with both my ankles fractured from my boots up, yet I'm standing before you now, ready and capable to jump."

"But legally incapable. We can't insure you to jump—"

"I'm already insured."

"Until December. But after that, there are too many risks… risks Metrics Insurance isn't willing to take."

"Metrics Insurance or you?" I step closer to her, so close, we share the same air. "I've been cleared from doctors across the country. I've undertaken endurance test after endurance test. I even jumped with the supervisor of your division strapped to my chest, yet those still aren't enough hoops for you, are they, *Ms.* Burgess? You still want me out on my ass."

"This isn't about what I want. It's merely protocol."

"Protocol?"

When she nods, I glare at her. She's full of fucking shit, and I'm about to rat her out as the conniving vermin she is. This has nothing to do with protocol. It's the butt-sniffing stiffs who don't understand what I do. The ones who think a thrill is cracking open a bottle of wine before five o'clock or sneaking a sniff of their wife's dirty panties when she leaves for her bi-daily church sermons. The butt-clenching motherfuckers who want society wrapped up in bubble wrap to ensure we don't get any boo-boos. Protocol my ass. I'll show her protocol.

"W-w-what are you doing?"

Her stammer is just as cute the second time around as it was the first. Pity I'm too frustrated to let it calm me down. "You've got a bee in your hair. Quick, spin around before it stings you."

Squealing, she pivots, her hands shooting up to her hair as quickly as I hook my harness into hers. I roll my hips upward, hoisting her feet from the ground as if my crotch is a big crane.

It is, but I figured you'd already know that by now, so I didn't need to spell it out for you.

I shouldn't like the meow that purrs from her mouth when her backside gets friendly with my crotch, but I do. It never gets old, no matter how often it occurs. "You don't believe my ankles are capable, so how about I show you they are?"

Jamie tries to dig her heels into the sandy soil beneath my feet when I commence moving. It does her no good. I've got eight inches on her in height, let alone the fact I'm clutching her thighs like my crotch is attached to her front instead of her back.

When her physical endeavor to stop me fails, she resorts to words. "Colby. No. Don't. Please. I'm scared of heights."

Her words are separated by the big pumps my legs do when I break into a sprint. She thinks I'm running for the plane Tyrone is in the process of filling with willing participants. She's dead wrong. I'm wearing a single parachute, meaning we need to stay close to the ground to get her rocks off.

"Colby, Jesus Christ, don't!"

This plea didn't come from Jamie. They're Tyrone's frantic begs for me not to siphon our business down the gurgler. He's spotted the direction of my sprint. He knows I'm charging for the sheer cliff edge that borders The Drop Zone. I've told him for months its ideal for base jumping, so Jamie isn't the only one learning a lesson today. Tyrone is as well.

"Oh my God. I'm going to die before I've even lived. I wanted a puppy and kids with hippie names and dirty faces. A house with a plunge pool, and a car that doesn't overheat once it hits forty. I haven't achieved any of those things yet. So, please, God, don't kill me."

The fact Jamie missed mentioning her fiancé during my

sprint should slow me down. Unfortunately for all involved, I've been accused more than once of having more than a screw loose.

"Open your eyes, Prim, because this is as close to heaven as you're going to get for another sixty-plus years," I say a mere second before leaping over a three-thousand-foot rockface with a screaming insurance assessor strapped to my chest.

CHAPTER 4

JAMIE

I scream the first thousand feet of our jump where we tumble like a tennis ball in a dryer. Then I curse blue murder for the next thousand feet where we soar like eagles. Now I'm summarizing how I'm going to kill Colby McGregor in my mind. It will be a slow and painful death occurring after I've ensured his insurance coverage has only one beneficiary—me. The millions of dollars he's in the process of draining his bank account will make a nice indent in the counseling I'll need after this ordeal.

First, I had to act nonchalant to his hands running up my inner thighs like he was a gynecologist about to give me a pap smear with his tongue, then I had to sidestep his interrogation knowing everything he was saying was true. Now, I'm gliding in the air, struggling to ignore a girth the world's biggest belt buckle couldn't detract from.

Today has been a horrible day, and it's only just beginning.

"Land or sea landing, Prim? I'll let you pick."

"For one, stop calling me Prim..." I pause to wipe away the dribble I wasn't expecting since my lips are flapping more than Mick Jagger's would if they got stuck in an air vent, "... my name is Jamie or Ms. I'm-going-to-sue-the-pants-off-you Burgess." I stop again when Colby snickers so I can curse my stupid adrenaline-thick blood for mistaking his witch-like cackle as sexy. "Two, land wherever the hell you like. It won't change anything. I'll murder you whether you're on the land or in the sea."

"Wow, *Ms.* Prim has a personality. Where do you hide it? Behind those hideous glasses that slipped off your nose during our first tumble? You should wear contacts. Keep those pretty eyes uncovered for the world to see." I peer back at him over my shoulder, wondering how the hell he can see my eyes from his vantage point. I fall straight into his trap—again. "Ah, there they are. I was right. Much better without the glasses."

I roll my eyes as he tugs on the tethers of the micro-strip of material between us and the beautiful, yet equivalent of concrete if-you-land-on-me-the-wrong-way beach below. "You're buying me a new pair."

"Of balls? Or..."

I fold my arms across my chest with a huff, giving Colby the response he wanted. After securing his arms around me in the same manner, he discharges the parachute saving us from rejoining God's dirt in an unpleasant manner.

"W-w-what are you doing?"

I swear my vocabulary is usually more extensive than this. Unfortunately, I've got too much adrenaline surging through my veins to think of better responses. And yes, I had it before Colby threw us off a cliff's edge like a deranged man. I'm also panicked out of my mind. I wasn't joking when I said I'm afraid of heights. I am reasonably sure I left my heart somewhere back at The Drop Zone because there's no way it's with me right now. If it were, I'd be flapping my arms like a beheaded chicken before saying my final goodbyes. I guess you can't really fear death when you're halfway there.

"You seem hot. Figured I'd cool you down. Plug your nose, Prim, or you'll have more than horniness as an excuse for the wetness of your panties."

"I swear I'm going to *kill you.*" My last two words are muffled since I plugged my nose with a scream.

"Now straighten those sexy legs of yours. Keep them nice and still."

I go as straight as a board, not because he asked me to but because of how close his lips are to my ear. Is it just me, or is it odd he smells like pepperoni and cherry lip gloss?

"When we land in the water, I'll swim us to the surface before untethering our harnesses. You don't need to swim. Leave the leg kicking to me. I like my nuts where they are."

If you push aside the sexual ambiguity in every comment he makes, he's treating our jump as if it's something particularly uneventful. It's as if this is something he often does. If it is, we'll have more issues than we already do. He didn't just step over the line today—he's broken rules I haven't even thought up yet.

"Here we go, Prim. We're about to hit the water. Remember... no kicking."

I nod a mere second before the surprisingly refreshing water of the California coast swamps my ankles, surges up my body, then drenches my hair. We pierce through the water so deeply, my legs instinctively kick out, praying I'll reach the surface before the minute bit of air in my lungs runs out.

Colby groans, mumbles something I can't understand since

we're immersed in salty water, then commences our swim to the surface. Mercifully, the two broken ankles he suffered while landing him and Mr. Celest doesn't impede his swimming capabilities. Our heads bob out of the water just before my lungs start screaming about a lack of oxygen.

"You owe me a new pair of nuts."

I wait for him to release me from his front, spin around, then splash him with a heap of water. "Since they're already smashed, I may as well take advantage."

He looks at me confused. It's settled when I use his crotch as a springboard so I can commence my swim to shore. Well, I hope I'm heading in the right direction. I don't wear glasses to hide my appeal as Colby seems to think. I damn-well need them to see.

Several strokes later, and a near coronary from something brushing past my leg, Colby floats up to my side. "Jump on." He nudges his head to his back that somehow lost its harness and jumpsuit between our landing spot and me.

"No. I'm fine."

Picture a set of dentures floating in the bathtub after your grandma spat them out laughing. That's the halfhearted splash my arm does when I endeavor to swim away from him. It's weighed down with exhaustion. Who knew such a rush of endorphins was so energy-draining?

"Prim—"

I shoot Colby a wry look that not even the midday sun glaring off the ocean can hide.

"Ja-*mie*." He says my name as if he hates it as much as me. "Get on. I'm responsible for your midday swim, so I should make sure you get back to the shore safely."

"Are you sure my safety should be your utmost priority?

Because once we get back on solid ground, I'm going to crash every fantasy you've ever had—"

"Like you already are?"

I tread water, both shocked and upset. He didn't ask his question like he was seeking an explanation. He said it like it's factual—like not jumping will literally kill him.

Before I can demand a better explanation, he jerks his chin to his back. "Get on. I'm not asking. I'm telling."

I've heard you appear weightless in water, but it's proven in the most ridiculous way when he seizes my wrist, drags me toward him fast enough I create a wave, then tosses me onto his back. I cling to him as he swims us to shore, thrilling body surfing and all.

When we reach the water's edge, I wiggle, requesting to be put down. He ignores me, his trek through the white sandy beach proving his ankles are more than capable of withstanding impact during parachuting. I already know this as the many medical reports I've read the past four months reiterated that, but there are too many risks associated with The Drop Zone's insurance renewal that aren't sitting right with me. If there is any chance Colby will make Metrics Insurance liable in the future, I have to squash it before it occurs.

Throwing me off a cliff without a signed insurance indemnity waiver is *not* a good start.

CHAPTER 5

COLBY

"*A*re you sure you want to catch a cab home?"

I pace away from Tyrone and Jamie, certain I'm not up for more glaring. I get it. I fucked up, so Tyrone doesn't need to keep glaring at me like he is. Not going to lie. I'd do it again tomorrow if given the opportunity. Yeah, Jamie is freaked. Her eyes are wide, her lips are trembling, but the width of her pupils reveals a glint I'm not even sure she's seen in her eyes before. She's got that sheet-clenched, toe-curling, just-screamed-my-lungs-out gleam all women wear when leaving my presence. She just didn't get it from wrestling with me beneath the sheets.

Pity. She might have gone a little easier on me if that were the case.

All the flirty sweetness her face was harboring when Ice T told us about his bitches is gone, replaced with a lady I'd usually play hooky with. It's probably because she's lost her snooty attitude right along with her shimmy shirt. Her messy locks are even messier since they're sitting on top of her head in one of those buns college students make sexy. Her cami—that's still drenched from our escapades—is peeking out of the jumpsuit Tyrone promised would remain on solid ground at all times, and her wiped-clean-by-a-saltwater-blast face can't hide the tiny freckles that adorn her nose. With the dorky business-woman look cleared away, she's got a cute, funky vibe going on.

As Tyrone escorts Jamie to the foyer, she peers up at him with her big aqua-blue eyes in full force—the same eyes that stared at me in awe only an hour ago. "I'm fine. Really. Once I'm in a fresh set of clothes and washed the ocean out of my hair, I'll be good to go."

Great. Now I have images of her in the shower playing through my head. Like I need to add more fuck-ups to my catalog today. I already told Jamie her legs are sexy, her eyes are pretty, and I pretty much insinuated I dumped us into the ocean because she was 'wet' for me.

I guess it could be worse. She could have come out of the ocean swinging like she warned before I threw her on my back. I fully expected her to, so you can imagine my surprise when she placed herself between Tyrone and me when his arrival at the beach came with a threat to beat me until our skin tones matched.

Can you blame a man? Not Tyrone's response. Mine. Every-thing I said was true. Metrics Insurance isn't riding my ass because I pulled a stunt like I just did. They want me out of the game. Sidelined. Fucking benched. I live for this life. I aced business school, sucked up the board members asses at Attwood Electric to lease the land The Drop Zone is situated on, and ate my greens like a real fucking saint to get my business off the ground. And now, I'm set to lose everything because a man's ticker couldn't stand a rush of adrenaline.

If Fabian went into cardiac arrest at a strip club in Vegas, nothing would have been said. But because it happened doing a sport—yeah, you heard me right, what I do is a sport—he not only has the right to sue me for millions of dollars, he could also stop me jumping altogether.

When the insurance company came at me with the news I was being sued, I was shocked. Fabian's accident occurred two years ago. He's all but recovered now, and he's one hundred pounds lighter, so to say I was shocked would be an understatement. A major one. I tried to reach out to him at the start of the proceedings, but my attempts were forever shut down by his lawyers—yep, you heard me right this time around too. Lawyers, with an 'S.' He has over a dozen of them, and they don't want my money, they want me.

I followed the rules. I borrowed a button-up shirt and tie from my brother, rocked up to court a good ten minutes before the proceedings started, then offered a chunk of cash that would have me living without an allowance until I was dead for half a century.

What did I get for it?

Nothing.

Sweet fuck all.

Zilch.

Fabian didn't even show up. That's when I began ignoring my lawyers, insurance consultants, and business partner's advice. I went back doing what I did best—feeding the adrenaline junkies of America. It was a good four months until the email of one *Ms.* Jamie Burgess landed in my inbox. Now it's specialist appointments, business proposals, and phone consultations where I'd rather stab a pen in my ear than be marked off the attendance roll.

Do you know not even a billionaire can operate a company in this great country of ours without insurance? No, me neither. I found that out the hard way.

Before you get excited. I'm not the billionaire. My brother is. It's technically the Attwood Electric fortune, but with his name at the top of the list, he gets the right to be called a billionaire. I'd feel sorry for him if it wouldn't risk the burden being placed on my shoulders. Cormack is good at what he does. He keeps America's love of energy on the go, so they can blare his little side business' records out of their speakers. Cormack owns Destiny Records. His love of music has always been as diverse as my love of adventurous sports. He wouldn't be half the man he is if he didn't pursue his dreams—just like I won't be if Jamie pulls the rug out from beneath mine.

If only she didn't have that big sparkly ring on her finger because then my fate would be sealed with a big shiny bow.

Talking about fate, I better dodge this one. With my adventurous morning taking up a portion of Tyrone's time he doesn't have, I am sure he's failed to exterminate the rodent left in my loft. Stage-Five Clinger is making her way down the stairs with her eyes locked on me. They leave no doubt of my horrid miscalculation yesterday afternoon, but even if they did, the three buttons she left undone on the shirt I mentioned borrowing from my brother earlier all but confirms it.

It's three buttons, you say.

So why are you so freaked out, you say.

Because three buttons on a male shirt are the equivalent of having no buttons done up on a female shirt. This couldn't get any worse if I tried.

"You shouldn't take a cab home in your condition. Let me drive you."

Jamie's groan sounds like an orgasm leaving her lips. It has me picturing things I shouldn't be picturing, things I shouldn't be thinking about much less imagining in cock-thickening detail. I know what you're thinking too. What changed between me throwing her off a cliff—*not quite that, but you get the idea*—and now? *Heaps.*

For one, do you have any idea how much buzz you get from base jumping? It's as addictive as skydiving, but the edge of danger it creates makes it more thrilling. Add that to the fact Jamie followed my every demand without so much of a whim. She crossed her arms, straightened her legs, and plugged her nose like she's been under my command for years.

That's thrilling.

It has me thinking recklessly.

And has me hearing her sexy-ass groans as moans.

Jamie shoots me a look as if she'd rather jump off a cliff again than accept my offer of a ride. With Olivia's target locked and loaded, her thoughts are appetizing, but I don't have time to rig us up. We need to leave, and we need to leave now.

"Come on, this way. My car is out back."

I replace Tyrone's arm that's clutching Jamie's shoulder a little more dotingly than a helpful employee would with my own before making a beeline to the back entrance of The Drop Zone, missing Olivia's entrance in the foyer by a mere nanosecond.

"The cab is already on its way. I can't cancel it."

"Sure, you can." I walk quicker, kicking up dust with my boots. "You came, you saw, you conquered. Sidestepping a cabbie is the next step. With how quick you're learning you'll be skipping restaurant bills before you know it."

She gasps like there's no possibility of that ever happening, but the dip of her body into my low-riding car steals her reply. Jamie's mouth falls into a shocked 'O' when I slip into the driver's seat before jabbing the start button. My ride is fast, sleek, and sexy. If you minus the fast part of my comment, it represents its owner to a T. No girl wants to play Sheet Twister with a guy who blows his load quicker than it takes to unfold the board. If he fucks you faster than he undresses you, it's time to get yourself a new man.

As we skid out of the backlot of The Drop Zone, Jamie slides her phone out of her leather satchel. She swipes the screen before her finger taps on gleaming glass. She doesn't have those manicured nails that make a *tap tap tap* noise. They're clean and clipped without the slightest bit of polish. I already knew she wasn't a girly girl, but now it's cemented in concrete.

"There. Done. Canceled." Jamie spins her uncracked phone around to show me she canceled her cab before the driver left the depot. She appears pleased with herself. "Now we've avoided one disaster, how about we face another?"

I roll my eyes at her question before increasing my speed. Yeah, it's immature, but did you expect any less?

"Ignoring this won't make it go away, Colby."

My eyes stray from the road to her. "I know that." When she gives me a look as if I told her I'm shy, I add, "I do. I just..." *fucking hate that I'm paying more attention to your lavender scent than the fact you're trying to castrate me,* "... don't like talking about myself."

"Colby McGregor, entrepreneur, youngest member on

Forbes' watch list, and all-round playboy with seven hundred thousand Instagram followers doesn't like talking about himself? What's the world coming to?"

I flash her a wink, loving that she did her research on me. "That's all an act. The real me is a dorky Sci-Fi freak who'd rather watch *Star Wars* than interact with members of the public."

"Ha! You, shy? *Please.* Don't think I don't know what that was all about." She wiggles her finger in a rolling motion like my sprint from Olivia was done with a firing gun, white lines marked on rolled turf, and my competitors wearing spandex no man should *ever* wear. "If you're shy, I'm Mother Theresa."

I arch a brow, mocking her for stroking her brush on an already-finished masterpiece.

"You think I'm Mother Theresa?" Her voice could only be higher if she had balls, and someone was crushing them. "Why? How?"

"Where are we heading?"

She peers at me in shock, stunned by my swift sidestep of her interrogation. That's not what I'm doing. I'm just trying to work out if I should give her a short answer or a long one.

When I say that to her, she rolls her eyes, having me wondering if she is as old as I first thought. I was putting her in the mid-to-late-thirties bracket—she doesn't look that old, she just acts it.

"Considering I'd most likely get fired turning up to work like this, I guess I should get changed."

There she goes again, reminding me she's about to get naked.

She chews on the corner of her lip in a cute One-Button Barbie way while inputting an address into the map app on my console. After she has her details entered, it tells me we have twenty minutes to fill with conversation. *Great.*

"Question for question is the only way I operate. And I get to go first because it's rare for me to *come* first."

Jamie makes a face like she vomited a little. "Those lines don't really work, do they?"

"What did I just say? Let a man be first for a change. Jesus, woman! It won't kill you."

As she struggles not to laugh, her lips tug into a grin. "Fine. You go first."

She thinks by caving to my demand, I'll keep things professional. She's dead fucking wrong. "Does your fiancé love you?"

I swear I hear her neck pop when her head jack-knifes to me so quick, she gives herself whiplash. She blubbers out a string of unintelligible words before anger clears her sentences of gibberish. "Yes, of course, he does. Why would you ask something so ludicrous?"

"Big ugly overstated ring." I nudge my head to the monstrosity on her ring finger. It's at least six carats but has a handful of imperfections that shows he didn't pay any attention when picking it. He just went for the flashier one, signs he is as disinterested in his wife-to-be as he was choosing her ring.

Jamie covers her ring with her opposite hand, protecting it from the bitterness of my words. "It was his grandmother's!"

Her lie doesn't eat me away, but it does her.

"He *said* it was his grandmother's." Her tone is less harsh this time around, de-volumized. "I found a receipt last month. It wasn't for a resize. That doesn't mean he doesn't love me, though. He just wanted to ensure the ring was big enough for guys to get the hint." She wiggles her hand in the air, sending rainbow hues bouncing around the cabin of my car. "Did it work?"

Yes, yes, it fucking did, is what I want to say. Instead, I go with, "But you would have preferred something more understated, prim, and feminine." *Something more like you.*

I begin to wonder if she heard my thoughts when she asks, "Why? Because I'm understated, prim, and feminine?" She doesn't express her words as I did, instead she says them in a tone that's as low as her shoulders have now sagged.

"You're feminine. There's no denying that. *Right?*" That brings back some of the smirk my interrogation lost. "We already know you're prim, Prim, so we can cross that one off."

Jamie folds her arms in front of her chest with a huff. "So that only leaves understated. The most mundane, minimalist way to explain someone who bores you to death."

"Or…" I leave her hanging a little, not willing to show my hand too quickly. "Someone who doesn't require bling to show their true self. They stand out even without the glitter. They don't have to be the life of the party. They simply want to enjoy the party."

My reply cuts her deeper than she'll ever admit. She even gets a little misty-eyed, exposing I've hit the nail on the head. That's why I asked the question. I don't even know her, but I do know Jamie hates the ring she will be wearing for the rest of her life.

"Tell him you hate it."

Her eyes snap to mine quicker than a rocket. "What? *Nooo!* That's straight-up rude."

"No, it isn't. Asking someone to marry you with *that* ring is rude."

Jamie laughs, assuring me she heard my comment as I had intended—obnoxiously playful.

"Brad can't help it. He's showy like you."

Ouch! There's a slap my ego never saw coming.

I try to play it cool. "So... Brad, hey? Sounds pretty douchey." Okay, that wasn't quite cool, but I'm not known for being smooth when it comes to discussing gents. I save that for the ladies.

"Yeah, Brad." It sounds gross even in his fiancée's tone. "What about you? Did you get the four-button clinger's name before you fornicated with her? Or is that not the 'in thing' right now?"

She did just say fornicated, didn't she?

Who the fuck says fornicated in this century?

Oh, that's right, women who also use slogans like 'in thing.'

"We didn't fornicate... today. That was all handled last night... depending on what basis you consider fornication to take place?" Why am I rambling like a teenage idiot? I hand out orgasms like a two-dollar hooker hands out chlamydia. I am *not* a fumbling reject. "We fucked last night. This morning, she only sucked my dick. I didn't come, but it was pretty close. Is that fornicating enough for you?"

"You didn't come? Why not?"

I wave my hand at her, looking all prissy in a jumpsuit that should make her look frumpy, even though it doesn't. "Because you turned up."

"*Ohhh.* Now everything makes sense. I thought you threw me off a cliff because you were determined to show me you still have what it takes to be a jumper. In reality, you were just pissed I interrupted Miss Sweet Thing going to town on your... your—"

"Cock? Schlong? Captain America? Penis? Womb raider? Tonsil tickler? Pee-pee?" *Too much, Colby, way too much! You're supposed to make your cock sound manly, not like a kid's tugboat in a bubble bath.* "Shall I continue, or did you get the hint?"

"I think I got the gist of it. You came. You saw. You *didn't* conquer."

"Hey!" She couldn't have shocked me more if she slapped me with a cold fish. "I conquered. I *totally* conquered like King Kong climbing the Empire State Building, banging my chest and all. She was so conquered she was left dying for more. That's why I ran as I did."

"Ha! So I was right? You did *only* offer me a ride home to escape her clutches."

I make a *pfft* noise. "That isn't close to the truth."

Jamie folds her arms in front of her chest, her white cheeks reddening. Her attempt to act angry is as cute as fuck.

"It may have appeared that way at the start, but now I've gotten to know you a little better, I would have offered you a ride home… eventually. I like you. You're cool and hip. I may even have a little crush on you."

What the fuck!

I stop seeking the closest ditch to bury myself in when she squeaks out, "Really?" Just as quickly as her surprise arrived, it leaves. "I mean… *really!*" This one is delivered with a sarcastic eye roll and an ear-piercing tone. "Like I'd fall for that. Nice try, buddy, but I'm not that type of girl. You can't woo a lower insurance premium out of me."

I might have believed her if she stopped seeking confirmation from my eyes. I'm reasonably sure if I told her my dick was a throat lozenge, she'd be complaining about a sudden sore throat.

"Yeah. Ha! You busted me."

My voice replicates the one I had when I reached puberty but still lacked the 'pubic' side of the saying. Every word I spoke is true, micro-crush part included, but her insurance premium comment reminded me quick smart she's not a woman I should be messing with. And let's not mention the big-ass rock that started our conversation.

CHAPTER 6

JAMIE

*Wh*y in the world am I getting jealous? I'm engaged, angry, and bubbling with so much jealousy, I'm considering a second jump into the ocean to cool down. Jesus. I need to shut this down, and I know the perfect way to do so.

"Without the amendments we're suggesting, Metrics will not be able to provide insurance indemnity for The Drop Zone."

Colby tightens his grip on the steering wheel before spitting out, "Then I'll find another insurer."

Ha, like I'm not aware he's tried that very thing multiple times over the past four months.

"Our stipulations aren't the end for your business, Colby. For all you know, stepping back could benefit it greatly. Put those years of business studies to use from *behind* a desk."

"My business is what it is because of me. I'm embedded in it.

People don't come to The Drop Zone just for the thrill. They come for me."

"And a chance to get in your bed?"

I thought I said my comment in my head, but the narrowing of Colby's eyes reveals I didn't. "And that right there is my point." He jerks his head at me as if I'm more than one person. "This isn't about risks. It's about the stiffs who can't understand how anyone can enjoy life without anti-depressants. I'm not talking out my ass when I say if they had found a well that served them a million dollars before they turned twenty-two, we wouldn't be having this conversation. This isn't about risks, protocols, or any of that other shit you emailed me. This is purely about knocking me down a peg or two." His eyes stray from the road to me. "And they're using you to do it."

"No one is using me, Colby. I made an informed decision from the facts presented before me."

"Facts?" He waits for me to nod before continuing, "Were they better served than the one I just gave you? My ankles are up for the task."

"But your tact isn't. Today proves that without a doubt. You take uncalculated risks which endanger people's lives—"

"Today. I did that today! And that was only because it was you." It suffices to say I'm shocked, not just by the heat of our conversation, but because of what he says next. "I started The Drop Zone specifically for people like you. The ones who can't find themselves even when standing in front of a fucking mirror. People who are so goddamn lost, jumping out of a plane is their *second* jump location. You think it's all about the thrill and the endorphins, but what about those people who just want to feel alive for an hour. That's why they come to me. That's why they beg and plead with Tyrone for me to be their instructor because if one-tenth of my personality rubs off on them while they're sailing in the air like an eagle, they have more than enough reasons to live."

Before I can fathom a reply, he pulls into an apartment building that doesn't have the standard thumbnail size crash pad most apartments fringing LA have. The street is leafy, the vibe hip, and the price tag way above an insurance assessor's salary. I share my apartment with my fiancé.

Share, such a weird word for me to use when referencing the man I'm set to spend the rest of my life with.

Like I need any more clues that he can't wait to see the back end of me, Colby reaches over to open my door for me, giving me my marching orders without shutting down his engine. "You can deny my coverage claim all you want. I'll still jump."

I grit my teeth, holding back my remark. I have half an ocean of sand in my hair, my clothes are thinner than a sheet of paper, and my heart is whacking out a tune I've never heard it play before. Now is not the time for arguing. I honestly don't know if any time would be right.

"Thank you for the ride." I nearly add on, *and the near coronary*, but lose the chance when my slip out of Colby's car concedes with his foot getting friendly with his gas pedal. He zooms down the street using the wind from his brutal speed to slam my door shut.

Once his taillights blur into a sea of many, I spin around to face the doorman whose shocked expression jumps onto my face when I realize I left my satchel in Colby's car.

"Need me to buzz you in?"

Nodding, I give Raguel my best could-today-get-any-worse

face before following him into the lobby of my building. It's a boastful space with fresh flowers, crystal chandeliers, and glistening tiles that have no issues displaying my low-hanging head. I've read many reports on Colby McGregor the past four months. Most were the ones from physio specialists whose aspirations to remain in the Attwood's family dynasty's good graces was seen all over their reports. I doubt half of them physically attended a meeting with Colby. They just let him blind them with his good looks and charisma as unwisely as I did.

After sliding his key into the elevator dashboard and hitting 'P' for the top floor, Raguel slips back out. "Mr. Valeron is home."

"He is? Oh." I could have sworn he said he had a meeting today.

Shrugging off my confusion, I thank Raguel with a smile before the elevator commences its eighteen-floor climb. I would give anything for it to be Friday afternoon. A soak in a tub with a chocolate swirled sundae with crushed nuts on the top would be ideal right now—and I'm not even fussed if the nuts don't belong to Colby. What he said before tearing away from my building makes sense. I feel more alive now than I did when my eyes fluttered open this morning, which isn't great form considering I was awakened by my husband-to-be with a fresh mug of hot chocolate and a beaming smile.

Am I a terrible person? I certainly feel like one right now.

When the elevator doors ding open, I trudge down the long, elegant corridor. The first time I walked this hallway, my feet didn't touch the floor. Brad carried me to the door of the apartment he purchased as a surprise for me. I was shocked. Not just because he bought an apartment way above our league, but the way he bent on his knee after carrying me over the threshold. That day was a little over three months ago—exactly four months after we began dating.

Ignoring the painful twist of my stomach, I lower down the gold-leafed handle of my front door. It doesn't budge an inch, indicating it's locked.

"Brad."

I tap on the door two times, eager for both a shower and to reacquaint with the lips who had avoided mine like I had a cold sore this morning. I can't blame him. Even a man with panty-wetting features like Colby wakes up with morning breath.

"Princess? Is that you?"

I roll my eyes at Brad's hideous nickname. I love when my dad calls me princess, but when it's coming from Brad's mouth, it is cringeworthy. "Yes, it's me. Who else would it be?" I'm reasonably sure my dip in the ocean didn't just wipe the makeup from my face. It dug out an attitude I haven't utilized in a very long time. My question wasn't snappy, it was down-right rude.

"What are you doing home so early? Didn't you have a meeting today?" His words are jutted by big breaths like he's jogging.

"If you open the door, I'll tell you all about it." I will after I work out what the hell he's up to. "Brad!" I jiggle the handle again as if it will miraculously pop open. "Why aren't you letting me in?" I stare down at the lock, certain my adrenaline-thick blood is capable of kicking it open, but before I can, it flings open.

"Hey, there, princess. Sorry, I was getting dressed. You know what Ms. Rosa is like. If I answered the door in a towel, she'd have us kicked out of the building."

Everything he's saying is true, but that doesn't stop me from storming into our apartment like I'm about to take down a drug operation being run in my kitchen. I race through the living room and past the kitchen on my sprint to our bedroom, finding not a thing out of place.

"Princess?" I spin around to face Brad, who's eyeballing me like a freak, even with his eyes not lowering to take in the ridiculous outfit I'm wearing. "Who are you looking for?"

"Why are you showering at one thirty in the afternoon?"

He takes on a defensive stance, unappreciative of the interrogation in my tone. "Because I left the ranch Mr. Kemp wants zoned as commercial smelling like a piggery. I don't know about you, but I'm reasonably sure those wealthy investors you despise schmoozing at every corporate function wouldn't appreciate me turning up to a meeting reeking of manure."

"Ah. Good point."

"And you, Jamie?" He says my name with the same stinging scorn Colby used earlier. "Why are you home at one thirty in the afternoon looking like *that*." When he spits out 'that,' he glances down at the jumpsuit Tyrone gave me after promising to have my skirt and blouse dry cleaned and returned to me later today.

I wait for Brad to finish raking his hand through his inky black hair that curls around his ears before replying, "I also had a meeting with... pigs."

Brad's icy stare pins me in place. It's the same daring look he gave me across a conference room floor only seven months ago. It's fierce and impenetrable, much like its owner. Brad could never be accused of being cruisy. He's masculine, cultured, and hungrier for success than any man I know.

"I thought you had a meeting with an adventure capitalist today. What's his name? Col—"

"Colby McGregor. I did." I follow him out of the bedroom, not surprised his interrogation ended as quickly as it started. Brad Valeron would never believe little old me would deceive him. He's so sure of himself, even if he had someone as ritzy as Gigi Hadid on his arm, he wouldn't be worried. "It didn't go according to plan."

Brad snags his leather briefcase off the round table in the foyer before pivoting around to face me, his lips hard-lined. "He's responsible for you looking like that?" Once again he highlights my outfit with his head.

"No." I draw out my lie as if it is an entire sentence. "This was all me." I hate dishonesty, but Brad knows people who know people who know my boss. If word gets out that Colby strapped me to his chest before throwing me off a cliff, The Drop Zone won't be just shut down, I could lose my job. "My car overheated again. When I walked, I fell in a ditch. It rained last night. So..." I drag my hand down my body, letting my messy-self answer on my behalf.

Brad doesn't hear my lie as I hoped. "So you turned up to your meeting like that? If you want to be taken seriously, Jamie, you need to act accordingly."

"But I'm fine, so don't you go fussing." Some of the southern heritage I nearly forgot I had rings true in my tone.

"Don't be like that, Jamie. I know you're safe. I can see, you know. I'm more talking about how many hours you've put into this request for coverage when you should have just stamped it ineligible and moved on."

Brad is talking about Colby's insurance indemnity like he's handled it as closely as I have. We may have discussed it in passing, but he's one of the people Colby mentioned earlier—the stiffs who wouldn't know a good time if it were to slap them in the face.

"It isn't as simple as it seems. Colby made a lot of good points today... points that deserve assessing."

Brad stares at me with his brow cocked and his jaw tight. "Colby? You refer to your clients by their first name now, do you?"

His jealousy is unexpected but highly appreciated considering the hot mess I'm currently in.

"He's very laid back, Brad. Nothing like the media portrays." That's not entirely true. Colby is cocky, self-opinionated, and arrogant but in an endearing I'm-going-to-hell type of way. "I've got until the end of next month to decide, so a few more hours of deliberation won't hurt anyone."

"Jamie.... Princess..." He cups my cheeks like two names aren't enough to reveal how stupid he thinks I am. "You've deliberated over this claim for months. It's time to let it go. The risks far exceed any premium amount Metrics could draw against them. Do you really want to be the woman who single-handedly loses thousands of jobs this close to Christmas? Nice guy or not shouldn't come into it. This is business. Nothing more."

Why do I get the feeling he's talking about us more than The Drop Zone's liabilities?

"Now, have a shower, fix your hair that's all types of wrong, then get this wrapped up like the responsible, smart woman I plan to marry." When he swoops down to kiss me goodbye, I stupidly pucker my lips. He isn't going for a mouth peck, instead he kisses me on the forehead like we're saving my virtue for our wedding night, which is scheduled to occur on New Year's Eve. We're not, but it certainly feels like it has been over the past two months. "I have a meeting in Santa Clara for the rest of today, so I'll be home late. Don't wait up for me."

With that, he leaves our apartment, tapping out a message on his cell phone on the way out the door.

CHAPTER 7

COLBY

I tiptoe into the foyer of The Drop Zone, unsure if the extermination company I regularly utilize for pests got the silent signals I was shooting his way during my fast departure. It has the same lackless vibe it usually has each Monday afternoon when the nuns have finished collaborating with God. The trained jumpers are in the break/games room playing X-box and talking smack about what they did on the weekend. The cleaning staff is ridding the toilets of the nerves nearly every jumper gets before they're shoved into a tin can we call a plane, and the safety officers are checking each chute—including the one I disengaged while soaring over the Cali coast earlier today.

Not going to lie, my blood is still pumping. Not just from my base jump, but from my exchange with Jamie after it as well. I shouldn't have snapped at her like I did. Even if everything I said were true, making out I threw her off a cliff just to bring her out of her shell was a lie. There's no doubt she's uptight, but if she were as stiff as I first perceived, I would have been charged with attempted murder by now.

My next sneaky step lands with a thud when Tyrone says, "She's gone. It was easier than I thought." He rounds the counter, making me anxious since there's no longer a big clump of wood between us. "And I didn't even have to make out you had an STI." He drags his hand across the stubble responsible for the only bit of roughness on his face, hoping it will hide his smile. "I've caused you more issues than a little ole STI lie. Serves you right, too. You fucked up today, man."

"I know. I'm sorry. I don't know what I was thinking."

"I know what you were thinking with, and it wasn't with this." He taps my temple, his pat strong enough to inform me he's still pissed as fuck. "You like her... so much so, you had to bang your chest like a fucking moron."

It's sufficed to say I'm shocked. "What? Whatever! You've got rocks in your head. Today was *nothing* about liking anyone. I was merely proving a point."

"That you want to get into her floral panties?" Tyrone moves past me to restack the pamphlets that make most jumpers' eyes water. It isn't a list of injuries they most likely will never endure during a jump that has them almost sobbing, it's our pricing catalog. "They were floral, right? I'm guessing paisley pink with a cute little bow at the top. She probably smells like flowers, too."

I take a step back, shocked as fuck. "Who likes who? Silly me, I thought your are-you-okay-Ms.-Burgess routine was about keeping our business afloat, not getting your dick head wet."

Tyrone stacks the pile a little too roughly. It bends the brochures more than it straightens them. "It *was* about that." He licks his lips, his smirk picking up. "Until I saw the gleam in her eyes. She became an addict after one jump. Who does that?"

"Women who jump with me, that's who." I peer past my shoulder, wondering where the fuck that alpha macho voice came from. It was all possessive and virile like I'm warning Tyrone to step the fuck back from Jamie without words. "If you saw the gleam in her eyes, I'm guessing you didn't miss the big-ass ring on her finger. She's engaged, douchebag, so she isn't wetting anyone's dick any time soon." I stop in just enough time to hold back my final six words—*not even her fiancé's, I hope.*

He smirks a wolfish grin. "Yeah, I saw the ring. Why do you think I'm imagining what her panties look like?"

My teeth grit when he emphasizes 'panties' as no man should. Unlike me, Tyrone has no issues mowing another man's turf. As far as he's concerned, it should be in the bro-code. He believes he's doing his brothers a favor by plucking out the weeds messing up their pristine lawns. In a way, he's right. No one says a woman has to sleep with a guy because he flirts with her, but I'd rather he defend that logic to anyone *but* the woman who could decimate our business.

"She still wants to ground me, you know? Says I'm a liability to the company."

Tyrone shrugs. "You are, but that isn't necessarily a bad thing. The Drop Zone isn't for the faint at heart. If clients are coming here expecting a polished, safe afternoon, they entered the wrong address into their GPS. It's your edge which exposes that for all to see, even women who don't realize their missing something until you show them."

My tongue peeks between my teeth when I attempt to stifle a grin. "Thought you said I only base jumped with her as I want to get into her panties?"

Tyrone arches a brow. "Thought you said you would quit pretending every memory was your last when you turned twenty-four. That happened months ago, yet I'm still waiting for you to uphold your pledge." Once he has the pamphlets in a presentable order, he heads for our office to do the businessy-shit I pretend doesn't exist, so I don't have to gouge my eye out with a pencil. "By the way, I wouldn't recommend logging into social media any time within the next century."

"Why?"

Tyrone enters our office, slamming the door behind him. His eagerness to shut down our conversation has my back molars grinding together. That man should have been born as a woman in his eighties as he loves to chat.

"Goddammit, Tyrone! What did you do this time?"

He wasn't joking when he said he makes out I have an STI to exterminate my loft. With how many so-called infections I've had the past year, I'm shocked I have any bed companions left to notch on my bedposts. I guess I can thank the he'll-change-his-ways-the-instant-he-meets-me girls for that. Every woman wants to tame a playboy, even when the odds are stacked against them.

While climbing the spiral staircase of my loft, I dig my phone out of my pocket and fire it up. It's cracked like an Easter egg, but the many messages I get each day are still visible. The first two dozen texts are the standard, *hey, wanna hook up* ones I get a hundred times a day. The next twenty are GIFs of women in all stages of crying, and the last five are straight-up, *You're engaged!* comments.

My pulse spikes to a dangerous level. "Are you serious, Tyrone? Engaged! What the fuck!"

Even with me reaching the top of the stairwell, I can hear

his chuckle. It's thick and full of mirth. "You did see that big-ass ring, right? Easy explanation as to why you went running. No one wants their fiancée to run into the woman he just messed his sheets with."

I grip my phone harder, fighting with all my might not to throw it at the glass box he's hiding in. I'd march down these stairs right now if I were unaware he had fixed the lock into place the instant he slipped into his shelter. Sly fucker most likely reinforced the door with his chair too. Coward.

"I would have preferred another STI story."

"Yeah, well, I would have preferred for you not to jump off a cliff with our business strapped to your chest like napalm, but we can't always have what we want, can we?"

He has a point—somewhat. Won't ever let him know that, though.

After a silent *"fuck you"* directed at his door, I weave through my loft that smells of sticky sheets and someone packing in a hurry. I don't know what Olivia had to pack, but I'm certain that's the scent I'm smelling in the air. As I make a beeline to the bathroom, I log into my emails to delete the hundreds of requests I get for an interview every time a scandalous event unfolds about me. Then I'll reply to my brother's one email assuring him the rumors aren't true. Cate will blow up my phone once the stories reach her ears, and Clara is too busy being Clara to worry about what her little bro is up to.

Cate and Clara are my sisters. Cate is the baby of our family, two years younger than me, and Clara is three years older. Up until a few years ago, I would have straight-up said Clara is a thorn in my backside. Thank fuck she met someone so unlike her, she had no choice but to change. Cate is still a thorn in my ass but in a good, mischievous type of way. She's pretty much a female version of me. She's in her final year of college after taking a year off to do whatever people do when they take a year off.

My steps into the bathroom halt when I discover an unexpected email weaved through the riff-raff. It's from Jamie.

Dear Mr. McGregor,

It appears as if I misplaced my satchel somewhere between the foyer of The Drop Zone and the boardroom where our meeting was held. I've organized a courier but thought best to seek an appropriate time for him to arrive. We don't want another incident like the one we had this morning, even with him assuring me he's wearing a non-buttoned shirt.

I will await your reply.

Ms. *Jamie Burgess.*

Her email makes me smile. It's formal with a hint of cheekiness. It suits her well.

After shrugging off my shirt, I punch out a reply, my mood rather playful considering the way we departed.

*Dear **Ms.** Jamie Burgess,*

I found your satchel haphazardly dumped on the carpet pile when I returned home from our rendezvous today. Let me say, it was a somewhat unexpected surprise—much like its owner.

Cancel the courier. I'll bring your satchel to you. I'll let myself in since I have your keys.

See you once I've showered!

Colby   Can't-Wait-To-Hear-You-Scream-My-Name-Again McGregor.

PS: For future reference, the flooring between The Drop Zone's foyer and our boardroom is in rustic wood. I guess you missed that fact since your focus was on anything but the decor.

Her reply arrives faster than I can remove my jeans.

You can't come here. It's inappropriate.

I smirk like the smug prick I am.

Inappropriate is emailing me while I'm naked. What would happen if I accidentally hit the video call button? The bathroom is extremely foggy. An error could occur.

Can you hear someone's annoyance over an email? If you had asked me an hour ago, I would have said no. Now I'm certain you can.

You're incorrigible!

I could formulate a reply, but it will be more fun this way. After dumping my phone onto the granite vanity, I slip into the shower, smirking about a frazzled insurance assessor and her impossible quest to get away from the big bad wolf.

After a quick shower and a change of clothes, I gallop back down the stairwell. Tyrone spots me coming, the smile on my face having him unsure of whether he should duck for cover or check me for a temperature. While I hosed off the salt making my skin more pasty than normal, Jamie sent email after email after email. They all followed a similar path about us needing to maintain an amicable, yet professional relationship.

That all changed when she switched from her work email to her private one. Not going to lie, her email tag already had my lips curling, much less the threats she sent. Who knew Ms. Goody Two Shoes had it in her?

"I'll be out for the rest of the afternoon, doing damage control for the avalanche you started."

Yep, that's what I'm running with. I'm not visiting Jamie at her place of residence because I'm dying to know why she plays the dorky insurance assessor when her insides scream 'wild child.' I'm doing it purely to soothe the volatile waters Tyrone started.

Yeah, right.

If you believe that, sit down, I have a heap of tales to tell you, none of which are true.

With traffic gridlocked, it takes me longer to get to Jamie's apartment building the second time around. After snagging her satchel off the passenger floor, I toss my keys to the valet before hot-footing it into her foyer, barely making it through the big wooden carved door when my elbow is seized in a tight grip, and I'm dragged back out.

"I told you not to come!" Jamie must have a drawer of hideous glasses as the glare she's giving me only hits me with half its strength since it's blocked by thick, ugly frames. "I'm supposed to be at work, not waiting around for you to gallivant across town."

"Then why aren't you?" When she peers up at me in surprise, I add on, "At work? If you really didn't want to see me, your doorman could have told me you weren't home." When I stray my eyes to the large man with a gentle smile eyeballing our exchange from the side, he dips his head in agreement. "Seems to me you were eager to see me... *again.*"

She whacks me in the gut, snatches her satchel out of my hand, then whacks me again—with the satchel this time. "If I recall correctly, you're the one who drove off in a tizzy like the head cheerleader who didn't win the prom vote, so why the hell would I sign up for a second round of that?"

"About that…" I'm over being eyeballed by her doorman, so I guide her to the side of her building. "That's why I said to cancel the courier. I wanted to say I'm… *sorry* about what happened earlier today."

One of my words is barely a whisper, and Jamie knows it. "Did you say something?"

"I said, I'm… *sorry* about what happened earlier today."

"Nope. You need to speak up. With everything going on, I can't hear you." She waves her hand around the empty street like we're standing in the mosh pit of a heavy metal concert.

"I said I'm sorry about what happened today." If she missed this one, I won't be just replacing her glasses, I'll be booking her in for hearing aids as well. "I acted like an ass, which is pretty much how I act around all my friends. You're welcome. It usually takes a good two to three months of courting for me to treat you the way I did. You brought out my assholery within minutes. You could quite possibly be a new record."

She whacks me again. Lucky my abs are made of steel, or I might have crumbled by now. "Don't act like you know what courting is. The only court you know of is the one a basketball bounces on."

Jamie has me there. "True, but the way I acted was wrong, so you deserve an apology."

She appears shocked and she isn't the only one. I can't remember the last time I gave an apology, much less two in a row.

"And…"

Before I can shock her for the second time, the flash of a camera bulb steals my words. When it arrives with a barrage of questions, I bundle Jamie under my arm, enter the foyer of her building, then make a beeline for the elevator banks.

"Colby, is this your fiancée?"

"When's the wedding?"

"How'd you two meet?"

"Does she know about the recent chlamydia claims?"

Out of all the questions, Jamie only hears the last one. Her eyes rocket to mine as her mouth falls open.

"It's not true." I shove her into the elevator before gesturing for Jamie to hit a button. It doesn't have to be her floor, but anywhere is better than here. We're like goldfish in a bowl being eyed from all angles.

After selecting 'P' for the penthouses, Jamie spins around to face me, tapping her foot like K does anytime I'm in trouble. K is my grandmother. Don't say a bad word about her, or I'll never speak to you again.

"I don't have chlamydia. Never have."

Either she has faith in me not even I have, or she's not bothered about my STI denial because she knows we'll never mess the sheets together. I'm not sure which one I prefer the most.

"And the engagement rumors, are they true?"

Don't make me place my hand on the Bible, but I'm reasonably sure she's jealous. Her pupils are as wide now as they were when her head bobbed out of the ocean, but steam is billowing out of her ears like she's about to blow her top.

"Not true… but the paps *think* we're engaged."

She chokes on her spit. "*Us*! Why would they think that?" I only rub a kink in my neck, but it tells her everything she needs to know. "You made out we're engaged!"

"Not me, specifically." Her foot tapping doubles, urging me on. "When we fled—"

"The blonde saw us leaving together and assumed I was your fiancée."

She's not right on the money, but it's close enough. "Yeah."

I could throw Tyrone in the deep end with me, but since my nuts are still attached to my body, I let him sidestep this throwdown. It's the least I can do after what I've put him through the past few months.

After the elevator arrives at the top floor, I shadow Jamie down a long hallway. My nose screws up when we enter the fancy-schmancy foyer of her home. The vaulted ceilings with crown molding aren't responsible for my ghastly response. It's the scent lingering in the air. Much like my apartment, it reeks of dirty sex and someone leaving in a hurry.

Now that I think about it, Jamie's hair is wet, and she's changed out of the clothes she was wearing when I dropped her off earlier. Her fiancé must have been so excited about her unexpected return home in the middle of the day, he took care of her needs—in under an hour. Loser.

"Anyway, now that I've said I'm sorry, and you know about my second dumping of the day, I better get going." There's nothing like the scent of another man's spawn to make you eager to leave. "Don't worry about the paps. As long as we stay away from each other, they'll die down in a week or two."

"A week or two?"

I don't hear anything else Jamie says as I'm out her door faster than a bullet being fired from a gun.

CHAPTER 8

JAMIE

"Colby?"

I stare at my door for several minutes, certain I didn't imagine his visit. I can smell his manly scent lingering in the air. It's mixed with another not-so-scrumptious smell but undeniable all the same.

After checking the hall, which is empty, I move to the large bay windows that face the street below. It appears to be as it generally is—until the quickest blur of blond darts between the alcove of my building to an idling sports car the valet just brought to the front. I could mistake him for any of the dozen Hollywood heartthrobs who live in this building if Colby didn't peer up at me staring down at him for the quickest second. It's him. I'm certain of it. But why did he flee? I'm not overly presentable in a plain black skirt and satiny blouse, but I'm certainly putting a better foot forward than the one I walked away from him only an hour ago. Perhaps it's my hair? I let it dry out naturally, meaning its ringlets of curls makes it appear half the length it does when I straighten it.

Shrugging off my confusion, I move to my walk-in wardrobe to replace my shoes that are harboring seaweed. Halfway there, my phone dings with a text message.

Brad: *Do I need to turn around?*

I'm confused by his message until I spot a link attached to the bottom. I don't need to open it to know what it's about. The headline tells the story.

Forbes Top Man to Watch is Engaged

Me: *It isn't as it seems. You know reporters, Brad. They're rarely accurate.*

Take the many times they cited you as having an affair for an example. That comment wasn't for Brad. It was to appease my anger.

Me: *They photographed me leaving his office, saw my ring, and assumed wrong.*

Brad's message pops up just as I slip my feet into a swanky pair of Milano pumps.

Brad: *Okay, then explain this.*

Fuck!

I'm not a fan of curse words, but there isn't a more appropriate one for the image attached to Brad's text. It shows Colby and me in the foyer of our building.

Me: *He was returning my satchel.*

I don't get any words with his next message. Just a picture of Colby following down the hallway that leads to our apartment. I should be panicked, but more than anything, I'm mad. This photograph wasn't uploaded by a member of the media. It's from the security cameras positioned around our building for the safety of its residents.

My fingers fly across the screen of my phone so fast, I'm certain my stubby nails are scratching the screen.

Me: *Are you spying on me?!*

Brad: *Spying entails being sneaky. I was merely checking in on my fiancée.*

I grip onto my phone for dear life while sucking in big breaths. My endeavor to quell my anger does me no good. Instead of replying to Brad's text, I send my phone flying across our walk-in closet. It smacks into his pricey suits that line one wall before landing in a heap on the plush carpet that fortunately saves it from being smashed to smithereens.

I'm not overly angry at Brad. For once, it's nice for him to think he has competition. I'm just confused. Today has been one major commotion after another, even with me feeling the most alive I've ever felt. I heard adrenaline does wonders for your heart—I assumed it was only needed once it stopped beating.

After a few big breaths, I gather my phone from the floor, spotting my amethyst stud earring on the way. I must have bumped it off when getting dressed in a hurry earlier. The backs are so loose they come undone all the time.

My confusion intensifies when I attempt to slide my earring back into my ear. I'm not missing an earring. They're both in my ears where they belong. I peer down at the shimmery purple rhinestone Brad gifted me for my thirtieth birthday, utterly confused. It matches my pair in every way, but it's *not* my earring.

With my heart in my throat and my suspicions high, I snap a picture of the earring, send it to Brad, shut down my phone, then dash out of my apartment. I have a job to do—a job I can't afford to lose when I wring my husband-to-be's neck.

"You weren't caught kissing the lead singer of Wanting Wombats again, were you?"

After hustling through the half dozen paparazzi who tailed me from my building to my workplace, I shoot a wry glare at my best friend and co-worker, Athena. "Not this time."

I bump her with my hip, taking in how her curvaceous frame gains more than a few admired glances from the men milling around our work building. Metrics Insurance has the top floor of the skyscraper Brad's firm built last year. It's an eyesore who's monthly premiums match its sky-high stature. This building was approved a mere week before a new capita height was introduced by the state.

"So... how did it go?" Athena hands me an iced chocolate with triple swirls before twisting around to jab the button for our floor. "Was he everything I thought he'd be?"

"Yep!" The 'P' pops from my mouth. "He's an arrogant, self-assured asshole who doesn't have a clue what's in front of him."

The first half of my reply was in reference to her question— she knows about my meeting with Colby as she organized it— the second half was for Brad. Not even a forty-minute commute has cooled my turbines. I'm still fuming mad.

"What did he do this time?" Athena's voice is as hot as her face.

I hold out my hand palm side up. "Have you seen this before?"

Some of the heat on her face cools, believing what I first

thought. "Did you almost lose it again? Jesus, J, you need to get tighter backs. Those puppies cost a fortune..." Her words trail off when I pull back my crazy curls to show her the earrings I'm wearing. "Oh, cupcakes. This isn't good. Where did you find it?"

"On the floor in our walk-in closet."

Athena shadows me out of the elevator. "And what was his excuse this time?"

"He hasn't given me one yet. I sent him a picture, then shut down my phone. Let him stew on those apples for a few hours." We push through the revolving double door of Metrics Insurance before making a right. "I'm sure he has a reasonable explanation."

"Uh-huh. Like he always does." Athena's voice is as sarcastic as mine, her anger just as palpable. "I don't know why we're still doing this to ourselves, J. We both know you deserve better, so why aren't we stepping back?"

Her inclusion in my relationship is nothing new. She's been my friend for donkey's years, so if you want me, you get her too —much to Brad's annoyance.

"Because he's Brad, and I'm me."

Athena almost rips my arm out of its socket when she tugs me back. "Excuse me. What do you mean, you're you? Of course, you're you, who else would you be?"

"You know what I mean."

She whips back so quickly, she slaps me with her fiery red hair. "Hell, yes, I do. That's the issue. You were fine for years before Brad came into the picture, and you'll sure as hell be fine within minutes of him leaving... not that he deserves even a second of your remorse."

My chance to reply is lost when I hear someone calling my

name. I'm relieved when I notice it's Hugh. He may be my supervisor, but he's a great guy. "Can we see you for a minute?"

"We?" I lock my eyes with Athena's big brown eyes, wondering if she heard Hugh in the same manner as me. If the dragging of her teeth over her bottom lip is anything to go by, she did. "Sure. Just a minute."

I thrust my satchel into Athena's chest, my cell into her hand, then shimmy the nerves out via my shoulders before turning to face Hugh. His glistening blue eyes, cut jaw, and handsome face remind me a lot of the man I was wrangling this morning. Instead, he has a platinum band around his ring finger instead of platinum blond hair.

"Everything okay?"

Bile scorches the back of my throat when my arrival at his office door has me coming face to face with the head honcho of Metrics Insurance. I'm not talking Hugh's boss. I'm talking Hugh's boss' boss' boss. Mr. Luis has the same fierce cutting edge as Brad but in an entering-gates-hell way. His hair was inky black at once stage, and his eyes are blue and razor-sharp.

"Mr. Luis, what a pleasure to see you again. It's been so long."

After kissing my cheeks with his thick lips, leaving a wet spot on each side, he gestures for me to take a seat across from Hugh's chair he's seconded for himself. "I'm afraid this is a formal visit."

I'm tempted to say, *when isn't it?* but settle with, "That's a shame. I've sure missed the stories you like to share." Lying is occurring way too easily for me today.

"I'm short of time, so let's get this underway." With a jerk of his chin, Hugh jumps to the snapped command in his tone by sliding a picture onto the desk in front of me. It's a printout of the article Brad showed me earlier. "Are you aware of this?"

After a quick swallow, I nod. "Yes, but it isn't as it seems."

"This is the company we're in the process of reassessing for coverage, is it not?"

"That's correct."

Mr. Luis' pepper gray brow shoots up high into his hairline. "And that's the man at the helm of its operation, is it not?"

"Once again, that's correct." He attempts to speak again, but I beat him to it. "But we're not engaged. That was a ghastly horrendous misunderstanding that occurred today while in the presence of The Drop Zone co-owner to discuss the stipulations you..." when he shoots me a wry look, I try again, "... *we* added to his claim for coverage."

"So it's fictional?"

I nod again. "Very much so."

"And Mr. McGregor is aware coverage for The Drop Zone will not be approved if he continues to helm the operation?"

"Ah... not entirely." Sweat beads on my top lip when two sets of powerful eyes glare at me. "Col... ah, Mr. McGregor believes there are extenuating circumstances we've yet to assess. I'd like to look into them a little closer before finalizing this claim."

"Extenuating circumstances as in what?"

I twist my torso to face Hugh, the questioner of my query. "He doesn't believe he's a liability, and that his company will most likely collapse shortly after he's dismissed as its face."

Hugh's expression makes it seem as if his stomach just gurgled as mine did. I don't care how heartless you are, no one wants to add dream killer to their job description.

"He's probably right—"

"None of this matters," Mr. Luis interrupts Hugh. "We, as insurance consultants, are to only look at figures. Personal matters should not factor into any decisions we make. This man has already cost me millions of dollars. I'm not willing to risk anymore." With that, Mr. Luis stands from his chair, gathers his coat as if it isn't ninety-plus degrees outside, then exits Hugh's office.

Hugh waits for him and his bodyguard to be chauffeured into a waiting elevator by his assistant before he shifts his focus back to me. "Did your face-to-face meeting cause a change of heart?"

I want to say no as an agreement would give him too much satisfaction, but I've reached my quota of lies today, so I nod instead. "It's not necessarily what they do, but the reason why they do it. I'm also beginning to wonder if the reports on Colby's physical capabilities are true. He certainly didn't lack an ounce of strength today." *Not even while piggybacking me up sand dunes that would kill even the fittest of men.*

"Then why aren't your reports reflecting that." He gestures his head to the email I sent him during my commute.

"Because that's what Mr. Luis wants."

Hugh props his hip onto his desk before folding his arms in front of his chest. "What Mr. Luis wants and what Mr. Luis can have are two entirely different things. He may be my boss—"

"Your boss' boss' boss."

Hugh rolls his eyes in a manner way too sophisticated for a man in his thirties. "Whatever. He doesn't run the show here. I do. And if you think The Drop Zone's coverage should be renewed, we'll renew it."

"And when you get fired? What will happen to you and that pretty wife of yours?"

His eyes gleam when I mention Kate. "We'll move into your penthouse with you and Brad. Your walk-in closet alone is bigger than our house." After moving around his desk, he slides into his chair, looking more at home than Mr. Luis did in it. "Remember that trip I mentioned? The one where the blue-eyed wonder boy is billed as the opening act?"

"The adventure-packed weekend The Drop Zone sold out within a day of them going on sale, even with the event costing over ten K per recipient?"

"Yes, that one." He slouches low in his chair before making a triangle with his fingers. "I have a ticket with your name on it."

My eyes bulge out of my head. "Say you don't."

"I do."

"How? They're sold out. You may be many things, but we all know your only magic trick was tricking Kate into thinking you're charming."

Hugh throws his head back and laughs. "She thinks I have other skills, too, but since I don't want a sexual harassment claim filed against me, I'll leave it at that."

I pick up a wad of pencils out of their brash holder and peg them at him. Two hit their mark. The other four fall short. "I'm not going. This is way above the pittance you pay me."

He shrugs. "It's too late. I already told Mr. Luis you're attending as an assessor. If things aren't safe, you'll be expected to shut them down."

I gag in an extremely unladylike manner. "Really, Hugh? Like things could get any more awkward?" I slap my hand over my mouth. I said too much—*way too much.*

"What do you mean, 'more awkward'?" Hugh quotes his last two words like a man purchasing seasonal tickets to *Cats,* the musical.

I nudge my head to the printout on his desk. "I'm referring to that."

"Bullshit, Jamie. We've worked together for years, so I know your bullshit face. That's your bullshit face." He wiggles his finger in front of my face. "Now out with it. What awkwardness?"

I exhale a deep, nerve-penetrating breath. "That picture was taken in the foyer of my apartment building." Hugh gives me his *duh* face. "After Colby dropped me home so I could change since he landed our base jump in the ocean instead of on the sandy shore..." My brow becomes lost in my hairline. "Why are you smiling? What about anything I just said is funny?"

He drags his teeth over his lip in a way I shouldn't find cute, but totally do. Not sexually—*God.* I've never looked at Hugh like that. Not even when we were both single. He's like a brother to me, so you can get those images out of your head, thank you very much. "What was his excuse for landing your jump in the ocean?"

Someone call the fire department as my cheeks are burning.

"*Ahhh.* Just as I thought." He gives me a wink revealing he knows exactly what transpired between Colby and me today. "Still not letting you out of it, though. This getaway will be the perfect opportunity for you to see Colby in all his glory."

Is it just me, or did that sound wrong to you too?

"Hugh—"

He shoots me down with a stern glare, one that's really hard for him to pull off. "Who do you work for?"

He wants me to say him.

He's shit out of luck.

"Metrics Insurance."

His lips tug into a smirk. "Okay. Then who signs your paycheck every week?"

"The payroll lady."

Since he refuses to let his groan out via his mouth, it comes out his ears. "Pack your shit, Jamie. This negotiation is over." A normal person would think he's firing me. I'm not normal. "You have an adventurous getaway in a little over six weeks. If you're anything like my wife, you better start packing now."

Hugh picks up his phone like he has important calls to make. He's full of shit, no one uses a landline phone anymore. He's simply giving me his silent marching orders.

"When I return from my soiree with a truckload of reports showing how Colby McGregor takes uncalculated risks after uncalculated risks, don't say I didn't tell you so."

I hear Hugh's receiver click back onto its base before I'm even halfway out his office door.

Unfortunately for Athena, my steps into my office are soundless. "One, get your feet off my desk." She pulls a cherry sucker out from between her painted lips before removing her pumps from my desk. "Two, is that my phone?" She has a cell phone in her hand—one that looks remarkedly similar to mine. It even has Jamie stitched on the edge of its leather case.

"Yep. Had to see what asshat had to say for himself." If you haven't worked this out yet, Athena isn't a fan of Brad. "He was very inventive this time around. Did you know he's so nimble, he can replace lost earrings while you're sleeping? And… wait for it, here's the golden ticket… he purchased three sets of identical earrings so he could replace them anytime you lost one without making you feel bad." She drops her bottom lip into a pout before she gags.

When I attempt to snatch my cell out of her hand, eager to

see Brad's excuse firsthand, she *tsks* me. "Don't be rude. I'm in the process of a very risqué email-a-thon."

"With who?" Jesus, that was loud. "That's my phone, so anyone you're emailing thinks they're from me."

"Bullseye, bitch." She launches out of my seat with her eyes bulging. "Holy shit! Do you think this has been photoshopped?" When she spins my phone around to face me, a very impressive penis fills the screen. "Who knew frosty had it in him. He's hung like a donkey."

Suddenly, I feel sick. That's been her nickname for Colby since we were handed his claim for assessment four months ago. "You're emailing Colby McGregor?"

When she tears her eyes away from my phone—it's a long-ass two minutes—she nods. "Yeah. He's cheeky."

My racing heart is heard in my squawked reply, "Cheeky enough to send you a dick pic?"

Hold on, if he thinks he's talking to me, does that mean he *thinks* I want to see his manhood? Furthermore, why does the thought intrigue me more than it sickens me? My nonexistent social media presence is precisely for this reason. I saw more penis profiles than headshots before Brad took me off the market. For the record, none were as impressive as the one Athena just showed me.

It feels like the planet circles the sun a hundred times before Athena confesses, "He didn't send the pic. I Googled it after he shot down my request by saying he didn't want to give me my second heart stutter for today." She dumps my phone onto a pile of papers on my desk before pressing her hands on each side of it. "First things first. What heart stutter did he already give you? And two, will your story include the word 'multiple'?"

She makes an 'O' with her lips like I'm a brain-dead idiot who won't understand what she means.

After moving around my desk, I guide her out of my office. "One, heart stutter is too kind of a word for what he did to me. Two, multiple wasn't mentioned, but I was so wet by the end of it, every inch of me was drenched... even my hair."

Athena wants to ask more, but the quick slam of my door in her face stops her. I have an adventurous weekend to get out of. I don't have time for anything else.

Except perhaps discovering what Colby said when he thought he was talking to me.

CHAPTER 9

COLBY

"Y#ou probably shouldn't go out there." Tyrone steps into my path, his hands coming to rest on my shoulders. "Might be a little awkward."

"For who? Nothing makes me uncomfortable. I thought those chocolates I gave you last Christmas proved this."

Before he can respond to the mirth in my tone, I spot Jamie standing at the side of The Drop Zone's foyer. She's fidgeting with the hem of her skirt, acting as nervous as she was the first time she stepped foot in here. I've experienced a different side of her the past two weeks. She isn't one the wickedly deviant women I usually correspond with, but her emails assure she's undeserving of the saint title my initial assessment awarded her with.

Don't misconstrue. Excluding the first dozen emails we shared, she's kept things professional, but with a playful edge that shows she isn't the bore I thought she was. When her name pops up in my inbox, I don't groan as I once did. More times than not, I look forward to her daily snips of wittiness.

I sidestep Tyrone, my swagger extra notable as I make my way to Jamie. I could blame two broken ankles for the sway in my walk, but that would be a lie. I've never been shy about being boastful. I just shouldn't be parading like a peacock when it's happening in front of a soon-to-be wedded woman.

We don't just talk about The Drop Zone during our multiple-times-a-day correspondence, snippets of our personal lives come up as well, including Jamie's upcoming nuptials. I like that we've stuck to a stone-age tradition for communicating, but it sucks not being able to hear her tone in her emails. Half the time, I think she's head over heels in love with her fiancé. The other half, I'm certain she's looking for an out. Since it's not my place to step between anyone, I veer our conversation back onto neutral ground—such as when will she let me toss her out of a plane instead of a cliff's edge.

Fingers crossed that's what she's here for today.

"Jamie, hey. You all right?" My last two words come out with a crack like a teenager going through puberty. It was high and cringeworthy, and one hundred percent understandable considering the amount of moisture flooding Jamie's eyes. "What's going on?"

My hands instinctively veer for hers, more to stop her from fidgeting than to hold her hand in public. I'm not a hand-holding type of guy, but even if I were, I don't hold a taken woman's hand.

"I'm so sorry, this is awkward."

I lose the chance to give her the same assurance I gave Tyrone seconds ago when a shouted voice gains my attention. "My fiancée paid for me to jump, so what do you mean it isn't booked?" A guy with black hair, wide shoulders, and a massive fucking chip on his shoulder flips the daily schedule board into the air. "Check it again because I'm not leaving until I get what she paid for."

I'm about to toss his ass to the curb when a faint voice next to me whispers, "When he saw your emails in my private inbox, I told him I was organizing for him to skydive on his birthday. Today is his birthday. I tried to book, but your website had no openings for the next six weeks."

I give Jamie a look, one that says way more than my words ever could. Our emails have been nothing but platonic, so she had no reason whatsoever to hide them from him. But I guess if this is how her fiancé acts in public, who knows what he's like behind closed doors.

After squeezing Jamie's hand, assuring her I have her back, I make my way to the douchebag asshole I'm about to have strapped to the front of me. "That was my error. I forgot to add him to the books after my *friend* requested a last-minute special." I overemphasize the word 'friend' ensuring he and everyone else gawking at me understands that I don't mow another man's turf—even if he *is* a douche.

Brad sizes me up as much as I am him. "And you are?"

"Colby McGregor." *Your worst fucking nightmare.* "Nice to meet you, Brad."

He's taken aback that I know his name. I would have preferred for him to introduce himself, it makes men feel less inferior when people don't know who they are, but it would have foiled Jamie's ruse that we're only emailing each other because she wanted to give him a thrill on his birthday. If this is the only thrill he'll get, I'm down with stroking his ego.

"Fill this in." I toss a clipboard with the safety indemnity form onto his side of the desk as aggressively as he flicked up the daily schedule. "Don't bother reading it. You're jumping with me. You'll be safe." *For the most part.*

Jamie peers at me over Brad's shoulder, her eyes begging. If she's worried I'm going to pull a stunt like I did with her, she doesn't need to be. She took my near-heart-attack stunt like a champion. Brad has the nervous-shitter vibe pumping out of him.

"Weight? I'm guessing around one forty, one fifty max."

Brad's almost black eyes peer up at me in disdain. "One eighty. These aren't made out of marshmallows." He jack-knifes up to show off his guns—emasculating muscle shirt and all. Once the college girls stop giggling, he returns to filling in the paperwork.

With his insurance forms filed in the trash, I walk him into the locker room as I did Jamie only two weeks ago. "Because it's your first time skydiving, we'll tandem jump." When he makes a face as if he's going to be sick at any moment, I say, "Don't worry, this will be just as awkward for me as it for you."

I lower my assholery when his grin relaxes the aggressive lines tainting his face. I don't even know the guy, yet I'm already hating him. I can't help it. He has a hateable face. "Do you have any preference in suit colors? We have black, blue, green, rainbow—"

"Black."

After jerking up my chin, advising I heard him, I move into the cage to gather our parachute and jumpsuits. While he gets changed, I add him to the next flight manifest. It's technically at capacity, but since most of the jumpers going up are college students, the weight allowance has some leeway for an additional two people.

As I'm heading out of the office, I bump into Jamie. "I'm so sorry about this, Colby. I honestly didn't think he'd jump even if I had purchased him a ticket."

"It's fine. It's all good. I don't mind taking him up."

Jamie steps closer to me, engulfing me with the lavender smell still embedded in the passenger seat of my car. "Are you sure? I don't want to make things awkward?"

I slant my head and cock a brow. "And how will this make things awkward? If anything, this will benefit me." When her brows scrunch, I add on, "If you trust me enough with your fiancé, I figure you won't be so quick to judge my abilities with other patrons. He is, after all, your most valued possession. Right?"

In normal circumstances, the wife-to-be would nod without a second thought. It takes Jamie more than a few seconds to bob her chin, and even then, it remains balancing on her chest instead of coming up to finalize her nod, proving I heard her tone right during our emails.

After lifting her chin back to its rightful spot, I rejoin Brad in the locker room where, for the next thirty minutes, we go through the safety video, jump expectations, and rules he will be expected to follow during our jump. Once I'm confident he's been stepped through the process, we join the rest of the jumpers in the holding room while the safety crew completes the preliminary checks the plane undertakes before each run.

Jamie hovers at the side of the room, her eyes more on me than her fiancé. Don't paint her with the wrong brush like I did the day we met. She's not eyeing me with ogling eyes—I've got plenty of them from the college girls—they're more like apologetic ones. For some reason, she feels it's her responsibility to apologize every time Brad says a lewd comment to the girls vying for my attention. He's not flirting with them. He's just—I don't know how to explain his actions. Believe me, I know cocky, but Brad is in a league of his own.

Once the 'skydiving school' is finalized, and the plane is prepped, Brad follows me to the tarmac, surprisingly minus a goodbye kiss to his fiancée. My reasoning for disliking him from the get-go is proven with merit when his eyes drop to Claudia's backside during boarding. Claudia is one of the safety instructors I mentioned earlier. Her short height and tiny weight mean it will take her more than three hundred freefall hours to become an instructor at The Drop Zone, but what she lacks in size, she makes up for with enthusiasm. She handles the nervous shitters and pukers like their body products are water all while keeping their adrenaline pumping.

"Are you guys ready to have the time of your life?"

After dragging his eyes down her body in a I'm-a-fucking-creep way, Brad joins me at our spot on the plane. "If she's here for entertainment purposes, I have no doubt I'm about to have the time of my life." When I swing my eyes to his, certain he didn't just say what I thought he said, he holds his fist out for me to bump. "Am I right? She's *fine*."

With my teeth grit, I leave him hanging by taking my seat. While Tyrone buckles us together, Brad keeps his eyes firmly planted on Claudia's ass. I can't see his face, but his gaze is so white-hot, I'm on the verge of calling in a skin specialist to check Claudia for burns.

Brad twists his neck to face me before nudging his head to Claudia. "Is she single?"

"Yeah, she is, but you ain't."

He wiggles his left hand in the air. "Do you see a ring?"

He can't be serious, can he?

He knows I'm aware Jamie is his fiancée, doesn't he?

"I must have heard wrong. I thought you were engaged."

His lips twist into a sly grin. "Yeah. I'm *engaged*, which means I'm free to sow my oats for a few more weeks." His last two words come out with a grunt from Tyrone tugging on his harness to make sure it's tight. I made sure before we entered the plane, but when forced between tugging on his straps or punching him in the face, Tyrone went for the former.

I really wish he had chosen the latter.

"Once you're married, what happens then? You lock up the zipper to anyone but your wife?"

Brad makes a *pfft* noise. "Who practices monogamy these days?"

Now I'm more interested than angered.

"So your girl is down with this? You have an open relationship?"

"What? No! But what she doesn't know won't hurt her."

Since he's strapped to the front of me, I'm reasonably sure he felt how I stiffened from his comment, but since we've commenced takeoff, my chance to reply is stolen.

Once the plane is at the desired height, the five jumpers before us have evacuated and my anger has subdued to one-tenth of its strength, Brad and I make our way to the escape hatch. When Brad's eyes stray to Claudia for his hundredth glance the past twenty minutes, I snap his eye protection into place, then leap out of the plane minus the countdown I usually do. He screams like a fucking bitch the first fifty-five seconds of our jump. That might have more to do with the fact I extended our freefall by an additional ten seconds, bringing us much closer to the ground than the jumpers around us.

Certain I have him fearing death, I release our parachute.

The pilot chute soon catches the air and inflates, awarding us a more peaceful and surreal feel. This is usually when I instruct my students to marvel at the wonderous surroundings. There's nothing more addictive than seeing the world we live in from this altitude in this situation, but Brad doesn't deserve to marvel. I don't even shoot his big toothy grin in the webcam strapped to my wrist. If he wants to rehash this experience, he'll have to jump again—with another instructor.

I swoop low and fast, more eager to get our jump over than give Brad an additional thrill. He must not feel the anger pumping out of me. He hollers into the air like a wolf before begging for me to do it again. I do, only to lower our time under parachute from five minutes to three. The quicker our jump is over, the better it will be for all involved.

"Prepare for landing." I pull down on the steering toggles causing the parachute to flare out like wings of a plane. "Stretch your legs out straight."

As we reach the drop zone, I parallel my legs with Brad's before preparing my ass for impact. We skid across the thick-grassed ground, stopping nearly in the bullseye all instructors aim for. I'm quick to unleash him from my harness, and he's even quicker to leap up from the ground.

"That was fucking unreal!"

I smirk, grateful Brad at least has enough manners to advise he enjoyed himself.

It's wiped straight off my face when he slaps my back before charging toward the group of families filming their loved ones in the sky. His mouth collides with Jamie's so fast, even with my ears still ringing from the whoosh of the freefall, I hear their teeth crash together.

I won't lie, I'm jealous as fuck. Not just that he's kissing Jamie, but the fact he thinks he's worthy of her kisses.

Brad is a dog, and if I were more of a man, I'd ensure Jamie is aware of that. Since I'm not, I push the pang of jealousy to the background of my mind and remember who I am.

I am *Ms.* Burgess' client. Nothing more. Nothing Less.

CHAPTER 10

JAMIE

When Brad's lips collide with mine, I'm too stunned to do anything. I don't return the lashes of his tongue or the nips of his teeth, I just stand still, motionless, peering in the direction where Colby once stood but no longer does.

Today is Brad's thirty-fifth birthday, but that doesn't mean our past two weeks of bickering has been forgotten. Yes, he gave a mountain load of excuses as to why there was a random earring found in our walk-in closet, but I don't believe him. His mannerisms are off—more than usual—and I'm confident it isn't cold feet as our wedding date creeps closer. He's keeping something from me. I just don't know what it is.

"Did you see me up there soaring like an eagle." Brad sets me back onto my feet before nudging his head to the sky he just fell from. "Bet you thought an angel was falling from heaven for the second time in your life."

Tandoori chicken never tastes as good the second time

around. "I'm shocked you jumped. I didn't think you'd have it in you."

"Me, scared? *Please.*" When Brad curls his hand around mine, his sweaty palm foils his calm ruse. He's scared, but doesn't want anyone around us to know.

"Why did you jump? When I told you I was being handed this claim, you said the only way you'd ever jump out of a plane was if it were already in the process of going down."

Brad escorts me into the room Tyrone took me to after my unexpected base jump two weeks ago. "Figured I should try something new. There's no harm mixing things up occasionally."

My skin crawls when he drags his index finger down my bunched-up nose. I know what you're thinking. If he gives me the heebie-jeebies anytime he touches me, why am I with him? The short answer is I love him. The long, it's a lot harder to fall out of love with someone than it is to fall in love with them. Every time we fight, I remember the good times, the days where he made it seem as if the sun shined out of my ass. In the beginning, he was attentive, kind, and made me feel like a princess—hence the nickname—but the instant he slid a ring on my finger, it was as if a switch inside of him turned off. He no longer tries to impress me, preferring to bask the stray cat in our building with attention instead of me.

Athena tells me to walk away like it's the simplest thing in the world to do, but our lives are intertwined together so profoundly the past seven months, I'm having a hard time knowing where Brad's ends and mine starts. Our house, cars, and even my parents' mortgage are in both of our names. Our bank accounts are joint, and we're down as each other's beneficiaries.

I thought it was cute he didn't want to keep our money separate, even more so since he earns a lot more than me, but now I'm realizing it's weighing me down even more than the ball and chain he plans to strap to my ankle a few weeks from now. I can't even splurge on a second iced chocolate without him being alerted. I shouldn't complain. Things are only tight because he had my mom moved to the best assisted-living facility in the state.

God—now I feel terrible. I lied to him before refusing his request to sleep in our room, so he could wake up next to me on his birthday, and now I'm trying to snuff his high not even two weeks could siphon from my veins.

"I'm glad you had fun. Perhaps Colby isn't as incompetent as you believed?"

Brad peers up at me mid-strip. "My instructor was *the* Colby McGregor?"

I return his glare, equally confused. Colby introduced himself when Brad first entered The Drop Zone. I know this because not even the nerves in my stomach could stop me feeling the ripple when Brad balked during his introduction.

"He did introduce himself to you… full name and all."

Brad screws up his face. "I thought he was pranking me. My instructor was a baby. He'd be lucky to be twenty—"

"Four? Yep. That's how old Colby is." I could also divulge his weight, height, and the circumference of his ankles for him to authenticate, but Brad's flaring nostrils are warning me it would be the wrong thing for me to do. "He had help, but pretty much everything you see before you is compliments to the drive of Colby and his business partner, Tyrone."

Brad pulls a shirt over his head before raising the cuffs, so it shows off the biceps he was shamefully displaying earlier.

"You're sounding a little too smug for the woman who's about to tear this place down."

"Who said I'm about to tear it down?"

He arches a brow sardonically. "You know what Mr. Luis wants."

"What Mr. Luis wants and what Mr. Luis can have are two entirely different things. If there's no reason for me to deny The Drop Zone's request for insurance, I won't deny their application."

Birthday or not, I'm five seconds from slapping his face when he murmurs, "Spoken like a woman who doesn't bark on command."

Brad pats my head to amplify his comment before pacing out of the room, dumping his jumpsuit and harness on the floor on the way. I'm too shocked to go after him—even more so when a deep rumbling voice at the side asks, "Did you mean what you said? Will you go against Mr. Luis on my behalf if you believe I am competent?"

I spin around to face Colby, my footing unsteady. I'm not shuddering with anger, I am jittering with nerves. The last time we stood across from each other like this, he threw me off a cliff—literally.

"Yes. Despite what Brad says, I'm not a dog who performs tricks for a treat."

Colby moves out of the shadow he was hiding in while spying on my interaction with Brad. "You know he's a douche, right? Not just what he said now, but in general. He's a douchebag in all forms of the term."

"Yes, I'm aware of that." I should be defending my fiancé, but in all honesty, I'm tired of taking up the fight. It's been nonstop since we got together, not just from my friends, but my family as well. I swear no one likes Brad, not even me right now.

I weave my fingers in front of myself, praying it will hide the shake of my hands. It does, but Colby doesn't need to see their spasms to know I'm worked up. I'm confident he can see it in my eyes.

"But you're still going to marry him?"

I bite on the inside of my cheek, praying it will stop the moisture looming in my eyes before nodding.

"Why, Jamie?"

"Because it's complicated. This isn't real life." I wave my hand around his business premise that also seconds as his residence. "Adults have—"

"*Adults*? Am I not an adult?"

I roll my eyes as if I'm not one. "You know what I mean."

Colby steps closer to me. I really wish he wouldn't. I'm struggling to speak now, so I can only imagine how much harder it will be when poor lighting isn't hiding his eyes. "No, I don't, Prim, so why don't you spell it out for me."

"You're young—"

"You mean I'm a baby, right? That's what doucheface Brad called me."

I continue as if he didn't interrupt, "So you don't understand the responsibilities someone my age has."

"Someone your age. What's that again?" He says 'again' like he knows my answer, but he wants to make sure I know he knows.

"Thirty."

Air whistles between his teeth. "Jesus. That's nearly halfway to the grave already, no wonder you're so uptight."

He thinks he's teasing me, but I don't see it that way. "Yep.

You're exactly right. I'm halfway dead. Does that make you happy?"

That stumps him. Not enough to stop me from leaving but enough to shelf his retaliation to my question. "Jamie…"

I shouldn't like the way Colby makes my name sound sexy. I should hate him and everything about him and his youth, but for some stupid reason, I don't. My life is so mundane, my every thought the past two weeks was wondering what witty comment his next email might contain.

"I like you…" he nudges his head to the door Brad just walked through, "… but I can't stand him. He's not right for you."

"You don't know that, and you're also not the first friend of mine to dislike Brad. That's okay. You don't have to like him to be my friend." He cringed at the first friend comment, so you can imagine his response to the second one, but before I can work out what his look means, my name is called by the very man we're discussing. "I have to go."

"Back to doucheface Brad. Yippee for you."

"Now you're just acting immature instead of being immature." Ignoring his juvenile eye roll, I lean in to place a kiss to his cheek before realizing that isn't something I'd usually do with a client. But that's okay, isn't it? We're friends. I kiss my friends goodbye all the time. "I'll be in contact later this week with details on the specialist I want you to visit. If she gives you the all-clear, you're one step closer to having full coverage again."

When he attempts to protest, I push my finger against his lips. "You agreed to my terms earlier this week. *This* doesn't change anything." I wave my hand between us as if we're a 'this.'

After a second cheek peck and a stern warning to myself to

back the hell up before I ruin not just my life but those I care about the most, I dart out of the room.

"I still think you should tell him his ring sucks," Colby shouts as I break into the foyer.

"Yeah, well, I still think you shouldn't judge girls by the number of buttons they have undone."

His laugh warms up the icy cold glare Brad is giving me. Lucky, or I may have been dead by now.

"You ready?"

After accepting the coat he's holding out for me because he's too warm with adrenaline to wear it, I nod. "Yes, lead the way." *Like you always do.*

CHAPTER 11

JAMIE

"*If* we keep meeting like this, rumors about our engagement will return."

I stop swirling a cheap glass of merlot around my glass to raise my eyes to my greeter. I recognize the voice accosting me, I'm just too stunned not to act surprised. "Like you wouldn't like that. Women chase harder when they think they're close to losing something."

Colby slots onto the stool next to me before requesting a shot of tequila from the bartender. "Is that why you chase after Brad like a lost puppy?"

I set down my glass, no longer in the mood for company, let alone bitter wine.

"I'm joking. Don't go. Sit." His hand darts out to seize my wrist like he did Saturday. "I promise I won't mention his name again."

I stray my eyes to his. "Unlike the hundred times you brought it up in our emails over the past four days?"

Guilt crosses his features before a smirk swipes it away. "Yeah. Like that." He bumps me with his shoulder, his mood playful for a Wednesday night. "What are you doing out this way, Prim? Thought this type of establishment would be below your standards." Colby swipes his finger down my nose to amplify a point I don't have.

"You can be assured I'm not here for the wine."

He grimaces. "That bad?"

Nodding, I hand him my glass. "You'll never believe how bad without experiencing it for yourself."

I expect him to reject my offer, so you can imagine my surprise when he downs a hefty mouthful. As heat roars through my body, my thighs press together. I'm not burning up because it's a humid night, it's from the way Colby's lips brushed the lipstick smear on my glass when he took his sip. It wasn't accidental. He lined it up like he's dying to taste the flavor of my lip gloss.

After swishing the red concoction around his mouth, he swallows. "It's not the worst I've tasted. With the right palette, I could handle it."

Colby hands my glass back to me, then arches his brow, requesting me to answer his original question. Nerves twist my stomach. I didn't skirt his question for no reason—it's because he swore only seconds ago not to mention Brad's name again. I don't see him keeping that promise when I tell him why I'm hanging out at a bar alone on a Wednesday night.

When his glare reaches a point I can't ignore, I swish my tongue around my mouth to loosen up my words. "We were supposed to be taking a dance class."

"We?" His brittle tone reveals he knows my answer, and he's just being an asshole.

"Brad and me. He doesn't want me stomping on his feet during our bridal waltz, so he requested me to get lessons beforehand. I agreed on the stipulation he came with me. He's not keeping his end of the deal."

"So why sit here? Why not go home?"

"And wallow in an empty apartment like a loser? I'd rather drink nasty wine." Which I do rather quickly when the taste of Colby's lips hit mine. He hasn't even downed his tequila yet, but I can still taste the lemon and salt lingering on his plump lips. "So why are you out alone on a Wednesday?"

My eyes rocket to his when he answers, "I'm not alone."

"You're not." You know those super cute little girls with high piggy tails and dimpled cheeks? Imagine them crying. That will give you an indication of the expression on my face. "Who are you here with?"

When he nudges his head to the left, I peer past his shoulder. An attractive young woman with pixie blonde locks, wintry blue eyes, and a plaid shirt undone at a precise three buttons smiles when she catches my eye. "She's cute."

Colby laughs at the highness of my tone. "You're cute... when you're jealous."

"I am *not* jealous!" I am, which is utterly ridiculous, but there's no denying it. Even after all the awkwardness on Saturday, we continued with our email communications for the past four days. Once again, they're strictly platonic, but still the highlight of my day. "But I do feel guilty I stole your attention from your date."

Humor flames Colby's cheeks. "She's not my date."

"She's not?" Someone remove the wine from my hand, I'm clearly over my limit.

He shakes his head, sending sprinkles of blond locks into his eyes. "No, she's my sister."

After waving for the blonde to join us, she slips out of her booth and makes a beeline for us. Her steps are so fast, not even her tiny frame stops me from feeling her thunderous stomp. "Hi, Jamie. I'm Cate with a 'C' McGregor. It's a pleasure to meet you."

"Hi, Cate." I can't hide my shock she knows my name. "The pleasure is all mine."

Cate is a bundle of excitement, but her presence has things slipping into awkward quickly. Not because she's annoying, but because it's taking everything I have not to grill her on what Colby has told her about me and for exactly how long he spoke about me.

Determined not to let unease steal the show, Cate asks Colby, "Did you find out why she's here alone?" She swings her eyes to me. "He's been watching you for ages, but was too chicken to come talk to you."

"I wasn't chicken." I smirk when Colby's high tone doesn't back up his claim. "You appeared to be enjoying the solidarity, so I didn't want to disturb you."

Cate leans in real close. "He's a chicken."

My nose screws up when I laugh. I love their dynamic. They have very similar personalities—nearly as perverse as their looks.

I throw Colby a lifejacket. "I was supposed to be taking a dance class with—"

"Brad stood you up, didn't he? You're right, Colby, he's a douche." Cate's eye roll suits her age, which I'd guess to be around twenty-two.

"That's not entirely true. He's just..." *always disappointing me,*

"… busy. His work is very important." I freeze as I'm hit with a second wave of confusion. "Hold up, how do you know about Brad?"

Cate slaps Colby in the chest. "I'm his little sis. He tells me everything."

Now I really want to grill her.

"We're as thick as thieves. That's why I'm confident he really wants to do this even though he'll deny it." She plucks Colby from his seat before placing his hand in mine, her strength admiring for how tiny she is. She's the size of a fairy. "Time to learn the foxtrot."

When she nudges her head to the dance studio across the street, I choke on my spit. "Colby doesn't want to dance with me, do you?" Someone call up losers anonymous as they've got a new recruit in training—me.

I expect Colby to chuckle out a 'no' before telling me he'd rather saw off his arm than be caught dead in a couples' dance class with Mrs. Valeria Palencia. Instead, he downs his shot of tequila and jerks his head in the direction Cate gestured before saying, "Lead the way, *Ms.* Burgess."

"Really?"

I don't know why I'm surprised. Only someone related to him by blood could accuse him of being a chicken.

CHAPTER 12

COLBY

*J*amie's big aqua eyes pop out of her head when Mrs. Palencia straightens her spine with the cane she's been tapping on the scuffed wooden floor the past fifty-five minutes. "Bum in, chest out, chin up."

The nipples I've been striving to ignore brush my torso when Jamie pushes her chest out as instructed. Since her breasts are natural, they're not as in my face like some women I've dated, but their ripeness ensures I can't miss them every time they get friendly with my torso, arm, or back during the many routines we have stumbled through the past hour.

I've lost count of the number of times I've told myself she's taken. Her perfectly plump titties stroking my chest should be as disturbing as a man's ass landing in my crotch every time we execute a perfect landing, but it isn't. And no matter how many times I tell myself to back the fuck up, Mrs. Palencia forces us back together. I would hate Cate for putting me in this position if it weren't against the rules.

I'm not here purely because I'm a closet dancer who used Jamie's predicament to my advantage. It's because Cate is kicking my ass in the dare game we've been running the past four years. I was already a dozen or so points behind her tally before I refused her dare to approach Jamie three times before finally succumbing to the pressure. It wasn't that I didn't want to talk to Jamie, I just don't want to give her the wrong idea.

Like emailing her two dozen times a day is perfectly acceptable, fuckface.

When Mrs. Palencia floats to the couple next to us, Jamie lifts her eyes to me. "Sorry."

I act ignorant of her remorse. "For?"

Her throat works hard to swallow before she gestures to the minute snick of air between us like I'm unaware of the little peaks peering up at me, begging to be touched.

After sending a warning to my cock to stay flaccid, I flash her a cheeky grin. "I'd rather their collision than your big hoofers stomping on my toes again."

Jamie's pout is as cute as fuck. I'd twang her lip if our dance instructor didn't just position us for our next dance. The way the male dancers' faces surrounding us lit up when they were informed what our next dance was has my interest piqued. They're wearing the look all men get when their date admits they enjoy giving head—and they mean it.

Mrs. Palencia taps her cane onto the ground two times, demanding the group's attention. "The Bolero is a slow, expressive dance that evokes romance and love. Through both music and movement, you'll make sensual love to one another. Yes?"

Everyone but Jamie and I reply with a hearty, "Yes!"

"Good. Let's dance."

As Mrs. Palencia makes her way to the music player in the corner of the room, I glare at her like she's an untouched bottle of water, and I was born in a country without clean drinking water. I'm Colby fucking McGregor—adventure capitalist, inductee into the Playboy Mansion Hall of Fame, and have a cock half an inch bigger than my brother's, but I can't do this. This is above me or below me or whatever the fuck level is needed to get me the hell out of here. I don't make love—not even with my clothes on.

Mrs. Palencia sees my panic, but she leaves me hanging. I don't know whose grandmother she is, but I'm confident they're ashamed of her right now. Who does that? Who leaves a man hanging when he's not even drying his own laundry?

I stop glaring at her like my eyes are able to burn her at the stake when Jamie says, "We can go. It's fine."

"What?" How is it she can feel my unease, but a lady who deals with couples all day can't? "I thought you wanted to do this?"

"I do. I just don't want you to feel uncomfortable."

When she attempts to lower her hands, I tighten my grip. Now I understand how she knows I'm apprehensive. Don't worry about water. I've got enough wetness on my hands to fix the drought in Australia.

"I'm good." I'm not, but I sure as fuck am not letting Jamie down like her douchebag fiancé. "I've just never done this before. It's a little daunting."

"To you? *The* Colby McGregor. Surely not." Even with music floating in the air, we remain perfectly still, attached at our chest, hips, and crotches. "Don't you know dancing is just like sex—"

"Only slower and more tempting." Mrs. Palencia's polish accent is nearly as thick as the hair on her top lip. "For a man known in the media for his moves, you're as stiff as a board." Any worries about me getting a stiff are a thing of the past when she unpeels Jamie from my front to take her place. "Watch the other couples, mimic their movements until the music eventually overtakes you."

I will never see the roll of my hips in the same light again when Mrs. Palencia uses her grip on my ass to grind herself against my crotch. I'm reasonably sure she's not dry-humping me—she's so old, her orgasms would have dried up right around the time I was born—but the color of her cheeks has me suspicious. It's muggy tonight, but her dance studio's cooling is so adequate, my balls tucked inside myself when we entered to ensure they didn't get frostbite.

"Be the bull, Colby, and I'm the matador."

What? Is she asking me to ram her?

"Follow the fluidity of the matador's cape... lithe and free."

Ohh, I much prefer that analogy than her earlier one.

"Loosen up and float with the music... slow and sensual."

When she weakens her vice-like grip on my ass cheeks, Jamie moves closer before she eventually returns to being my dance partner. With my worries about getting a boner a thing of the past, I move more freely than I have the past hour.

"Yes. Like that. Perfect!"

My body isn't plastered to Jamie's as it was earlier, but the almost-touches as we move similarly to the dancers around us are just as arousing. It's a teasing, carnal dance that's slow pace shouldn't be sexy, but somehow is. It's similar to the waltz but more fluent with near-touches instead of constant contact.

"Slow, quick, quick, slow, quick, quick."

Within minutes, Mrs. Palencia's instructions fade into the background. We're still novices, however I need nothing but the electricity bristling between Jamie and me to guide my steps. It is as blistering as the smiles on the faces of the people surrounding us when I switch our moves from the slow, controlled pace of the bolero to ones you'd expect to see at a rockabilly event. We twist and bob around the dance studio like Sandy and Danny in *Grease* without a care in the world. I'm sure we look like we've been smoking crack to the people milling past the dance studio's windows, but I don't give a fuck. I've never had so much fun with my clothes on.

After blowing a raspberry, Mrs. Palencia slices her hand through the air, permitting the rest of her students to dance freestyle with Jamie and me. They immediately jump to her command, with their dance moves as risqué and as random as ours. Even Mrs. Palencia gets in on the act. She takes Mr. Gardner for a whirl around the dance floor, her style a cross between the raunchy rumba and the jive. For a lady in her seventies, she's got *all* the moves.

"Oh my God, look!" Jamie points out a couple in their fifties just as the husband tosses his wife into the air. She lands with her legs curled around his waist and a mammoth smile stretched across her face. They've clearly done this before, but it doesn't stop me from wanting to get in on the action.

"Wanna give it a whirl?"

"*Nooo.*" Jamie backs away from me with her head shaking and her eyes wide.

It's a pity for her I haven't let go of her hand for the last twenty minutes. "Come on. What's the worst that could happen?"

"Oh, I don't know... I could break my neck?"

I give her a look. Don't ask me which one. I'm too exhausted to explain my facial expressions.

"If you hurt me—"

"I won't. I promise." I drag her closer to the couple with all the moves, pretending my vow didn't have a double meaning. "We'll go slow. Not just for your benefit but mine as well. I like my nuts where they are. They wouldn't look good dangling next to my Adam's apple."

She giggles. It's ten times cuter than her pout.

We watch the couple for a few minutes before attempting to mimic their dance moves. Our joint laughter roars over the music every time our attempts to spin around each other has our knees and heads knocking, but we continue with our mission, determined the rockabilly couple won't steal our thunder. We're younger and fitter, so we should be able to kick their asses.

Several long minutes later, "No! Not like that. Ugh!" Jamie bobs in just enough time to miss the leg I can't raise above my waist. With her laughter no longer containable, she bends in half and howls in hysterics. "I can't. Oh God... we need to stop. My gut is killing me."

"Fine!" I throw my hands in the air like I'm pissed. In reality, I need to expand my lungs so they can suck in some much-needed breaths. "But their asses are ours next week. Deal?"

Jamie knocks her fist against the one I'm holding out. "Deal."

With us bowing out of the dance-off, the party-like atmosphere dies down within minutes.

"Now that's what dance is about... fun, music, friendship,

and love." Mrs. Palencia's eyes shift to Jamie and me. "*Thank you*." Although she only mouths her praise, it doesn't lessen its impact.

"*You're welcome*," Jamie mouths back before straying her eyes to mine. They're as mischievous as the dance moves we just tried to master. "Pizza?"

I scoff, disgraced. "Pizza? It's Wednesday. What are you, a food dictator?"

Her brows furrow as her smile makes my skin even stickier. "If only dictators are allowed to eat pizza on a Wednesday, then yeah, I'm a dictator."

I grimace at her sweaty palms when I help her up from the ground, but mine are just as sweaty, but hey, I've got someone to blame, so why wouldn't I use it? "Everyone knows Wednesday is waffles and wings night."

Jamie dries her hands on her skirt before snagging her purse off the floor. When she spins around to face me, her skirt flares out, showing inches upon inches of smooth, flawless skin. For a dorky numbers cruncher, she has a stellar pair of legs that would only look better—*no, Colby, don't go there!*

I'm snapped from my uncalled for thoughts when Jamie asks, "Why waffles and wings? Because they start with a 'W'?" Although she's asking a question, she doesn't wait for me to answer. It's for the best, I'm still too busy checking out her legs to formulate a reply. "Are you five?"

I remind myself for the hundredth time tonight that she's a taken woman before asking, "What's wrong with coordinating you're eating schedule according to what day of the week it is?"

"Ah, it's boring and repetitive, for one."

"Like bunkering down with a dude you can't stand for the

rest of your life?" *Goddammit, Colby! You weren't meant to say that out loud.* "I didn't mean that."

"Yeah, you did, and it's fine." Jamie's face doesn't match her words. For the first time tonight, her lips are pointing to the floor instead of the sky. "Thank you for stepping up to the empty plate tonight. I had a lot of fun."

After pressing a hurried kiss to my cheek, she says goodbye to Mrs. Palencia, then scurries outside. I should let her leave, then collect a medal of valor for keeping myself in check, but the look in her eyes before she fled has me doing something I never thought I'd do. I'm doing the chasing for a change.

"Jamie..." She continues walking as if she didn't hear me, but I catch her before her slumped form is lost in a sea of many. "The waffle house is that way."

Even with a waffle place only half a block in the direction she's traveling, I nudge my head behind me. I need more than half a block to calm her down before giving her an instrument that could carve out an appendage I'm very fond of.

When she remains cautious, I try another tactic. I lie. "I didn't mean what I said..." My words trail off when her brow arches. "Okay, I did mean it, but I won't say it again." Jamie's brow arches and arches and arches until it's lost in her hair. "I won't, but *if* I happen to have another slip of the tongue, which we both know will most likely occur, I'll wear a traditional Latin dance suit to next week's class."

Really, Colby? You have millions of dollars in your bank account, yet you offer up that?

I swear on my mother's grave, the world slows when Jamie's lips curl into an uneasy smile. It already seals the deal, but she adds words into the mix just in case I'm not getting the full picture. "Are we talking the male version? Or a skin-tight dress with a sequin bodice?"

I curl my arm around her shoulders and spin her to face the opposite direction she's traveling. "Does it matter? They're both as emasculating as each other."

When she laughs, the world feels right again—even with the ridiculously hideous snort that comes after her laughter.

CHAPTER 13

JAMIE

"Try it on."

Faking a gag, I stray my eyes to Colby, who's wrangling an overloaded taco into submission. "No. I couldn't wear something like that on a good day, much less when my waffle baby is past its due date." My gag turns real when I shake my belly to amplify my statement. We ate enough waffles tonight to ward us off eating for a week, so I have no clue why Colby needs to add a taco to the mix.

Today was our third dance class with Mrs. Palencia. I still have two left feet, but I'm certain we're getting close to whipping Linda and Royce's butts during the end-of-class dance-offs. They might have years of rockabilly dancing under their belts, but that's nothing on Colby's and my competitive streak.

Colby is so determined to beat them, he suggested we add additional hours of practice during fiesta Fridays at a Spanish restaurant near The Drop Zone. I love Mrs. Palencia, but no amount of classical training comes close to the gritty rawness you get dancing amongst people who grew up doing the salsa. Winter is approaching, but my Friday nights the past three weeks have been the sweatiest I've ever had.

After Colby pays the street vendor, he joins me at the front of the boutique which has a one-of-a-kind Jenni Holt creation in the window. "I know that designer. Nice girl. Got a couple of kids."

"Not yours, are they?"

He bumps me with his hip. "Ha ha. Wouldn't have mind tapping her if she weren't related to Isaac. I almost had my nuts hung out to dry a few years ago when I crushed hard on his girl. Doubt I'd survive a second brush with death if I tapped his little brother's wife." Red-hot jealousy shouldn't hit me like a bolt of lightning, but it does. "Come on. I'm not taking no for an answer. You said last week that you need a dress for a gala, this place sells dresses."

"Colby..." My whine doesn't slow him down the teeniest bit. With a taco hanging out of his mouth and his hand clamped around my wrist, he drags me into the fancy boutique, gaining the attention of the store assistant. "Don't get up. He's so broke he can't fill his bicycle. Get it? You fill a bicycle with air, but he can't even afford that."

Colby rolls his eyes, dissing my joke without words. Unfortunately, the store assistant doesn't take a page out of his book. She blubbers like an idiot when she realizes she has a celebrity in her midst. Colby isn't famous in a way a lot of people in LA are, but his name alone opens plenty of doors. I've learned that the glamorous way the past three weeks. We've dined at restaurants that usually book out months in advance, and I read my favorite author's latest release before it had reached her editor's desk.

"Jamie would like to try on the dress in the window." I peer at him when Colby's voice squeaks at the end. "And that."

When I follow the direction of his gaze, I slap his arm. "Do I look like a prostitute?"

He strays his eyes away from a seductive lingerie set that leaves nothing to the imagination so he can lock them with me. "In that outfit, yeah, you could be." He returns his eyes to the sales assistant. "Do you sell trench coats? With the right pair of shoes and something to return the kink to her hair, I might be able to afford the bike she mentioned by the end of the night."

I laugh when she nods, stupidly believing him. "He's joking... on all accounts. Have a pleasant night."

Colby stops me from walking away by snagging my wrist for the second time tonight. "Thank you." He plucks the dress I was eyeing out of the store assistant's hand before redirecting me toward the back of the boutique. "Still up the stairs and to the left?"

Colby doesn't wait for her to answer, he continues walking and shoving until we reach a long set of dressing rooms on the second floor. "Need me to come in and help, or do you have all your bases covered?" For someone talking through a mouthful of taco, his innuendo can't be missed. It's been the same the past three weeks. He's flirty but never in a way that would be unacceptable for friends.

Snarling, I snatch the dress out of his hand before entering the first room. My mouth falls open. It's bigger than my office at Metrics. After dumping my glasses onto the bench stretched across one wall, I peel out of my clothes and replace them with the dress I was eyeing, certain I'll have to buy it even if it doesn't fit. I'm still sweating from the rumba, meaning my wish to subdue Colby's need to do everything at a hundred miles per hour puts its satin teal design at risk.

"Come on, Jamie. What's taking you so long?"

"I think the zipper is stuck... Jesus Christ, Colby! What if I were naked?" I shout the last two sentences when he enters my dressing room without warning. The naughty parts of my body are covered, but that's not the point. We've grown close the past few weeks, but we're not *that* close.

"You're not, Prim, so we're good, right?"

My brows join from the bitterness in his tone. "What's gotten into you? You've gone from cruisy to pissed-off in under sixty seconds. Was the Tabasco sauce on your taco not hot enough again? I told you I carry a bottle in my purse to save the embarrassment of the waffle place having 'non-authentic goods.'" I air quote my last three words, smiling when I recall how mortified he was when he found a generic branded hot sauce on our table three weeks ago.

"It was fine..." He stops when his eyes stray from something outside my dressing cubicle to me. "Jamie." I almost squirm. He's never said my name like that before, all hot and needy. "You look..." I wait and wait and wait for him to finish his sentence, praying my patience will pay off for a change. It's proven worthwhile when he murmurs, "Beautiful."

"Really?" I don't know what I'm shocked by more. What he's just said? How it made me feel? Or the high pitch of my tone. It could be a combination of all of them.

Nodding, he spins me around to face the mirror before snatching my glasses off the bench. "See."

I have to wait for the condensation of his high body temperature to clear from my lenses before I can take in the whole picture. This is conceited for me to say, but he's right. I do look beautiful. The satin flows over the parts of my body I'm not a fan of while holding onto the areas some women pay good money for.

"You have to buy it."

I shake my head. "I can't. It's too expensive..." My words trail off when a husky moan sounds from the dressing room next to us. I shoot my eyes to Colby as my teeth rake my lower lip. Busting someone doing the deed in public is almost as embarrassing as doing it. "What was that?"

I'm anticipating for him to add to the mischievousness heating my blood, so you can imagine my surprise when he shrugs like he didn't hear anything before he curls his arm around my shoulders and guides me out of the dressing room. "I'm beat. We should call it a night."

"Okay, but I have to get changed first. I can't leave in a dress I don't own."

The waffles I scarfed like a piggy flip in my stomach when he gallops us down the stairs like a man on a mission. The cashier's eyes light up when she spots us, confident she has this sale in the bag. Her excitement is proven spot on when Colby says, "Give yourself a nice bonus when you place her dress onto my tab."

"I can't let you buy me a dress. It's not appropriate."

Cool, late fall winds whip up around me when he throws open the boutique doors and shoves me onto the sidewalk. He then moves to flag down a cab, his efforts double since we're in Los Angeles and not New York.

"Colby, what's going on? Did the taco upset your stomach?" He told me about a horrid experience he had at a Mexican restaurant earlier this week. It ended with him fleeing from his date while clutching his stomach. I should have felt bad for him, but all I felt was relief that he left his date stranded. "You might need to step away from spices for a few days until your tummy recovers."

"It's not the fucking taco!" When I step back at his roar, the panic I'm wearing jumps onto his face. He drags his fingers through his thick blond locks before saying more respectfully, "I just need you to go, okay?"

"Okay." I only say one word, but the relief that crosses his face makes it seem as if I said much more. "Will you be all right getting home?" Cate dropped him off after their weekly dinner date, so he doesn't have his car here.

"I'll be fine. Tyrone will pick me up." After helping me into the taxi he hailed, he glances over his shoulder, back at the boutique, then he returns his eyes to me. "I'll talk to you tomorrow."

Colby slams the back passenger door shut before I can reply. Then even quicker than that, he disappears into the shadows.

CHAPTER 14

COLBY

"You lying piece of shit. You told Jamie you couldn't attend dance class because you had a meeting." I stray my eyes to the blonde plastered to Brad's side with kiss-swollen lips and ruffled hair. "Does she know you'll be married this time next month?"

I nearly add on, *to a woman ten times more beautiful and one hundred times smarter,* but I stop myself when I realize the blonde could be as innocent in this predicament as Jamie.

My thoughts are proven right when the blonde stares up at Brad with wide, ashamed eyes. "You're engaged?" When guilt crosses his features, her strike to Brad's cheek bellows down the alleyway I've been camped in the past twenty minutes waiting for his cheating ass to show up.

When she shoves a couture boutique bag into his chest, I say, "No, sweetheart, take the dress. It's the least he could do after his less-than-stellar performance." She may have kiss-swollen lips, but there's not an ounce of satisfaction on her face.

She flashes me a mammoth grin before ripping the bag out of Brad's grasp. "I think you're right." With a huff, she pivots on her heels and dashes out of the alleyway as fast as her hooker high heels can take her. "Lose my number, gherkin dick!"

I stop watching her exit when Brad steps up to me. "What the fuck is your problem, man?"

With my anger unlike anything I've ever felt, I push him back. "For one, don't call me 'man.' I am not your friend, associate, colleague, or anything that would have us tied together in any way whatsoever. Two, why the fuck are you messing around on Jamie? She could have any dick she wants, but for some fucked-up reason, she picked an asshole instead. You should be relishing that, not screwing around with a woman way below her league."

Brad smiles a slick, conniving grin. "What or *who* I do has nothing to do with you."

"Bullshit! Jamie is my friend."

"Friend?" While chuckling a mocking laugh, he steps closer. The smug gleam in his eyes pisses me off more than his attempt to stand taller than me. "That there is the *real* reason you've got your panties in a twist. You've got looks and money and a name that opens doors, but not even those can have Jamie looking past the scared little boy no amount of adrenaline can remove from your eyes. Step back from the plate, Colby. You're not man enough to play in my league."

The blonde's slap has nothing on the crack my fist makes with his eye when I sock him in it. I'm rearing back for my second punch when I'm grabbed from behind.

"Colby, what the fuck?" Tyrone needs all of his one hundred and eighty pounds to wrangle me back from Brad when Brad mocks, "Don't worry. I'll keep our foray between us." He wipes the sweat off his brow like he isn't sporting a swollen eye. "Wouldn't want Jamie knowing you're only associating with her, so she'll keep your little business afloat."

"Please, tell her because I won't stop smiling when she kicks your ass to the curb."

Brad's witch-like cackle is barely heard over my pulse shrilling in my ears. "If that doesn't prove you don't know Jamie, nothing will. She'll *never* leave me, just like she'd never believe you over me. If you doubt my beliefs, do it, call her, and watch your business go bye-bye. I have more influence over her in my pinkie than you'll ever have."

I fight against Tyrone's hold, getting to within a foot of Brad before he is back between us. "Colby, calm the fuck down." After dragging me to his four-wheel drive, he pins me to it by my shoulders, his breaths coming out ragged. "He isn't worth it. Breathe it out." He locks his dark eyes with mine, the sincerity in them shocking. "Breathe it out."

"She was right fucking there in the dressing room next to his, yet he still couldn't keep it in his fucking pants!"

"I know, man. I know."

Tyrone's reply reveals he understands where my anger is coming from. I'm not just ropeable at Brad's claim he can puppeteer Jamie, I'm pissed at how similar he is to my father. My father was a horrible man. He married my mom for one reason only—her inheritance. When he thought he had that, I caught him in compromising position after compromising position. His secretary. The housemaids. My fucking nanny. If she had a pulse between her legs, he endeavored to spike it— all while my mother lay in a hospital bed suffering through an illness a woman as wonderful as my mom didn't deserve to have. I guess I should be thankful a disease took her memories because I doubt any she had with him were worth rehashing.

With Brad no longer in the alleyway and my anger somewhat contained, Tyrone steps back. "We good?"

I jerk up my chin. "Yeah, we're good." I crack the throbbing knuckles I wish I could have split on Brad's face. "But can you believe the hide of that guy? Making out he can manipulate Jamie to do whatever he wants..." My words trail off when the sincerity in Tyrone's eyes switches to doubt. "You think it, too?"

"No. It's just..." He scrubs at the stubble on his chin, his next words coming out in a hushed whisper. "What if it's true? We've got a lot riding on this assessment, Colby."

"Are you fucking serious? You've met Jamie. You know she's stronger than this." I wave my hand in the direction Brad just was. "She said she'd have my back if I proved I was competent."

Anger flames my face when he says, "Before she left with her fiancé who she lied to regarding your correspondence."

"She did that because... because..." I've got nothing.

"Because he could have a hold over her you don't know about?" Tyrone steps closer to me, his stance non-aggressive. "She agreed with you when you said he was a douche, yet she still left with him after telling you she plans to marry him." He licks his puffy lips that get all the girls' heads in a tizzy. "If you think she's bigger than this, why didn't you let her bust him tonight? You didn't have to whisk her off like you did. You could have let her see the truth firsthand, saving us from worrying he'll fuck over everything we worked for just to prove a point."

I speak before my head or heart can battle. "I don't want to hurt her, Ty. The life in her eyes is only just being lit. I don't want to douse it."

Tyrone appears as shocked by my declaration as I felt expressing it. They evoked strange feelings in me—ones I'm certain I've never experienced before. I could blame the cocky bastard inside of me that's certain I'm God's gift to women, so lighting flames in women's eyes is the reason for my existence, but the sentiment behind my tone would make a quick liar out of me.

"You care about her as more than a friend." Tyrone isn't asking a question. He's stating a fact.

I shake my head, denying the voice in my head agreeing with him, incapable of backing down. Jamie and I have epic chemistry, but we've never stepped over the barrier the ring on her finger propped between us—*physically.* Mentally is an entirely different story, but I'll save you that tale for a day when my heart isn't sitting in my throat.

Tyrone acts as if he didn't see my head shake. "I don't know how I didn't put two and two together sooner. You've been different since she walked in The Drop Zone."

"Because I have no intention of playing Sheets Twister with her. I don't chase taken women. I'm not my father."

He doesn't even look pissed by my lie. "Don't put this on his shoulders, Colby. You know as well as I do that your backpedaling has nothing to do with him and everything to do with the stupid pledge you made." He steps closer to me, his smile making it seem as if he just found a pot of gold under the rainbow. "If it's true, if she has broken through the façade others couldn't, fuck Brad and Metrics Insurance. It's time to take a risk that doesn't involve a parachute for a change."

I hit him with a stern finger point before jabbing it into his chest for good measure. "I swear to God, if you give me the same crappy line you've given me every day for the past five months, I'll use it to wring your scrawny neck."

He gives me a look as if to say, *I'd like to see you try,* but I don't back down. I'm fucking pissed, my gut is swirling from wolfing down a taco as if I hadn't already eaten my weight in waffles, and I'm about to say something I'm certain I'll regret within ten seconds of saying it, "I'll step back."

"From?"

The panic in Tyrone's eyes is washed away when I say, "From Jamie. I'll take our friendship down a notch. Let nature take its course, so to speak. Then you won't need to worry about her douchebag fiancé fucking us over, and the ridiculous notions in your head might fuck off right along with him and his bogus claims."

For the record, it didn't even take two seconds for regret to hit me like a ton of bricks. I like Jamie. The more time I spend with her, the more I realize how misunderstood she is, but she also has me breaking rules I swore only months ago not to break. I can't do that anymore. My rules were created for a reason, and I refuse to break them for anyone. In the long run, Jamie will realize I did her a favor by pulling back.

Worry skates across Tyrone's features, hardening them. "You don't want to do this, Colby, any more than I don't want you to."

"It doesn't matter what I want, Tyrone. It's about doing the right thing. She doesn't deserve that." I point where Brad once stood before dragging my hand down my body. "But she doesn't deserve this either."

He steps closer to me as fury overtakes his worry. "She *deserves* the right to make her own decisions."

I agree with him, but I'm a missile locked on its target.

When I've made up my mind, there's no stopping me. "You can't play on both teams, Tyrone. You have to pick a side. Your business or your stupid beliefs I'm more deserving than the hand I've been dealt."

He steps closer to me, his eyes watering. "I choose for my best friend to stop acting like he's already fucking dead. That's what I choose." His heaving chest connects with mine when he brings himself so close to me there's no way I could miss his hushed words. "You say you're not scared of death, that you started our business because you aren't afraid of anything. You lied. You're so scared of dying, you are letting it kill you long before you've lived."

CHAPTER 15

JAMIE

I stop staring at the empty inbox on my phone when Brad enters our walk-in closet. His pricey suit looks cheap since his left eye is still holding remnants of the black eye he got two weeks ago when he was mugged on his way home from a meeting. Raguel said the chances of finding the perp are low since Brad refused to get the police involved.

"Only those with nothing steal from others," he said when I urged for him to contact the authorities. If someone were foolish enough to rob him at knifepoint, what chances would someone like me have if I venture outside after dark?

But no matter how hard I pleaded, he didn't give in. That isn't unusual. If it isn't Brad's idea, it's a bad idea. I guess that's why he shot down my many requests for us to stretch our wedding date to one more suitable for two people who haven't even known each other for a year.

Expensive cologne filters through my nose when Brad bends down to press his lips to my temple. "What are you doing home so early? I thought you had a desk of assessments to get through."

"I did. Hugh sent me home to pack. I head north tomorrow morning."

He jerks back, his brow etching high. "He still wants you to attend the getaway he organized?" When I nod, he shouts, "What for? I thought you made your decision on The Drop Zone's application weeks ago?"

"I did," I reply with a nod. "Hugh still thinks I should attend. He's hoping firsthand claims to go with my reports will have Mr. Luis understanding why I cleared The Drop Zone for insurance."

"You cleared them for insurance?"

I wiggle my finger in my ear. "Jesus, Brad. What's with all the shouting?"

When I stand from the daybed, his hand shoots out to grab my wrist. "I thought we were done with *this*."

By 'this' he means Colby McGregor. Not even being mugged the night before could douse his fury when the *Los Angeles Chronicle* ran a full-page spread on Colby and me dancing. Supposedly, our "happy, loved-up faces" reignited the story that we were on the verge of wedded bliss. The press has been so hounding the past two weeks, I used them as an excuse for Colby's lack of contact the days following him bundling me into a cab in a hurry. When our dance class arrived and passed without a word from him, I realized there was nothing wrong with my email hosting provider. He had cut contact with me.

"You said this silly thing was behind us."

I suck in a big breath before cranking my neck to Brad. "It wasn't silly. It also wasn't a *thing*. He was a friend, Brad, nothing more."

"A friend who just happened to drop you the instant your assessment of *his* coverage was finalized?"

When he sees the truth in my eyes, he smirks a cunning grin. As much as it sucks to admit, he's right. The morning I emailed Hugh the all-clear for The Drop Zone to be sheltered under Metrics' giant insurance umbrella, Colby stopped returning my emails.

"Convenient, wouldn't you say?" Brad releases me from his hold, somewhat aggressively. "I guess his ploy worked, didn't it? Before your little foray of emails, you were prepped to deny his application. Who knew a little flattery was all it took for you to bark when commanded?"

He re-catches my wrist when I attempt to slap him across the face. This hold is firmer than his first. It sends pain zapping up my arm as quickly as it spikes my panic.

"Let me go." My voice is smooth and calm considering I'm seconds from going on a rampage. Brad's moments from discovering I'm not programmed to jump on cue. Murder, though, I'm reasonably sure that's a command I can immediately snap to.

When he releases me from his grip, which is longer than it takes for my wrist to start throbbing, he pushes me back, sending me toppling onto the daybed with a bang. "Embarrass me again, and you'll have more than this on the line." He gestures his hand around an apartment many would consider luxury where all I see is a prison without bars.

After a final sneer, Brad leaves the walk-in closet without so much of a backward glance.

I pack my belongings and leave just as quickly.

"I want out."

I hear Athena tell a cab driver to pull over before the hustle and bustle of LA comes roaring down the line. "You need to speak up, sweetie, I thought I heard you say you want out."

She sounds surprised. Rightfully so. We've had this code for years. If either one of us say, 'I want out,' it means we're ending a relationship. For the past nine years, those three words have only ever been spoken by Athena.

"I do. I want out. Do you still have contact with that divorce attorney? I know we're not technically married, but our assets are too intertwined to do this without assistance."

"What did he do?" I swear China will be able to feel her anger. I'm not even in the same zip code as her, yet I can still feel it. "I swear to God, if it's any of the things your crackling voice is putting in my head, I have a blowtorch at the ready."

For the first time in two weeks, I smile—then I cry.

"Oh, honey… where are you? I'll come to you."

"I'm okay." I slip into the backseat of the cab Raguel is holding out for me before handing him the twenty fisted in my hand. "I'm going to see my parents before I leave. They'll make everything better."

"Okay…" I can tell Athena wants to say more, but she's stumped for a reply. She's not the only one. I've been dying to say those exact words to her for months, and they arrived with as much relief as I predicted. "While you're away, I'll get everything started. You don't need to worry about anything, okay?"

"Okay. Thank you. I appreciate it."

"Call me if you need anything."

I drag my hand under my nose before nodding. "I will."

"I love you, sweetie. It will get better, I promise. The first step is always the hardest, but you've done that now, so it's only onward and upward from here."

I nod, agreeing with her. "I know. I love you too. Bye."

It feels like a good thirty seconds pass before Athena eventually hangs up, and thirty minutes later, I arrive at the assisted-living facility where my mom resides.

"How is she today?"

My dad's big worldly eyes pop over the newspaper he's reading. He's in his favorite position in the corner of my mother's room, watching over her as he has every day for the past eight years. "She's good, sweetheart, real good."

The joy in his tone makes me smile. "How many times today?"

He waves his hand across his hulking frame like he's shooing away a fly. In reality, he's more in love today than he was the day they wed. "Only four. It's been a slow day."

"It's still early. Give her time." After being wrapped up in a smell that reminds me of flannelette sheets and stovetop brewed cocoa, I pad closer to my mom's bed. She glances at me blinking and confused. That isn't unusual for someone with severe Alzheimer's. "Hi, Mom."

The broken heart I anticipated when I made my decision to leave Brad hits me full force when a single tear rolls down her cheek. She's not crying because she doesn't know who I am. She's spotted my dad standing behind me.

"James." She holds out her hands for him, sobbing more when he balances his forehead against hers. They stare into each other's eyes for what feels like a lifetime before my mom says, "We should get married?"

"We should," my dad replies as if today isn't the fifth time she's suggested they renew their vows. "Do you think Jamie could attend? She could be our witness." My dad holds out his hand, inviting me into a duo hug so tight not even Alzheimer's can break it.

"Yes, that would be lovely. She's very beautiful." My mom stares at me like she's seeing me with the curls I straightened this morning. "Do you look like your mother? I think I know her."

When I nod, it's the fight of my life not to let my tears fall. "My dad says that all the time. Except her hair is wilder than mine." I run my hand down the entanglement of curls curtaining her beautiful face.

For the briefest second, hope flares inside me that she's remembering. It's quickly dashed when she shifts her eyes back to my dad and says, "James, we should get married."

CHAPTER 16

COLBY

"*D*on't give me that face, Casper. She's here as a ticketholder, so you sure as fuck better treat her like one."

"Ticketholder? *Right.*"

I don't believe a fucking word Tyrone speaks. He all but glued my hands to the keyboard in an endeavor to get me to return one of the many emails Jamie sent the past two weeks, so I'm supposed to believe she's here solely for an adrenaline-packed weekend.

"I wasn't born last week."

"With how many brain cells you seem to have lost over the past month, I'm beginning to wonder." He shoves the bag of a pretty blonde with fake boobs and clothes way too skimpy for the miserable weather into my chest before making his way to help Jamie with her luggage. "And yeah, that was a low blow, but you deserve it."

Grunting, I toss the blonde's Prada bag into the back of the van we're loading like its trash before giving Tyrone the one-finger salute. We've barely spoken since our 'conversation' in the alleyway two weeks ago, but he doesn't need words to project his annoyance. He's refusing to fumigate my loft of pests, he's not scheduled me for a solo jump in weeks, and anytime I try to get an invite to his tequila and taco Tuesdays, he tells me he doesn't eat according to what day of the week it is anymore. Who under the age of fifty doesn't follow a weekatarian diet? That would be like saying not to throw candy bars at women during their menstrual cycle. Both notions are ridiculous.

I wind down my upstanding finger when a big pair of aqua eyes lock with it over Tyrone's shoulder. Jamie's eyes are narrowed into tiny slits, but their thinness can't hide the roll they do. I return her stare, pretending I'm not pissed I didn't treat her like every other woman I've come across. I should have worked her out of my system when I had the chance. Fucked her until the smile she wears while dancing no longer highlights my dreams. I should have chewed her up and spat her out, then the sadness in her eyes wouldn't affect me like it is.

She's a taken woman.

Engaged.

Soon to be wed.

Not on my fucking radar.

But even if she were, I doubt I would have treated her like every other woman I've bedded.

Tyrone was right. I was different around her. It's amazing how much you can be yourself when you're not trying to impress somebody. We were only friends and doing the most mundane tasks, but the time she was in my life before I said I'd step back were some of the best weeks of my life.

This is Cate's fault—stupid fucking dare.

After reluctantly handing her suitcase to Tyrone, Jamie shadows him to the van assigned to take us to a cabin in the dense forest in Northern Cali. Her narrowed eyes taper even more when she takes in the women flanking me. They're fluffing their hair and checking their makeup for the hundredth time this morning, unaware the only people they'll see for the next four days signed a contract agreeing to keep things professional at all times—myself included. I don't recall a non-fraternization policy being discussed when we dreamed up this trip, but since I rarely pay attention during meetings, who was I to call Tyrone out as being a lying two-faced back-stabbing motherfucker.

What? It's been a hard two weeks. You have no clue how hard it is to decipher the number of buttons a woman has undone when she's wearing a cashmere sweater over her shirt, then face the risk of booting them out yourself if your calculations are off. Screw that. That wasn't a risk I was willing to take, so not only has Jamie's smile featured in my nighttime dreams, it's taken up a good chunk of my daytime ones as well. You can imagine how well that's going down with the python in my pants?

Tyrone places Jamie's luggage into the van before shifting on his feet to face me. I tighten my jaw when his smug grin tells me I won't like what he has to say next, "Colby, you remember Jamie, right? The insurance assessor you threw off a cliff but somehow managed not to get sued."

I give him a look, one that warns we'll be having words with our fists real soon. "Of course, how could I forget having her fiancé strapped to my chest? It's a pleasure seeing you again, Jamie."

Yep, Colby McGregor turns into an asshole when the woman he thought was smart enough not to be manipulated is, *and* he hasn't been laid in weeks.

Jamie leaves the handshake I'm offering hanging, her devotion fixed on Tyrone. "There's still time." When he peers at her in confusion, and with way too much admiration for my liking, she adds, "To sue him. The standard statute of limitations is one year, so I've got plenty of time to decide since the charges brought forward would be much more severe than a standard civil suit."

When she climbs into the van to find a seat, I mumble, "You better hurry, my insurance runs out next week."

She gives me the same doe-eyed look Tyrone gave her, but before she can voice a single word I see in her eyes, I slide the van door shut so we can commence our six-hour commute to a cabin with open fireplaces, a twelve-man jacuzzi, and not a single person to enjoy it with. *Boo-fucking-hoo!*

"If you're planning to continue your I-don't-like-her ruse for the next four days, you better quit staring at her. It's getting very creepy real quick."

After dumping two weeks' worth of Twizzlers, Milk Duds, and M&M's onto the passenger seat of the van, I shoot Tyrone a warning look before devoting my focus back to Jamie. She's standing in the middle of a puddle-drenched lot, wrangling a bent umbrella and a cell phone as she endeavors not to let brutal winds give the truckers eyeballing her a peek of her no-doubt cotton panties.

"What's she doing? Trying to get electrocuted?" I strive to make my voice sound hopeful. I should purchase a one-way ticket out of LA—I'm a shit actor. "If she wants cell service, she'll have to wait until we arrive at the cabin, and even then, it'll be sporadic."

Tyrone waits for the gas pump to click before placing it back on its holder. "She said it was too important to wait."

"Probably giving her fiancé his tenth update for the morning." For a man who swears he doesn't work out, Tyrone has a lot of *oomph* in his whack when he hits me in the stomach. "What the fuck was that for?"

He hands Claudia three Benjamin Franklins to pay for our gas before shifting on his feet to face me. "For a man who hasn't quit staring at her for the past four hours, your observation skills are shit." I glare at him, a little lost—even more so when he says, "She's not wearing her engagement ring, douche canoe." His smirk turns smug when my heart rate skyrockets. "Ah, look at you perking up like I just inserted an IV of coffee into your veins."

I make a *pfft* noise, trying my best to play it cool. "She's probably getting it cleaned in preparation for their wedding." That hurt to say more than I care to admit. "We saw them at the gala last week. They were *very much* together." *Even with her wearing the dress I bought her mere seconds after busting her fiancé kissing another woman.*

"I didn't see shit. Couldn't past your stalker watch. They don't hold masked balls so the freaks can mingle without fear of prosecution—" His interrogation bomb misses its target when I steer it off course with my fist. He doesn't stay down for long.

Once his lungs are replenished with air, he recommences his campaign to take me down. "Maybe her wearing the dress you purchased was her way of trying to reach out to you when you cut her off."

"I didn't cut her off. I..." *Ran like a fucking coward.* "It doesn't matter what I did. You were right. I don't know her like I thought I did."

Tyrone squeezes my shoulder, his firmness convincing it's more to maim than offer support. "If you truly believe that, I'm not the only idiot standing under this awning."

After a second squeeze, he advises our clients their twenty-minute pit stop is up and to return to the van. Most follow through with his request, but Jamie pleads for another five minutes. She's more drenched than she is dry, but Tyrone approves her request as if her happiness is more important than the other two dozen people who paid to spend a long weekend surrounded by wilderness and not smelly cattle trucks and roadkill.

"We need to go. It will be dusk soon, and the rain is already slowing us down."

Jamie takes a giant step to the left, clearing the girth of Tyrone's shoulders so she can lock her eyes with mine. I can barely see hers through the fog on her lenses, but from what I can see, she's fuming mad. "It's five minutes. I'm sure it won't kill you."

"If I give you five minutes, I have to give everyone five minutes. That will add up to a whole heap of minutes no one wants to waste at a gas station."

"Yeah. Let's go. It stinks here, and the toilets are..." A gag finalizes the blonde's whine.

I can't recall her name even with her advising me of it many times the past four hours. She's an attractive girl in her early twenties, and she has the perfect three-button combination, but her voice alone gives me a headache, not to mention her numerous stories about the television pilots she has coming up. I didn't realize how unattractive ditziness is until I became friends with Jamie. We talked for hours after our dance classes, and not once did I want to shove my head into an oven. Within ten minutes of the blonde talking, I am seeking a blunt instrument to gouge out my eardrums.

"No one asked for your input, Barbie, so why don't you shut your—"

"Jamie!"

I arch my brow, praying it will hide the excitement flaring through me that she finally stood up to the Playboy Mansion wannabee. She's been snickering nasty comments about Jamie all morning, but since putting catty bitches in their place isn't in my job description, I let her comments slide—for the most part. I may have requested Tyrone to schedule her to jump with Dallas. He has the looks needed to encourage more female jumpers to visit The Drop Zone, but he comes as quickly as an average man sneezes.

"Fine!"

Jamie wrangles her umbrella into submission, forgetting she needs it to keep her sheltered from the rain before marching toward the awning I'm standing under. With how hard the rain is pelting down, she looks like a drowned rat in under a minute. She isn't feeling it, though. She's too mad to worry about a little bit of wetness.

After thrusting her umbrella into my chest, she climbs into the van. With the only hostile client seated, the rest follow suit. Since Jamie took my seat, the one facing the opposite direction to which we're traveling, I fill the spot her backside was planted on in the previous four hours. It's better this way. I can watch her without wondering if my position is the cause of the queasiness in my stomach. If it occurs this time around, I'll know its churns are solely her fault.

———

Jamie remains quiet the first forty minutes of our trip. I would like to say so does everyone else. Regrettably, that would be a lie. Unlike the first section of our trip, this time, it isn't the blonde bombshells snickering about Jamie. It's men—grown men who should know women don't find derogative comments about their bodies appealing.

Yes, Jamie's nipples are braced against her shirt that's clinging to her chest. Yes, she's cold enough the little bumps circling her areola give a great indication on how perky and firm her tits are. No, you don't get to request for the driver to turn up the AC because 'you're burning up everywhere.' And no, motherfucker, you do not get to murmur about the many ways you plan to warm her up when we arrive at the cabin.

When I twist in my seat, preparing to rearrange the face of the douchebags behind me, Tyrone pins me to the seat with his arm. "They're paying customers." His words are whispers, but we're in a van, so everyone can hear them.

"Just because you pay for something doesn't mean you get to be an *asshole.*" I practically shout my last word.

"It does if it lowers the chances of us getting sued. You know what O'Donnell said... this weekend is our last chance."

That lowers my turbines as much as it tightens my jaw. O'Donnell is our last hope. If he doesn't find a broker willing to insure us, our planes will be grounded from five o'clock next Friday afternoon. I wasn't lying when I said I didn't know the real Jamie. Not even twelve hours after my confrontation with her fiancé, an email arrived in my inbox. It advised The Drop Zone's request for coverage had been denied on the grounds I refused to stand down as its face.

Not going to lie, her email gutted me. It wasn't because she couldn't see through the bureaucratic crap others thrust in her face, it was the fact she couldn't see the weasel of a man directly in front of her. I thought she was a good judge of character, the way she had my back after my jump with Brad proved this, but I guess I'm also learning there's only one person I can trust. Myself.

CHAPTER 17

JAMIE

A long grateful moan rolls up my chest when I peel my long-sleeve shirt over my head. It was stupid of me to stand in a storm with a jacked-up umbrella and my cell phone thrust out like I was Benjamin Franklin praying for a lightning bolt, but what I told Tyrone was true. My desire to untwist the knot in my stomach couldn't wait another two hours. I'm shocked I managed to reel back the desire for the first four. I wouldn't have if I hadn't stupidly housed my cell in my suitcase.

"Whoa... I'm so sorry." Tyrone's hands shoot up to cover his eyes when he realizes I'm wearing nothing but soaked trousers and a lace bra. "It took me a bit to find, but I discovered the landline." He jingles a brick-like phone in his hand before peering over it to check the coast is clear. It is, but my crepe-paper-thin cami doesn't alleviate the situation. White tissue-paper material and lace aren't the best items to cover rosy pink nipples.

I pace to my suitcase to replace my wet shirt with a sweater. "Is it in order?"

Tyrone waits for me to drag my sweater over my head before stepping deeper into my assigned room for the weekend. "Yeah. I'm not sure how long the battery will last, but it has a dial tone."

"Great. Thank you." I accept the cordless phone from his grasp while pretending my cheeks aren't on fire.

That would be a heap easier to do if he didn't say, "I was wrong about you." My arched brow encourages him to continue. "I said what you lacked in the front you made up for in the trunk. I was wrong." I'd be on the verge of sobbing if a gleam in his eyes didn't tell me everything will be all right. "You should wear fitted clothes more often. Let people see you've got the goods both front and back."

I smile like we're at Macy's, and the Thanksgiving parade just started.

Tyrone's smile matches mine. "I'm glad you came, Jamie. I'm sure it wasn't an easy decision to make."

"I didn't have much choice."

He shrugs, not believing me. I understand. Even a stranger would have heard the deceit in my tone. "Still, you're here instead of out there." He swings his eyes to the window that shows the howling storm hasn't let up for the past three hours. My smile takes on a new meaning when he cringes. "Let's hope that clears by tomorrow, or I'll have a heap of bouncing checks to write."

His long strides out of my room slacken when I say, "Climatic events are covered with most travel insurance policies. As long as your contract was worded right, you have no reason to offer refunds."

"I wasn't talking about our clients." He rubs his hands together like he's suddenly cold. "I was referring to Colby. If this weekend doesn't pan out the way I'm hoping, I'll most likely have to buy him out. The money is there, I'm just not sure it's something I want to do." Tyrone's not unsure. His eyes reveal he straight-up doesn't want to travel this path.

"Is this what Colby wants? Does he want you to buy him out?"

Tyrone shakes his head. "No, but being at The Drop Zone and not jumping may very well kill him." He looks like he wants to say more, but something stops him. "Anyway, I'll let you get settled in."

I want to tell him everything will be okay, that it isn't as it seems, but until I unjumble the confusion in my head, I can't be expected to clear it from others.

With that in mind, I sit cross-legged on the massive bed in my ginormous room before dialing a well-used number on the borrowed phone. Hugh answers three rings later. "I thought we agreed to a communication ban this weekend?"

I pull the phone down to check it's still the brick Tyrone handed me before squashing it back to my ear. "How'd you know it was me?"

"Who do I know in Bigfoot territory?"

When a long, controlled breath follows his question, my jaw quivers. "Are you smoking?"

"No!" One word shouldn't call him out as a liar, but it does.

"Hugh Bartholomew Barnett, you quit smoking six months ago. If Kate finds out, you'll be in big trouble, mister."

"Kate won't find out, will she, Jamie?" I picture him stubbing out the butt with his shoe when jutted breaths shrill down the line. "I need something to take the edge off. Things are hectic down here."

"Then why did you force *this* on me?" I thrust my hand around my room that's the size of most log cabins but in a money-will-make-you-happy type of way.

"Because you need *this* more than I need the occasional hit of nicotine." Because I've worked with him for so long, I know his 'this' is more regarding my personal life than our professional ties.

"I left Brad."

He sucks in a breath that's withdrawn with a cough. I'm about to lecture him on better lung health, but his next set of words alter the direction of our conversation. "I gathered that's why he was stomping around here this morning like he owns the place."

"He came to Metrics?"

"Yes." I hear an elevator ding before his voice starts to echo. "I didn't speak with him, but he and Athena shared words."

"Is she okay?" My high heart rate is heard in my question.

"Yes." Who knew so much suspicion could be voiced with only one word? "Why wouldn't she be?"

I'm saved from his interrogation by a second beep. This one isn't from Hugh's side. It's the brick in my hand announcing it's low on battery.

"Listen, I'm about to lose charge, and this can't wait until Tuesday."

"Jamie—"

"Hugh, I swear to God, I'm fine. I've never felt more at ease, but I need your focus on something else."

He sighs. "Okay… but when you get back—"

"We'll have words. I get it." I wait for him to sigh again, this one more in agreement than annoyance before advising Hugh of the reason for the breach in our no-electronics-weekend contract. "Colby is under the impression The Drop Zone's renewal was denied by Metrics. Do you know why he'd believe that? I sent you my reports with the recommendation that they were clear for coverage."

"I know that. I forwarded your reports along with my own the same day. As far as I'm aware, they're covered." I hear papers being ruffled. "It's here somewhere." Another twenty seconds pass before his search is awarded. "Yes, here it is. Coverage was extended for another five years with the stipulation it could face a new investigation if any claims were brought forward within the first year."

"So it was approved, and they have coverage?" The hope in my tone can't be missed.

"Yes. It's here, right in front of me."

"Can you forward it to me?"

I cringe before apologizing to Hugh for my ear-piercing squeal. I'm not excited this evidence will get Colby off my back, I'm just eager to use it to show him what an egotistical asshole he is. I get why he's angry, he did everything I requested to have his application approved, but if this accidental miscommunication is the reason he cut contact with me, Brad was right. He's a user who only befriended me because he thought it would benefit his quest for coverage.

If I were even a smidge of the woman both he and Brad think I am, I could ignore the oversight and let Colby believe his coverage was denied. Regrettably, what Mr. Luis said weeks ago is true. As an insurance assessor, my personal feelings should never enter the equation. They didn't when I recommended that The Drop Zone be covered under the Metrics Insurance umbrella, just like they won't be now.

"How do I get a sheet of paper to you in the middle of nowhere?" Hugh doesn't mean figuratively. He has no clue how to send documents since faxes were decommissioned from our office five years ago.

"Give it to Athena. She'll handle it."

"Okay."

When feet-stomping sounds down the line, I imagine him running through our office, holding the sheet of paper in front of him as if it is a dirty diaper. I hear him advise Athena he needs something faxed to me before the line goes dead a mere second before the lights.

"Goddammit."

With the light on my cell phone leading the way, I make my way into the main living area where the rest of the guests are congregating. Blow-Up Barbie hisses at me like a cat when I walk past her, and the two men who stared in the van could have dried me if they didn't arrive with a heap of drool making gaga faces at me. After the week I've had, I'm more pleased by their attention than frustrated—regrettably.

"The power will be back on within a few minutes. We need to wait for the generator to kick in. Until then, why don't we gather around the fireplace to stay warm." After handing Blow-Up Barbie and her friends a blanket, Tyrone makes his way to me. "You all right?"

"Yeah. This died just before the lights. Figured I should put it on its charging base for when the power comes back on."

He jerks up his chin. "It's in the office." Tyrone gestures behind me before motioning for me to follow him.

As we glide past the kitchen, little rays of sunshine beam through its windows. "The rain is trying to let up."

"Finally."

When we enter the office, which is just as quaint and beautiful as the rest of the cabin, I gasp at the picturesque mountain backdrop. "Wow. Who wouldn't live without cell service for a view like that?" My comment pops a brilliant idea into my head. "What's service like at the peak?"

"Too dangerous to consider trekking today to find out." These words didn't come from Tyrone they came from Colby, whose shoulder is propped on the doorframe, acting casual even though his face shows he's still the grumpy-ass I've been dealing with the past eight hours. "*If* the rain holds off, and power doesn't return, we'll consider a hike tomorrow morning."

Pissed at the superiority in his tone and still harboring anger from our earlier tussle, I get extra snarky. "Or I could go now? Find out for myself?" I skirt past Tyrone, acting like he isn't urging me to listen to Colby's advice without words. "I've got important matters to attend to."

"Like ensuring you don't miss your fiancé's check-in deadline?"

Can you kill someone with a death-stare? Please say yes because I'm about to murder Colby McGregor with one.

When I exit the office by a door on my right, Colby calls my name in a deep, grumbly tone. I don't stop. I'm too pissed to listen to reason, especially when it's coming from an immature insensitive jerk.

"Jamie, I swear to God, if you go out that door, I'll..."

While shoving my feet into a pair of big muddy gumboots I found by the back door, I stare up at Colby. His voice was threatening, but I'm not the slightest bit worried. He'd never hurt me—physically.

"You'll…"

When he fails to answer me, I push through the door like a loud clap of thunder didn't just rumble above my head. Trees with big umbrella-size leaves canopy my trek, but nothing can ease the chill running down my spine. It's not just cold, it's below freezing.

My teeth chatter out of control, but they're barely heard over the squeal I emit when I'm suddenly grabbed from behind. "Are you fucking insane? That's not rain, it's sleet. Do you want to catch pneumonia?"

"It'll be worth it when I prove you're a using piece of shit."

Like I did in the ocean, I use my feet to propel myself away from Colby. He falls back with a groan, his hands shooting down to protect the package my body failed to ignore rubbing against me even when I warned I'd withhold its orgasms for the next century if it didn't commit. It probably would have listened if it had any clue what it was missing out on. I can't recall the last time I orgasmed, but I'm reasonably sure it wasn't with Brad.

With Colby on his knees, he devises a new tactic to take me down. It's as dirty as the sneer he wears when he snags my ankle to tug my legs out from beneath me. I land with a splash, my mouth, nose, and glasses bombarded with muddy water.

After screaming blue murder, I flip onto my back then give as good as I'm getting. I thrash out with all my might, ensuring some part of my body connects with Colby's. I kick and kick and kick when he crawls toward me in an attempt to pin me to the ground with his big, imposing body.

Once he has my legs and torso subdued, he secures my

hands to the side of my head, then lowers his wild eyes to mine. I can barely see them through the slosh on my glasses. "Stop it! You're acting like a lunatic."

"Get off me..." I sound like a mental patient, but now my anger is being unleashed, I can't reel it back in. I'm aware not all my frustrations should be directed at Colby, but since he's the only one here challenging me, he's receiving the brunt of it. "Before I sue you for every penny you have."

Colby's grip on my wrists tightens. It doesn't hit me with one-tenth of the pain Brad's clutch did. He's not holding me down to hurt me, instead he's trying to contain me. "As I said earlier, you better be quick. Would hate for you to lose the chance when my insurance runs out."

I scream my frustration into his face. "I don't know why I bothered. You're such an idiot, even if I were to thrust the truth in your face, you still wouldn't believe it." I kick and buck like I'm not on the verge of climax from having his panty-wetting face so close to mine. "Let. Me. Go!"

CHAPTER 18

COLBY

"Colby..." Tyrone only says my name, but it's the words he doesn't speak I hear the loudest. *Breathe it out.* "You need to let her go."

I lower my eyes to Jamie, all red-faced and on the verge of crying. "I will when she takes it down a notch." I hate seeing her like this, but I'd rather have her kicking and screaming at me than fighting for her life when she catches pneumonia.

"No, Colby. You need to let her go. *Now.* Don't make me ask you again."

My eyes rocket up to Tyrone who's pissed as fuck. I'd never hurt Jamie, but he's making it seem as if I'm digging a knife into her ribs.

All my daggers miss their mark. Tyrone isn't looking at me, he's glaring at something above me—something that makes my stomach recoil when I follow the direction of his gaze.

"Fuck."

I scoot back, horrified by the circular bruise on Jamie's

wrist. She's too worked up to understand my quick retreat. She thinks I'm threatened by Tyrone's tone, having no clue the tantrum she just threw will barely be a rumble to the storm I'll rain down on the person responsible for marking her when I find out who. That bruise isn't newly formed. It didn't happen during our tussle.

After picking herself up from the mud-soaked ground, Jamie yanks off her glasses before thrusting her cell phone into my face. "Look what you did. Are you happy? You ruined it." Sludge drips off her phone even more than her glasses. It must have fallen into a puddle when I tripped her. "Now, I can't show you how much of an idiot you are." With her voice on the verge of cracking, she shoves me in the chest before storming back toward the cabin.

"Jamie..."

Tyrone blocks my path with his six-foot-three frame and wide shoulders. He gives me a look that warns he'll hold me down like I did Jamie if I don't follow through with his nonverbalized threats.

"I didn't do that to her." I point in the direction Jamie just stormed, my hand shaking more than my words.

The anger in his face recedes. "I know that, but if it happened the way we're both panicked about, pinning her to the ground won't help matters. Hell, it might even make them worse."

"What if there's more? What if that isn't the only one on her body?"

He crouches down in front of me, bringing his dark worldly eyes level with mine. "What if she's stronger than either of us are giving her credit for? What if that's the reason she's no longer wearing her ring? There are a lot of what if's, Colby, and only one person who can switch them from theories to facts." He nudges his head to the cabin that's once again lit since the emergency generator kicked in. "You said you were her friend—"

"I *am* her friend," I correct.

Tyrone smiles, exposing that I interrupted as he had hoped. "Then be her friend."

"It isn't that simple. If I get close, she'll get hurt, Ty." My use of his nickname exposes how badly my emotions are teetering. It wasn't easy staying away from Jamie the past two weeks, but I did it because it was the right thing to do. It was the only way I could ensure no one would get hurt.

Tyrone looks into my eyes, so I can see how serious he is. "Did you see her face? She's already hurting." His words whack me in the gut, making me want to bend in half. "Besides, you're the only egomaniac who thinks people won't forget you as easily as you'll forget them. For all you know, she may not even remember you next week. You're not that memorable."

I smirk at the mirth in his tone before shaking my head. Confident I got the message, he messes my hair like it isn't filled with muddy slosh, then re-enters the cabin. I take a few minutes to center myself before following after him. The silence when I walk into the main living area reveals my exchange with Jamie wasn't solely witnessed by Tyrone. Pity for them, I don't give a fuck what anyone thinks of me—*except perhaps Jamie.*

As I make my way to the shower, they glance at me sympathetically, clueless to the secret Tyrone and I now share. Jamie's sleeve hides her bruise so well, I may not have discovered it if my ego didn't get the better of me. I didn't just storm after her as I didn't want her to get sick, I wanted her to take me seriously for a change. I'm a goofball but not when it comes to my business. That's why I was so surprised she denied my claim for insurance. I did what she asked. I jumped through all her hoops, and I did it without letting my frustration about bureaucratic bullshit tag along in our friendship. During business hours, she was Ms. Burgess, my insurance assessor. Outside of those hours, she was my friend—*is my friend.*

After taking a shower and changing my clothes, I head to the office to finalize our itinerary for tomorrow. With the recent rain, it would be smart to switch our whitewater rafting expedition from Monday afternoon to tomorrow morning. I'm also hoping for a bit of solidarity. I want to talk to Jamie, but I need to get my headspace right first. I'm reasonably sure I know who bruised her, but without the means to set motions in play to take him down, I've got plenty of time to ensure they're the right steps to take.

I freeze halfway into my office. Jamie is sitting at my desk, tinkering with a computer that's almost as old as me. "If you're searching for games, you're shit out of luck. Tyrone had them removed last year. Said something about playing snakes and ladders isn't the same thing as predicting profits and loss." Her smile isn't half the one I was aiming for, but it's better than none. "Jamie, about—"

She cuts me off by slicing her hand through the air. "Don't apologize. I shouldn't have reacted as I did. It was highly unprofessional. It won't happen again." Her tone is the same proficient, ball-stomping one she used the day we met. I fucking hate it.

After a halfhearted smile, she returns her focus to the computer monitor. "Ugh! Come on." She rattles the box-like contraption, praying it shakes some sense into it.

"Gentle. She's an old thing. She doesn't like being rough handled." When she peers at me over the rim of her hideous, but once again clean glasses, the heaviness on my chest weakens. It's faint, but I swear a glimmer of the Jamie I stood across from while dancing is igniting in her eyes. "I meant the computer, not you, *grandma*." I whisper my last word loud enough she'll hear me, but soft enough she'll think I didn't want her to. If she's insurance-assessor Jamie, she'll act unaffected. If she's the Jamie I'm hoping, she'll smack me on the up side of the head with one of the many instruments in front of her.

My hope grows when her hand creeps toward a brick-like cordless phone.

They're dashed when she picks it up and squashes it to her ear. "There's my issue. No dial tone."

My brows shoot up. "You need a dial tone to use the computer?"

Jamie huffs while slouching low in my chair. She looks good in my space, like we've stepped back in time before internet connections and cell service. That probably has more to do with her wild, crazy hair than her clothes. Our tussle in the muddy field un-straightened her hair that should remain kinked. Her natural hair is beautiful, so I have no clue why she 'irons' it every morning.

"You do when it's dial-up."

"Dial what?" She laughs like I'm joking. I'm not. *What the hell is dial-up?*

She balances her elbows on the desk, her eyes more sparkling than they were thirty seconds ago. "Let me guess, you've never heard of a rotary phone either?"

"A whatta whatta?" I take a mental note to make up a hundred fake words after she smiles at the pathetic one I just

153

made up. When she nudges her head to a hefty-looking contraption next to the antiquated computer she's attempting to use, my brows furl. "What the fuck is that?"

"It's a phone." Jamie talks to me like I'm mentally challenged. It reduces the tension suffocating the air even more. "Try and use it."

I almost fall for her trick. "Nice try. It's one of those electric buzzing machines, isn't it? Tyrone pulled a swift one on me last year. I'm not falling for it again." I'm reasonably sure I'm right as it has a silver circular piece in the middle. That's most likely the part that will zap my pubic hairs off my balls when I touch it.

With her eyes watering, this time from laughter instead of tears, she picks up the clumpy object on top that looks remarkedly similar to a phone receiver. "It won't zap you... unless you use it in a storm." After thrusting it my way, she nudges her head to the bottom half. "Try and dial a number." When I snatch her hand off the desk, she balks. I hate the move-ment even more than the bruise on her wrist. "What are you doing?"

I act cool, calm, and unaffected even though I'm anything but. "If it zaps me, it's going to zap you, too. Electricity travels through bodies. Believe me, I tested the theory on electric fences many times in my youth." Her smile makes up for her flinch. "So this is your last chance, Prim. If you don't want to be electrocuted, speak now or forever hold your peace."

Without warning, she spins the circular thing in the middle of the 'phone' before screaming like someone just stabbed her. After laughing at my whitening face—which is only white because her scream ripped my heart out of my chest—she releases her hand from mine, stands from her chair, then makes her way to the door. "You're such an idiot. It's *only* a phone" Before she exits, she cranks her neck back my way. "About your insurance renewal—"

"It doesn't matter."

She peers at me like I have two heads. I'm beginning to wonder the same thing. I thought my world would come tumbling down if I were denied the opportunity of jumping professionally. Although her email stung my ego, it was nothing on the burn I felt when I noticed her injured wrist.

"Your company had stipulations they required me to follow. I didn't agree with them, so you had every reason to deny my request."

She steps closer to me, seemingly confused. "I didn't deny your claim, Colby. I approved it." The honesty in her eyes could only be more shocking if she told me she loved me. "Yes, we had stipulations, but after meeting with you and hearing your side of the story, it became apparent we weren't being fair." She flexes her fingers as if she feels uncomfortable about her next set of words, but hopes the gain will far exceed the unease. "But please don't think our… *friendship…*" she says the word like it made her stomach roll, "… had anything to do with my decision. I sought advice from practitioners, specialists in your field, and other agencies before making my decision. It wasn't done lightly or without due diligence."

"Not that it matters, but I got an email from you stating our claim had been denied. Here, I'll show you."

When I dig my hand into my pocket to retrieve my phone, she returns to my side of the desk. I thought providing proof of my claim would ease the groove etched between her brows. I was wrong—very much so.

"Oh, look, you could read my supposed email with the

subject 'insurance application,' but all the others remain unread." She flicks her finger up the screen, showing unread email after unread email from her personal account. If that isn't bad enough, my inbox reveals I opened plenty of emails from women not named Jamie. "I can't believe I'm going to say this, but Brad was right about you."

When she turns to leave, I grab her wrist, which I drop like it scorched my hand when I realize it's her bruised one. "Brad doesn't know me." I impress myself by only expressing his name with the slightest sneer.

"No, he doesn't, but he predicted *that* weeks before I worked it out for myself." She points to the open email during the 'that' part of her comment. "He knew whether your insurance was approved or denied, you'd drop our so-called friendship within hours of my decision." When her hands fall to her side from air quoting 'so-called,' she spreads them across her hips. "Was it even hours, Colby? Or was it as fast as your eagerness to get away from your previous four-button clingers?"

I'm shocked she's referencing herself as one of my bed companions, but it doesn't stop me from retaliating. "My insurance application had nothing to do with my absence of late."

When she *tsks* and rolls her eyes, my brain screams at me to tell her the real reason, not to let her leave here thinking our friendship meant nothing when it was some of the most carefree weeks I've had, but no matter how loud it yells, no matter how often I call myself an idiot, I let her walk away not having a clue what she means to me.

CHAPTER 19

JAMIE

"Good morning, Jamie, how'd you sleep?" Tyrone adds a big beaming smile to his greeting. It should be illegal to be so chipper at this time of the day.

"Remarkedly good... considering." My eyes light up when he jingles a jar of hot chocolate in front of me. "Yes, please." After plopping into a seat in the middle of the country kitchen, I stray my wary eyes around the cabin. "Where's everyone?"

"Claudia took them for a hike. If her underhanded scope comes up trumps, we should be set for whitewater rafting later this morning." I mouth a 'thank you' when he hands me a cup of warm cocoa. "What do you say, are you up for some water activities that don't involve wrestling in the mud?"

I glare at him sardonically. It doesn't even singe his eyebrows. Tyrone laughs it off as if I poked out my tongue instead of glaring at him like I'm attempting to kill him.

"Will Colby be there?"

"I'd say so since he scouts the expeditions." He moves

around the kitchen as if he were born to be a cook instead of feeding the adrenaline junkies of the state. "Is what Colby said true? Did you approve our request for insurance?"

I stop sipping on my delicious drink to peer up at him. "Yes, but it wasn't because of my friendship with Colby—"

"You can stop right there. If I had the slightest inkling you could have been wooed into siding with us, I wouldn't have left the task up to Colby. His idea of romance is letting you shower first after he has..."

When he glances at me with wide, apologetic eyes, I laugh. "I get it." I take a large gulp of my hot chocolate being setting it down. "So, the whole 'are you okay, Ms. Burgess' after my base jump was how you treat all your clients?"

Tyrone's embarrassed cheeks are super cute. "Not at all. But can you blame me? You had the adrenaline junkie gleam after only one jump." He tugs on the collar of his shirt. "It had me thinking all sorts of naughty thoughts... thoughts Colby wanted to pummel me for after he drove you home."

Okay, maybe they aren't his embarrassed cheeks.

"Now that I've been honest and stopped wondering how many floral panties you have in your lingerie drawer—"

"Seven."

"Huh?"

I wait for a bead of sweat to stop rolling down his cheek before saying, "Seven floral panties, half a dozen thongs, twelve boy legs, and an infinite number of lace panties. They're my favorite." I raise my mug to my mouth to hide my smile. "Oh, and let's not forget those monstrosities no one wants to talk about, but hey, when you're cramping, you don't care what your panties look like." I shoot my eyes to the left when smoke burns them. "Tyrone?"

"Yes, Ms. Burgess…" He stares at me like I'm holding a treat, and he's waiting for me to throw it.

I point to the retro oven. "I think the bacon is on fire."

"Oh, fuck… shit!"

After pulling the skillet off the hotplate, he yanks a tea towel off his hip to fan the smoke outside. When alarms start hollering, Colby charges into the kitchen with a fire extinguisher in his hands and a fretful expression on his face. Although the flames have been doused with water, he coats the extra crispy bacon with a product no amount of rinsing will remove. He's gone and ruined breakfast—along with my appetite for the rest of eternity. I doubt anything will be appealing after seeing him in nothing but a teeny tiny towel, *although I've never been more thirsty.*

"What the fuck, Tyrone? The only time I've ever seen you burn bacon was when…" He stops speaking, his eyes colliding with mine after a quick scan of the premise. "Jamie…" He grits his teeth before shifting his focus back to Tyrone. *"Jamie?"* This one is more a growl than a word.

"Woah. Step back. It's not what you're thinking." Tyrone steps back when Colby does the opposite of his demand. "She told me about her panty collection. You know what I'm like with panty collections."

"She told you about her panty collection?" When Tyrone nods, Colby's wide eyes snap to mine. "You told him about your panty collection?"

I shrug like my heart isn't racing a million miles an hour. "Yeah. So?"

"So? *So?* You never told me about your panty collection, but you told Tyrone? Why?"

My lips twist like I'm considering a reason. I'm not. I just want it to appear that way. "I like Tyrone. He's my friend." I stand from my seat, taking my cocoa with me. "You are not." Just before I exit the kitchen, I sling my head back their way. "Furthermore, his heated cheeks are *really* cute."

An hour later, Tyrone knocks on my room door. "Come on, you and I have a meeting with some firewood."

"I'm good." I return my eyes to the book I'm reading.

"I wasn't asking, Jamie. I was telling. Let's go." He jerks his head to the right. "After the mess you left me to clean, the least you can do is gather resources with me."

I would continue with my stubborn stance if his reply didn't hammer me with guilt. I didn't mean to throw him into the deep end. I just couldn't help but use him to annoy Colby. It returned some of the confidence I lost last night when I realized my emails were the only ones Colby had ignored the past two weeks.

"Fine. But if I get a splinter—"

"I'll call you an ambulance. Yeah, yeah, I get it. Girlie shit 101."

Tyrone guides me to the mudroom at the back of the property before handing me boots, a thick coat, a beanie, and a pair of leather gloves. Once I'm dressed, he gives me my last item for the morning. An ax. "You're serious about the firewood?"

"You bet your ass I am."

I whine like a teenage girl being told the internet is getting cut off. "This isn't the experience I signed up for."

He shoves me out the door. "Join the club, sister."

Several clumps of wood later, I sit on top of a pile we've barely made a dent in before rubbing the kink in my neck.

"Feeling better?" Tyrone splits a large chunk of wood like it's made out of Jell-O before raising his eyes to me. If my head weren't clouded with a heap of confusion, I'd pay more attention to his thick, bulging biceps and ripped stomach not even a padded jacket can hide.

"That I have enough wood to keep warm?"

He laughs at me like I'm an idiot. I am, but I'd rather him not spell it out for me. "That you worked out some of your funk. It's not a boxing bag or jumping out of a plane, but no matter how you get them, your body gobbles up every hit of adrenaline it gets like its crack and you're an addict."

Although I'm exhausted, there's some truth in his comment. I do feel better now than I did when waking this morning. "Yeah. I'm feeling better."

"Good." He splits another chunk of wood before tossing it into the pieces we worked through the past hour. "Now, you might be willing to listen." I attempt to interrupt him, but he keeps talking like he hasn't seen my arms wailing in the air. "Colby didn't back away from you because he wanted to. I forced him to."

"Huh?" That was not what I was anticipating for him to say.

"We had words, I expressed that maybe you weren't who he thought you were, so he backed away to prove a point. I was wrong. I fucked up, and I'm sorry."

Wow. I don't think I've ever had a man be so upfront before. It's unusual, but something I could get used to.

"The thing is… Colby is stubborn. Even with me telling him

I made a mistake, he won't back down. That's why I need you to step up to the plate." I recoil back like he threw the towel he cleaned his face with into mine. "I know I'm asking a lot, but he needs someone like you in his life. You got through to him like no one ever has."

"That's because he wanted something from me..." I swallow my words when Tyrone glares at me. I've never felt lucky to be a woman until now because if his glare is anything to go by, my vagina saved me from sporting a new bruise.

"Even if that were true, isn't that the way friendship works? Everybody wants something. Fun. Commitment. Understanding. That's why we seek mates our entire life because we crave something we can't give ourselves."

"That may be the case with relationships, but it isn't what Colby and I had."

There he goes with his glare again.

"We weren't friends. We were just..." I pause, having no clue how to explain what we had. It was crazy and unreal and some of the best weeks of my life.

"You were more than friends."

I shake my head, denying the accusation in Tyrone's tone. "We never stepped over the line." Physically. Emotionally is a whole other story.

Tyrone stops to stand in front of me. "I never said you did, but you don't need sexual contact to have a soul connection with someone. That's why it's called *soul*mates because it isn't embodied."

"We're not soulmates." I raise my confused eyes to his. "Are we?"

Relieved he appears to be getting through to me, the panic

162

on his face switches to hope. "I don't know, but you'll never find out if you stay on the path you're walking."

Even if everything he's saying is true, real life doesn't work like this. "I just came out of a relationship, Tyrone. I can't trust my feelings right now."

He cocks a dark brow on his ridiculously handsome face. "Can you trust a friend?"

I think about his question for a moment before nodding.

"Then you have nothing to worry about. Friendship is the only thing that holds everything together when you think it's falling apart." He crouches down in front of me, his eyes more gentle than his large height and frame should be able to pull off. "He's scared, Jamie. I thought it was because of the hand he's been dealt, but only now am I realizing he's more scared of losing you than anything."

CHAPTER 20

COLBY

*T*yrone freezes halfway into the living room, seemingly surprised to see me. "Hey, is the forecast good?" He nudges his head to the rafting planner in my hand before dumping a pile of recently cut wood into the fireplace.

I lift my chin. "Yeah, the waves are long and unpredictable, but we have more experience rafters in our group than novices, so I say everything will be okay. Claudia and Dallas are preparing the van. We'll head to the river in around an hour."

"Sounds good. I'll get cleaned up, then go assist them..." His words trail off when Jamie enters the living room clutching a second pile of wood. "Thanks, just set them at the side. We'll add them when needed." When she does as instructed, he gives her a smile that has me wanting to stab him in the throat. "We're about to head down to the river for some rafting. Are you up for it?"

Although her head doesn't swivel my way, I can feel her eyes on me. I'm anticipating for her to say no, so you can imagine my surprise when she says, "Yeah. Why not?"

"Great." Tyrone leads Jamie toward her room with his arm wrapped around her shoulders in a super chummy way. "Change into something synthetic and tight. It dries quickly and makes maneuverability easier."

When she leaves the room, it's the fight of my life not to get up into Tyrone's face and demand an explanation for their coziness. The only reason I stay put is because I fucked up earlier by showing Tyrone my hand. If I had acted unaffected by his rile, he wouldn't be eyeing me with suspicion like he knew I wasted the last two hours searching for his signed non-fraternized policy in my office. In case you're wondering, I never found it.

"Jamie helped you gather firewood?"

What? I said I wouldn't get up in his face. No one said anything about not grilling him.

"Yeah." Tyrone restacks the pamphlets on the coffee table, incapable of sitting still. "She's got more *oomph* than I realized. She must be wearing her superpower panties today." His eyes pop up to mine when I growl. "What? I thought you said you had no interest in her like that?"

"I don't, but that doesn't mean I want you to. She's engaged, man, that's already stepping over the line, not to mention the fact she's our client." I'm such a fucking liar. This has nothing to do with our business ventures. I'm two seconds from ripping him a new asshole simply at the thought of him liking Jamie as more than a friend.

"She *was* engaged. She's not anymore."

I take a step back, shocked, but try to play it cool. "Still, that's all types of fucked up. Do you really want to be the rebound guy?"

He looks at me as if I'm an idiot. "Have you seen her? I'll be any guy she wants me to be. The rebound guy. The cry-on-her-shoulder guy. The let's-fuck-him-out-of-your-system guy."

I scrub my jaw, tracing its tick. "While you were out there working out all the ways you're hoping..." *more like fucking dreaming* "... to ease her through her heartbreak, did you find out who bruised her?"

The smug expression on his face clears away in an instant. When he shakes his head, my jaw tightens. "So you don't really care about Jamie at all. You just want to get into her panties." I'm not asking a question, I'm telling him how it is. "I haven't asked much of you the past two years, Tyrone, but I'm going to need you to follow this demand. You need to step back from Jamie. If you can't do it for me, do it for the IOU you owe me."

The shock on his face morphs onto mine when he shakes his head. "I'm sorry, Colby, I can't. She may be worth more than my outstanding IOU."

Before I can demand how, where, and why, Jamie returns to the living room. She's dressed as Tyrone requested—it's ten times tighter than even my deviant mind could have predicted. One of my superpowers is being able to imagine what women look like naked when they're still dressed. Jamie's visual was mighty enticing, hence why it was so hard to keep myself in check the past few weeks, but there must have been a flaw with my powers that day because as she stands before me now, she's even more tempting.

Jamie's cross-runner gym pants hug every one of curves, and the crop top she's wearing as a bra showcases her tits in the same painstaking detail her drenched shirt did yesterday. It's clothing most women wear to the gym, but since it's Jamie, a woman I shouldn't be looking at the way I am, it feels wrong but in a totally right I-want-to-fuck-her-brains-out way.

"What?" Her nervous eyes bounce between Tyrone and me. "Is it not right? I don't have much synthetic clothing." She swallows harshly before pivoting on her heels and heading in the opposite direction. "I'll get changed into something else."

"No! It's fine. You look great." Tyrone bridges the gap between them, all eager and shit. "You might get a little nippy. It's cooler up this way than LA." After banding his arm around her waist, he directs her toward his room. That frustrates me more than him having his hands on her for the second time in under five minutes. I don't want them alone anywhere—much less in the room he swears he creates magic in. "I have a spare long-sleeve shirt I usually wear when rafting. It will swim on you, but if we tuck it into your panties, it should be okay."

I stare at the hallway they walked through for several long minutes, shocked as fuck. Our IOU has been dangling between us since we started The Drop Zone. Usually, Tyrone performs like a dog begging for a treat when it's up for negotiation. Its importance is immense for him, yet he's willing to give it up for Jamie, a woman he's only just met. If that isn't enough to cause a heart stutter, I'm so hard from taking in Jamie's tight body up close, if my pants were to catch a breeze, I'd sail to the Antarctic without breaking into a sweat.

What the fuck? I'd be pissed if my cock hadn't been on hiatus the past few weeks. I know he works. He's just favored the solo route the past month—much to the dismay of every female jumper I've had.

I'm stunned for the second time when a pair of nails rake my torso. "What do you think? Claudia hooked us up with some merchandise." Barbie Number One twirls on the spot, showcasing an outfit oddly similar to the one Jamie was just sporting. It has more material in the top half, and The Drop Zone's logo is stitched in the waistband and across her left breast, but it has my cock lowering its mast.

"Thought we'd represent our favorite company." She all but shoves her breasts into my face when she wiggles her cleavage to amplify the logo that's so stretched over the mounds on her chest, it's barely legible.

"You look great, but I'd hate for you to catch a cold." I pinch the zipper pull tab that's dangling precariously in Silicon Valley before yanking it up until she represents a One-Button Barb. "There you go, much better." When her lower lip drops into a pout, I tap her backside with my clipboard, playing the role I'm paid to play. "Now, how about we go get you all wet?"

She giggles a laugh I've heard a million times in my short twenty-four years.

Today is the first time it's made me nauseous.

"Dig your blades low, the current is heavier beneath the surface. We need to cartwheel this boulder."

When my crew does as requested, and we spin around to bounce off the boulder instead of impacting it head-on, I raise my eyes to Tyrone's raft. They're leading our second flotilla for the day. I'm seeking guidance, but I'm also eager to see if Jamie is still enjoying herself. She didn't stop smiling on our first run, even with the rapids being a little hairier than anticipated.

She's still smiling—at Tyrone. He's been glued to her side all day, and it's frustrating me more than Jamie's request to ride with him this time around. I'm both the scout and organizer of this activity, so I could have said no, but for another reason I've yet to work out, I didn't. I've spent my entire life in the fast lane, but this is one trip I don't want to rush as I'll most likely hate the outcome.

Just like in the bedroom, women aren't done after one round. They could be covered head to toe in cum, but they'll continue seeking their next orgasm until the person handing them out has exhausted all avenues.

The same can be said for hits of adrenaline. Tyrone served her one, so now she'll be craving another from him, and another, and another until they run out of activities that don't require a condom.

I hate that more than anything.

My eyes stray from Jamie when I spot a flurry of blue in the corner of my eye. The ghost boat we send down the rapids unmanned is wrapped around a smaller boulder downstream. Its hang-up can only mean one thing—classifications have changed.

"Brace. We could have a smoker on our hands." A smoker is an extremely violent rapid that should only be run with extreme caution.

We get hit with a wave breaking back on itself a mere second before "Swimmer!" is sounded from the boat in front of us. A swimmer means someone has gone overboard. I scan the whitewater, seeking the blue oar and helmet our rafters are required to wear. With conditions volatile, it takes several scans to find them, and when I do, my heart is in my throat. I'd recognize those wild curls anywhere, much less the beautiful face they curtain.

Jamie's head bobs out of the water for a mere second before

she's dragged under by the current for the second time. In her panic, she tried to stand, which caused either the undercurrent or a concealed object to wipe her feet out from beneath her. While Tyrone alerts the safety boats downstream that we have a man overboard, I snap off my life vest, then dive into the water. I'm a strong swimmer, but the feeling of being tossed around in a washing machine hits me when I spear through the surface of the rapids. With the snow on the mountain caps melting in today's warmer conditions, the water rushing downstream is extra volatile—and fucking freezing.

Thanks to the safety beacon flashing on Jamie's life vest, I locate her remarkedly quick. After curling my arm around her waist, I swim us to the surface before adopting the position we teach all rafters before letting them anywhere near the rapids.

"Feet up, Jamie. Lawn-chair position, remember?" The rapids have moved us too far from the flotilla to return. We'll have to follow the rapids until we reach the safety boats. "Jamie?"

When she fails to respond for the second time, I stop using one of my arms as an oar so I can raise her head to mine. She's out cold, and blood is gushing down her cheek. She either discovered a sleeper beneath the surface, or one of her fellow rafter's excitement saw her being struck with an oar. That's usually the cause for swimmers not immediately resurfacing following a dismount from the boat.

I blame the icy conditions we're emerged in or the shake of my hands when I check her for a pulse. It's there, although declining with each second we spend in the water. "You'll be all right, Jamie. I won't let anything happen to you. Just hold on, okay?"

With my butt high, my toes above water, and my feet

pointing downstream, I successfully guide us down the rapids in a safe, yet fast manner. By adopting a lawn-chair position, I am able to use my feet to bounce us away from any rocks that come into our path.

After grabbing the safety rope Dallas throws out, I curl it around my wrist three times before signaling for him to pull us in. As they drag us across less violent waters, Tyrone and the rest of the flotilla arrive at our meeting point.

"Careful, don't move her too much. If she's going into hypothermic shock, we need to keep her as still as possible," I demand when they pull Jamie into the safety boat. Once I'm on board, they race to the shore where Claudia is waiting with a van full of medical supplies. "I need blankets, warm water, and scissors. Have the EMTs been called?"

Nodding, Claudia rushes off to gather the supplies I requested.

"Condition?" Tyrone drops to Jamie's side before checking the response of her pupils with a small torch.

"She has a pulse and is breathing unaided, but has been unresponsive since surfacing." I take a quick look at the cut on her head, grimacing when my inspection causes it to bleed more. "Her wound is straight, indicating it was most likely caused by the blade of an oar."

"I agree. It was quick, but I saw contact just before she went over."

When Claudia returns with the supplies I requested, I nudge my head to the rafters mingling around us, watching the show. "Move them back." I'm about to cut Jamie's clothing off, so I doubt she'd want witnesses. "I don't believe her knock to the head is the cause of her drowsiness. I think she's going into hypothermic shock." I don't know why I'm explaining myself to

Tyrone. We're both extensively trained in this type of first aid. It just feels different since it's Jamie.

"Once again, I agree. She's showing reduced circulation, and her lack of response could be more from confusion as her body fights not to shut down." He lifts his eyes to Dallas. "Fold down the seats in the van. We need to get her back to the cabin."

My eyes rocket to Tyrone's. "EMTs are on their way."

"If we don't get her warm now, they may arrive too late."

The honesty in his tone kickstarts both my heart and my feet. "Bring me the back brace."

I snatch it out of Dallas' hand before laying it beside Jamie, then carefully guiding her onto it. Once we have her strapped to the brace, Tyrone and I slide her into the back of the van being extra cautious not to move her more than necessary.

When I swing my eyes to Claudia, she slices her hand through the air. "We've got this. Go."

She barges me into the van before slamming the doors shut and tapping on the window, giving Tyrone the signal to leave. While I work on cutting off Jamie's soaked clothes, Tyrone races us back to the cabin. Mercifully, we purchased this cabin because of its close proximity to the locations our activities are undertaken, meaning we're only a few miles from the equipment needed to ensure Jamie's hypothermic shock remains mild.

Halfway there, Jamie's eyes begin to flutter. "Colby...?" Her body brutally shudders as her organs fight to stay warm chops up my name.

I want to fist-punch the air that she said my name instead of Tyrone's or her ex-fiancé's, but I've got to keep my game face on. Now is not the time for cockiness. "I'm right here, Jamie. It's okay. I'll get you warm real quick."

After dragging my scissors through the wire refusing to buckle from my jabs, I dump it and her crop top at my feet, then cover every inch of her with the blankets and towels, leaving only her face peeking out. Most people would rub the patient's arms and legs in an attempt to warm them up. Trust me when I say that's the worst thing you could do. Excessive jarring movements can cause hypothermic patients to go into cardiac arrest. The best thing is keep them warm and alert, so that's what I do. I talk to Jamie and ask her questions all while pretending I'm not on the verge of a panic attack. Jamie rarely responds, and the times she does it barely makes any sense.

Several long minutes later, Tyrone skids the van to a halt at the side of the cabin. "We're here." He throws open the driver's side door before racing around to the back of the van to help me carry Jamie out.

Once we have her lying on the table that usually houses twenty for dinner, he gathers the heat packs from the storage closet and places them into the microwave. We seamlessly work together for the next fifteen minutes, monitoring Jamie's condition while ensuring Claudia and Dallas have everything handled at the river. I'm panicked out of my fucking mind, but also understand this is my moral obligation since I'm the lead instructor for this trip.

When Jamie starts to stir a few minutes later, I nudge my head to the stovetop kettle. "Boil some water. A warm sugary drink will help."

Tyrone's brows draw together. "Coffee?"

I shake my head. "No. It can't have any caffeine. Just sugar and water."

When Jamie groans, I peer down at her. Her eyes are wide and alert but clearly confused. "Where am I?"

I gather a pair of her glasses Tyrone found in her luggage and place them on the bridge of her nose before moving into her line of sight. "We're at the cabin. You fell overboard. Do you remember that?"

She nods before attempting to caress the nasty gash on her head. "Leave it. We need you to stay as still as possible."

"We?"

Tyrone answers her question by arriving at her side with a mug full of warm water and sugar.

She groans again when she peers down. "Am I naked?"

I cringe. "We needed to get you warm."

"*We?*" This one is more a sob than a question.

"Me. I cut them off while Tyrone drove the van." When she attempts to sit up, I carefully push her shoulders back down. "You need to stay horizontal."

I remove the mug from Tyrone as sirens filter through the air. When I peer at Tyrone, he jerks up his chin, understanding my request with no words needed to be shared between us. While he alerts the EMTs to our location, I lower the mug to Jamie's mouth. "Can you sip on this? It will help."

She licks her blue-tinged lips before raising her head enough so she won't choke. Although her nose screws up when the sugary concoction hits her taste buds, she continues sipping it until she drinks half the cup, and two paramedics enter the kitchen.

"She's alert and responsive, that's good."

The male paramedic pulls out a chair from underneath the table Jamie is sprawled on to check her pulse and the response of her pupils while a female paramedic removes a foil blanket from her kit to curl it around my shoulders. "How are you feeling? Any blurred vision? Impediment of speech?"

I peer at her in confusion. "I'm not the patient."

"You're saturated head to toe on a below-freezing day, and your skin is extremely pale."

I'm about to tell her I have Finnish heritage, so my whiteness is nothing out of the ordinary, but before I can, she shoves me into a seat and sticks a thermometer into my mouth.

CHAPTER 21

JAMIE

"I really wish you would reconsider. Even if your condition is mild, hypothermic shock isn't something to take lightly."

The paramedic isn't speaking to me. She's talking to Colby, who's sitting on the back step of the EMT truck I'm being monitored in. Despite the pretty brunette's efforts, Colby hasn't left my side the past hour. I'm okay. I also have a mild case of hypothermic shock and five pretty new stitches in my head. I'm just not being fussed over by my caregiver since he has a wedding band wrapped around his finger. Don't get me wrong, he's been extremely helpful, but he's kept things professional. The same can't be said for the naughty nurse who can't take a hint.

"Take two of these three times a day for the next few days." The male paramedic hands me a bottle of pain medication. "They'll make you drowsy, but I'd pick drowsy over a throbbing head any day." He lowers the guard rail he raised when my eye roll nearly had me falling off the bed. I wasn't getting sassy with him. My eye roll was from overhearing Blow-Up Barbie's assurance she could warm Colby with nothing but her lips. "If your condition worsens, or you feel disorientated—"

"I won't hesitate to seek medical assistance." I spread my hand across his chest before locking my eyes with his nurturing ones. "Thank you. I really appreciate your help."

"You're very welcome." His reply is as humble as the man behind his kind eyes.

Noticing my approach to the back of the EMT truck, Colby stands, then aids me down. "Everything okay?" With the hand not clutching mine, he checks my stitches by carefully brushing away the ringlets sprouting down my face with his pinkie. "Are you sure you don't want to go to the hospital?"

When I shake my head, he drifts his eyes to my EMT. He assures him in a way I can't since his hands are on me. They're making me even woozier than the pain medication the medic offered before stitching me up. "She's fine. Just needs rest and to be kept warm for the next few days. I don't think she's concussed, but I'd still like you to keep an eye on her."

My eyes rocket to the male paramedic as quickly as his side-kick's do. "They're not together." When he arches a brow at her, she murmurs, "What? They're not."

"Come on, Cassie. It's time to go." She appears as if he's just told her they're taking her puppy to the farm, but she does as requested. When she storms toward the passenger seat of their truck, he returns his eyes to Colby and me. "I expect you to take care of her. If I'm called back here, I add more than a comped jump to my list of requirements."

My confused eyes dance between Colby and him when Colby says, "Deal." They seal their agreement with a handshake.

"Thanks for taking your time with her, Nixon. She's ah…" I stare at him, waiting impatiently for him to finish his sentence.

Unfortunately, Nixon is more clued on to his inner workings than me. "I understand." He moves deeper into the truck to prepare it for departure. "But next time you're up this way, you better come visit. Eden has been baking a storm of late."

"I will." Colby rubs his tummy in anticipation. "I would have come out this weekend, but you know…" he nudges his head to me, "… I've got drama queens to take care of." He laughs when I sock him in the stomach, relieved I'm well enough to return his banter.

After a final wave, Nixon and Cassie return to base while Colby guides me inside, still holding the hand he didn't relinquish after helping me down from the medic truck. I don't mind. I'm still a little rattled from my time underwater, although I'll never tell Colby that. His eyes are holding enough guilt, so there's no way I'll add more to them.

"Are you hungry?"

I screw up my nose. "Not really. I'm too tired to eat. Nixon failed to mention my pain medication would knock me on my ass within twenty minutes of taking it until after I swallowed them."

He laughs. It's a nice thing to hear considering how tense he is. "Hot cocoa, then?"

I don't really feel like that either, but since he's peering at me with pleading eyes, I nod. He's quick to shut it down, but relief crosses his features when he spots my agreeing gesture.

Compared to last night, the cabin is quiet. "Where is everyone?"

Colby taps the itinerary on the table before suggesting for me to take a seat at one of the many empty chairs. "Even in the event of a near death, activities must continue as scheduled." He sounds frustrated. I don't understand why. If I paid ten thousand dollars for a four-day getaway, I'd want my money's worth even if someone did pass away.

"I wasn't on the verge of death. I just bumped my head."

Colby places a pot of milk onto the stovetop before spinning around to face me. "I wasn't talking about you. I was referring to you discovering I cut off your clothing while lying next to dangerous instruments."

When he nudges his head to a knife block on my right, I laugh. It hurts my lungs, but the pain is worth it. Not only does it remove some of the worry in Colby's eyes, it loosens the knot in his shoulders.

"I might have castrated you if you had removed them where you had originally planned."

From the information I've gathered over the past hour, he almost stripped me in front of everyone. I would have died a thousand deaths. I'm comfortable in my own skin, but I'd rather not be paraded naked in front of women who have had their assets enhanced with a surgeon's knife. I would have also preferred for Colby not to see me like that, but I guess you can't have everything you want.

Before my cheeks bloom to half their natural hue, Colby says, "Can I ask you something?"

"Isn't that already a question?" Damn, my pain meds are nearly as good as a few glasses of wine. I'm feeling witty and friendly, a stark contradiction to the cranky cow I woke up as this morning.

Colby gives me a look as if to say, *smartass* but remains quiet. I wait for him to add cocoa and sugar into the simmering pot of milk before jerking up my chin, granting him permission.

"The bruise on your wrist." As he drops his eyes to my left wrist, his tongue darts out to replenish his dry lips. "Did you get that from the raft?"

I could lie. I could pretend it occurred when I attempted to grab the safety rope circling the raft, but he just saved my life, so doesn't he deserve more than a lie?

With my eyes facing the tabletop, I shake my head. They pop back up when Colby exhales a relieved breath. *Why is he relieved?*

When I ask him that, he says, "You could have lied to me. You didn't." He fills two mugs with steaming hot cocoa, places one down in front of me, then sits in the chair opposite me. "Was it caused by Brad?"

"Yes, but not in the way you're thinking." He doesn't hear the last half of my sentence. All he hears is me admitting my fiancé bruised me. "He's stronger than he realizes." When he growls like he's seconds away from lecturing me about the pathetic excuse I gave him, I quickly rush out, "But that doesn't excuse what he did. Accident or not, he has no right to mark me."

While taking in what I said, he works his jaw from side to side. "Is it the reason you left him?"

I shake my head. "Not entirely. It's been a long time coming."

"I thought you were only together a few months?" He sounds confused. I understand why. We corresponded a lot about my relationship at the beginning of our friendship, so he's well aware I haven't been with Brad for even a year.

Colby must see something on my face I can't work out how to express. "Time slows when you're miserable?"

Sighing, I nod. "Is that why you do this?" I gesture my hand around the cabin.

"Because I'm miserable?" He looks as panicked now as he did when I woke on the table we're dining at.

I shake my head. "No. To hasten time."

He smirks. It doesn't belong to a man who's happy. "No. It's quite the opposite actually."

I wait for him to elaborate—it's an extremely long two minutes.

"Come on, drink up, then I'll show you your new room."

That perks me up as much as him dumping another two marshmallows into my drink. "My *new* room?"

He nudges his head to my cocoa, demanding for me to drink before nodding. "Nixon said I had to keep you warm. I know the perfect place to do that." Stuff blankets. The innuendo in his tone has me heating up everywhere.

After two mugs of cocoa and way too much silence, Colby guides me into my new room. Just like mine, it's the size of most log cabins you'll find in this region of Northern Cali, but it has a roaring fireplace and a bed fit for a king.

When I spot a suitcase near the entrance door, I shift my eyes to Colby. "Whose room was this before it became mine?" I hate the thought of anyone being inconvenienced by me. I already cut their rafting expedition short. I don't want more annoyance added to the list.

My heart does a crazy dip when he answers, "Mine."

I step deeper into the space, taking in its quirky features which should have revealed it was his room from the beginning. A three hundred hours of freefall certificate is tacked to the side wall. It's just above original *Star Wars* figurines that would make Sci-Fi freaks cream their pants, and a box of specially made chocolates are on the nightstand.

"I still can't believe you did that. Who gifts their family chocolates molded from their... *rectum?*" I whisper the last word.

"People who aren't afraid to say rectum out loud." Laughing at my mortified face, he moves to the nightstand. "Want one?"

"*Eww.* No thanks." I don't know whether to barf or laugh when he pops a demented seashell-looking chocolate between his lips before chewing it. "You're disgusting."

After cleaning smears of chocolate off his teeth with his tongue, he nudges his head to the giant bed in the middle of the room. "Go on, try it out. Let's see what you think."

"Are the sheets clean?"

Colby cocks his brow. "Yes. No one has slept in this bed but me."

"Once again, are the sheets clean?"

His growl is more sexy than threatening. "Prim..."

"Fine! I'm going."

After toeing off slippers no woman under the age of sixty should wear, I shimmy my pants down my thighs then climb onto the mattress. Yes, I said climb as it's so high off the floor, I'm afraid I might get altitude sickness.

"If you hadn't ruined my cell phone, I bet I could have gotten reception up here."

It takes Colby a good three seconds to remove his eyes from my thighs, and even then, the heat of his gaze is felt for many more. From the way he's eyeing me, anyone would swear he hadn't seen me naked only hours ago. It's that knowledge that saw me stripping out of my pants without a worry in the world. He's seen me at my worst, so why act coy about being without pants?

"I'll replace your phone when we go to town tomorrow, then you can test the theory."

My brows spike as quickly as my heart rate. "We're going to town tomorrow?"

Colby joins me on the mattress to remove my glasses like I'm incapable of doing something I've done since I was eight. It does stupid things to my insides, but I'm too woozy to sit down and decipher what it means. "Yes. While the group goes skydiving, I thought we could do a run for supplies." He locks his dazzling baby blues with me. "If you're up for it."

"Sounds good, but are you sure you don't want to go skydiving? I can get supplies by myself. I'm a big girl who knows how to take care of herself." When his eyes lock with the split in my head, I screw up my nose. "That wasn't my fault. Lumberjack Bill has more brawn than brains."

"Terry?"

I sink into the super-soft pillows, being extra attentive not to bump the part of my head I can no longer feel. "Who's Terry?"

Colby waits for me to finish yawning before explaining that the man I nicknamed Lumberjack Bill is Terry Fousser, a big-time banker who's worth millions of dollars. "He feels so guilty about what happened, he offered to reimburse you for this trip."

"Did you tell him no?"

A sprinkling of blond hairs fall into his eyes when he shakes his head. "I told him I'd wait and see what you want to do first."

I roll over so I can spoon the softest pillows I've ever laid my head on. They smell scrumptious too. Manly and pure—much like their owner. "I don't want to be reimbursed."

The smell I'm sucking in like the first day of spring amplifies when Colby adjusts the pillows around me, so I'm cocooned like a newborn baby sleeping on its parents' bed. Once he has everything in order, he lies opposite me. "Why wouldn't you accept his offer, Prim? You haven't experienced anything you paid for. You didn't hike, you only had one run down the rapids, and now you're out for the rest of the week. Why wouldn't you want to be compensated for that?"

"Because despite all of that, I've lived more the past two days than I have the previous thirty years." His smile is gorgeous, but I can barely see it through my sagging eyelids and poor eyesight. "Tell Terry I appreciate the offer, but I'm okay. I'm happy just the way I am..." I'm out cold before my reply completely leaves my mouth.

CHAPTER 22

COLBY

*W*hen a knock sounds on my bedroom door, I yank my hand away from Jamie's cheek like I'm not a creep confirming the softness of her skin while she sleeps. Jamie is beautiful as she is, but when she's dozing, the term takes on a whole new meaning. With it being late in the day, the low-hanging sun sends streaks of orange over her face, amplifying the redness the tip of her nose got when she almost froze to death. She's huddled in the fetal position, so the shirt she slipped on when Nixon moved her from the kitchen to the privacy of his EMT truck is riding high on her luscious thighs, and she's snoring.

Snoring should never be classed as adorable, but like many things I'm discovering about Jamie, she's not close to ordinary. Her snores are soft and cute and arrive with the occasional snort, which makes them even more adorable. I stayed with her because I thought her sleep would be restless. She went through quite the ordeal today, yet she sleeps as if she has the world at her feet. If that doesn't show her fighting spirit, I don't know what will.

After scampering off the bed as quietly as I can, I twist to face the door Tyrone's standing outside of. His arms are folded in front of his chest, but the confused crinkle popped between his brows reveals he isn't angry. He's as shocked now as he was when I said I'd stay with Jamie instead of attending rock climbing as scheduled.

Usually, I never volunteer to stand-down from adrenaline-packed activities. With Tyrone's interests in Jamie as obvious as the sun hanging in the sky, I expected him to put up more of a protest to my request, so you can imagine my surprise when he merely agreed with a head bob before loading our clients into the van as if Jamie's hacked clothes weren't tangled around their feet.

"How is she?" His voice is thicker than usual, more controlled.

"Good. Nixon gave her some strong pain meds. She's been out for a few hours." I join him in the hall. "How was the rock climbing? Any incidents?"

He shakes his head. "Kendall got a grazed knee, but other than that, we're in the clear." He should sound happy, but he doesn't. I think I know why.

"What happened to Jamie wasn't your fault."

Air whizzes out of his nostrils. "She was in my rig, Colby. That makes her my responsibility."

"She got a blade to the head. You activated the safety measures as you were taught. How is it your fault?"

"I should have dove into the water."

I backhand his chest, my head shaking. "I only went in because I had experienced guides on my crew. If I didn't, I wouldn't have." That's a lie, but if it makes him feel better, I'll run with it. "Do you know what Jamie said before she went to sleep?" I wait for his worldly eyes to drift to mine before saying, "That this is the most alive she's ever felt. That's why we do this, Ty. It's not to get rich or to feed off the hype. It's for responses like that." I hook my thumb to Jamie, who's still resting. "She doesn't blame you for what happened. Heck, she doesn't even blame Terry, so you sure as fuck shouldn't be feeling guilty."

When his chest rises, revealing I'm getting through to him, I slather more cream onto my ego-inflating pie. "If you want to make it up to her, keep her smiling like you did before she went for a swim."

I don't know why, but that was hard for me to say. Probably because I don't want to hand that task to Tyrone, I want to make Jamie smile. Mrs. Palencia spent more of our dance class checking the firmness of my butt-cheeks than teaching me how to dance, but those nights boosted me with more adrenaline than any jump I've had since. Inside those walls with Jamie, I was just me, Colby McGregor. I wasn't trying to impress anyone or rewrite the stars. I was the closet Sci-Fi geek who had a crush on a taken dorky insurance assessor.

My heart must have fucked-up notions on what it thinks is romance. The only other girl I've ever crushed on was also taken. I like keeping things interesting, but this is messed up, even for me. But, even if you were to exclude those heinous facts I just disclosed, I'm the one who snuffed the life in Jamie's eyes, so shouldn't I be the one responsible for returning it? I've taken some steps this afternoon to commence that process, but I've got many more to take. While I'm being honest, I'll also admit, she scared me today. So much so, the hang-ups I've had about our friendship don't seem as perverse. She's no longer taken, but even if she were, why can't we be friends?

Because you can't fuck your friends, doofus, and you've had too many improper thoughts about her to pretend you don't find her attractive.

I grow worried Tyrone is a mind reader when he says, "I will if you will." He shifts on his feet to face me, the crinkle between his brow weakening its cinch. "And before you give me some bullshit excuse that you don't do attachments and yadda yadda yadda, remember I saw your face when she was pulled out of the safety boat. Attachments have already occurred, so you may as well run with it. If you don't, I will."

"Like fuck you will."

He slaps my shoulder three times like I didn't speak a word. "Dinner will be ready in around an hour. Scrub up and join us... both of you. I'm sure you can fit more than one person in your shower if you're worried you'll be short on time."

Tyrone hits me with a playful wink before pivoting on his heels and stalking down the hall. I wait for him to disappear into thin air before returning to Jamie's bedside. She's sleeping peacefully with her hair fanned across my pillow. Because she went for a swim, it's back to its usual kinky self. I like her hair au naturel. It's as wild as the woman she tries to hide with a professional demeanor and ugly-ass glasses.

While staring at her beautiful face, I summon images of hairy armpits, festering pimples, and teeth that haven't seen a toothbrush in a decade. The visuals which usually make my stomach recoil don't work this time around. I'm still having improper thoughts about a woman I swore I'd never be more than friends with. If that isn't bad enough, I'm as hard as a pensioner who took an entire prescription of Viagra instead of just one.

After leaving Jamie a note to say I'm in the bathroom if she needs me, I head to that so-called bathroom to drown my inappropriate thoughts down the drain. I could shower in one of the guest bathrooms, but since they're on the other side of the cabin, and I want to be within earshot of Jamie in case she suddenly clues on to the fact she almost died today, I'd prefer to use my own.

I undress and throw my clothes into the hamper before entering the shower. The water hasn't had time to heat, but it's better this way. Maybe the chill will subdue the python between my legs long enough I can shower without poking my eye out.

As I scrub the funk from my skin, I ignore the object that appears to have its own blood source separate from my body. It throbs with want while sending needy messages to my brain. Those statistics that claim men think about sex almost one hundred percent of the time are true—except now, it's one hundred percent on my mind. It hammers into me on repeat, not giving in until my soapy hand is wrapped around my shaft, and I'm imagining the woman in my bed is no longer sleeping. She's in the shower with me, wearing nothing but a smile. She rakes her teeth over her lower lip when she realizes what I'm doing, liking the thought of me jacking off thinking about her.

I stroke my cock faster, giving her the show she deserves. No, the show she *needs*. She wants this as much as me. That's why her nipples are always strained against her shirt when I'm around. Why her lavender scent is stronger. She wants to fuck me as much as I want to bang Brad out of her brains, but she also knows that isn't something friends do. Friends don't kiss, touch, and fondle each other, and friends most certainly don't fuck.

Lucky for me, this is just a fantasy. There are no rules when you're dreaming, no barriers, no obstacles, and no stupid family shit that dictates every fucking step I take. It's just her. The geeky risk calculator with kinky hair and snorting snores. And this isn't our first fornication.

My cock throbs in my hand when I imagine how wet and tight her pussy is, and how she'll moan my name when she clamps around me. She's a screamer. I guarantee it. You can't be as controlled as her in real life and not release it in the bedroom. She'd probably want me to pull her hair and spank her ass. I'd do it too. I'd give her a right royal fucking—one where she won't walk properly for days afterward. She'll be all bowlegged and shit and thinking about me every time she sits.

I brace one of my hands on the steam-covered tile before pumping my hips faster, my strokes tightening. It usually takes more than a hand to have me on the express train to coming, but I'm playing on a new field today. I'm so fucking close, the world no longer exists. Everything fades—blacks out. I'm on the final stretch.

I tug on my dick harder and faster, punishing it for not being able to take a backseat today of all days. She almost died, yet here I am, jerking off to the image of her peering up at me when she realized I undressed her without an audience.

The image is even better. She's naked now. *Really* naked. She's not the Jamie I imagined the past five weeks or the one I jerked off to when I told my date the Mexican meal we shared gave me the runs. She's the Jamie I undressed earlier today. The one with the squishy belly and the curvy hips. The perky tits and kissable lips. I didn't pay any attention to how perfect she was earlier. I was too panicked to look at her how I am now, but I can't go back. She's too perfect. Beautiful, smart, and funny—*my fucking friend*.

I shouldn't be doing this, but I am.

I'm too far gone.

I'm aching to come.

To hear her shout my name.

As my balls tighten, a jolt spasms down my spine. When I come hard and fast, her name leaves my throat in a whispered roar. I can't have her know what I've done, that just the thought of fucking her sucks me of enough energy to light the country. Except she does know because she's no longer asleep. She's standing just outside the partially cracked open bathroom door with her mouth open and her wide eyes not concealed by her foggy glasses fixed on the stream of cum dripping from my palm.

CHAPTER 23

JAMIE

"I'm so sorry."

I step away from Colby like his cock is a machine gun, and it's aimed at me. It is. You should have seen the way cum shot out of his crown. It was mesmerizing and seemingly in slow motion since a good ten minutes of my brain screaming for me to look away didn't have me complying with its request until it was too late. If I'd have listened, he might not have busted my perverted stare.

Can you blame me for hanging around to watch the finale? I've never seen such a riveting sight. Colby's body is already dynamite, but his cock—Mind. Blown! Picture the best cock you've ever seen in your life—Colby's is bigger and better. It's sexy too. Long, thick, satiny, and with so much girth, I'm wondering why circumferences aren't brought into the equation when discussing the perfect male appendage. If his performance didn't match his tremendous anatomy, I'd be demanding an encore. Since it went above and beyond, all I'm seeking is a cigarette, and I don't even smoke.

"Jamie..." Colby steps out of the shower, covering himself with a towel during the process. It's okay. I don't need to see the evidence of his performance to remember it. I'll never forget it. "Are you all right?"

"I'm great!" *Less crazed stalker, Jamie. More professional. Please.* "The mugs of cocoa have caught up with me." I point to the toilet and say, "I need to pee," like my first hint wasn't juvenile enough. "I should probably shower, too. I'm... *sticky.*" Someone kill me, please. This can't get any worse.

Some of the brain cells I lost watching Colby bring himself to climax return when I see an amused twinkle in his eyes. He's loving the fact he has embarrassed me.

"Why are you smirking? I just busted you masturbating. This..." I swivel my finger around my inflamed face, "... should be on there." I make the same gesture to his face.

"Why would I be embarrassed?"

A toilet break is the last thing on my mind when I shadow him into the main section of his room. "Ah... 'cause I just busted you masturbating. *Duh.*" My last word isn't needed, but I'm still low on brain cells.

"And? There's nothing wrong with taking care of business, Prim. If you did it more often, you probably wouldn't be so uptight."

"I can't do... *that.*" My last word is nothing but a gurgle. I'm not choking on my spit because I've never masturbated before. It's from Colby dropping his towel. Even flaccid, his cock is stupendous. "I could probably give it a whirl. There's no harm trying something new."

193

I curse myself for talking out loud when Colby cocks his head to the side. "You've never masturbated? *Ever?*"

When he steps closer to me, his cock swings like a pendulum in a grandfather clock. I'm not a fan of giving head, but it's the fight of my life not to fall to my knees right now. I wouldn't hold back if I weren't afraid of being rejected.

"We're not having this conversation with your dick hanging out." I pretend to stray my eyes to the wall. In reality, I'm giving myself eye strain. I can't take them off him. The visual is too much. I'm burning up everywhere, my near-freezing a thing of the past.

Colby tugs on a pair of gray sweatpants. "Better?"

I want to yell, *no!* Instead, I nod. "Much, although we're still not having this conversation. I just said that so you'd put on some clothes. It's cold today. I don't need you to explain yourself."

"Explain myself? What exactly am I explaining?" He stalks my way, his walk arrogant. "That I have a cock half an inch bigger than my brother's? That there's nothing wrong with stroking one out in the shower on the quiet days?"

Jealousy smacks into me from his 'days' comment. I would have preferred months but would have settled for weeks.

"That you're so fucking worked up right now, I'd give anything to switch the tension on your face to relief."

Colby's hot breaths fog up my glasses when he pins me to the outer wall of the bathroom with his crotch. In case you're wondering, gray sweatpants may as well be tissue paper when it comes to containing the manhood I'm striving to ignore. "What did you hear, Prim?"

"Hear?"

He jerks up his chin. "In the shower, what did you hear?"

194

"I didn't hear anything." I'm not lying. I was so close to climax watching him pleasure himself, blocking out his moans was the only defense mechanism I had not to make a fool of myself.

"You didn't hear anything?"

I shake my head. "Who goes to an art gallery to hear brush strokes?"

He appears confused, but still answers, "No one."

"Exactly. I wasn't watching for the pleasure of my ears." I gulp before cringing. I just threw myself into the deep end without a lifejacket. "Not that I was watching."

"Oh, you were watching, Prim." Colby steps back, unpinning me. "Why do you think I put on such a riveting performance?"

He doesn't wait for me to answer. Instead, he stalks out of the room, his walk as cocky as ever.

"Jamie, over here. I saved you a seat." Tyrone stops coercing the skillet into being his bitch to point to a chair at the end of the dining table. It's directly across from Colby. "How are you feeling? Did a nap help?"

"Yeah. I'm feeling wonderful." I smile a greeting to Terry, who's peering at the stitches in my forehead with remorseful eyes. "How was rock climbing?" Pretending I can't feel Colby's eyes taking in my recently straightened hair and scrubbed-cleaned body, I slip into the seat Tyrone referenced before twisting around to face him. "You should take Colby next time. I've heard it's great for working out stubborn kinks."

Thank God the table is wide or I'd be wearing the drink Colby was in the process of swallowing. I wouldn't have minded. My first shower was nowhere near as riveting as Colby's, but I'm willing to give it another shot. I'm buzzed all over, so not only will the high pressure of the spray give relief to my tight muscles, the coolness will soothe the burn of Colby's white-hot glare. He's not glaring at me in anger. It's the same sexy hooded stare his eyes held just before he came.

Colby and Tyrone's closeness is proven without a doubt when Tyrone replies, "It's a great stress reliever, but some of us only need a bit of hot water to see us through the day." He plops down a bowl of bread rolls in front of me before hitting me with a playful wink. "How do you like your steak?"

"Medium rare, please." As Tyrone heads back to the skillet, I ask, "Any news on the landline?"

Although my first thought was annoyance when Colby showed me the supposed email I had sent him, once my anger settled down, suspicion took its place. The IP address attached to the email proved it was sent from a server at Metrics, which means someone in the building sent it. I just can't understand who or why.

"Not yet. The phone company said a technician could be out anytime within the next seventy-two hours."

I stop grimacing when Colby asks, "Who do you need to call, Prim?"

A quick-witted comeback sits on my tongue, but with the events of earlier today overtaking the stimulating one from this afternoon, I go with honesty instead. "My parents."

"Do you want to go home?"

The worry in his eyes floats away when I shake my head. "My mom has been unwell, so I want to check in."

My reply isn't a total lie. My mom will never get better, but she's been battling more than Alzheimer's the past few weeks.

When my dad gave me a full report Thursday afternoon, I immediately suggested canceling my weekend getaway. He, just like Hugh, wouldn't hear me out. For some stupid reason, he believes I need time away from LA. Only now am I beginning to wonder if he was right. It's been an eye-opening starter, that's for sure.

Colby nods in understanding. "Once you've eaten, I'll drive you into town. Service can be sporadic in winter, but old-man Fishburne has a satellite phone." He strays his eyes to Tyrone during the last half of his statement, seeking confirmation.

"Yeah. He'll charge you out the ass to use it, though."

"It'll be worth it," Colby and I say at the same time.

I squeeze Tyrone's forearm in thanks when he sets down a perfectly cooked steak with a jacket potato and a generous helping of steamed vegetables. It's more than I'll ever be able to eat, but with my hunger rampant from Colby's pre-dinner entertainment, I'll give it my best shot to clear my plate.

"Is this the town we're visiting tomorrow?"

Colby's eyes stray from the road to me. "No. There's nothing here but an overpriced pub, angry locals, and a big-ass cell tower." He points to a steel monstrosity on our right during his last word.

After pulling into a dusty gravel lot, he digs his switched-off cell phone out of his pocket and hands it to me. "You don't want to check it first?"

Colby twists his lips in a sexy way. "Who do I have to worry about?"

I want to say me, but that would be pretty pointless considering I'm sitting directly in front of him. "Cate? Clara? Or any of those other 'C' names I can't remember." When he snickers, the world feels right again. He's been quiet since I walked in on him in the shower, which is surprising considering how cocky he was afterward.

When I switch on his phone, it vibrates nonstop for the first minute, announcing we have service. "Ignore those. They won't be anyone important."

He leans in real close so he can decline to open the seventy-three text messages and one hundred and forty-three emails. One inch closer and his lips would be tickling the shell of my ear.

My breaths hurry when Colby inhales deeply, smelling the body wash I lathered myself in. It's a more manly palette than I'm used to, but since it replicated the scent surrounding me when he brought himself to climax, I wanted to be doused in it.

When I feel his heart racing in his chest, I flick my eyes up to his to see something vulnerable flashing through them. They're different—more controlled than usual. The gleam in them brightens when he notices my nipples strained against my shirt. They're budded and hard, begging to be fondled. No part of his body is touching mine, but I'm burning up as if we're back in the bathroom, and I'm in the shower with him instead of watching from afar.

While licking his dry lips, he raises his eyes to mine. They're still vulnerable, but also hungry. But I don't think it's a hunger for food. "Do you know the number you need to call, or do you need the directory?"

"I know it."

My reply comes out with a quiver, exposing my wavering constraint. It was like this throughout dinner—little glances and almost touches. It's been electrifying and oddly compelling. I've always said I hate being teased, but Colby is making a quick liar out of me.

Nodding, he clicks the phone app before sinking back onto his side of the van's bench seat to crank open his door.

"You don't have to go."

"It's okay. I don't mind. I need a breather." He sounds the most honest I've ever heard him, but he also sounds like he's in pain.

I take a few moments watching him kick up dirt before dialing my dad's number into his phone and squishing it to my ear. My dad answers a few rings later. It's late for him. After apologizing for not calling yesterday, I request an update for Mom. He sounds optimistic, which fills me with hope the doctors are wrong.

"How many times did she request your hand in marriage today?"

His chuckle warms my heart as effectively as Colby's closeness heats my body. "Only half a dozen." Dad's laughter dies down as a strong sense of sentiment zaps down the line. "She asked about you today."

"Really?" My eyes burn from a sudden rush of moisture.

"Yeah." His voice wobbles like he too is on the cusp of crying. "She wanted to know where the crazy-haired lady went. You were supposed to be our witness."

It's not quite the reply I was seeking, but it still sends tears toppling down my cheeks.

My dad groans when he hears my quiet sniffles. "Princess... ugh. This is why I told you not to call. You're supposed to be having the time of your life, not worrying about us."

"I'm not crying." I wipe at my cheeks, hating that they're

forcing me to lie to the only man I've ever loved. "I'm crying, but they're happy tears. I swear." I brush away the blobs slipping down my cheeks before Colby can see them. It's bad enough my dad heard them, much less having them witnessed. "I went whitewater rafting today."

I don't expect Dad to fall for my quick change in conversation, but he follows along nicely. "Yeah? How was it?"

"Ah..." I think back to the moment where my life flashed before my eyes. It was an extremely short and boring twenty seconds. "It was good. Interesting."

His hearty laughter beats his crackling voice any day of the week. "Let me guess, you were too worried about getting your hair wet to have a good time?"

"You know me, Dad, all about the glamour."

"I wish that were the case, princess. It would make a nice change instead of fussing over us all the time, eh?"

"Dad—"

"No, Jamie, enough of this. Go... have fun. I'll be here waiting for you and your stories when you get back."

"Daddy." He sighs. He's a sucker for 'daddy.' "I love you. I'll see you on Tuesday when I bring a shortlist of candidates for you to look over."

"Okay. I love you too. See you on Tuesday."

After pulling Colby's cell from my ear, I hit his email app. I log him out so I can enter my details. Although Colby believed me when I said I approved his claim, I still want him to see the proof firsthand. I'm also interested to see if any of the assisted-living facilities I emailed Thursday night replied to my request for an emergency transfer. I didn't hold back any punches after my exchange with Brad. I left my engagement ring on the entryway table, had my mail redirected to Metrics Insurance, and commenced the process of having my mother's care returned to my custody. I'd love for her to stay in the facility she's in now, but it isn't feasible. It costs more per year than I make.

My heart whacks out a funky tune when I discover the response has been better than anticipated. There are a number of facilities capable of an emergency transfer, and some are well within my budget. I flag their emails as unread, so I can find them quickly when I return home Tuesday before scrolling down to an email from Athena.

In true Athena form, it's not a standard here's-the-attachment-you-requested email.

To: The sexy bitch who finally realized her worth

From: The sexy bitch who always knew it

Subject: Have you banged him yet?

If you say no, I'll show you how to get the job done when you get back, but for now, we'll go with the basics. Take Frosty's *ginormous* carrot. Shove it into the warm pie between your legs. Rinse with wetness. Then repeat until you scream his name at the top of your lungs. Easy peasy.

Oh, yeah, and there's supposedly something *really* important attached to this email.

Love ya face.

A xx

I laugh before forwarding the attachment to Colby's email address, minus Athena's instructions and subject line. Once it whooshes into the world wide web, I return Athena's email.

To: The sexy bitch who needs to stop calling herself a bitch

From: Someone who needs recordable spy glasses

Subject: Are steamy shower activities classed as banging?

I'm joking. Calm down. The only banging was my heart

when I was caught watching something I shouldn't have been. I'll explain when I get home.

Thank you for the attachment and so-called instructions, but if you really have a pie between your legs, I suggest you seek urgent medical attention.

In other news, I hope Brad's visit didn't dampen your day. It will be a thing of the past soon. I promise.

I love *your* face.

J xx

If you think discussing the dissolution of my engagement is stabbing my heart with pain, you'd be wrong. What I said to Colby earlier was true. I feel more alive now than I ever have. My bad days with Brad were far exceeding the good days, so I would have left him eventually. His rough handling just sped up the process. Shouted words are understandable, we both have stressful jobs, but nothing will ever excuse violence. A shove always turns into a slap. An open-handed slap always turns into a punch. Just like a violent-tempered man will always blame others for his actions. I know this firsthand. Not because I was in an abusive relationship but because I helped my best friend escape one.

I stop reminiscing about days that should have been golden when a tap sounds on the glass next to my head. While smiling at the worried crinkle between Colby's brows, I wind down the window.

"Are you okay?" His thumbs clean my tears before I get the chance to nod. "Why are you crying?"

Trying to think of how I can explain the craziness of my life right now, I'm a little stumped. My body's response to his meekest touch has me finally understanding why Tyronc requested him to cool our friendship two weeks ago. We never stepped over the line, but things between us became very chummy very quickly. I was confused about the feelings I was developing for him, so I could imagine how bad it looked to those outside of our bubble.

I would feel sorry for Brad if he weren't such an asshole.

Even with my cheeks dry, Colby keeps his hands close by. It triples the heat creeping up my neck. "Is your mom okay?"

I lift my chin, aware the panic in his voice most likely resides around the emotions he tries to keep hidden. Even if news of the McGregor children being orphans hadn't circulated in the media when his brother married last year, I'm still aware his mother died when he was a teen, and his brother was appointed his guardian instead of his father. Stuff like that was mentioned in the psych examination Metrics Insurance made him undertake to ensure he was mentally capable of being a skydiving instructor.

"She's been ill for a long time, so I've grown accustomed to anticipating bad news. I'm just not sure I'll be ready to accept it when it does come. If that makes any sense?"

"I get it. If I didn't, I'd give you a shit line about how talking about it will make it better."

Colby's reply makes me smile. The first line I'm always given when I tell people my mom is sick is that "talking will make everything better." It doesn't. No amount of words will fix what my mom has. Not even medicine can help her, so telling me to talk about it won't change anything. She will still die, and I'll still be left picking up the pieces her loss leaves behind. It sucks, but sometimes life does.

I stop twisting my skirt around my fingers when Colby says, "That doesn't mean I can't listen, though, Jamie. Whether about your mom, work, or even Brad..." I laugh at the gag he does when he mentions my ex-fiancé. "If you need to vent, I'm more than happy to hear you out."

"What if I need to let off steam about a really annoying adventure capitalist who grates my last nerve?"

The worry on his face switches to humor in an instant. "What could you possibly have to whine about him? He sounds like a great guy. I bet he's handsome, too. Probably hung like a donkey. All adventure capitalists are. It's what brings in the big bucks."

His words shift to laughter when I sock him in the stomach. "Sounds like someone has tickets on himself."

When I poke him low in the stomach, right near his tattoo, the humor in his eyes burns away for egotism. "Ah... I was wondering if you took in more than my cock sliding in and out of my fist when you watched my performance in the shower. Are you sure you need glasses, Prim?" Colby slides the glasses he's referencing back up my nose with his index finger. "Or are they just an excuse to conduct *in-depth* examinations without your suitors' knowledge?"

My nipples press up against his chest when I slide out of the van with more gusto than I used to enter it. "I hated having glasses when I was a kid. The bullying, the four-eyes comments, and the assumption I was a nerd made me wish I had never told my mom I couldn't see the chalkboard in the fifth grade." I tilt closer to him like my heart isn't racing a million miles an hour. "Now, I love them. Not just because I could see how every vein in your cock pulsated when you caught me *enjoying* your performance, but because even with my pulse shrilling in my ears, I could read the word you whispered just as you came. *Ja-mie.*" I mouth my name like he did in the shower—all virile, hot, and spaced by a needy breath.

Pretending my legs aren't close to buckling, I skirt past Colby and head toward the bar on my right. "After the crazy day I've had, I could really use a drink or seven. Do you think this place knows what a cosmo is?"

"Jamie..."

Colby's voice is as hot and husky as it was in the shower but with a hint of worry my lusty head is refusing to listen to. Only days ago, I would have never articulated the words I just said, yet here I am, talking freely without a care in the world. That probably has more to do with the member I felt growing between us the longer my body was pressed against Colby's than newfound confidence, but I'll gobble it up no matter what it is.

Dust covers the exposed toes in my pumps when I spin around to face Colby. "Are you coming, Colby? Drinks are on me." Even in my voice, my tone is dripping with the sexual innuendo Colby uses in his day-to-day activities.

"I don't think this is a good idea." His mouth is telling me no, but his legs are walking toward me—rather quickly too. They're pumping as fast as the pulse beeping in my clit.

"It's just a drink. What's the worst that could happen?"

CHAPTER 24

COLBY

*P*lease, please, please, let her be wearing panties. I'm not strong enough for this. If Jamie straddles my lap sans underwear, I'm san morals. She's drunk, and I'm as sober as the nuns who jump every Monday to get close to God, but that won't stop me. She's been teasing me all night. Daring little touches and flirting one-liners which have kept my dick in close contact with my zipper at all times. She all but ear-fucked me on the drive home. She told me how wet watching me in the shower made her, and how she wants to do it again but that she'll replace my hand with her mouth.

Now she's shoved me on my bed, telling me she can't wait a second longer.

"Jamie..."

Her hands are around my neck, then in my hair before her lips are on mine.

Fuck. Me.

Even if she's wearing panties, I won't be able to stop this.

There isn't a battle in the record books that could explain the level of fight I'd need to stop this.

She kisses me furiously like her lips aren't laden down with the half bottle of tequila sitting in her gut. Her mouth should taste salty or sour—perhaps even bitter. It's neither of those things. It tastes sweet like watermelon on a blistering summer day. It will quench my thirst no matter how dire it is.

I guess I should just kiss her then. Bang out the thoughts that have kept me awake the past few weeks. Take back some of the control she stole.

That's what I'll do. I'll kiss her until my thirst is satiated, then pull back.

Easy.

I'm an idiot. There's no returning from this. Our tongues dance too intricately to pretend one taste will ever suffice. I'll be left begging for another and another and another until I've pleaded so much, I'll be on one knee instead of two.

With that scary notion in the forefront of my mind, I inch back. It's more painful than my ankles snapping upon landing two years ago. When I shake my head, denying the plea in her eyes, I hear a familiar crack. It's not my ankles fracturing, though. It's Jamie's heart.

"Please, Colby. I want you." She says my name on a moan like she's on the cusp of climax after nothing but a kiss.

With words eluding me, she hoists her skirt up her thighs, then cuddles them around mine. She's wearing panties, but since they're lace and soaked through, she may as well not be. I groan when the heat of her pussy braces against my dick. It's fighting my zipper, endeavoring to be freed and sunk into the scent that's kept it restless for weeks now.

We kiss for a few more minutes, moaning with every intimate grind of our bodies. We're dry-humping like teens at the prom, but it's the best make-out session I've ever had. I fuck, and I fuck good, but this is different. I don't feel like I'm performing an act. I'm enjoying this as much as Jamie, like my dick doesn't need to leave my pants for me to come.

That will never happen, though.

All men fuck for pleasure, but real men ensure it's for both him and his lady.

Every sweep of her tongue against mine has my hips lifting off the bed more. We lick and rock, lick and rock until I'm not the only one waving a white flag in defeat. With her head burrowed in my neck, and my name huskily leaving her lips, Jamie does one final grind before the moans I've imagined in vivid detail fill my ears. She stills as an uproar of devastation overtakes every inch of her. She's hot all over, my earlier worries about her hypothermic state done and dusted. She's the sexiest I've ever seen her, and I can't wait for stage two.

I wait patiently for her to come down from the cloud. I'm a gentleman like that. Why exhaust her of something I plan to make her do at least five times tonight?

When thirty seconds pass with no signs of life, I drop my eyes to Jamie. When another ten seconds tick by, I peel her off my chest by her shoulders. When her nose is dislodged from my neck, I realize what a fucking idiot I am. She's not floating on a cloud. She's sleeping on one. Or should I say, snoring on one?

Keeping my disappointment on the down-low, I use my crane-like dick to hoist her from my crotch to her pillow. She snuggles in close, my name leaving her mouth in a moan similar to the one she released while coming. It tightens the front of my pants even more, while also reminding me about how close I came to royally fucking things up tonight. As if it isn't bad enough she heard me murmur her name while cum streamed out of my cock, I nearly slept with a drunk girl.

I don't do that.

Consent is sexy

Consent is right.

Fucking someone when they're plastered isn't, especially when you care about that someone enough you want to save them from the misery that will become your life.

After pulling a blanket over Jamie's shoulders, I walk into the bathroom to clean my teeth and scrub my face. I could take care of the throb behind my zipper as I did earlier today, but I won't. Its ache is a reminder that Jamie won't be the only one who'll forget our kiss. It will disappear from my mind eventually too. It just won't be because of an excessive amount of alcohol.

———

The following morning, I'm awakened by the hum of excitement. Usually, I'd relish a noise that guarantees a day of adrenaline-packed fun. This morning, I'm not so eager. I've been sidelined from activities to ensure Jamie complies with Nixon's advice on her having a low-impact weekend. I'm not annoyed, far from it, but it's that notion that's panicking me just as much as the fact I didn't run for the hills last night.

Things with Jamie have always been complicated. We've had a natural, unexplainable connection from day one, but last night ramped it up to an entirely new level. Even knowing no matter which path I take, it will always be the wrong one doesn't have me reaching for the brake. That's inconceivable. Un-fucking heard of. It has me wondering if she's the reason my cock's been disinterested in the game it's been playing the past eight years. I guess faking a stomach bug so I could go home and stroke one out about my 'supposed' friend should have been the first sign I was swimming in unchartered waters.

I wish things could be like they were in the shower, that nothing but my insatiable horniness matters. Unfortunately, this is real life. It isn't a romantic movie, much less one of those raunchy novels Jamie talked about incessantly during our many 'dates.'

That's probably half my issue. Her excessive gloating about her book boyfriends had me thinking how awesome it would be to be one. Picture this—a four hundred and fifty-page paperback novel with a foldout section so the readers could visualize my cock in all its glory.

Just thinking about buying this book brightened your morning, didn't it? You're welcome.

With my steps no longer weighed down with misery, I make my way into the living area of the cabin. This is the standard type of cabin you'd expect to find in the foothills of Northern Cali. It's boastful, gleaming of money, and capable of attending to numerous guests' needs at once. It once represented its owner to a T.

As I make a beeline to the coffee machine, my eyes lock in on a visual I didn't anticipate seeing until the sun was high in the sky. Jamie is at the side of the kitchen, looking over some paperwork with Tyrone. She acts like she hasn't noticed my gawking stare. I'd be inclined to believe her if I hadn't seen the goosebumps on her neck rising. They're as strained as her nipples are budded—a telltale sign she's sensed my presence.

"Morning." I help myself to a mug of coffee before joining them at the dining table. My swagger is awfully cocky for a man who was left hanging last night. "What are you looking at?" They have a heap of forms on the table—official-looking forms.

I freeze with my mug halfway to my lips when Tyrone says, "Jamie is signing an indemnity waiver so she can jump with us this morning."

Although I've been dying to take her on a jump since we landed in the ocean seven weeks ago, she can't jump today. "You can't jump, Prim. You're injured... and hungover, aren't you?" My last two words are brimming with suspicion. Her eyes are the clearest I've seen them, and although her hair is a wild mess, her face isn't harboring a single side effect of a woman who drunk half a bottle of tequila.

"I'm fine. I feel great."

You have no clue how fucking hard it is not to bang my chest right now. What did I tell you? Backed-up orgasms weigh a ton. She may have only had one last night, but she's light and flighty.

"And I paid for an adventurous weekend, so aren't I entitled to one?"

"There's plenty of fun we can have without putting your safety at risk, Prim."

There I go again with a needy, underhanded comment that reveals why I had no chance of sidestepping the event that occurred last night. My tone could have only been more insinuating if I bent her over the table and swiped my cock across her clit.

"Once your stitches have been removed and you've been given the all-clear, I'll take you for a jump."

This is the only time in my life I wished skydiving was referred to as anything else but jumping. I want to jump her all right, just not out of a plane.

One of the many things I admire about Jamie shines in her eyes when she says, "Colby, you're being silly. I honestly feel fine." She's not buttering me up, she's being straight-up honest.

I can't say the same thing about Tyrone. "She also signed a waiver, so she's good to go."

I glare at him, revealing we'll have more than words if he doesn't get his hands off Jamie. He may only be rubbing her arm to assure he has her back, but my fucked-up brain isn't seeing it that way.

"I don't give a fuck what she signed, she can't jump." I stare at Tyrone for another ten seconds, expressing the words I can't say in front of witnesses before shifting my focus back to Jamie. "Altitude can increase cerebral blood flow, meaning you risk further injury if you had even the slightest concussion yesterday. I'm not willing to risk your safety for a stupid jump."

With her silence revealing she's teetering toward my side of the argument, Tyrone places himself between us—*again*. "This isn't your choice, Colby."

"Yes, it is," I roar at Tyrone, startling Jamie and the handful of people who have gathered to watch our exchange. "You're only encouraging her defiance to prove a point."

He thinks this argument will have me admitting I'm developing feelings for Jamie. I am, but there's no fucking chance in hell I'll admit that in a room full of spectators.

"Safety is more important than the stupid game you're playing, Ty."

I shift my eyes to Jamie. She's peering at me with the same stunned expression the blonde bimbos behind her are wearing, it's just different. Like she's more pleased than shocked. "I'll take you skydiving when the time is right. Now is not the right time. You know me. You know I'd rather have my nuts crushed in a grinder than give up an opportunity to jump, so you also know you can trust that I'm not denying your request for no reason. It's not safe. I can't put it any simpler than that."

I want to punch myself in the throat when a collective sigh rolls out of the mouth of every female surrounding me— excluding Jamie. From their reaction, anyone would swear I'm down on one knee proposing instead of doing the job I'm paid to do. This is my event. I am the head coordinator, but even if I weren't, my opinion wouldn't change. This isn't a risk I'm willing to take. I'd rather tell Jamie my deepest, darkest secret than have her jump so soon after an injury.

Some of the heaviness on my chest lifts when Jamie steps closer to me. "If we're going to miss out on an adrenaline-packed day in the sky, I'm going to need your guarantee our day will be just as adventurous on the ground."

I'm about to say "deal," but she presses her finger to my mouth before I can. "I haven't finished with my demands just yet." My lips raise against her finger, loving her sassy attitude. I can't believe I ever thought she was a stiff. "The next time 'The Git Up' comes on, no matter the time or the place, your ass better be next to mine doing the hoedown. You let the team down last night, Colby. That's unforgivable."

The seriousness in her tone makes it seem as if we competed against Royce and Linda last night. In reality, it was a handful of drunken teens who most likely still have their heads hanging in a toilet bowl.

"Deal?" She holds out her fist for me to knock, her eyes sparkling with more life than I've ever seen them show.

I should add my own negotiations into our deal, but for the first time in years, I let my heart win the battle it's been waging with my head since I was a teen. "Deal."

CHAPTER 25

JAMIE

*E*xcitement roars through my body when Colby bumps his fist against mine. I want to say because the most arrogant, boastful man I've ever met just agreed to my every whim a mere second after admitting my safety is more vital to him than an activity he'd rather die than live without, but that would be a lie. It's from having my finger pressed against his mouth—a mouth I was staring at differently only yesterday. My God, if my vivid imagination is anything to go by, Colby McGregor is a stellar kisser.

Eager to leave before the many eyes gawking at us see my heated cheeks, I drop my hand from Colby's mouth. "Give me five minutes to brush my teeth, then I'll be good to go."

When he waves his hand across his body, signaling for me to lead the way, I arch a brow. "I need to brush my teeth, too." He swivels his finger around his ridiculously handsome face. "This alone has girls looking past ghastly morning breath, but as I said earlier, I don't want to take any unnecessary risks today."

His last few words are garbled when I punch him in the stomach. "You're a pig."

Colby grunts like one before shadowing me into his room. I move through the cabin remarkably quick for someone who should have a hangover. My head is throbbing. It's just barely felt since the rest of my body is thrumming with a delighted zap. It's a hard sensation to explain, one I'm certain I've never experienced before.

After wetting a toothbrush and loading it with paste, I twist to face Colby. "Did I say or do anything stupid last night?"

"Depends on what you class as stupid?" The quickest flash of disappointment flares in his eyes as he joins me next to the vanity. "What do you recall about last night?"

I poke my toothbrush into his stomach. "That Mrs. Palencia needs to encourage you to work on more than your rumba."

"That fucked-up shit they were doing last night wasn't dancing." He snags his toothbrush out of the holder before squirting a generous helping of paste on it. Once he's dunked it under the stream of water, he pops it into his mouth. Even doing something as mundane as sharing a vanity sink is exciting when it's happening with him. "How did you even know the moves they were doing? Never saw you as a line dancer, Prim."

"Uh... Blanco Brown tells you what to do in his song. It's not hard."

Feeling playful, I do the two-step, then the cowboy boogie, breaking out the moves Colby refused to do last night. Before he can deny my request, I swing him around as Blanco is demanding in my head before scooting back to do the dorkiest form of the hoedown, spasming knees and all. After throwing down my toothbrush, I take a sip out of the imaginary cup in my hand.

"Come on, Colby. The song might only be in my head, but you're not keeping your side of our deal, which means I have the right to enroll in jump school."

I'm anticipating for him to deny my request, so you can imagine my surprise when he steps to the left before stepping to the right. For someone who can fake apprehension like he's vying for an Oscar, he has no problems boogying to a song we can only hear in our heads. When we're instructed to take it down, he gets his ass closer to the floor than I do.

By the time 'The Git Up' finishes playing in my head, I'm sweating like a pig and smiling as I've never smiled before. "Why didn't you do that last night? We could have won if you weren't scared about performing in front of an audience."

Colby rinses out his toothbrush before spinning around to face me. "I'm not scared about performing in front of an audience. Just figured you'd rather have a private show... *again.*"

When he hits me with a flirty wink, it isn't just my skin that gets extra sticky, so do my panties. It isn't the naturally ingrained ambiguity in his tone making me hot all over, it's memories too real to be fake.

Colby's steps out of the bathroom freeze when I say, "We kissed." He's not the only one turning solid when reality dawns. "Sorry, let me correct that. *I* kissed *you.* Here... in your room... on your bed." I've always hated my mom's condition, but I loathe it even more now. Having any memories blurred is horrendous, much less ones I'd give anything not to forget. "Why did we stop? What happened? Did I do something wrong?"

Colby squares his shoulders before flashing me his infamous smirk. "No. You didn't do anything wrong. We just—"

Colby stops talking when my mouth falls open. "I fell asleep. Oh my God. Please kill me."

I'm serious this time. This isn't a drill.

Colby steps closer to me, all casual. "It's not a big deal."

I shove the rest of his assurance into the back of his throat with a stern glare. "It's not a big deal? How is this *not* a big deal? I kissed you. Then I brought myself to climax on your zipper."

Colby scoffs. "Don't give my zipper all the credit. Some of your moans rightfully belong to my cock. He's sporting battle wounds today, so the least you could do is stroke his ego."

I continue talking as if he never interrupted me. "Then, I fell asleep. My God. This is *really* bad." I crawl under the blankets to hide my inflamed cheeks, beyond mortified. "You can go now. Let me die of embarrassment in peace."

"You were drunk, Prim. Crazy shit happens when you're drunk."

He joins me under the sheets, smiling in a way that makes me want to kiss him again. If I didn't know any better, I'd swear he's relieved I remembered our exchange. I wonder if he'd still be smiling if he discovered I would have kissed him even if I wasn't drunk? Alcohol might have fueled my motives last night, but tequila isn't the sole reason I kissed him. It just made me brave enough to put motions into play I've dreamed about for weeks.

Taking my silence as mortification, Colby says, "If it makes you feel any better, you can return the favor tonight. I promise to be snoring the instant the first squirt of cum leaves my dick."

I whack him—hard. "You're an asshole."

His laugh slicks my panties with moisture. "Says the lady who left me hanging. It's lucky I know how to take care of business, or I might have woken as a cripple."

Colby is joking, but my stupid body doesn't register it like that. It grows heavy with sweat as images of him pleasuring himself filter through my head.

"Now, come on. We've got non-brain-swelling adrenaline-packed activities to undertake." He nudges his head to the door like my embarrassment is nothing but water under the bridge. "If you're not waiting for me in ten minutes—"

"You'll leave without me, so I can die in peace?"

He pushes my glasses up my nose so I can see the honesty in his eyes when he says, "I'll dig my belt buckle out of my suit-case. It will ensure not even a gallon of tequila will steal your memories."

Colby taps my ass two times, having no clue how invaluable his comment is for me. When you have a parent with Alzheimer's, you never stop worrying that one day you'll force your loved ones down the painful track you'd give anything to stop walking.

"Come on, Prim. I thought last night settled the score between us. I came. You came. Everyone fucking came. Now we're even, so there's no reason to be embarrassed."

That pops my head out of the blanket. "Everyone? Who else came?"

He laughs at my inability not to pry into other people's lives even when I wish mine were close to the end. "Figuratively, Prim. I wasn't listening out for any moans that didn't have my name associated with them."

Clearly, he hasn't ventured to the other side of the cabin the last two nights. The moans I heard may have come with a hefty amount of vibrations, but there was no doubt it was his name being murmured—even with him passed out several rooms away.

"Ten minutes?"

The weight on my chest eases when he holds out his fist for me to bump. "Ten minutes."

Once we've sealed our agreement with a fist bump, he leaves the room. I waste a few minutes under the sheets gathering my composure. I'm still embarrassed, but Colby's reminder of the compromising position I caught him in before my shameful attempt to seduce him makes it not as palpable. At least I was clothed. Colby wasn't.

After fanning my heated cheeks, I slip into a pair of knee-high boots, snag my coat and beanie out of my suitcase, then march out of my room like my ass is on fire. I may have kissed Colby, but there's no doubt he kissed me back. He wouldn't have done that unless he wanted to. Believe me when I say there are many ways a man can avoid being kissed if the idea disgusts him. My relationship with Brad makes me an expert on the subject matter.

With my mood only just improving, I increase my pace, eager to avoid anything that will sour it. The hype coming out of the living room matches the buzz roaring through my veins. The participants are sitting through an impromptu 'jump school' in preparation for their scheduled events today. I'm disappointed Colby denied my request to join the festivities, but I'm secretly looking forward to spending the day with him. I'll get to jump one day. His eyes held too much promise for it not to be in the cards, so for now, I can enjoy our first full day together.

Don't misconstrue. I'm not anticipating anything like the event that's slowly trickling back into my head, but I hope it's similar to the nights we spent together before he pushed the brakes on our friendship. We have a bizarre, unexplainable connection, but I need his friendship more than anything. It's been a crazy few years for me, and it feels like I'm only just coming up for air.

When my mom was diagnosed with Alzheimer's, my first thought was that I could never force anyone through the maze my dad and I were about to navigate. I closed myself off, not just from friendship but love as well. It was only as my mom's condition worsened did I realize how silly I was being. My dad could have given in. He could have walked away, but he didn't. He loved her too much to do that. He stuck by her side throughout it all, and now his dedication is being awarded in the most beautiful way. She may only remember the man he once was, but she undoubtedly loves him with every snippet of her being. She loves him so much not even Alzheimer's has her forgetting him. That's a love I was determined to find—a love I craved. It's also the reason I fell for Brad's tricks so quickly. I told him about my mom's condition from the get-go, and despite that, he still asked me on a second date. I thought he understood my want of a love greater than the world's hardest circumstances.

I was wrong.

You can't force someone to love you any more than you can't force yourself to love someone who isn't right for you. It took me a few months to remember my pledge, but now that it's back, I'll give it my best shot to make it come true—although with some slight variations. I don't have to fall in love to have the best life possible. I simply need to learn to love myself. It will be a slow process, but this weekend has been a great starting point. Colby's cockiness is a wonderful way to show how there's nothing wrong with self-love. Whether sexually or mentally, there's no shame in self-care.

While I'm being forthright, I'll also admit a small part of me, the dorky, insurance-consultant side, loved that not even a guarantee I wouldn't sue if I were injured saw Colby being lenient on the rules. If that doesn't prove I made the right decision in approving his request for coverage, I don't know what will.

My brisk speed slows when Colby's eyes lift from a sheet of paper in his hand to me. He drifts them up my body and over my face before taking in the springy locks still bouncing from my thunderous steps. My hand shoots up to my hair, suddenly embarrassed. With my body thrumming from what I thought was excitement, but now understand is orgasmic bliss, I brushed my hair with a wire comb this morning before returning its ringlets with a healthy scrunch.

"I've got a beanie to cover them up." Colby snatches my beanie out of my hand before tossing it out the window. "What the—"

"You won't need a beanie where we're going. Besides, I don't iron my clothes, much less my hair, so why should you?"

"Uh… because my crazy ringlets fail to show me as the professional businesswoman I'm supposed to be?" Those are *not* my words. They're Brad's. I only commenced straightening my hair six months ago when he pointed out numerous times how childish they make me look.

"My point exactly. I like wild, carefree Jamie. She's almost as fun as tequila Jamie."

His teeth grit as if he said too much before he shoves the sheet of paper he's clutching into Tyrone's chest. I eye him curiously when he arches his brow at Tyrone. They must be able to communicate without words because not long after Tyrone jerks up his chin, Colby curls his hand around mine to lead me outside. It's chilly today, but I'm not feeling it—even more so when Colby walks me toward a four-wheeled motorbike. It's big and bulky and has a black steel cage on the back. It looks like an all-terrain vehicle a hunter would have.

"Aren't we taking the van?"

Colby shakes his head before gathering two helmets off a shelf at the side of the carport. "This will be quicker." He smirks a cunning grin. "And more fun." He hisses while placing my helmet on. The band is nowhere near my stitches, but his panic makes it seem as if he's jabbing a screwdriver directly into my wound. "Is that an okay fit? It's not too loose for you, is it?"

"Let me guess, those aren't words you articulate often?" Colby laughs at my comment, but the worry in his eyes remains. "It's fine. I'm more fretful about how I'm going to handle that girth." I nudge my head to the widespread of the quad's seat. "I'm wearing extremely tight jeans that don't have much stretch."

"Now, those are sentences I often hear."

I'd whack him in the gut if it wouldn't reveal how jealous I am. I am green with envy, but I've got lost ground to make up for, so I can't give him more ammunition. "You know what they say about guys who brag, don't you?"

A throb descends to the lower half of my body when he purses his lips. I kissed them—more than once. "That it isn't bragging when you have the goods to back it up?"

I roll my eyes before mounting the ATV remarkedly well considering I didn't stretch beforehand. When Colby requests for me to scoot forward, I peer at him in confusion. "Aren't you driving?"

He shakes his head. "Hell no. You don't get to insult my manhood and not expect it to have it rubbed against you for the next hour. Scoot forward, Prim, things are about to get extremely chummy."

"You're being ridiculous," I murmur, acting like I'm not on the brink of climax from the thought of us getting friendly —again.

"How? Because I want to prove a point?"

I must still be drunk, otherwise how else could I explain leaning in real close to his side to whisper, "Because I was wearing tequila goggles last night, not a hazmat suit. I know what your packing."

I see confidence roar through his eyes a mere second before he winks. "Then you know as well as I do that you're more than eager for a second round, so scoot. I'm not asking, Prim. I'm telling."

CHAPTER 26

COLBY

*J*amie tries to act annoyed by my request, but I can see the excitement in her eyes. Why do you think I'm so determined to ride shotgun? I won't lie, my peacock feathers were already fanned when she sided with me instead of Tyrone, but I was nearly whacked on my ass with a bolt of cockiness when memories of our kiss slowly trickled into her hungover head. I barely showcased the moves I'm more famous for than my billionaire surname last night, but not even half a bottle of tequila could push them into the background of her mind. I can understand why. Our kiss was too fucking sexy to forget. The way her lips parted just before my name came tumbling out in a throaty purr. Fuck. Me. That's the stuff wet dreams are made of.

After donning my helmet, I mount the ATV behind Jamie before my cock swells so much I become a brain-dead reject —*years earlier than predicted.*

I shake my head to clear it of negative thoughts before

focusing my devotion on Jamie. "Have you ever ridden a quad before?"

She shakes her head. "No. That's why you should be driving."

"It's easy. You'll get the hang of it in no time."

Prickles on her nape rise when I guide her hands onto the handlebars. The way her body forever responds to mine doesn't make sense, but tell me one time you've sat back and thought, *Fuck me. That makes perfect sense.* Some things are meant to be unexplainable—that's what makes life interesting. It would be one dead ritual after another if everything were understood the first time around.

"This bike is fully automatic." I press the start button to fire her up before giving Jamie a basic rundown on how it operates. "The thumb throttle on your right controls your speed, and the brakes are just like the ones you find on any bike. When you yank them back, the quad will slow down."

"So I just push on the throttle, and we will go?" I don't know why she sounds surprised by the simplicity of my instructions. A bike is just like a woman—with the right amount of pressure and a little bit of patience, she'll take you on the ride of your life.

"Go slow. You don't want to throw me off." I scream like a bitch when she presses on the throttle so severely I'm thrown backward. "If you want to slow down, ease off the throttle, then slowly apply pressure to the brakes." My teeth grit when my helmet headbutts the back of hers from her locking up the brakes.

"I'm sorry. I suck at this."

She has to shout so I can hear her over the ATV's revs and perhaps the snickering of the snooty women eyeballing our escape from the front porch of the cabin. Even hearing Jamie moan my name last night hasn't dampened their campaign to treat her like an outcast. If anything, it's increased their bitterness. They're pissed my dick was taken off the itinerary of activities, and they're more than happy to place the blame for that on Jamie's shoulders. In a way, they're right, but I'll never let them know that.

"Let's switch places."

I grip Jamie's thighs like my cock is plastered to her crotch instead of her ass when she attempts to hook her leg over the bike. "We're not switching places. You're going to ride this quad like the bad bitch you are. Hit the throttle, Prim, and this time, do it with enough power you'll add a mud bath to their list of activities for today." When her eyes collide with mine in the side mirror, I jerk my chin to the group watching us without the slightest bit of remorse on their faces.

Her pupils dilate. "I can't do that."

"Why? Because they have been nothing but nice to you since you arrived?"

I feel her sigh more than I hear it. "What if they sue you?"

"How can they sue me? I'm not driving." I can't see her mouth, but I know she's smiling. I can feel it in my bones, not to mention the way it lights up her eyes. "Unless you have millions of dollars I don't know about, it's time to give as good as you're getting."

Her chest rises and falls three times before she jabs her thumb onto the throttle. The backend of the ATV swivels out of control, skidding in the mud for several long seconds before rocketing toward the exit.

Jamie squeals the entire time, her panic about our brutal speed having her missing the muddy mess she left in her wake.

Not only did she spray the snickering women with smelly mud, she also got Tyrone, who's watching our departure with the biggest grin on his face. I doubt he'll still be smiling when we get hit with a dry-cleaning bill in the thousands.

Still worth it. I'd spend millions of dollars if it guarantees Jamie's heart will continue beating the tune it is now.

Five hours later, Jamie's big aqua eyes lock with mine. "What are the rules again?"

I laugh at the competitiveness in her voice. If anyone ever accused her of not being driven, you can be assured they're a liar. Even standing shoeless in a muddy paddock with a lard-sodden pig staring her down hasn't had her backing away from the many activities we've undertaken so far this morning. We ate our weight in scrambled eggs, undertook two rounds of archery, and ziplined across ranges that make this region of the country some of the best for adrenaline junkiness.

Now we're wrestling pigs. By we, I mean Jamie. I was booted in the first round.

"Tackle the pig, Prim. That's all you've got to do. If you win this round, you'll be crowned champion pig wrestler for this region."

Nodding, she buries her feet into the sloshy mud while waiting for the buzzer to announce the final round has begun. When she suggested we join the pig wrestling competition at Clement River's agricultural show, I agreed on the assumption we'd be out in the first round. I had no clue she'd make it to the finals. Not even a healthy coat of mud smeared across her glasses slowed her down the past five rounds. She has a competitive streak as long as my cock.

"Come here, Prim." When she joins me at the side of the fenced pavilion, I adjust the bull- riding helmet I demanded she wear so it protects her bandaged stitches. Nixon gave her the all-clear to participate on the agreement he bandaged her cut so she wouldn't get any mud in it. He's here with his wife, Eden. She and Jamie sparked an instant friendship. If the baking competition hadn't started, I doubt anything would have torn them apart.

"Do you need the glasses, Prim?"

"Ah… yeah." Her brisk nod doubles the assurance in her eyes. "Unless you want me groping the other contestants as I hunt for the pig? They smell about the same."

I laugh as if my gut isn't aching from how many times I've laughed the past five hours. "They'd probably let you win if you gave them a quick feel-up."

My laughter halts when she says, "Then remove my glasses and point me in the direction of contestant number six. He has sexy bedroom eyes."

Jealousy roars through me like a big, hot beast. "Prim…"

She pokes her tongue out when the buzzer announces the start of this round, and even faster than that, she's chasing a pig almost as big as her around a sloshy pit. I nearly fall off my seat laughing when she dives headfirst into a massive puddle. She slipped straight off the hindquarter of the pig, revealing the oil they lathered him in is doing its job.

"You won't catch him down there. Come on, Prim. I'm craving some bacon."

That jumps her into action. "That's why I'm going to win. So I can set him free."

With a grunt like she's double her size, she shoves the contestant she said had dreamy eyes onto his ass before elbowing another opponent in the ribs. When she jumps onto the pig's back, she holds on like he's a bull, and she's striving for the clock to reach eight seconds.

"I'm trying to help you," she screams at the pig, sending laughter across the pavilion. "I won't let anyone eat you. I promise."

The roar of the crowd subdues when she miraculously gets the pig's four hooves off the mud. To the organizers of this competition, it's all that's required for a win.

"Yes!"

Jamie jumps into the air like she isn't soaked head to toe in mud. She does the moonwalk before ungraciously gloating to the losing contestants that they're not having pork chops for dinner tonight. I don't have the heart to tell her that just because the man she's organized to take her pig is an organic farmer doesn't mean her pig won't be turned into pork at some stage in his life. He'll simply roam free before he meets with his creator.

After snatching her winner's sash from the organizer and handing the pig to her farmer, she bolts my way. The smile on her face has me misreading her happiness. Jamie's not dashing my way to give me a hug of congratulations, she wants me covered with as much smelly mud as she is.

"Jamie… don't."

My command is separated by big breaths from me launching out of my seat to bolt in the opposite direction from where she's coming from. I make it to the edge of the pavilion before my feet are wiped out from beneath me. Jamie isn't responsible for me hitting the slosh-covered ground like a bag of shit. It's the damn pig she saved from being slaughtered tonight. He's racing for the exit like he's outrunning a firing squad. Since he is, his dash for freedom is understandable.

"Run, George, run!" Jamie screams before 'accidentally' stepping into the farmer's way, blocking his exit long enough that George disappears into the dense forest bordering the showgrounds.

Once he's nothing but a haze on the horizon, Jamie helps me off the ground. "My job here is done. Next!"

I shake my head with a laugh. I always knew there was an adrenaline junkie hiding deep inside her. "We'll get booted out of more places than welcomed with you looking like that." She pouts when I tug on one of her springy locks. They're being weighed down by mud, returning them to the flat, lackless style she usually dons. "Come on, let's get you cleaned up."

When I guide her to the only clothing store in Clement River, the store assistant greets us with a beaming grin. "Howdy, y'all. What happened here?" Her accent is way too south for this far north. "Pig wrestler?"

"Champion pig wrestler," I correct, the pride in my tone unmissable.

The cashier slaps her knee. "You're the reason I saw the town's supper for the next month running past my back window just now?" She tilts in real close to Jamie, who's throat is struggling through a brutal swallow. "I'm glad. If it isn't bad enough they are wrestled multiple times a day, then they face being eaten, too. It almost has me wanting to turn vegetarian. Alas, I like my meat too much for that ever to happen."

She winks at me, ensuring I can't miss the double innuendo in her comment. Don't judge her—she's not flirting with me, she's just being playful. The gold ring on her left hand assures this, much less the brute of a man eyeballing our exchange at the side. He has the alpha male I'll-squash-you-like-a-bug-if-you-dare-look-at-my-woman-the-wrong-way vibe. He's got nothing to be worried about. His wife is a knockout, but even without her wearing the mud suit Jamie is donning, she can't steal Jamie's limelight. She's Clement River's Pig Wrestling Champion.

Why does that get me so excited, you ask? If she can wrestle a pig into submission on a muddy paddock, imagine her prowess when she gets one between the sheets? *Oink oink.*

"There are spare towels under the vanity, and the mat is hanging on a hook behind the door." Belle, the cashier slash owner of Clement River Boutique places the clothing we've purchased onto the bed before nudging her head to the only door in the loft apartment above her store. "The hot water takes a little while to kick in, but the pressure is good." She smiles at Jamie while running her hand down her muddy locks. "There's shampoo in the stall." She pivots away from us, still smiling. "And the bed has clean sheets, you know, just in case." When she offered for Jamie to use her loft to shower and change in, she hinted multiple times that her loft was a thing of magic while peering at her husband with gaga eyes. "If you need anything—"

"I'll find you at Smitty's next door, right?" I guide her to the spiral staircase like I own the place. "Thanks for everything."

The jeans, boots, long-sleeve shirt, and jacket Jamie purchased set me back a whopping $83.72, including tax, but Belle is acting like she hit the jackpot.

"You're very welcome." After a playful wink directed at

Jamie, she gallops down the stairs where her final leap has her landing in the arms of her husband, Darby. Even from this angle, their differences in height and width is undeniable. Darby is massive. Belle isn't.

I stop watching them suck face as they exit the boutique via a back door when Jamie calls my name. It was all needy and hot like she wants me—urgently. She does, just not in the way my wicked brain is thinking. She's tugging at her zipper—a zipper that's refusing to budge since it has a truckload of dried mud embedded in the teeth.

"Do you need me to get my scissors... *again?*"

She peers up at me with her big doe eyes out in full force since her glasses are on the bedside table. "Considering the fact I smell like manure, I'd rather you bust the zipper. I'm sure it's not the first time you've done that."

I peer down at the floor, so she won't see my grin. The only time I busted a zipper was when she had my cock wrestling it last night and during our multiple dance-offs, but I'll keep that snippet of information to myself.

After sitting on the edge of the bed, I tug her toward me, instruct her to lift her shirt until it sits in the middle of her stomach, then wrangle her zipper like my cock did my jeans last night. "You don't have a wild bush that will take out my eye when I get this undone, do you?" She smacks me up the side of the head, sending my laughter barreling around the room. "What? Have you seen your hair?" *I have, and I fucking love it.*

"Excluding the seventies shag rug on my head, there are no carpets in my building, Colby." Now she says my name how I've been fantasizing. Probably has more to do with the brutal yanks I'm doing on her zipper than the electricity zapping between us. "Figured you would have known all about the décor since you undressed me only yesterday."

"I was trying not to look." *Unlike now.* "I'm all about consent, Prim. When your dad frames your brother for rape, you get a little cautious with protocol."

When her zipper finally gives way to my tugs, I lower it until it sits at the sexy apex between her thighs, then raise my eyes to hers.

She's standing frozen, peering down at me. "Your father framed your brother for rape?"

I'd laugh at the shock on her face if she weren't dead serious. "Do you own a computer?" When she nods, I ask, "Have you heard of Google? It was a long time ago, but it was all over the media."

She rolls her eyes. It is as sexy as fuck. "I don't read gossip. I prefer fact over fiction." I almost correct her, but she beats me. "Except when it comes to romance novels. No one wants to read about a guy with a hairy four-inch penis. Women handle enough disappointments in real life, we don't need them in the books we read." Her comment has me wondering if the name the blonde called Brad while storming out of the alleyway is accurate, but before I can ask, she murmurs, "Do you need to talk about it?"

I take a second to consider her offer before shaking my head. I still can't believe what my dad did to Cormack, but as I said earlier, it was a long time ago, so it doesn't affect me now as it did back then.

"All right. If you change your mind, you know where to find me."

There she goes again reminding me she's about to get naked.

"I'll be out in twenty. Do you think that will be enough time to take care of that?"

After dropping her eyes to the massive bulge not even horrid memories of my father could contain, she winks then enters the bathroom. *Tease.*

When I guide Jamie into a café at the end of Main Street, I'm anticipating a voracious applause, multiple pats on the back, and for the old ladies playing Canasta at the back to include me in their wills. It's the least I should be given for keeping myself in check while Jamie showered mere feet from me—*naked*. I didn't think I'd last ten seconds. I held out for eighteen minutes and thirteen seconds. Yes, I counted. And yes, I was hard the entire time.

I'm still stiff now—hence my eagerness to slide into the first booth I see.

"Today's lunch specials are vindaloo or shrimp and quinoa salad," the waiter advises, handing us the menu in case the specials don't sound appetizing.

"I heard the spices in vindaloo make it seem as if you aren't eating pork."

Jamie glares at me over her menu. With her hair still drenched, it's darker than normal and more contained. "You think you're hilarious, but since George is free, I'm happy to return to my regularly-scheduled eating program."

She hands the waiter her menu before ordering a steak sandwich with a loaded sundae as a side dish. I order the same before balancing my elbows on the tabletop.

"Thought you didn't follow the weekatarian diet?"

"Thought you said I wouldn't win the tequila contest last night and look how that turned out." She taps her chest like she's wearing the fake medallion she was awarded last night when she ate the tequila worm as if it was a gummy worm. "There's a lot you don't know about me, Colby McGregor."

If it were anyone but her dropping my last name, my defenses would rise as quickly as my cock did when she touched her boobs, but I don't need to be anyone but me when I'm with her. It's like she sees a side of me that's for her eyes only.

I'd be scared by my comment if my hope wasn't higher.

"Tell me something I don't know about you."

I give myself a mental pat on the back for keeping our conversation in safe waters. A lesser man would have bowed out of the fight before Jamie climbed into the shower. I would have too if there weren't something in her eyes telling me this weekend is about more than having a good time. I wish I knew her well enough to decipher exactly what it was. If it's Brad and all the shit he comes with, she doesn't need to worry. Tyrone and I set the wheels in motion to fix that as soon as the landline has a dial tone.

Jamie pops a chunk of bread into her mouth before arching her brow. "Turn for turn, right? It's the only way you operate."

"That's right."

She purses her lips in a way I can't help but notice how plump they are. They're as soft as a cloud, and they taste even purer than that. *Take it down a notch, fuckface! She needs a friend, not a sex fiend who's about ready to jump her leg.*

With how many concentration lines are scoured on Jamie's forehead, I'm anticipating for her to say something more profound than she does. "I can make fart noises with my knees."

I throw my head back and laugh. "Now that's something I need to see."

"Sorry, I'm wearing jeans, so I can't."

I shrug in a cocky, egotistical way. "Then it's not true. Unless you have proof, it's merely a myth."

"Says the guy who claims he has a dick half an inch bigger than his brother."

"I do have a dick half an inch bigger than my brother!" If anyone missed Jamie's sentence, they surely couldn't miss mine. That's how loud I shouted it.

Jamie slouches low in her chair, not the least bit confronted by the number of eyes we now have on us. She's loving that she's passed the uncomfortable baton to me for the first time in history. I don't get embarrassed, but I swear I can feel my cheeks heating.

"Without proof, it's merely a myth."

I scoff. "How am I supposed to prove it? Take side-by-side comparison photos with a ruler?"

Any embarrassment left lingering on my cheeks clears away in an instant, replaced with anger when she murmurs, "Now there's an idea."

Although pissed she wants to see my brother's wang, I play it cool. "Cormack would never go for it. He's not—" I stop when I struggle to find a word to describe myself. I need more than one.

"Arrogant, boastful, *thinks* he's right about everything?"

I roll my eyes. "I was leaning more toward *as well hung as me,* but whatever."

When she tosses a bread roll over to my side of the table, I snatch it up before tearing a chunk out of it like I'm as wild and free as the pig she wrestled to save its life.

Jamie waits for me to swallow the extremely dry clump of bread before asking, "Really, what's the half-an-inch thing about?"

I almost give her the same line I give everyone—*because it's true*—but once again, the light shining in her eyes has me bringing out a side not many people see. "Cormack's always been taller, bulkier, more handsome, and successful than me. I wanted to be better than him in just one aspect. Considering my claims have only ever been denied by the woman he married, I'm reasonably sure I picked the right thing to gloat about."

The first half of my reply was straight-up honest. The second half was to douse the sympathy in Jamie's eyes. It's like she's tapped into my inner workings, so she knows there's more to my story than I'm willing to share. There is something I have that Cormack doesn't. It's just something I'd give anything not to have.

CHAPTER 27

COLBY

Tyrone grunts when my fist gets friendly with his gut. "What the fuck was that for?"

I give him a stern glare before returning my eyes in the direction his were just facing. "I don't recall Jamie's eyes being anywhere near her ass."

His smile is more stirring than joyous. "Can you blame me for looking? Her ass in that skirt is... *roar.*" When I whack him again, his smile turns blinding. The same can't be said for his breaths. They're as wheezy as fuck. "So what's the go? Have you two sorted your shit out? You seemed awfully cozy when we returned this evening."

"We were watching a movie."

"With the lights turned off while sharing *one* blanket." He thrusts his index finger in the air to amplify his statement. "If that isn't code for 'please play with my sausage, Jamie,' I don't know what is."

"Nixon said she had to stay warm." I try to keep the smirk

off my face. I miserably fail. What can I say? I'm a cocky bastard. "I'm all for following orders when it comes to our clients."

The innuendo in my tone makes it seem as if more happened between Jamie and me today than it did. We hung out, wrestled pigs, and talked more than we did the first three weeks of our friendship, but the closest we got was her head resting on me when the pain medication I forced her to take made her eyelids heavy. Still, it was one of the best days I've ever had. Jamie is unlike any woman I've ever known. I don't have to woo her with my wit or throw out tacky one-liners. She likes me for me. Weirdo.

My thoughts snap back to the present when Tyrone says, "So nothing is going on between you two? I'm good to ask her on a date when we arrive back on home turf tomorrow morning?" I fist his shirt before I can stop the brutal knot of jealousy twisting in my stomach from responding to his rile. "Should I take that as a no?"

I scoot to the edge of the couch before straying my eyes to his. "Take that as a warning. I'm not playing your games anymore, Ty. *If* this is meant to happen, it will occur without your interference at a time that's right. She just broke off her engagement, douche canoe. She's not ready for anything right now."

Ignoring the little voice in my head screaming out in denial, I make my way to Jamie. When I reach her, she sets down the bottle of wine she was replenishing her glass with before facing the congregation of hyped-up people in the middle of the living area. "Is it always like this after a jump?"

"Crazy?" When she nods, I do too. "Pretty much so. There's a thrill you get from skydiving you can't get anywhere else. For years, I thought it was all about the freefall. Only over the past few months have I realized I was wrong. There's something surreal about the minutes you have under the chute once it's been deployed." I swing my eyes to Jamie's, my smile picking up when I catch her staring at me. I've noticed her not-so-inconspicuous glance many times today. "You'll be as crazy as them one day."

Her laugh is full of nerves. "Yeah... one day."

"You don't have to jump if you're scared, Prim. It's okay to say no."

"I'm not scared. I'm..." She swivels on the spot, fanning out the skirt I've admired for way too many hours tonight. When we returned from Clement River, she changed into clothes more suitable for her personality, and even though the length of her skirt should make her look dowdy, it doesn't. "Fine. I'm scared. Happy?"

Not at all. "Depends? Are you scared because of fear? Or are you worried you'll become an addict after one jump?"

Jamie smiles in a way that shouldn't stop my heart, but it does. "A bit of both." Her smile slips away as the light I've been striving to keep alight in her eyes dims. "There's also guilt associated with having fun when those around you aren't."

Although she doesn't mention her parents, I know that's who she's referencing. They popped into our conversations many times today. She's never directly said what's going on with her mom, but the pain her eyes holds every time she talks about her reveals it's hurting her as much as my mother's illness affected me—*affects me.*

"Grab your coat." When Jamie peers up at me with big, wide eyes, I nudge my head to my room, pretending I can't feel the eyes of over a dozen people on us. "Grab your coat, or I'll staple

Moosey's skin to your shoulders." Jamie's face whitens when I nudge my head to a hideous moose skin I need to ensure the decorators remove when they bring my cabin into this century. "The choice is yours, Prim. Which is it? Moosey or your c—"

"I'll get my coat" She pushes off her feet with a huff. It does little to weaken the smile breaking across her face. Jamie's so eager to discover what I'm up to, she's back at my side before I've slipped my feet into a pair of gumboots by the front door.

After donning my own sleet-resistant clothing, I help Jamie into hers before adding additional layers of protection. I'd rather keep her curls exposed, but a beanie and scarf will keep her head and neck as warm as her toes will be in wool-lined boots. I should probably ask her to switch her skirt with a pair of jeans, but since her coat almost hits her ankles, I let it slide. We won't be outside long, and it gives me the perfect excuse to get cozy with her as we did on the couch earlier.

Tyrone wasn't lying. We did look 'awfully comfy' when he arrived back to the cabin because I scooted across the sofa so Jamie's head could rest on my chest instead of my shoulder. For the first time in a long time, I sat in silence while the world raced by me at a million miles an hour. I always thought silence was my enemy, but the hour Jamie slept on my chest had me realizing it isn't an empty void of nothing. It was full of the answers I've been seeking but were too busy to stop and listen to.

After opening the door we're standing next to, I gesture for Jamie to exit before me. Since the sun set a few hours ago, it's chillier than I was anticipating. "Keep in close, Prim. I don't want to—"

"Overstretch when you trip me?"

When our eyes meet, I'm at a loss of a witty comeback. I

didn't even speak, yet it's as if she heard the crazy thoughts in my head. "Maybe."

My reply awards me a bigger smile than I'm anticipating. It also has her arms wrapping around my waist. I feel like an A-grade moron when she buries her face into my chest. I thought she was snuggling in because she was eager to sniff my cologne, not because it's fucking freezing.

Halfway up the hillside we're trekking, Jamie asks, "Are you disappointed?"

"That the boobs squashed up against my arm aren't bare? It's a little disappointing, but my imagination is wondrous."

She squeezes me instead of punching me like she normally would. "I meant that you didn't skydive today, perve."

"It's my middle name." I wait for her to finish laughing before answering her question. "Shockingly, no. We had fun, so I don't feel like I missed out."

She peers up at me with her big aqua eyes. "I doubt pig wrestling and skirmish come close to the high you get skydiving."

"It does when I'm doing them with you." I scan the horizon, waiting for a drove of gentlemen to welcome me into their elusive club since I articulated my reply without an ounce of ambiguity. When they fail to arrive, I devote my attention back to Jamie. "We kicked ass this afternoon. Those punks didn't know what hit them."

She laughs again. "Still can't believe they booted us out. If he weren't such a brat, you wouldn't have shot him between the eyes."

I smile as memories of our afternoon filter through my mind. I thought Jamie was a force to be reckoned with in a muddy field. It had nothing on her determination when we went three rounds of paintball with a group of teens who thought they had us suckered. "Bet he'll think twice before he calls anyone four-eyes again."

"Hopefully…" Her reply falls short when a cloudless night steals her words. "Colby." She sounds like she's about to sob. "It's so beautiful. I've never seen such a star-filled sky."

I bring her closer to the peak before dragging my hand across a pure, uninterrupted skyline. "Now picture it from fifteen thousand feet in the air. You're up there amongst the stars and the clouds."

"Wow." She smiles as brightly as the sea of stars stretching for as far as the eye can see. "I can see how it becomes addictive." She shuffles on her feet to face me. "Have you ever jumped at night?"

I twist my lips to stifle my grin. "Are you asking as my insurance assessor or my friend?"

She laughs before whacking me in the gut. After rolling her eyes, she shifts her focus back to the view. I'm tempted to snuggle up to her back, but since I'm not into all that fancy shit guys do when they're endeavoring to get into a girl's panties, I act like a creeper by sliding my phone out of my pocket so I can take sneaky photographs of her to jerk off to later. I've been hard all day, so there's no way my balls will make it until tomorrow without exploding. Jamie looks insanely sexy in the moonlight, so my pictures will be a great incentive.

"Colby," Jamie says on a groan, spinning to face me. "Don't take my photo. I look wretched."

With my brow cocked, I snap her picture again, doubling the groove between her brows.

"At least let me take my glasses off."

She jumps when I shout, "No! Leave them on. They're you." I

stop in just enough time. I almost said, *They make this Sci-Fi geek want to cream in his pants.* "If you're going to remove anything, take off your beanie. Let those crazy locks of yours spring free."

Jamie peers at me with hesitation for a good twenty seconds before her hand creeps up to her head. After dragging her beanie off, she shakes out her curls. My dick hardens when her lavender scent streams through my nose. It has nothing on the smile stretched across my face when she lets me fake the role of a photographer for a good thirty pictures before she snatches my phone out of my hand.

"My turn." After hitting the rotate button on the screen, she curls her arm around my waist then takes a selfie of us standing near the cliff's edge. Because it is so dark, nothing but our beaming smiles are seen. "Can you forward that to me? My friend, Athena, is a whizz on photoshop. She'll add a fake sky background and make it all jazzy and shit."

I jerk up my chin. "All right, but only if she promises to forward me a copy."

Since I'm not taking no for an answer, I remove my phone from her grasp before hitting my email app. My brows furrow when the arrival at my inbox has me stumbling onto a small handful of emails. Usually, my inbox is hammered with hundreds of emails per day. This one only has eight messages sitting unread. Excluding the one at the top, the rest follow a similar pattern—they have availability for an emergency transfer from Freedom Care.

I swallow the bile burning the back of my throat when my brain clicks as to why Freedom Care registers as familiar. It was one of the assisted-living facilities my dad tried to dump my mom in when she got sick.

The hits keep coming when I click into each email. They're

all addressed to Jamie, and they all state the same thing—they'd be honored to assist in the care of her mother.

"Your mom has Alzheimer's." I'm not asking a question. I'm stating a fact as it's presented to me.

When Jamie's eyes snap up to mine, tears glisten in them a mere second before anger dries them. She's peering at my phone, at her emails I just opened. "Why are you reading my emails? How do you even know my password?"

"I don't. You must not have logged out when you borrowed my phone."

Her cheeks redden with anger like this isn't the first time her privacy has been invaded. "That doesn't give you the right to read them."

When she attempts to snatch my phone out of my hand, I pull it out of her reach. "Does your mom have Alzheimer's?" My voice is dark and dangerous as the shadow I struggle to conceal surfaces at a rate faster than I can shut it down. I'm shaking all over, unhinged, and on the verge of being sick.

"Why does it matter to you if she does? I've been tested. I don't have the APOE-e4 risk gene."

"You can still get Alzheimer's even if you don't have the gene!" I don't know why I'm yelling. It won't change anything. It will still be misery and heartbreak and a brutal reminder of how many ways I fucked up the past seven weeks.

Jamie's eyes fill with pain and anger. They mimic the despair in my gut to a T. "You don't think I know that! God, Colby, you can be a real insensitive jerk sometimes."

When she charges down the hillside, I follow after her. "Me? *I'm* the fucking jerk. You're the one who kept this secret. You're the one who's been lying." Some of my anger should be directed at myself, but I've discovered an out, so I'm running for it. It's what I do.

Jamie whips around so fast, even with her hair tightened by ringlets, it still slaps her cheek. "I didn't keep it a secret. I told you my mom was sick."

"Yes, sick! You didn't say she was dying."

She slaps me hard across the face. It's not felt. I'm too gutted to feel something as meager as a slap of a woman in denial. "She's not dying!"

I hate that she's crying, and for the horrid way I'm expressing myself, but she needs to learn the truth quickly. If she doesn't, the light in her eyes will be extinguished years before her heart stops beating. "She is, Jamie. She's dying a miserable, undeserving death that will steal more than your heart when it happens. The sooner you learn that, the easier it will be."

She shakes her head so rigorously, tears fling off her cheeks. "I don't have to learn anything. New research is conducted every day. They're on the brink of a cure."

"There's no cure for Alzheimer's. Anyone who tells you otherwise is a liar."

I steal the chance for her to retaliate with one of the many lies I've heard the past five months by storming back to the cabin and slamming the door behind me.

CHAPTER 28

I glance up from the check Tyrone just handed me, blinking and confused. "I told Terry I didn't want to be reimbursed." I glance at Terry whose wealth is more notable now than it was at the cabin. As he paces to a chauffeur-driven Bentley, he's flanked by two bodyguards and a personal assistant. "It was kind of him to offer, but it's not necessary."

When I attempt to hand the check back to Tyrone, he refuses to accept it. "The check isn't from Mr. Fousser. It's from Colby."

I grit my teeth with all my might, warning my eyes they better not spill a drop of moisture. I doubt they'd listen if anger weren't roaring through my veins just as quickly as devastation. Colby hasn't spoken a word to me since our exchange last night. He hasn't even given me the pity look I usually get when people hear about my mom's diagnosis, certain I'll soon fall through the rabbit hole her brain went years ago. Come to think of it, this is the first time I've had someone respond as angrily and bluntly as Colby did.

"Tell Colby I don't want nor need his money."

No matter how many times I thrust the check into Tyrone's chest, he refuses to take it. "You paid for a service. You didn't get the service you paid for, so you're entitled to a refund."

"I didn't pay for anything, so if you truly believe a refund is necessary, it should be made out to my boss, Hugh..." My words trail off when a flare detonates in Tyrone's eyes. He's quick to shut it down, but not quick enough for a woman suspicious of everyone's motives. "What aren't you telling me?"

"Nothing."

Tyrone scrubs at the stubble on his chin when a squeal rumbles in my chest. He shouldn't test me today. I didn't sleep a wink last night. The ride back to Los Angeles was long and full of hushed whispers on what supposedly happened between Colby and me last night, and I'm hormonal. Now is not the time to piss me off.

Incapable of withstanding my glare for a second longer, Tyrone mutters, "Mr. Barnett purchased your ticket—"

"Exactly, so *he* deserves to be reimbursed for it."

He continues talking as if I never did. "But a majority of the payment was made from the checking account of James Burgess."

I freeze, my heart rate cantering. "My dad? Why would he do that?" I don't know why I'm seeking confirmation from Tyrone. Other than knowing my dad's name, he knows nothing about him.

"A lot of people owe you an explanation, Jamie. Just none appear to be willing to give it to you right now." His eyes stray to Colby, who's sitting in the van, acting like we didn't arrive back in LA over thirty minutes ago. "He didn't mean what he said."

His eyes return to me when I reply, "Yes, he did. And it's not okay."

Needing to leave before the tears I've been keeping at bay the past sixteen hours fall, I remove my suitcase from Tyrone's grasp, shove the check into my purse, then make my way to the cab I organized on the way home.

Although I want to confront my dad about Tyrone's confession, my heart isn't up to the task today. Instead, I ask the cab driver to take me to Metrics Insurance. I have days of missing work to catch up on and a separation to finalize. That should keep me bogged down long enough I won't have time to think about a single thing that occurred this weekend—not even the good parts.

"You wanted to see me?" I barely placed down my suitcase when Hugh's assistant came barreling into my office, demanding my immediate attendance in Hugh's office. "If it's about the weekend, I'll need a few minutes to process everything before I can give you any type of report... personal or business-related."

Hugh's eyes snap up from a recently drafted indemnity form. When he realizes who's standing in his doorway, his face goes deadpan, and my heart freezes. He's an adrenaline junkie, so usually he'd be chomping at the bit to be updated on my weekend. Instead, he slouches into his chair before requesting me to close his door.

When I do as he requested, he jerks his head to the right. "Coffee?"

I gag. To me, coffee is the equivalent of drinking the sludge at the bottom of the Hudson. Disgusting with a capital 'D'! But Hugh is aware of my dislike of coffee, so why is he offering me a cup?

My question is answered in an unfavorable light when my eyes sling in the direction of his state-of-the-art coffee machine. Mr. Luis is helping himself to a shot of espresso. You know those micro-shots that should be inserted into your vein instead of your mouth. He's having one of those.

"Mr. Luis, twice in two months. You better be careful, or your other businesses might think you're favoring us over them."

He doesn't respond to my jest with the same kindness he did last time, nor does he greet me with dual kisses on my cheeks. He glares at me, a stealthy, you're-costing-me-money stare. "I thought my last visit portrayed my wish for Metrics Insurance to stop draining me of millions of dollars in unnecessary claims."

I don't recall him explicitly stating that, but it was the gist of his conversation.

"Yet here I am, only weeks later having a claim drawn against me for the amount of thirty million dollars."

My eyes stray to Hugh, confused as to what Mr. Luis means. Thirty million is excessive for the coverage we generally insure. There's only one company I handle that has that amount of liability—*oh shit.*

"Someone filed against The Drop Zone?"

When Hugh nods, my heart falls into my stomach. I'm not

just frustrated for Colby and Tyrone, I'm panicked my job could be on the line. This is the last thing I need.

"Did they cite a defendant on the claim?"

Hugh's eyes answer me before his mouth does. "Yes, Colby McGregor. They're claiming gross negligence during a recent skydiving expedition."

My emotions are shut down, but mercifully that doesn't hinder the business side of my brain. "The Drop Zone's clients sign waivers before every jump. We brought those measures into place when Mr. Celest filed his claim."

Hugh shakes his head. "The claimant is stating although a brief rundown was given before his jump, no forms were signed, which means he has every right to sue."

"What about video footage of their jump? Mr. Celest's revealed he didn't get the experience he paid for, but if you have footage showing the claimant enjoyed his jump, it will greatly benefit both Metrics Insurance and Mr. McGregor."

I feel like I'm sucker punched when Hugh shakes his head. "Although the camera was switched on during their jump, it doesn't give any indication to the feelings of the claimant. You can't even see his face."

"Which means this case will be nothing but *his* word against the accuser." Mr. Luis spits out 'his' as if he hasn't greatly benefited from the ridiculously high premiums he's charged The Drop Zone the past two years. "I asked you to shut down this client's request for insurance."

"We had no reason to deny his request. That's why I approved it." I sound pissed. Rightfully so. I am. "I've worked for you for over eight years, Mr. Luis, and no disrespect, but when have I ever asked or needed your opinion when processing a request for insurance? This isn't ideal, but until

I've had the chance to properly investigate the claim of negligence, there's no use getting your panties in a twist. That's why you pay us, so you can sit in your ivory tower sipping sludge from the bottom of the Hudson." I storm out of Hugh's office, only realizing halfway to mine that I most likely just got myself fired. Thank God they have to give me four weeks' notice as I'll need every one of them to find a new position.

I bump into Athena as I enter my office. "Oh, thank God you're back. The Drop Zone—"

"Is being sued? Yeah, I just discovered that, while most likely getting myself fired." Athena balks, but I continue talking, stopping her from saying one of the many words I see in her eyes. "Do we know who the claimant is?"

Red hair falls into her face when she shakes her head. "The claim was filed under Holiday Free Pty Ltd."

I stop halfway around my desk. "The same travel insurance company Mr. Celest used?" When Athena's shake switches to a nod, I murmur, "That can't be a coincidence. Mr. Celest's settlement was just funded, and now they lodge another claim."

"Those were my exact thoughts. That's why I spent the past hour gathering everything I could on the new claim." She places a stack of manila folders onto my desk. "I hope you enjoyed your weekend away. I don't see you leaving your office for the next few days."

"Mel?" My assistant, Melanie Alonzo, pops her head into my office. "Hold all my calls. I don't care how urgent they appear, take down their details and tell them I'll call them back."

She looks panicked. I discover why when she asks, "Does that include Mr. Valeron? He's already called three times this morning."

I throw my coat over my desk before taking a seat. "It

includes everyone, both personal and professional. Tell them I'm still away, and that I don't get back until tomorrow." When Athena looks at me with wide, panicked eyes, I hit her with a stern finger point. "Don't. If I don't have a job, I'll lose more than a few Christmas presents this year."

"Okay. Fine." She hustles Mel out of my office before closing my door. "But once this is sorted—"

"We'll have words. I get it."

Several hours later, I finally get a break in the case. It wasn't any place I should have been looking, but it's undeniable proof that it isn't just The Drop Zone being played. I am as well. With reports, affidavits, and video footage going against my company, I took a five-second breather. That, like every other American, included a quick scan of my inbox. Since Colby 'read' a majority of my emails last night, one stood out more than the rest. It's a response from the travel insurance company Brad used for our honeymoon, granting my request for a refund. Although I asked him to use a subsidiary company of Metrics Insurance, he went with the broker Markham Properties Corporation uses. The trading name on the bottom of their disclaimer reveals it's umbrellaed under the same insurance company that's suing The Drop Zone.

Once again, I don't see this being a coincidence.

Athena hands me my glasses when I drag my laptop in close so I can input the trading number on the bottom of my email into my search engine. Since I'm logged into Metric Insurance's mainframe, my search returns more results than a standard Google search and adds even more evidence onto my pile.

"Markham Proprieties owns the insurance company suing The Drop Zone." Athena is confused, which is surprising. She is usually more suspicious of people's motives than me—especially when it comes to this man. "Brad mentioned Markham Properties wanted the land The Drop Zone is on many times during our relationship." I see the pieces clicking together in her eyes. "He also jumped with Colby a couple of weeks ago. What if this is his way of getting The Drop Zone's doors closed since he couldn't coerce me to bark on command?"

"Goddammit. I knew I should have packed my blowtorch today. I would have if someone hadn't already gotten to him before me."

Her reply lowers both my heart and my jaw. "What?"

She peers at me with wide, shocked eyes. "You don't know?" When I shake my head, she fills me in. "Brad 'supposedly' jumped again Saturday night. They messed him up a little more this time around. Made him as ugly as his insides." She stops talking, her brows joining. "Do you think the two could be related? When was the file claimed?"

I check the paperwork in front of me. "Sunday morning." My high heart rate chops up my next set of words. "I told Colby that Brad was responsible for the bruise on my wrist Saturday afternoon."

Athena leaps up from her seat. "He bruised you."

"It was an accident, and if what you're saying is true, blowtorches aren't required."

She rolls her eyes. "Oh yeah, they are. He was still walking. He won't be by the time I'm finished with him."

"You'll have to get in line." Athena watches me place my jacket on with her mouth hanging open. "This is my mess, so I'm going to clean it." After snagging my purse off my desk, I pivot around to face her. "While I'm gone, update Hugh on our findings before contacting Mr. Celest. If he was coerced by Markham Properties to sue, he could be entitled to a much higher settlement."

My brisk strides to my office door slow when Athena shouts my name. When I pivot around to face her, the panic on her face slips away. "You've got this."

Although she isn't asking a question, I answer her as if it was one. "I do. I promise."

After wrapping her up in a tight hug, I dash for the elevator banks. With Christmas quickly approaching, I walk to Markham headquarters instead of hailing a cab. Although it is many blocks away, I need the time to unjumble some of the confusion in my head. This is more than bogus insurance claims. This is my life, and how Colby placed himself in the middle of it if he's responsible for Brad's second mugging in two weeks.

When I walk through the rotating doors of Markham Properties Corporation my head is still woozy. I didn't sleep last night, and I only nibbled on the bagel Tyrone forced into my hand this morning, so it could be more than confusion clouding my judgment. I've never felt this way before. The weird twisting sensation in my stomach is more terrifying than the snarl Brad's receptionist gives me when I glide past her desk without waiting for her to give me the all-clear.

Brad is on a call, but he's quick to notice me. "I'll call you back." He doesn't wait for his caller to reply, instead places the receiver of his phone back onto its base before spanning the distance between us. For a man with a battered face and a cut lip, his walk is way too arrogant for my liking. "Jamie, I've been trying to reach you for days..." His words veer into a growl when he spots the stitches in my forehead. "What happened? Why are you injured?"

I hiss when his inspection of my stitches arrives with poky, explorative fingers. "I'm fine." I step out of the firing zone, away from him and his stupid beliefs I'm not smart enough to see through his ruse. "And shouldn't I be asking you that? You're more damaged than I am."

"This?" He waves his hand over a smattering of bruises the world's best concealer couldn't hide. "It's nothing. People grow desperate this time of the year."

"I wasn't talking about your face. I was referencing your *emotional* wellbeing."

When he acts clueless, I fold my arms in front of my chest. The disdain in his eyes grows when he realizes I didn't dress for the occasion. Since I went straight to Metrics after the cabin, I'm wearing snug jeans, a fitted shirt, and a cropped jacket. I'm casual, but in no way dowdy. He won't see it that way, though. Brad's always been about putting your best foot forward. He did gift me a makeover for our one-month anniversary. *Pig.*

"Should you even be working in your condition?"

"As I said, Jamie, I'm fine." The cockiness in his tone makes me sick.

"And as I said, *Bradley*, I'm not talking about your supposed 'mugging.'" I air quote the last word. "If you're so emotionally distressed you need thirty million dollars to recover, how can you adequately fulfill your role as the procurement manager for a multibillion-dollar company? Surely, you'd be on stress leave. Bedridden even."

Panic flares through his eyes, but he's quick to shut it down. "What are you talking about? What thirty million dollars?"

I'm about to hit him with everything I have, but before I can, a knock sounds through his office. "Mr. Valeron, I have an urgent call—"

"They can wait!" I feel bad about mistreating his receptionist when she jumps at his brittle tone. If the panic on her face is anything to go by, this isn't the first time she's been reprimanded by him.

"I'm sorry, Mr. Valeron, but he was adamant this can't wait." She races into his office, her steps thunderous even though her feet barely touch the floor. "It's Mr. Burgess." She strays her watering eyes to me. "He's seeking Jamie."

I snatch the cordless phone out of her hand, my mind spiraling. My father isn't a fan of Brad's, so he'd only reach out to him if it were extremely urgent.

"Daddy," I say down the line at the same time Brad requests for the valet to bring his car out front.

My dad replies, but I can barely hear him through his heartbreaking sobs.

CHAPTER 29

COLBY

*J*dig my thumbs into my temples when the brutal knock of someone banging on my hotel room door overtakes the thump in my head. They've been knocking for twenty minutes. I successfully ignored them for the first nineteen.

"I swear to God, Casper, I'll kick your ass if you don't open this door right now."

If Tyrone wants me to open the door, why the fuck is he threatening me?

"I've visited every hotel in this damn town searching for you, so I wouldn't suggest testing my patience. It's Christmas fucking Eve. I should be with my family, not seeking clues of your favorite haunts from Four-Button Betty's." A loud bang chops up his words like he's literally kicking down my door. "You better be alone. If you aren't, your ass will be as black as mine by the time I'm done with you."

After a final bang, the hinges on my hotel room door give

way, then Tyrone's big black ass comes storming inside. His nostrils flare while he scans the Presidential Suite of the Wiltshire, seeking the women he won't find. This isn't my usual type of bender. I'm still drowning my sorrows. I just used alcohol instead of women.

"What the fuck, Colby? Have you heard of a shower? This place smells like a homeless camp in Venice Beach."

Tyrone rips open the curtains, blinding me with midmorning rays, while also unearthing my companion of choice this time around. Nearly every surface of the thirteen-thousand-dollar-a-night suite is covered with beer bottles. A handful of whiskey decanters line the stained floor, and although most of my nutrients the past four days have been in a liquid form, flies are buzzing around half-empty takeout containers.

I want to say this is the first time Tyrone has seen me like this. Unfortunately, that would be a lie. This is our fourth foray into Drunkenville. The first time was when my mother died, the second was when my brother was charged with rape, and the third was when the man responsible for the fabricated charges finally relented to the dead cold organ in the middle of his chest. Some would call it a heart, but they'd be wrong. My father didn't have one of those.

I thought the misery in my life would be done and dusted when my father died. I was a fucking idiot. He left a legacy no amount of money could fix.

"Get up." Tyrone throws a towel into my face before nudging his head to the shower. "And get your ass in the shower before I fucking drag you there by the pretty blond hairs on your faultless fucking head."

"Jesus, Ty. Chill—"

"Chill? You want me to chill?" He drags his hand over his clipped afro, amplifying the furious shake hampering every inch of him. "I've always known you were arrogant, but I never thought you were heartless. I get your pissed, Colby. I understand you want a better hand than the one you've been dealt, but now isn't about you. Not every moment of every day has to be about you." He plucks me off the mattress before shoving me toward the bathroom. His movements are so quick, I stumble over my feet in my drunken state. "If Jamie doesn't get to drown her sorrows with gallons of alcohol and greasy Chinese, you sure as fuck don't get to either. Move your ass, Casper."

When he continues shoving me, I push back, my anger overtaking my confusion. "If this is the same shit you were preaching at the cabin, walk straight back out that fucking door, Ty. I told you I'm done. I told you it's over. So why the fuck are you still guilt-tripping me?"

"Because I'm not doing this for another forty years, Colby. I'm sick of bailing your ass out. I'm fucking tired of always needing to be one step ahead of you all the time."

I thrust my hand to the door he just stormed through. "Then walk. Fucking leave! I don't need you. I don't need anyone."

The anger lining his face doubles a mere second before he rams into me like a linebacker taking down a quarterback. Even with my head clouded with beer, I give back as good as I'm getting. I slam my fists down on him as I wish I could have Brad. I hated sending someone to do the job for me, but Isaac was adamant it was the only way I could keep my hands clean. Since he's good at doing precisely that, I took his advice.

Tyrone and I roll around on the floor of my suite for several minutes, going punch for punch. I loathe admitting this, but we're evenly matched, and if his ragged breaths are anything to go by, he will feel our fight for days to come as well.

The power behind my next hit is half its strength when Tyrone grunts, "You've wasted so much time making sure you don't get attached to anyone, but not once have you sat back and wondered how that affects the people already attached to you. You're the one who's going to forget, Colby, so why are you so worried about protecting your heart? It's not the one set to be broken."

His words hit me harder than his fists, and they have me rolling off him with a groan. Even though I've backed down, Tyrone doesn't understand the meaning of the words. "We're supposed to remember your love once you can no longer remember, but you're not giving us the chance to do that."

After dragging his hand under his wet eyes, he moves for a leather satchel he dumped upon entry. The sheets of stark white paper he digs out makes the red splits in his knuckles more paramount. "I had these drafted up months ago. I had hoped never to use them, but you've given me no choice."

When he hands me a transfer of assets form, I shake my head. "You're not buying me out."

"I'm not buying you out. I'm selling you my half."

My eyes snap up to his. "The Drop Zone is your family."

"No, Colby. You are. Or should I say 'were'?" Tyrone shakes his head, the disappointment in his eyes unmistakable. "Now, I don't know who *you* are." He scans his eyes over my trashed hotel room. "Was it worth it? Did it take away her hurt?"

He doesn't need to say Jamie's name for me to know who he's referencing. "I didn't want to hurt her, Ty. That's why I stepped back."

"And as I said before, that isn't your choice to make. It's also too late. She's already hurting." He dumps an opened *Los Angeles Times* onto the coffee table next to me before returning his eyes to mine. "The sale will be processed on close of business on the thirty-first of January. I'll continue running operations until then. You keep doing you... *like you always have.*" His last four words are whispers.

"Ty..." He stops just outside my suite door, but he doesn't turn around to face me. "This isn't what I want."

"Then fix it." He cranks his neck back to me before lowering his eyes to the newspaper he left on the coffee table. "Help her through this because she doesn't deserve the hand she's been dealt any more than you."

I stare at the door he walked through for a few minutes before snatching the open newspaper off the coffee table. Busted knuckles are the least of my problems when my eyes scan the half dozen funeral notices in front of me. One stands out more than the rest since it has a name I'd never forget in the middle of it. Ms. Jamie Burgess.

It's a notice for her mother's funeral, that's being held today, in not even an hour.

Fuck.

CHAPTER 30

JAMIE

Christmas Eve is supposed to be about feasts, tree-decorating, and the final finicky preparations every household undertakes before the fat man in the red suit slides down your chimney. It shouldn't be about funeral directors, coffin selections, and using the credit from your canceled wedding bouquet to purchase flowers for your mother's funeral.

Although it's an odd day for a funeral, the turnout reveals my mom was loved despite her inability to remember those she loved. The ten rows of chairs flowing from each side of her coffin are filled with a bottom. I recognize most of the people here. Just not all of them recognize me. They most likely don't even remember the person now lying in the white lacquered coffin which is suspended above the ground by black straps. They still came, though. Because they care—somewhat. Even Brad is here. Despite my many requests for solitude, he hasn't left my side since our arrival at my mother's assisted-living facility had us stumbling upon a cold and empty bed. People say Alzheimer's steals the life from your eyes years before God does. That isn't true. My mom's room always felt warm and inviting. Four days ago, it was miserable and bleak.

"Are you ready?"

I peer up at Athena with big, watering eyes before nodding. I gave my eulogy and said my goodbye, so I'm more than ready to crawl back into the bed I only left today because I had to attend the funeral of a woman I'll never stop loving. I can't imagine what my dad is going through. His heart must be in tatters. He's never been a man of many words, but even those infrequent few have dwindled the past four days.

"Where are we going?"

Athena's clutch around my waist tightens. She's right next to me, yet she still feels far away. "Back to your penthouse. Brad organized for the wake to be held there."

"Oh." Don't ask me if that is a good or bad 'oh' as I wouldn't be able to answer you. I'm so hollow right now, I can barely feel anything.

As we make our way to a procession of black vehicles, I scan the crowd one final time. Every pair of eyes I take in are brimming with moisture, but only one is filled with remorse. Colby stands at the back of the group. He either arrived in a hurry or his respect for me is so low, shaving wasn't on his to-do list today. His beard is thick, his eyes are sunken, and his hair is oily. He looks like the anger and grief that has festered inside of me the past four days.

I should walk away. I should acknowledge that the grief inside of me has me thinking carelessly, but instead of doing either of those things, I break away from Athena's side and charge for Colby. "Are you happy? You were right. This is what you predicted. She's dead! She died just like you said she would."

The remorse in his eyes doubles as he shakes his head. "This isn't what I wanted, Jamie."

"Then what do you want, Colby?" I scream at him like I wish I could scream at the disease that stole my mom away from me. "To gloat about how much better your life is than mine..." When my words become stuck by the thick black grief sitting where my heart once sat, my fists take up their campaign. I whack them into Colby's chest on repeat, hoping for just the slightest bit of reprieve from the heaviness drowning me.

"You did this. This is your fault. You killed her!"

Colby accepts both my beating and my blame without a word spilling from his lips, only moving when the exhaustion of not sleeping for five days crashes into me. When I slump into his chest, he wraps his arms around my torso, then buries his head into my hair. As the heavy stream flowing from my eyes unchecked doubles, he holds onto me tight, only stopping when his arms are replaced with my dad's.

"Daddy..."

"I know, sweetheart. I know. The pain will ease soon. I promise."

He tugs me into his side, sheltering me from the world that feels too cruel to live in. It hurts so much. Everything kills.

Once I'm seated in the back of the lead car in the funeral procession, he gestures for the driver to leave. We ride to the penthouse with Athena, the silence as unbearable as the look on Colby's face when I belted into him.

I don't want to attend my mom's wake, but since my dad will be there, and I want to support him as he has always supported me, I will, even if it makes me feel like I'm back below the surface, drowning in despair so thick I'll never be free of it.

Much like my mom's funeral, the next four hours pass in a blur. No one says anything about my breakdown at her gravesite or the fact Brad was noticeably absent for the first half of her wake. It's like every family gathering the Burgess' have had. Aunt Janet keeps attendees entertained with stories of when she tried to become an actress, while Uncle Irish seeks attention from anyone willing to sit through his hour-long recount about how he narrowly escaped a triple bypass with a strict kale diet and a diverse range of essential oils.

"Jamie, I really wish you'd rest. You look exhausted." Brad curls his arm around my waist, playing the devoted-fiancé ruse he never perfected when we were engaged. "Come on, let's get you into something more comfortable."

"I can't leave, Brad. It's my mom's wake."

He acts as if I never spoke, moving me from the living room to the walk-in closet without a single concerned glance directed our way.

"Satin or cotton. The sheets are satin, so you'll most likely want cotton, so you don't slip around." His laugh isn't cute, but I'm too tired to care.

"Thank you." He accepts a large mug of cocoa from our once housekeeper, Jeanie, before requesting for her to turn down the sheets on our bed. "I asked her to go easy on the marshmallows," he advises when I screw up my nose about the measly two floating on the top. "I don't want sugar keeping you awake."

Brad sets down the cocoa before moving to stand in front of me. "Up."

He has the hem of my long-sleeve shirt up and over my head before I realize what he is requesting. Once I'm standing in front of him in a bra and a tight-fitting skirt, he slides a cotton nightie over my head before lowering the zipper in my skirt.

"Figured it was best not to get any sneaky peeks until I've re-earned the right."

With a groan, I shimmy my skirt down my thighs before pivoting on my heels and entering the bedroom. I could go back to Athena's place to sleep, but I'm so exhausted, not even Brad's dry humor will have me turning down his offer. I'm so tired, I can barely see the bed I once shared with Brad.

"Will you tell my dad where I am..." My words are gobbled up by a big, drowsy yawn.

"Of course. Leave everything to me. I'll take care of you, Jamie."

Not even the alarm bells sounding in my head are enough to keep me awake.

I had hoped to wake up with my grief less heavy. If the weight on my chest is anything to go by, it worsened.

Yesterday was so final.

My mom is gone.

Buried.

I'll never see her again.

That hurts—a lot.

As if that doesn't have me wanting to bury myself in a deep hole, I feel the beady eyes of Brad on me. He's not in my bed—thank God. He's standing at the foot of it, watching me like a creep.

When he notices I am awake, he heads my way. "Hey, how did you sleep?"

"I slept." It wasn't restful nor nice, but it was better than nothing.

I begin to wonder if I am still asleep when he brushes away a curl hanging in front of my eye. This is the first time disdain hasn't crossed his features when confronted with my natural hair.

When his hand returns to his side, I notice the sheet of paper he's clutching in the opposite one. "What's that?" My nosiness can't be helped. It's a very official-looking document.

He sighs as if pained. "This is your mother's will."

"Then why do you have it?"

Brad gives me a look as if surprised by my anger. I don't know why. My mother's death didn't change anything between us. He's still an asshole I can't wait to see the back end of. "I have it because I was appointed as her guardian along with you."

"Only because I didn't have time to change it before she…" I can't finalize my sentence. It hurts too much to admit she's gone.

"Jamie." He looks like he wants to *tsk* me for being petty, but the tears in my eyes hold back his retaliation—barely. "That's why I'm here. We need to talk about this." He must have invested in acting classes this past week because he seems genuinely concerned. "Things aren't good."

I roll my eyes, acting as immature and hollow as I feel. "My mom died. I think it's pretty obvious how dire things are."

When he cups my cheeks to wipe away my tears, for some stupid reason, I let him comfort me. It isn't that I've forgiven him. It simply hurts too much to pretend I'm stronger than I am. I'm not strong. I'm weak and pathetic.

Once my tears are cleared away, Brad stands from his crouched position. "We'll save this for another day. It's Christmas. I don't want to worry you with this on Christmas."

"No." I stop him leaving by grabbing his wrist. "Let's do it now." Then I can commence the process of having him removed from my life just as permanently.

Excitement flares in his eyes when I tap the bed, offering for him to sit. "Are you sure?"

I jerk up my chin, my lips wobbling. I thought I had all my cards laid out correctly, but his tone is making me doubtful. It gave me the same dreaded feeling I felt the day my mom passed. It's thick and impenetrable like death isn't the worst thing that could happen to someone.

"Okay."

After handing me two tissues from a box on the bedside table, he updates me on my parents' financial situation. When he said things weren't good, he wasn't joking. Even with us contributing to my parents' mortgage the past seven months, they're at risk of foreclosure. My dad hasn't worked since my mom's diagnosis, and the therapy needed to improve her quality of life was in the high five figures long before she was admitted to an assisted-living facility.

"Your dad wants to sell, but I told him I wouldn't hear of it. If he sells now, he'll sell at a loss." Brad gathers my hands in his.

They're disgustingly sweaty, but I'm too dazed to respond. "I know things are rough between us right now—"

"Right now? Things have been bad for a while, Brad."

"But we can work through our indifferences, princess. It's moments like this that show how strong we are. I never held your mother's sickness against her. I never wished her ill harm to reduce the stress and financial strain on you. I've always supported both you and your parents throughout this horrendous disease." He doesn't say it, but I know he wants to say, *unlike Colby McGregor.* "And I want to continue supporting you. That's why I suggested for your dad to stay with us."

I peer at him as if he has two heads. "You did?"

When he nods, I balk. When Brad organized for my mother's care to be transferred to Freedom Care, I suggested my dad move in with us to save an additional rental payment on our already-stretched finances. Brad wouldn't hear of it. He convinced me it was more important for my father to be close to my mother than how much money we have in our bank accounts. He was right, but that strain was one of the reasons I stayed with him longer than I should have.

I stare at Brad, wondering who he is when he says, "Once your dad is back on his feet, I have some contacts in the architect field who'd love to meet him."

"He hasn't worked in years." I sound shocked. Rightfully so. I'm beyond stunned.

"Skills are like love, Jamie. They never go away." He drags his index finger down my scrunched-up nose. It doesn't sicken me as it once did. "He can have a life here with us."

"*Us?*" It sounds foreign even in my voice.

"Yes. *Us.*" He cups my cheek again, and once again, I let him. "I acted like a fool. I did stupid, foolish things because I was so afraid of losing you. I thought it would hurt less to push you away before you inevitably figured out you deserved better than me. I made a mistake." Before I can say it was more than once, he quickly adds, "Many mistakes. But, if you're willing to give me a second chance, I promise I won't let you down again. You're my world, princess. It's been so bleak without you in it. I don't think I can live another day without you."

"Brad…" I sigh. "This isn't an appropriate time to have this conversation. My mom just died." That hurt saying it as much as I thought it would.

He squeezes my hands before lowering his moisture-filled eyes to mine. "I'll do anything you ask. I'll drop the lawsuit against The Drop Zone. I'll pay for your mother's funeral. I'll even organize contractors to have your parents' ranch repaired, so if your dad still wants to sell, he'll get top dollar."

"You'll drop the lawsuit?" That shouldn't be the first thing I seek confirmation on, but for some stupid reason, it is.

"Yes." He locks his eyes with mine. They're full of shame. "I was hurt that he stole you away from me. I wanted him to feel half the pain that was eating at me." He drags his thumb along a vein pulsating in my hand, tracing the throb there. "I won't feel that way if you're once again mine."

"I thought you sued him because he had you beaten?"

Inky black hair falls into his eyes when he shakes his head. "No. That had nothing to do with it. I deserved that. I never meant to hurt you, princess. Sometimes I just forget how strong I am."

That should be my first clue that nothing has changed between us, but with my head foggy and my heart beyond shattered, I'm not looking at the world in the same light I did days ago. It's bleak and miserable and has me thinking foolishly.

"Okay."

Brad's dark eyes stare into mine as his brow cocks. "Yes? You'll take me back?"

When I hesitantly nod, he does something I never antici-pated for him to do. He falls onto one knee before producing a ring box out of his suit jacket.

CHAPTER 31

COLBY

"*D*id you see this?"

I dump a newspaper article revealing that Jamie plans to marry Brad in a twilight service on the Chinese New Year instead of New Year's Eve as originally planned onto the desk between Tyrone and me.

"She just buried her mother. Jamie is not in the right frame of mind to get married, let alone to a guy who's manipulating her. Do you know he refused me entrance to the wake? He even gave the security personnel printouts of me, so there wouldn't be any mix-up on who wasn't invited. It was a fucking wake. No one is invited to a wake."

Tyrone strays his eyes from the jump schedule board to me. "And here you were thinking you were saving her from an asshole, where in reality, you just shoved her straight into the arms of one." His tone is the same flat monotone one he's been using on me the past week. He wasn't joking when he said he's done dealing with my shit. Doesn't mean I can't use his fondness of Jamie against him, though.

"Do you want to see her married to Brad? You know he's the one who bruised her, right?"

Tyrone dumps his pen onto the desk more forcefully than required. "You're well aware I know what he did because it was my brother who paid him a visit."

"Then why aren't you annoyed about this?" I thrust the newspaper over to his side of the desk.

He scrunches it up before pegging it into my chest. "Because I'm not the person capable of changing her mind. You are, fuckface."

"She won't talk to me."

He glares at me across the desk before returning to scheduling our jumps for New Year's Eve. It's our busiest day of the year. "Can you blame her? You told Jamie her mother was going to die, then she did, the fucking day after you told her."

"That wasn't my fault. I'm not psychic. I can't predict the future."

"Funny, you seem to have done that numerous times the past five months."

Stealing my chance to reply, he grabs the schedule board off the desk and leaves our office. I'm not willing to back down this time around. If he wants to beat me, he needs to start using his fists again as I'm over the emotional shit he's been hammering me with the past week.

"What do you want me to do, Ty? I've emailed. I've called her. I've sent her fucking flowers. What else can I do?"

My attitude takes a step back when he shouts, "The truth, Colby! How about that? Or are you rich fucks too dumb to realize that's more important than anything you can buy?"

Tyrone acts like we don't have the eye of everyone in our crew on us when he takes a step closer to me. "If she understands why you said what you said, maybe she'll forgive you, then maybe, just maybe, she'll realize you aren't the asshole everyone thinks you are." He shoves the schedule into my chest with force. "Do something or do nothing, but whatever you do, if it isn't the truth, keep me the fuck out of it."

With that, he exits The Drop Zone but not before destroying the pamphlets stacked on the entryway table.

My eyes swing to the main desk when a deep voice says, "Is now a bad time?"

"No, not at all..." The fake businessman mask I'm wearing slips away when the man's receding hairline, rounded stomach, and kind eyes register as familiar. "Mr. Burgess. Hello. Is every-thing okay? Is Jamie okay?"

I stop peering out at the full parking lot when he replies, "Considering the circumstances, Jamie is doing remarkably well. It's been hard on all of us, but since we were prepared, it's been a little easier to wade through the grief surrounding us."

His strength is inspiring. "I'm sorry about your loss. From what Jamie told me, your wife sounded like a wonderful woman."

"Thank you. She was... very much so. She is who Jamie gets all her good qualities from." He smirks, revealing he isn't being totally honest, but before I can point that out, he recalls the real reason for his visit. "I'm here to return this to its rightful owner."

"Oh... ah... I can't accept that. That's your money. We didn't provide the service you requested, so you're entitled to a refund," I mumble like a reject when he thrusts a check toward me. It's the one I filled in almost two weeks ago when Tyrone let slip to the comment Jamie's dad placed in the description box when he deposited the funds for her ticket.

Bring my daughter back to life.

Everyone, including me, believed Jamie's inclusion in our tour was solely based on insurance matters. It was only when Tyrone looked further into Terry's request to refund Jamie did we realize our error. Her boss may have handed her a ticket under the assumption it was part of her assessment of The Drop Zone, but he was acting on behalf of Jamie's father and her best friend, Athena.

Supposedly, it wasn't just Jamie's mother's sickness that had stolen the light from her eyes. It was a range of things, including the man who should have been placing her on a pedestal—her douchebag fiancé, Brad. Her ticket was her father's last attempt to bring back the daughter he remembered before his wife was diagnosed with Alzheimer's.

I almost shake my head when Mr. Burgess says, "I wanted the light returned to my daughter's eyes, and you did that," but the image he holds out in front of me stops both my words and my heart. It's the photograph Jamie took of us the night I destroyed her. It's been digitalized as Jamie said it would be. Not a single star behind us can compete with our smiles, not to mention the happy gleam in Jamie's eyes.

I'm shocked he has this picture. I emailed it to Jamie after I saw how broken she looked at her mother's funeral. From her lack of response, I assumed it went unread.

"You don't know what I said. How I hurt her." My last four words are full of shame. "If you did, you wouldn't be offering me that check."

Mr. Burgess smirks at me as if I am an idiot. "Clearly, you don't understand the bond a father has with his only daughter.

As much as your words hurt her to hear, nothing you said was untrue."

"Still, I should have expressed myself better."

He twists his lips. "I agree, but young men have trouble expressing themselves as it is, let alone when they've faced the issues you have tackled and are still tackling." When panic makes itself known on my face, he squeezes my shoulder reassuringly. "Your mother was a brilliant woman, Colby. She was a pioneer in the Alzheimer's community, and her legacy has benefited many people since her passing. This disease is cruel and gutless, but it also brings people together in unexplainable ways *if* you're brave enough to look past the stigma attached to it."

"This isn't about Jamie—" He stops me before I speak the words I haven't said to anyone but Tyrone.

"I know." He nods like he truly understands. "Still doesn't change anything I said. She's stronger than you realize, Colby. You just haven't given her the chance to prove it."

"She's marrying another man." I thrust my hand around my office like he is able to see the newspaper I left dumped on my desk. "I can't stop that."

"Jamie is only marrying Brad because she thinks it will help me find happiness again." He steps closer to me, his eyes nurturing. "She's wrong. All I need is for *her* to be happy. After seeing the way you held her when you thought she hated you, I'm confident you can give her that."

"I can't. No matter what I do or say, she'll end up hurt." I've never sounded more weak and pathetic in my life, but he's not the least bit deterred.

"Yes, you can. You just need to remember that possessions

come and go, sometimes even memories do, but true love is the only thing that stays constant."

After a final squeeze of my shoulder, he places the check and photograph of Jamie and me onto the table scattered with pamphlets before heading for the exit, his footing lighter than it was upon entering.

He's almost in the clear when a question I can't hold back leaves my mouth. "Have you ever regretted it?"

A set of eyes identical to Jamie's in every way peer back at me before he shakes his head. "Not for a single second. Even if I knew back then what I know now, nothing would have stopped me from loving her. She was the love of my life. She still is."

With that, he leaves me with a tattered heart but a clear head.

CHAPTER 32

JAMIE

*M*y quick pivot has my nose crashing into Athena's shoulder. When I attempt to skirt by her, she shuffles into my way. "Nuh-uh. It's been weeks. I know you're still grieving, but I've sat by and watched you make mistake after mistake the past month. I can't do it anymore, J. It's time to face this issue head-on."

By 'this,' she means Colby McGregor, who's standing outside my office building, pretending he doesn't have the admired eye of many. He's done the same thing a dozen times the past three weeks, citing my failure to respond to any of his many emails and calls as the reason for his stalker stance. He doesn't approach me. He simply lets me know he's still around and has no intention of going anywhere any time soon.

"I'm marrying another man. This isn't appropriate."

Athena's auburn red brows furrow. "It isn't?" When I nod as if I'm believing the endless lies I've been spilling the past month, she snarls at me. "When did a marriage certificate arrive with a retraction of friends?"

"He's not my friend. He never was."

She huffs. "Jesus, this is worse than I thought. What has he been drumming in that head of yours?" The gag that arrives with her 'he' references whom she's speaking about without needing his name thrown into the mix. "You owe him nothing, Jamie. Not a single friggin' thing."

"I owe him more than I owe *him*." I thrust my hand at Colby during my last 'him.' "He wasn't there for me, Athena. He didn't wipe away my tears or promise that everything would be okay. He told me she'd die, and she did." Tears nearly spurt out of my eyes when images of my mother's coffin being lowered into the ground pop into my head. "He didn't kill her, but he didn't need to say what he did. He didn't have to be so cruel."

"Okay. It's okay." She soothingly rubs my arm, mortified by the amount of moisture in my eyes. "But no more tears. *Please*. I can't see you like this, J. It's breaking my heart."

"Then get me out of here," I beg through a sob.

Nodding, she pivots me around, so we face the entrance of Metrics Insurance. "Come on, Hugh mentioned something about bringing in leftover lasagna for lunch. If you're willing to risk a firing squad for a slice, I'm more than happy to steal it for us. It will beat a grilled pickle sandwich any day of the week."

She guides me into the foyer of our building with barely a second to spare. The first tear doesn't splash onto my cheek until we're in the safety of the elevator. I thought losing my mother would be the most devastating event I'd ever undertake, but the pain that flashed through Colby's eyes when I walked away from him is cutting it a close second.

281

Whoever said they feel peace in the rain obviously hasn't stood in a storm with nothing but a flimsy umbrella for shelter. My hair is dry, but I'm drenched from the waist down. Like I could be any more annoyed, Brad is late—*again.* Our rehearsal dinner has started without us. I'm starved since Athena hogged our shared lunch like a prisoner of war and it was her only meal of the day, and my dad is circling the block in my car, seeking a vacant spot.

"Fine! You have it," I yell at the wind when it whips my umbrella out of my hand and sends it tumbling down the street. "It's not as if my hair couldn't do with a wash."

My tantrum takes a backseat when a familiar-looking Polish lady hobbles down the footpath. Mrs. Palencia is as saturated as me, but for some inane reason, she's smiling like she's standing on a beach in Hawaii.

"Mrs. Palencia, are you okay?" I rush to her side to remove the large boombox she's carrying. It's more updated than the one she has in her dance studio but looks just as heavy.

"Oh, thank you, dear." Once I have her sheltered under the awning of the restaurant hosting my rehearsal dinner, she gestures for me to put down her portable stereo. I do, albeit hesitantly.

"What are you doing here? Are you working?"

She shimmies out of the cloak that protected her ballroom dress from the rain before raising her eyes to mine. "Dance will always be my first love, but it wouldn't exist without romance."

I peer at her in shock when she smacks her cane onto the ground two times before bending down to switch on her boombox. My heart falls from my ribcage when 'The Git Up' by

Blanco Brown roars out of the speakers. It isn't the memories it conjures up that has me stuttering, it's the way the empty street suddenly fills with bodies. The flash mob includes many faces I recognize. Royce and Linda, the rockabilly dancers Colby and I wanted to wipe the floor with. Tyrone and Athena. Even Blow-Up Barbie and Terry are here. But none are more influential than Colby and my dad. They're in the middle of the pack, dancing according to Blanco's instructions. They hoedown in the rain without a care in the world, hopefully believing the tears gushing down my cheeks are from the rain.

I shake my head when my dad gestures for me to join them halfway through the song. I'd give anything to pretend the pain and humiliation of the past month never happened, but I can't. I'm not the fun, carefree Jamie I was at the cabin—I'm nobody.

"I can't." I drift my eyes to Mrs. Palencia. "I'm sorry, I can't."

When I pivot on my heels, Colby shouts my name over the music blaring out of the speakers. I keep sprinting, only stopping when he discloses, "I have both the APOE-e4 risk gene and Presenilin 2. I was tested after a scan found amyloid plaque buildup on my brain." As I spin around to face him on extremely shaky legs, he continues confessing, "My mom was diagnosed with early-onset Alzheimer's when she was fifty-six. She died four years later. Although the disease is not fully understood, some scientists believe hereditary risks are higher between mothers and their sons—hence my request to be tested."

"What are you saying? You have Alzheimer's?"

He peers at my dad for the briefest second before shaking his head. "No, not yet, but the odds aren't in my favor."

"Amyloid plaque is usually only found on brain scans of patients with Alzheimer's."

He smirks, unsurprised by my knowledge. I read every article I could on the disease when my mom was diagnosed. "I know. That's why I act the way I do and keep everyone at arm's length—"

"And why you said what you said?" I interrupt. "Because you think that's what will happen to you? You think you'll die from Alzheimer's."

He steps closer to me like a torrent of rain isn't pelting down on us. "It isn't a probability, Prim. It *will* happen to me."

"That's not true." Heartache is heard in my tone. I think it's more from his nickname than his confession. "They're making advancements in the disease every day."

He looks prepared to fight back, but someone behind my shoulder stops him. I know who it is without needing to spin around. Colby's clenched fists are advising enough, not to mention the chill racing down my spine. Brad kept his word the past four weeks. He's been there for me more than he's ever been, but my skin still crawls whenever he attempts to touch me. I say 'attempt' because excluding the occasional peck on the cheek, we've not been intimate in months, much less the past four weeks.

"Is everything okay?" Brad slides his hand not clutching an umbrella around my waist just as the snap of paparazzi cameras announce Colby's flash mob gained him more than admiring fans. "Why are you crying?" He snaps his eyes to Colby, his growl loud enough to assure the hungry media they're about to be handed a scandalous story. "What did you do to her? Did you rough her up as you did me?"

Colby loses the chance to reply when the paparazzi's questions overtake Brad's. Regrettably, most of theirs center around his Alzheimer's confession than Brad's claim Colby had him rough handled.

Brad tugs me back when Colby steps closer to me. It tightens his jaw, but it doesn't shelf his reply. "I shouldn't have said what I did, or acted how I did, but I was trying to protect you. Only after speaking with your dad and Tyrone did I realize that was wrong of me. I should have been honest and let you decide if I were worth the risk." Colby steps even closer to me, making it seem as if we're the only two crazy people standing in the middle of a storm. "That's what I'm going to do, Prim. I'm going to step back and let you make your own decision." His eyes dance between mine and they're the mischievous pair I was used to seeing before my world was upended. "But not before I do this."

Like we're not being flanked by my fiancé, my dad, our friends, and members of the media thirsty for a story, he kisses the living hell out of me. I'm not talking a peck kiss I could pretend is perfectly acceptable for friends or a modest one you'd do in front of your grannie even after you've wed. I'm talking electricity-shooting-to-my-toes, fireworks-in-the-sky, I'm-melting-into-a-gooey-puddle kiss.

Colby kisses me with everything he has before lowering his lips to the shell of my ear. "How stupid was I to think a disease could ever make me forget that?" I feel his lips raise against my ear. It sends an excited zap racing down my spine. "Almost as stupid as developing feelings for a woman who's never been mine. I thought I could live without you, Prim. That I could live a full life without you in it. I was wrong." After inching back, he drags his finger down the point my nose doesn't have. "I'll be waiting for you. I'll never stop waiting."

With that, he steps back, shakes my dad's and Tyrone's

hands, then walks away. I'm bundled into the side entrance of the restaurant we're standing next to just as quickly. Not even a snippet of the confusion in my brain has been lifted.

Brad is so fuming mad, his spit sizzles my cheeks when he roars, "Who does he think he is? He had no right to kiss you like he did. I was standing right there!" He paces back and forth, ignoring the maître d's attempt to hand him a towel, so he can dry himself. "And as if you'd pick someone like him over me. He might have a name that opens doors, but that won't do him much good when his brain is an over-fried vegetable."

I snap my eyes to his, shocked as hell. "An over-fried vegetable? Is that what you thought about my mom?"

Brad rolls his eyes like I'm being dramatic. "You know what I mean. Look at your dad. He's beyond broken. He's barely spoken a word in the past four weeks." He thrusts his hand to my father standing solid in the corner.

My dad's more a lover than a fighter, but he looks seconds from blowing his top.

"He's grieving because he lost the love of his life. A love that was so strong, not even Alzheimer's could take it away from him."

"But it *did* take her away from him, Jamie. She's dead. His wife is dead." He talks to me as if I'm stupid and have no clue what's been happening the past four weeks.

"Yet, if given the chance to go back and never meet her, I guarantee you, he wouldn't change a thing." My dad nods without a second thought, backing up my claims. "That's true love, Brad. That's what loving someone for better or worse, for richer or poorer, and through sickness and health is about. You love them until *death* parts you, not women too stupid to see you're not worth the suit you're wearing."

When Brad tries to once again deny the media's claims he was seen dining with another woman last week, I shove my palm into his face before straying my eyes to my dad. "I'm sorry, but I have to go."

My dad smiles the grin he always wore when my mom asked for his hand in marriage. "Yes, you do."

I hug him fiercely before sprinting for the door Brad forced me through only seconds ago.

"Where do you think you're going?"

I slide halfway out before cranking my neck back to Brad. "I'm going to get a love that will be so strong, even if he eventually forgets me, I'll never forget how much I love him. That alone will be worth the heartache of losing him to Alzheimer's."

"I'll not allow you to do this to me, Jamie. I will not have you embarrass me again—" His words are stopped with a hand. It isn't mine. It's my father's fist. He punched him right in the eye, sending him stumbling backward until he crashes into the maître d's podium with a thud.

"Daddy..."

He smirks at the shock in my tone. I knew he had it in him to stand up to Brad, I've witnessed it many times the past four weeks, but I had no clue it would be showcased in such a brilliant way.

"Go. I'll take out the trash while you're gone, then celebrate your metamorphous with our guests." He nudges his head to the hub of the restaurant. The joy on the faces of the guests who were set to watch me marry Brad this weekend matches my dad's to a T. I wasn't lying when I said no one likes Brad—not even me.

"I'll be back... in a day or three."

Pretending my dad's face didn't just whiten, I dart into the street. It's still raining, but it hasn't dampened foot traffic in the slightest. The number of people in one space should lower my body's receptiveness of Colby. It doesn't. Not at all. That might have more to do with the fact Colby has his back braced against the outer wall of the restaurant. His knee is cocked up, and he's wearing the most arrogant smirk I've ever seen. He is one hundred percent the cocky man I know and am growing to love.

"What took you so long, Prim? I've been waiting forever."

EPILOGUE

COLBY

Two years later…

"Nu-huh. Don't let his growl fool you. He's really a giant teddy."

Jamie doesn't keep going to town on my cock like a four-button clinger would. She grazes her teeth along the vein feeding it before crawling up my body. I'd be tempted to kill Tyrone for the interruption if I weren't aware of its importance.

The happiness that spread across every inch of me when Jamie darted out of the restaurant doors three minutes later than I would have liked gets a renewal of energy when her head pops out of the sheets. Her curls are extra crazy today, the clutch I had on her hair when she gave me the best blowjob I've ever been given responsible for its wildness. I swear, every time we fool around, I'm convinced it's the best sex we've ever had.

Then, sometimes not even an hour later, Jamie proves me wrong. It's amazing how much you can enjoy something when you're not acting. I'm still a cocky bastard, but that's only because I'm smug that I nabbed the best girl on the market.

"What did you do to Tyrone this time? He sounds pissed."

When Jamie balances her chin on my sweat-slicked chest, I snag her glasses off the bedside table so she can see the honesty in my eyes when I say, "This time, it wasn't me. You're the one who has his panties in a twist."

"Me? What did I do?"

I send a quick prayer to God before sliding across the sticky sheets, leaving Jamie and her sexy body under them. I'm certain he heard my prayer when Jamie's eyes bulge out of her head. She loves eyeballing my cock as much as she loves being filled by it. Not even two years of constant, daily fucking has weakened the intensity of her stare. I'm only half-mast, yet she still stares, aware I not only have a cock half an inch bigger than my brother's, I know how to use it as well.

"My eyes are up here." I swing my dick like it's Tarzan's vine, ensuring her eyes won't lock with mine anytime soon.

After twenty seconds of teasing, I slide a pair of jeans up my thighs. I'm fucking wrecked, our three-hour-long make-out session this morning responsible for the tightness in both my thighs and my chest.

Once my cock is tucked away, Jamie falls back onto the mattress with a huff. "You suck."

She's right. I do suck—her clit into my mouth multiples times this morning.

I'd love nothing more than to spend the rest of our morning in bed, but Tyrone's bang on my loft door assures me I'm out of time.

"I'm pretty sure you were the one sucking."

I bend down to draw her protruded lip into my mouth before giving it a playful tug. After releasing it with a pop, I nudge my head to the stairwell now blocked by a reinforced door. Tyrone's one and only chance of seeing Jamie naked was when I cut off her clothes after she fell into the icy rapids. He won't get a second one.

"Come on. I need your help with something."

"*You* need *my* help?" Her high tone is super cute. "*The* Colby McGregor can't do something by himself. No way."

"Ha-ha, smartass. I could do this alone, but that would be like our first weekend at the cabin. Solo adventures are fun, but I'd rather recreate them while you're watching. I thought last week was proof of that."

My jeans tighten at the front when her cheeks inflame. "Tell Tyrone to leave. Give him another IOU or anything required to get your ass back in this bed."

I'm a cocky bastard, but the need in her voice nearly knocks me on my ass. It could only be hotter if she were climaxing while saying it. "I would if I could, but you know what Tyrone is like—"

"Smart. Intelligent. Somewhat stupid since he continues putting up with your crap?"

Laughing, I scoop down low to lift her into my arms. Two and a half years ago, I was driving in the fast lane, determined to ride it to what I was assured would be a bleak and bitter ending alone. Now, I feel like the luckiest bastard in the world. Jamie is the best thing that's ever happened to me. She's smart, beautiful, and comes with a guarantee even if I succumb to the disease that stole both our mothers, I'll never forget her. Every kiss, every moan, and every 'I love you' are locked in my heart.

Alzheimer's can't touch my heart. Excluding Jamie, it's untouchable. And since she unlocked it, she's its gatekeeper. Only she has the key.

"Ten minutes, then meet me downstairs." I set her down at the bathroom entrance before giving her naked backside a friendly pat. "And don't you dare touch those curls. Those curls are mine. My fingers created them, so my fingers own them."

I'm undeterred by the roll of her eyes. She loves my machoism, and her fantastic tits expose this. Jamie has a tight, firm body that gets more sweltering the longer I stare at it, but her nipples are always the first to give in to temptation. Like now. They're budded and strained, begging to be touched. I wish our plans for today took longer to organize than they did, but since they didn't, I'll place my needs on the backburner for another hour. Eternity will pass before my desires will ever overrule my moral compass.

Ha! Have you learned nothing the past two years?

As my mouth devours Jamie's with long dedicated licks, I curl her legs around my waist. I hate how fast this will be, but considering this is climax number three for her this morning, the heaviness isn't crippling enough to slow me down. She knows I'll take care of her, and that this won't be her one and only surprise for today.

The bathroom is still steamy from our earlier antics. It adds to the stickiness slicking our skin when I pin her to the wall with my crane-like dick before cupping her round tit in my hand. I circle my lips around the sensitive pink flesh before sucking it into my mouth. Her moans ramp up as she thrusts out her chest, begging for more. I love how hard her nipples get for me—tighter and more pointed with every suck.

While I adore her tits, she skates her hand down the hard

bumps in my abs, only stopping once she has the zipper of my jeans lowered and my cock in her hand. She drags her hand down my throbbing shaft, caressing the manhood she measured with precise accuracy only an hour ago. She didn't use a ruler. She prefers the old metric system—tongue and fingers. It was a glorious morning.

An anguished moan fills my ears, quickly chased by, "Please, Colby."

Jamie works my dick faster, matching the licks and sucks I do to her breast with long strokes. She jacks me off, each stroke having the head of my cock knocking at the door of her pussy. She's soaked, her wetness as evident as the glistening of my pre-cum.

"What do you need, Prim? Tell me, and I'll give it to you."

My chest swells with smugness when she says breathlessly, "I want you to go down on me. To eat me until I scream your name."

That confident, beautiful woman you just heard wasn't always that way. She was so shy the first time we were together, I wasn't sure she'd ever come out of the covers. I worshipped her then as I am now, but she had no clue of her beauty until I showed her. A peacock never wants his feathers plucked unless they're being used to shelter the woman who made him a better man.

The gleam in Jamie's eyes is now so bright, my ego feeds off her confidence.

I laugh when she adds a 'Please' to her request.

She watches me with wild, abandoned eyes when I lower her back onto her feet before falling to my knees—*both for now.* It's crazy how much I crave her. The need never ends. Even with just having her, my thirst feels unquenchable.

"Put your leg on my shoulder, Prim." When she does as instructed, I murmur in a groan, "Watch me."

Her pussy welcomes my tongue with delicious wetness when I spear it between her drenched folds. When she calls out as if her legs are close to buckling after only one full lick, I grip her thighs with my hands before kissing her sweet pussy as I just did her mouth. I've consumed her many times the past two years, and I know what she likes, so her train to Orgasmville reaches its destination remarkably quick.

Jamie's pussy coats my chin with juices as my name tears from her throat. She moans and writhes, her orgasm not holding back an ounce of strength even with it being her third one today.

Once she finishes shuddering, Jamie pulls my jeans over my ass, fully freeing my dick. It was already protruding well past the crotch of my jeans, but she wants the extra two inches only she can entice. I'm always thicker and harder with her, while somewhat gentler. We don't always fuck. We make love too.

Pre-cum seeps from my crown when she snags a condom from a box on the vanity sink before ripping it open with her teeth. Once she has the tip pinched as she's been taught, she rolls the tight latex down my shaft. Seeing her place protection on my cock has my urge to fuck at an astronomical level. I've never been harder, and Jamie appears more than aware of that. She stares down at my throbbing dick while her teeth graze her bottom lip. There's no chance in hell she'll be able to take all of me today, but I won't tell her that until I've given her the first nine inches, which I do in exactly 2.3 seconds.

"Fuck." Her curse word sounds more like an orgasm since its coming from her mouth. "Again."

I drag my dick back out, loving that her pussy quivers as she endeavors to keep me inside, before thrusting back in. Her moan this time around is just as good as the first. It's husky and ball-clenching sweet. When I draw back out for the second time, I add a swivel to my hips. I want her to come on my cock, to orgasm like she never has before, then I won't feel bad for this being the quickest fuck we've ever had.

When she took me to the very root, her face reminded me today isn't about me. It's for her, the woman I'd give up every memory I've ever created if I could only keep the ones that include her.

Jamie's moans heat my blood when my knob finds the sensitive spot inside of her. "Oh, God. It feels so good."

I drive into her on repeat, not caring who may be in the foyer of The Drop Zone. This morning's event is nothing out of the ordinary for them. With Jamie leaving her doucheface fiancé a mere day before they were set to meet at the end of an altar, and her dad relocating back to their family home to recommence finding himself—with some unknown help—she needed a place to stay. I thought my loft was an ideal answer. Jamie didn't see it that way. It's lucky I have persuasive techniques not even a geeky risk assessment calculator can deny.

Although she isn't on the lease, Jamie is very much a part of The Drop Zone. If it weren't for her, we would have never discovered Mr. Celest's sudden wish to sue wasn't his idea. It was that of Mr. Samuel Luis—Jamie's ex-employee. He was working in cahoots with Markham Property Corporation on the agreement he would have a fifty percent stake in the six-star, adult-only golf facility they planned to build here after bulldozing The Drop Zone's HQ. Their stupidity cost both companies millions of dollars and years in jail for those behind the scheme.

As much as it hurt Jamie to admit Brad only commenced pursuing her because he believed he could coerce her into doing anything he asked, it didn't linger for long. It wasn't just my hands, lips, and cock which assured her he was the only fool in their relationship, it was the fact that she didn't fall for his tricks. Yes, she moved in with him after accepting his proposal, but within weeks of us getting together, she realized what she thought was love wasn't. It wasn't close to the all-encompassing feeling we experience when we're together, and it was nothing like the sparks we're creating now.

Moaning, I grip her hips and fuck her faster. I need her to come even more than I wish Tyrone would stop banging on my door. Don't get me wrong. I'm grateful my groveling had him staying on as a co-owner of The Drop Zone, but I'm two seconds from whipping out the IOU that's been between us the past four years and tearing it up. He's killing my mojo, which is unacceptable when it comes to Jamie. I don't care how many times I make her come, if she's not quivering, I'm not doing my job.

"Come on, Prim."

Jamie inhales sharply when I notch in those extra inches she loves. My quads scream in pain as I fuck her like a wild animal, giving her everything I have. The way her pussy tightens around me is intense. She's wet and screaming, but not giving me the final shout I'm craving.

I drive into her harder and deeper, hitting her uterus with more force than I should, but too turned on by her gasps to stop. Her grunts turn feral as everything about her tightens. Her nipples tilt high, her breathing shortens, and her pussy grips onto my cock like it's the first time she's been fucked so brutally.

"Oh. Ohh. Ohhh."

As the most beautiful expression crosses her face, she calls out in a long, low groan that grips my heart as well as it does my sac. Cum rockets out of my dick, prolonging her whispered chants about how good I feel and how she's never come so hard before. They're closely followed by how she can't wait to do it again and again and again.

Now I just need to set up phase two to ensure that is the case.

The pilot chute catches the air and inflates without incident, awarding Jamie and me the peacefulness I feel anytime she shouts my name during ecstasy. Jamie has been working on the three hundred hours needed to jump solo, but she's only a quarter of the way there. Half of me thinks it is because she prefers to jump with me. Who wouldn't? She not only gets to feel the bulge not even the biggest belt buckle can deter from, she also gets to use it to double the adrenaline thickening her blood when we stumble into our loft like crazy teens who can't get enough of each other.

"I can't believe this was the big plan you needed help with."

I drop my eyes to Jamie, who's peering out at the horizon like she's seeing more than blurry blobs. "Are you disappointed?"

She peers up at me, smiling. "Never. I just don't know why you needed to keep it a secret. I'm still scared of heights, but I know I'm not in any danger skydiving. You'd never hurt me."

After dragging my hand down the little point she swears her nose doesn't have, I execute a swoop that will add to the thrill her comment just gave me. Once I have us on the right course, I loosen my grip on the toggles so I can dig out a black box I hid in the pocket of my jumpsuit.

Jamie's big aqua eyes compete with the oceanic background when I wiggle one of her many glasses cases in front of her face. "You need to see this. It's too beautiful to be blurred by poor vision."

"The view? Or your ridiculously handsome face?"

When I wink, pleased she answered as I had hoped, she accepts the case from my hand with a laugh. "I wouldn't endure eyestrain if I had the laser surgery Dr. Marco suggested."

"And have you lose your dorky insurance-assessor look? Never. It's too sexy to give up."

Jamie laughs again before carefully prying open the case, gasping when she realizes they're identical to the thick-rimmed ones she lost when I threw her over a cliff—literally. It took me weeks to find them since they're no longer manufactured, but I refused to do this without them. Her glasses are a part of our story.

The gasps keep coming when Jamie places her glasses on the bridge of her delicate yet noticeable nose. I'm not steering our landing for the manicured lawn at The Drop Zone. We're hovering like eagles about the ocean we had our first dip in.

That isn't the sole cause of her shallow breaths, though. It's the words Tyrone and Athena spelled out on the sand with rocks while I kept Jamie occupied in my loft. The words I have her father's permission to ask.

Will you marry me?

"Colby..."

I pretend I don't hear the nervousness nor excitement in her tone. "Straighten those sexy legs of yours, Prim. Keep them nice and still."

When she does as instructed, I release the parachute strapped to my back as I did a little over two years ago. It gives away without incident. My experience alone ensures we're safe, not to mention the fact I'd never hurt the woman strapped to the front of me.

"When we land in the water, I'll swim us to the surface before untethering us. Do *not* swim, Prim. Unless you want my cock decommissioned like it was when you first arrived in my life."

I feel her heart beat out a funky tune before she nods again. It's so robust, even crossing my arms over her chest to protect her before we pierce through the water doesn't slacken its intensity.

"Okay, here we go. Are you ready, Prim?"

She nods again before hollering in excitement. It's gobbled up when we break through a salty layer of water that removed more than the chip from my shoulders two years ago. It broke the wall surrounding my heart as well. I fell in love with a woman who took my breath away by lodging her heel into my crotch while submersed by gallons of water. Mercifully, the only crushed nuts I'll be handling today will be the ones on the sundae I plan to eat off Jamie's body if she accepts my proposal.

With Jamie's legs as straight as I hope her hair never is, I swim us to the surface. Since she failed to remove her glasses from her face, they're missing when her head bobs out of the water. She doesn't need them. She's peering at me now like she'll forever see me. For better or worse, for richer or poorer, and through sickness and health, Jamie will forever stand by my side as I will hers. Not a disease or a threat of forgetting will ever come between us.

While treading water like my muscles weren't exhausted to the point of seizing only a mere fifty-five minutes ago, I remove a beautifully 'prim' diamond ring from my pocket then say five words I never thought I'd articulate without a snick of hesitation crossing my face. "Jamie, will you marry me?"

Tears add to the wetness on her cheeks when she throws her arms around my neck and whispers a word more powerful than a thousand, "Yes."

BONUS EPILOGUE

I lied two years ago when I said nothing would come between Jamie and me. Something did—or should I say *someone?* She has wild blonde curls, dazzling blue eyes, and she snores just like her mother. Jamie will kill me when she discovers I caught her adorable snores on film, but I couldn't help it.

Our daughter's birth arrived with an incessant need to record every detail of her life. I don't want to miss a single moment. Her first cry. Her first step. Even her first snorty snore has been categorized and stored—both in my brain and digitally.

The plaque on my brain has increased slightly over the past four years, but I'm not worried. I haven't forgotten a single moment of my life since Jamie entered it. That's why Ziggy lies on her mother's chest with her curls unbrushed and her face grubby from Marley's obsessive licks.

Our mangy rescue mutt didn't leave a smidge of icing on Ziggy's face when we celebrated her first birthday at our house with a plunge pool and a top-of-the-line Lexus that doesn't overheat when it goes over forty.

Although I've ticked off every item Jamie requested when I threw her off a cliff, I plan to add heaps more. She failed to mention an outrageously handsome husband with a cock half an inch bigger than his brother's during our sprint, so I'm aware she didn't have the chance to vocalize all the top items on her hit list.

Fortunately for me, I have another sixty-plus years to work out what they are. You can put your money on it, ladies. I have this in the bag!

The End!
For real this time...

Did you know **Colby's** brother, Cormack, already has a book? You can find it here: Sugar and Spice. It is also a standalone! Continue reading for a sample!

Join my Facebook page:
www.facebook.com/authorshandi

Join my READER's group:
https://www.facebook.com/groups/1740600836169853/

Join my newsletter to remain informed:
http://eepurl.com/cyEzNv

My Amazon Page:
https://www.amazon.com/Shandi-Boyes/e/B01D8C13WU

If you enjoyed this book - please leave a review.

The Billionaire
& THE BAKER

Sugar & SPICE

and all things nice...

USA TODAY BESTSELLING AUTHOR
SHANDI BOYES

HARLOW

"*N*o, it's fine, really. I understand."

I don't, but what more can I say? My fourth employee of the month just up and quit. At least her excuse was more plausible than her predecessors'.

"My sister had a baby this morning."

I don't know about you, but I thought you had at least a few months' notice for that sort of event. I guess times have changed? My ovaries did shrivel up and die months ago—*right alongside my libido*—so who am I to judge?

"Can you still make your shift tomorrow morning? Renee called in sick earlier today, so I don't have other bakers available."

I'm not mad at the loss of staff—Fallon was a shit employee —I'm just frustrated by her lack of respect. My bakery may not be the mecca it once was, but without staff to serve customers, I'll descend even deeper into the sinkhole I've tried to ignore the past six months. I'm not asking for the two weeks' notice I'm entitled to, but I need more than two measly minutes.

"Umm. . ."

A huff spills from my lips. "I'll have your final pay wired into your account later this week."

"You're the best, Harlow! Thank you so much."

Not giving me the chance to respond, not that I was going to, Fallon disconnects our call. I place the phone receiver onto its console before slouching in my creaky office chair. I try to ignore the obvious, but I can't disregard them for a second longer. Not only is my heart rate spiked, so is the number of overdue bills on my desk. I'm literally weeks from financial decapitation.

Before venture capitalists made Ravenshoe's land value skyrocket, my bakery was thriving. It was never going to be a multi-million dollar empire, but it had a regular, steady income, capable employees, and a slew of customers. The customers still come, but they, just like me, don't have the means to purchase non-essential items. Thank god true-blooded Americans haven't given up their love of caffeine, or I would have closed my doors months ago.

With my determination wilting, my eyes drift to the thick white envelope a slick-grinned man handed me this morning. An easy way out of my predicament is hidden in that envelope. The amount cited on the transfer of assets isn't just triple what my property is worth; it's more money than I've ever seen, but no matter how generous the offer is, I can't accept it. This bakery has been in my family for decades. Before I took over the reins, it belonged to my great aunt. Treasured family memories are embedded deep in its core. That makes it invaluable. I'll never sell it. Not in a trillion years.

Recognizing that unwelcomed disappointment won't get me anywhere fast, I pull up my sleeves and get to work—literally. I have an order for six dozen cupcakes due first thing tomorrow morning. At four dollars a pop, I can't afford to leave the order unfilled. That's more than we cleared in sales today alone, and with Fallon calling it quits, that bequeaths the task to me. I'm the only baker left with the skills capable of getting the job done.

After pushing back from my desk, I flick on the coffee regulator I only just switched off, then head into the kitchen. Harlow's Scrumptious Haven doesn't look very scrumptious from this angle. The compact space is spotlessly clean, but the oven, countertops, and electronic appliances are well overdue for an upgrade. Only a few short months ago, I was gathering quotes to have them replaced. Now, all my savings have been depleted paying my staff's salaries. Without employees, I won't have any products to sell, but without the right equipment, I can't produce quality products. It truly is a lose-lose situation.

"But at least it's homey," I murmur to myself.

A few minutes later, I stop balancing packets of flour on my chest when a distinct bell chimes through my ears. I glare at the main entrance door of the bakery, certain I locked up hours ago. Sprinkles of flour dust my fitted Polly-knitted skirt when I dump the commercial-sized sachets onto the counter before making my way to the hub of my store.

"I'm sorry, we're closed," I advise my unexpected caller, my tone shocked.

Although the streetlights illuminate the bakery floor, the empty cabinets should alert patrons that the shop is closed, not to mention the late hour.

"If you come back in the morning, I'll have a fresh range of scrumptious products for you to sample. . ."

My words trail off when my guest spins on his heels to face me. If my tongue weren't laden with the excessive amount of sugar I consumed for dinner, it'd be hanging out of my mouth. This man. . . this man. . . I don't have a word to describe this man. I have many.

A chiseled chin hidden by the stubble of a hard day, glistening blue irises unconcealed by thick lashes, and blond hair that's well-groomed but free of products, that is what reflects back at me. Add those yummy elements to a fit body presented in glorious detail by a well-fitted suit and pristine shoes, and you've got an overall package that has my mouth drying up and my eyes going crazy.

Spotting my uncontrolled gawk, the man's lips tug high, making them even more enviable. If he weren't studying me just as closely, I'd be embarrassed he busted me for ogling him. Mercifully, I've never been referred to as shy.

When the stranger spans the distance between us, I eyeball him without shame. Even the way he walks is sexy. His strides are long and effortless, revealing the cut of his suit isn't the only thing enhancing his god-crafted body. Ravenshoe is known for its quality of men, but this man deserves his own unique category. One for him and him only. He's not just handsome; he's downright sexy.

When he stops to stand in front of me, a spicy scent lingers into my nostrils, mixing the sugary taste on my lips with an equally enticing palate.

"Cormack."

A platinum cufflink on a crisp white sleeve becomes exposed when he holds out his hand in greeting. I accept his gesture, forgetting my hands are gritty from the bags of flour I was wrangling before being graced with his presence. The contrast between my skin and his is evident, but I maintain my cool cat composure. I interact with hunky builders and tradesmen on a regular basis, so you can be assured I'm quite familiar with handling eye-catching men. Although none have ever been as stunning as this one.

"Harlow. It's a pleasure to meet you." I withdraw from his grasp, albeit reluctantly.

A grin furls on my lips when I notice he's accidentally dusted his thigh with a bit of flour. If he weren't wearing a midnight black suit, the powder could be overlooked, but since I'm as pretentious about messes as I am about wanting my bakery's glory days to return, I point to the offending product.

"You've got a little flour on you," I choke out. I'm not stammering because my mouth feels like the Sahara Desert on the hottest day of the year. It's from his hand brushing away the powder with a quick sweep.

I'm notorious for stalking Instagram in my spare time. I'm not looking for a date, merely inspiration for the numerous romance books I gobble up every week. I've found many suitable book-boyfriend candidates in my daily—*sometimes multiple times a day*—searches. Handsome men with straight teeth, blemish-free faces, and tight, fit bodies, aren't hard to come by, but rarely do I discover one who ticks all my boxes. I'm not fussy; I'm an everyday standard American mid-twenties romance lover extraordinaire. There is just one difference: I don't just want junk in the trunk, I want it in the hood as well.

This man has both. Not only are the creases in his trousers ineffective at hiding the swell of his crotch, but they showcase every perfect asset of his backside as well. My aunt thought a mirrored wall would give the bakery an illusion of space. She had no idea.

Is it possible to fall in love at first sight? If so, I've fallen head over heels in love.

Not with this man—with his tailor!

"Sorry," I mumble when a deep, penetrating voice breaks through the padded-cell silence surrounding me. "Did you say something?"

Cormack's smile exposes the pegs of his perfectly straight teeth. I didn't need an in-depth cavity search of his mouth to confirm he ticks every box in my ultimate book boyfriend list, though. His impeccably tailored suit, exceedingly shiny shoes, and zesty scent filled the gaps my lust-fired brain forgot to inspect. He's not a ten out of a ten. He's an eleven.

"My order? I was wondering if I could pick it up it this evening instead of tomorrow morning?" Chocolate dribbled on strawberries, honey smothering oats, or a dash of vanilla in a skinny chai latte—that's how heavenly smooth his voice is.

"Your order?" I repeat, somewhat lost between a lust-crazed idiot and a half-capable business woman.

My daft response can be easily excused. Excluding the one-off birthday or wedding cake requests, my customers are generally in and out in under ten minutes. And with sugary treats at the bottom of the totem pole when it comes to necessities, even those visits are becoming few and far between.

Just as Cormack nods his head, the business side of my brain finally kicks into gear. "Oh. . . you're Marshmallow Man?"

I try to iron out the immaturity in my tone, but I'm not fast enough. "When Fallon jotted down your order, she forgot to ask for contact details. Since you requested marshmallow fondue, we named you 'Marshmallow Man.' It was all in fun.

You don't look like a marshmallow—*not at all*. I'd be surprised to find an ounce of fat on you. Not with a body like that—all lean and muscular. Not a single lump to be found. Well, except in critically acclaimed areas . . ."

I'm rambling. Not an *I'm such a cutie-pie* ramble, but an *I'm as idiotic as I feel* ramble.

Pretending I haven't noticed an amused smile cracking onto Cormack's lips, I straighten my spine and assert a professional façade. "Anyhoo, your cakes aren't ready."

My laidback tone doesn't match my business-like stance. Once again, my response can't be helped. Any hope I have of sounding professional is destroyed by Cormack's ravishing grin. He has the *I'll cause you a whole heap of trouble, but in a way you'll never see it coming* smile down pat. It makes me both wary and excited. I love a challenge, and he appears as challenging as I could get. He makes me want to exercise the non-business side of my brain, which is so unfit from lack of use the past two years, our little tussle has already left me breathless.

If I weren't already suspicious of his wealth, his quick check of the time leaves no doubt. Either Scott upped the ante on the fake Rolexes he sells at the corner of my bakery for twenty dollars a pop, or this man is loaded.

"It's past nine," he advises, as if I'm unaware of the time.

"Uh-huh, it sure is." My eyes stray to the massive clock filling the silence with its loud clangs. "We here at Harlow's Scrumptious Haven pride ourselves on ensuring our customers receive the highest quality products. If that means I need to stay on site until 3 AM to produce the freshest and most scrumptious cupcakes you've ever eaten, that's what I'll do."

The first half of my statement is full of pride and certainty. The last half sounds like my voice when I have to book a pap smear. I arrived at work at 3 AM this morning. I don't want to be here anymore than I wish I hadn't kicked off my shoes nearly two hours ago. I'm not short, but my lack of heels has left me a good four to five inches shorter than the man smiling at me like I just told him his order is free. It isn't. I have until 8 AM tomorrow to fulfill his order because "it's on time or it's free" is our motto.

"You'll have your cupcakes, but not until the time Fallon promised. . ." I stop talking as my worry makes itself known. "She did give you a time for pick up, didn't she?"

A strand of platinum blond hair falls in front of Cormack's bright blue eyes when he briefly nods. "Yes, she did."

Although his reply seems hesitant, I murmur, "Oh, thank god. I was beginning to wonder if I had hired a dimwit with half a brain."

He unleashes his deadliest weapon when a wicked smirk crosses his face. He either finds me amusing or thinks I'm a twit. I really hope it isn't the latter.

"Teething issues?" The sass in his tone puts my worry to rest.

"Ah. . . if the issues stem from a ninety-year-old geriatric with a faulty pacemaker and glass eye, then yeah, we could go with teething issues." My reply reflects more on my outdated kitchen than crappy employees, but since it's the main source of my frustration, I work it into our discussion.

When he throws his head back and laughs, the lack of libido I informed you of earlier packs up and leaves town. I let out a yearning sigh, mesmerized by the raw sexuality of his mannish chuckle. It's gruff yet smooth, two usually contradicting features perfectly blended like sugar and butter.

Cormack uses his laughter to study me more closely. He

watches me through hooded lids, his lengthy perusal more attentive than carefree. His attention causes my stomach to somersault, but not in a bad way. It's flighty and free, as disentangled as the rope circling my heart.

When his eyes return to my face, I splay my hands across my hips and arch a brow, acting annoyed by his impish study of my body. I'm not annoyed, though—I'm far from it. I'm just praying he won't see the lust in my eyes caused by his prolonged stare. I'm a single woman living in the twenty-first century. I've been ogled in more ways than you can imagine, but this is the first stare to award me with excited butterflies rather than itchy hives.

Cormack doesn't buy my attempt to act coy. His sexy grin triples as his eyes glimmer with as much desire as mine. For every second he silently goads me, the curvier his lips become. His suit should come with a warning label: *only here to distract you from the defiant man beneath the expensive threads.*

I try to return his silent mock with an equal amount of grit, but I've never been good at lengthy bouts of silence. "I don't know why you're smiling. It's not funny. I've been up since 3 AM. I'm tired."

I wanted my reply to amplify the friskiness in the air, but my honesty has the opposite effect. I'm so tired, if the savage surge of electricity bouncing between us wasn't increasing my energy levels, I'd be on the verge of collapse.

My knees wobble when Cormack twangs my bottom lip. "Don't pout. You're not a baby."

"It takes one to know one," I fire back before I can stop myself.

It wasn't very mature, but when you catch me with minimal

sleep, you're destined to recognize my morbid dislike of mellowness.

Cormack's lips twitch as he attempts to stifle his reply. His pause is pointless when he snickers, "I know you are, I said you are, but what am I?"

My lips move, but not a syllable escapes my mouth. He just stole my line. "Well. . . ah. . . shit. . ."

Out of words—*and clearly oxygen*—I switch our verbal tussle to a physical one.

Cormack takes a step back when my fist lands in his stomach. My hit is barely a fairy tap, but firm enough for both of us to gasp in sharp breaths. I don't know why he's wheezing, but I obviously can't take it back. I just acted before thinking.

"I'm so sorry. I shouldn't have hit you."

I'm drowning in a cesspool of financial burden; I don't need a lawsuit to take away the half dozen pennies I earned last month.

I worry that his wealth wasn't acquired via hard work when he scans my bakery. If he's calculating my assets, he shouldn't waste his time. The chairs and tables nestled around the space are Ikea knockoffs because even flat-packed furniture is out of my league. The paintings gracing the walls are prints I doctored to look authentic, and my kitchen is older than me. Second only to Cormack, the highest thing of value standing in this bakery is me, and even then, you're not getting much bang for your buck.

When he returns his eyes to mine, the mischievous gleam brightening them divulges he isn't litigious. He's simply seeking a way to return my tease. How do I know this? The sting of my bra strap snapping my olive skin proves he was calculating nothing but revenge.

My jaw drops as my overworked brain struggles for an appropriate response. *He* just snapped my bra strap—a man whose suit alone could feed me for a year snapped *my* bra strap. *What universe am I in and how did I get here?*

Instead of taking a moment to consider all my options, I respond to Cormack's tease with an equal amount of immaturity. With a poke of my tongue, I stomp on his foot, spin on my heels, then dart for the kitchen. I should be screaming in alarm, alerting anyone in the vicinity that the Straight-Suited-Stalker who terrorized the residents of Ravenshoe in the late nineties has resurrected from his grave, but instead of hollering at the top of my lungs, I'm giggling like a juvenile twit.

My response can't be helped. The butterflies in my stomach already have me overwhelmed with giddiness, and don't even get me started on Cormack's bellowing laugh. He's loving this step back in time as much as I am. I can't remember the last time I acted so carefree, let alone freely frolicked with a man I just met. I wouldn't necessarily say dating sucks, but by the time I've spent hours primping my body to within an inch of recognition, I barely have the strength to leave my loft, let alone play nice.

When I enter my kitchen, I snag two eggs in my hand and pivot on my heels to face Cormack. I have no clue what I plan to do with the eggs, but with my brain on the fritz, I'm listening to my fun-loving heart instead of its more mature, rational counterpart.

He stops dead in his tracks. "Hey, whoa, hold on a minute." He raises his hands in the air like I'm grasping pistols instead of two lousy eggs. "We've only just met, but I'm fairly certain you're not a lady who does anything she'll regret in the morning."

I twist my lips, equally adoring and loathing the mirth in his tone. "Who says I'll regret it?" The sexual innuendo teeming between us can't be missed. It's so intense, I'm certain the eggs I'm clutching are now hard-boiled. "One stupid mistake can change everything, but who says all mistakes end badly?"

The air sizzles with sexual tension when he steps toward me, the crackling of energy between us making him seem closer than he is. "Think about this. For every action there is an equal reaction."

"Yeah, it's called retaliation." I give him a sassy wink.

When his eyes brighten with defiance, I raise an egg high into the air, wordlessly warning him to stand down. He angles his head to the side before furling his lips. He isn't berating me; he's merely authenticating my threat. I maintain my strong stance, even though his heated gaze makes me want to squirm. I don't back down when challenged.

With the smirk of a man who has nothing to lose, Cormack takes another step toward me. His prowling stops midstride when I peg an egg at a tile mere inches in front of his feet. It cracks on impact, splashing his expensive shoes with clear goop and bright yellow yolk.

Pretending I can't feel my heart jolting in my throat, I return my eyes to Cormack. He's staring at me in shock, and if I'm not mistaken, a smidge of awe. I accepted his challenge, wrapped a shiny red bow around it and served it straight back to him. He's probably used to high-class, *six months to make a decision* women. I'm a baker and a Libra. I think quick, respond even quicker, and dive into the shallow end without a second thought. My life is sweet, but my wittiness is even sweeter.

Some may say too much sweetness will leave a sour taste in your mouth. That isn't the case with me. I'm only here for a lifetime, so I plan to make the most of it. If you want to join the crazy-ass ride, you are more than welcome—the more, the merrier, but if you want a smooth, boring track without a single curve or dip in the road, you're associating with the wrong woman.

This is Cormack's introduction to my craziness. I'm expecting him to run for the exit without so much of a backward glance. Will I be disappointed when he flees? Yeah, I will be. Will I mourn his loss? Yes, just as much as I did my libido when it packed up and left town, but I played the game as stipulated in the rule book we call life, and I still came out a loser. That's why I turned a page five years ago.

Against the advice of family, friends, and anyone who has ever known me, I threw every penny I had into my business. Up until eight months ago, it was paying dividends. I was happy. *I am happy.* I'm just trying to find my work/life balance again since this recent decline in sales. Once I do that, things will once again be golden.

Cormack coughs, alerting me to his presence while also dragging me from my thoughts. I was so sure he would have fled by now, I stare at him with wide eyes. My frozen stance only lasts mere seconds, but it feels like hours.

"That was a warning." The sneer of my tone can't disguise my joy that he is still here. "I'll aim higher the second time around."

Spotting the fiery edge in my eyes, Cormack's smug grin turns into a mammoth smile. "I don't back down easily either." He reads me more expertly than a stranger should. "Not when it's something I desperately want and need."

I'm tempted to ask if there is any possibility that *something* will include me in the near future, but his charge across the room scatters my words as fast as my feet. I dump the egg on the ground so it doesn't weigh down my escape, spin on my heels, then make a dash for it.

The air in my lungs evicts in an ear-piercing scream when Cormack bands his arm around my waist not even two seconds later. Instead of requesting to be set down like a sane, sensible woman would, I scan my kitchen, seeking additional arsenal for my vault load of stupidity tonight.

It's also a great ploy to ignore the friendly fit of our bodies.

By keeping my focus on rejuvenating my veins with oxygen, I attempt to ignore the rigid bumps of Cormack's midsection splayed against my back. Or how him being a good four inches taller than me doesn't stop our crotches aligning perfectly. I'm not thinking about anything but the roguishness of our exchange. The rest can wait. . . at least another minute or two.

My impromptu scan of the area reveals nothing but bags of flour too heavy for me to maneuver in a hurry and my trusty tray of eggs.

"Uh-uh," Cormack grunts, hauling me away from my weapon of choice before more damage can be issued to his well put-together package.

My frantic lurch secures two eggs in my grasp, but unfortunately, it sends the remaining three dozen crashing to the floor. Lucky for me, I only need one to exact my revenge—so two is a bonus.

"Don't you dare." His warning holds no steam. His deep baritone is laced with too much amusement to convey anger.

A smear of flour to his expensive suit becomes the least of his worries when I crack an egg on his thigh before rupturing another one on his cheek. Like it could possibly get any bigger, my mouth widens even more. This man was a stranger only minutes ago, yet I've socked him in the stomach, stomped on his foot, then cracked an egg with his face.

What.

The.

Hell?

If I weren't on the verge of peeing my pants from laughing so hard, I would assess the situation with more diligence. Perhaps I'm dreaming? Surely that's a plausible excuse. Otherwise, what other explanation could I have for my stupidity? I'm cackling like I've never cackled before, but can a good time outweigh morals?

If you had asked me twenty minutes ago, I would have said you can't have both. Now, I'm not just doubting myself. I'm skeptical on my entire life plan. I took on this bakery because it's been in my family for nearly a century, but with its financial struggles sucking the marrow straight out of my bones the past six months, I forgot the real reason I won't fold. I'm not here to make a million dollars. I'm here because I love what I do.

The faint murmur when a customer sinks their teeth into a freshly baked éclair might not be the highlight of an average person's day, but when you're a baker, you worship it like liquid gold because for all I know, that may be that customer's only happy sigh for the day. Knowing that something so simple can give people pleasure makes the lack of fanfare worthwhile. It might leave me without a pot to piss in, but I'm rich with a substance money can't buy.

I land back in reality with a thud when Cormack's shiny shoes lose traction on the egg yolks splattered around his feet. He bows forward before slanting backward, his feet slipping out underneath him like Bambi the first time he skidded across the ice. I mimic his movements, praying the mess on the floor will be the only one I'm left cleaning tonight. Egg whites are great for combating oily hair, but yolk in hair as thick and wavy as mine...yuck!

For the umpteenth time in my adult life, my prayers are left unanswered. In an almost comical performance, Cormack's legs scissor high into the air before his backside impacts harshly with the tiled floor. Since I'm still wrapped up in his embrace, my fall is just as spectacular. I'm narrowly saved from landing on the rigid ground by his splayed thighs. My unladylike land in his crotch proves what I already knew: he has desirable assets front to back and back to front.

"Are you okay?" My words are scarcely heard through the giggle/moan I'm releasing. The entire situation is hilariously degrading, but no woman with a pulse could ignore the thickness of a *real man* bracing against their core.

When Cormack answers my question with a grunt, I scramble off him. The heat on my cheeks doubles as my eyes widen. With how slippery the ground is, I had no choice but to drag my ass over his crotch instead of respectfully holding my own weight.

Well, that's the excuse I plan to tell the cops when they arrest me for sexual assault.

I won't protest the charges. My boldness will be worth a night in lock up. I'd even do it again if it didn't make me seem desperate.

Rule 101: *Never show desperation.*

It's right above **Rule 102**: *It's not desperate if it gets you off.*

Like I'm not already on the verge of climaxing without stimulation, mayhem ensues. It isn't the greasy mess seeping through my skirt that has my clit thrumming. It's the scrumptiously delicious laugh of a man who was a stranger mere minutes ago. Cormack isn't chuckling a half-hearted *make your belly a little squishy* laugh. He has the full-blown *I'll shred your panties off by using nothing but my eyes* laughter. It makes me hot with need, but it also makes me laugh.

I honestly can't remember the last time I giggled without hesitation. I'm reasonably sure it was a couple weeks ago when I went out with Izzy and Brandon for drinks, and even then, it wasn't this madcap feeling. I was so out of my comfort zone, I nearly called it quits within an hour of arriving at the nightclub Brandon had chosen. Blessedly, Izzy gave me an out just as the alcohol settled in my gut. Thank god. If she hadn't, I might have accepted one of the numerous tacky one-liners I'd been issued all night. I'm desperate for adult company, but I'm not *that* desperate.

I already weaseled my way into Izzy and Brandon's duo by disclosing my fear of dying alone. I don't need more pity-me points. Izzy and I only became friends because she is a customer at my bakery. She accepts my witty personality no matter the time of day. In my book, that makes us instant besties. It's not every day you find an immediate connection with someone. Three months ago, it was Izzy. Today, it's Cormack.

"Eldest sibling?" Cormack questions, his words separated by chuckles.

I settle my laughter before nodding. "You?"

His eyes glisten as he matches my nod bob for bob.

"How many?" I ask, pretending I'm not on the verge of coronary failure from the mess surrounding us. I may be bat-shit crazy, but at least I'm neat.

He scrubs his jaw before answering, "Three. You?"

"Just one, but if he were here, we'd be wearing my entire pantry."

My last word comes out in a garble from Cormack brushing my cheek with the back of his hand.

"You had egg on your face," he explains, his rueful tone incapable of hiding his delight. He liked that my body bloomed under his touch nearly as much as I enjoyed his unexpected contact.

"I'm not the only one sporting shells. You look like a half-cracked Easter egg."

I scoot closer to him but keep my hands fisted at my side. Let me tell you, it's a battle worthy of the record books. It isn't that I don't want to touch him. I just don't want him thinking I'm using the tiniest bit of eggshell stuck in his blond brow as an excuse to get up close and personal. I am using it as an excuse—I just don't want him to know I am.

"May I?" I ask, pointing to his brow.

He slants closer to me, granting me permission without words. The milky white skin on his forehead bunches when I carefully pluck the shell from his brow.

"See?" I show him the microdot, acting as if it's a hundred times bigger.

"That's nearly an entire egg," he plays along, his tone lowering to match my lack of self-respect.

My lungs lose the ability to expand and collapse when his fingers return to my cheek. The sparkle in his eyes is a clear indication he isn't removing egg from my face. He's merely touching me without permission. I'm not surprised by his forwardness. He seems like a man who is used to getting his way, so why ask first?

"Harlow. . ."

"Yes?" I can't tell if his murmur of my name is a question or a statement, so I answer by asking one of my own.

His exploration of my face descends to my collarbone. "Is there a Mr. Harlow?"

The mad thud of my pulse tapping his fingertips should answer his question on my behalf, but in case it doesn't, I mumble, "No."

"Hmm."

My eyes dance between his brilliant baby blues, struggling to work out if that was a good moan or a bad one. Perhaps if I'd known him longer than twenty minutes, I'd have more chance of easing my confusion?

"Harlow. . ."

"Yes." This time I go with straight-up confirmation.

He tilts in closer, replacing the watery smell of eggs with a spicy cologne. "Can I kiss you?"

"W-W-What?" I bite on the inside of my cheek. That was worse than the blurted response I gave Arnie Frank when he asked the same question in middle school. His touch already has me heating up, so imagine adding his succulent mouth to the equation. *Mind blown!*

"Can I kiss you?" Cormack repeats.

"You want to kiss me?"

If I didn't need my hands to keep upright, I'd slap my face. I must be dreaming. Surely.

"Yes." He leans even closer. "Can I?"

I don't know what he had for tea, but it soothes the somersaults gurgling in my stomach, replacing them with a hungry grumble. I'm not hungry for food, though. I'm hungry for him.

"Yes." Our lips are so close, I practically kiss him when replying.

"Yes?" he double-checks.

"Yes," I reply, my voice one I haven't heard in longer than I'd care to admit.

My heart goes crazy when he locks his eyes with mine. They don't slowly flutter shut, and he doesn't lick his lips in preparation for our kiss. He merely devours me with his eyes, wetting my panties more swiftly than my skirt absorbed the three dozen egg yolks we're sitting in.

Just before his lips brush mine, the bells above my bakery door chime.

CORMACK

*H*arlow wrenches away, leaving me not just in a state of disrepair, but with a raging hard-on as well. As the scuffling of feet booms into my ears, she slaps her cheeks, trying to wake herself up. I'm tempted to do the same. I came here tonight with a game plan, only to leave with egg on my face—literally.

Getting messy isn't the only thing I achieved, though. I twanged a set of lusciously plump lips, flicked a bra strap, and acted like a man I once hoped to be.

It's fortunate the fire in Harlow's eyes matches her personality, freeing me from the worry of being sued—*again.* I can't recall the last time I acted so childish. I didn't even behave like a child when I was one. Harlow brought out a side of me I haven't seen in decades.

I've heard many things about the woman behind the helm at Harlow's Scrumptious Haven, but I was certain they were exaggerations. Very rarely are rumors true, but in Harlow's case, they're spot on.

Her hair, pulled back in a low ponytail, isn't quite red, but it's not conservatively brown either. Her eyes are as unique as her hair color: an eclectic green with brown flecks. And her body. . . sinful enough that ruining a three thousand dollar suit with egg yolk can't stop my zipper from biting my cock.

I guess that's my excuse for acting so idiotic? I either flicked her bra strap or removed it with my teeth. Considering the reason I arrived at her bakery well after closing hours is far from upstanding, I figured it'd be best to downplay my visit. Thank god my assistant Peta ordered a batch of unwanted cupcakes earlier this week, or I'd have no excuse for my late night arrival.

"What is it with unexpected visitors tonight?" Harlow mumbles to herself as she attempts to stand.

Her feet failing to gain traction on the tiled floor shouldn't be entertaining, but it is. I didn't just bruise my ass when I hit the floor with an almighty thump, my ego sustained a massive dent as well, so seeing her face the same issues is both refreshing and entertaining.

"I'll be right there." Harlow projects her voice into the main area of the bakery. Her tone isn't high nor overly nasal. Her perfect pitch reflects her elevated confidence but not in a snooty, look-at-me type of way.

Her visitor mumbles a reply, but since I'm too busy calming my raring pulse from her egg-soaked skirt sticking to her sultry hourglass figure, I miss what he says.

My heart thumps when Harlow balances on her hands and knees. If I were a gentleman, I'd offer her assistance, but with her backbreaking position amplifying the uncomfortable pinch in my crotch, I must remain seated.

After several near misses, Harlow stands to her full height, which I'd guess to be around five foot eight without shoes. She clears the yolk from her hands by dragging them down her loose-fitting sweater, then she offers them to me. I accept her assistance, fighting the urge to pull her back into my lap where she was seated mere moments ago. If my common sense hadn't arrived with her unexpected guest, I would, but with reality comes clarity.

I just need my body to get the memo that I'm not here for Harlow, and don't even get me started on my fucked-up heart. Instead of appreciating the extra thump our impromptu exchange generated, it's assessing every snippet as if they're signed guarantees of future exchanges. They aren't. I'm not in a position to take on more work, and Harlow won't just add issues to my current payload, she could completely obliterate them.

Furthermore, I don't chase my heart's desires. I beat them into a pulp.

"Thank you," I praise when Harlow drags me to a vertical position, proving her strengths aren't just internal.

With my tongue hanging out of my mouth, I slide across the egg yolk, using its gooey substance to my advantage. If I didn't loathe my father, I'd give him credit for my above-par skating abilities. Not every child gets to train with professional hockey players when they're only ten. It's a pity my father died years ago. It's also a pity I can't stand the guy—dead or alive.

"Good idea," Harlow murmurs, copying my skiing moves.

If you ignore our ruined clothing and sticky hair, we might look like a couple spending our first date at the Rockefeller

Center ice rink. We have the cliché Christmas movie vibe down pat—huge smiles and all. Harlow's nonchalant composure is refreshing. She's covered head to toe in goop, yet her toothy grin never waivers. She either has the world at her feet, or she's in the wrong industry.

Because the bakery's kitchen is so small, it only takes us a few glides to reach the other end. While I toe off my slosh-covered shoes, Harlow rolls neutral-colored stockings down her thighs. I don't bother hiding my hungry gawk. No sane man would. Harlow is drop dead gorgeous, and she has a body the devil would wear a halo for, so you can be assured I'm watching in full anticipation, praying her panties soon join her discarded stockings.

I'm left hanging when Harlow tosses the bunched-up nylon into a sink on her left. When her eyes drift to me, I nearly angle my body to the side to conceal a response a grown man shouldn't have over a pair of stockings. The only reason I stay put is because I remember her staring at my crotch earlier. Now we're even.

"Oh, for the love of sugar," Harlow mumbles, her voice void of shame as she stares at me.

I eat businessman for breakfast; I transfer assets worth millions of dollars multiple times a day, but I'm left void of a retort to her unexpected but highly sought-after praise. I can also feel my cheeks heating.

What.

The.

Fuck?

I don't blush. I'm a man, for fuck's sake. Men don't blush. We get red with anger or exertion. We. Do. Not. Blush.

Before I can conjure a plausible excuse for my red cheeks, a cough breaks the silence. When Harlow's eyes snap to the man standing at our right, the heat from my cheeks transfers to hers.

With clenched fists and a jaw just as firm, she growls, "You again! I told you this morning, my business is *not* for sale."

The man chokes on his response when I pivot on my heels to face him. He recognizes me as quickly as I identify him, but before he can credit our association, I slant my head to the side and glower at him. *Now is not the time for official introductions.*

After an inconspicuous nod, Levi returns his focus to Harlow. "I recall in utmost detail your response to my visit this morning." His tone indicates Harlow's earlier refusal wasn't as polite as this one. "I just figured there was no harm in popping in to see if you've glanced at the latest proposal yet. The company I'm representing has been *very kind* with their offer. I'd hate for you to mistake their generosity as desperation."

The way he snarls "hate" makes the throb in my cock extend to my jaw. He's not goading Harlow; he's degrading her. If I hadn't met her in person, I'd step back and let them handle their business—there are no friends in this fickle industry—but now it seems wrong to watch someone belittle her. I was literally seconds away from kissing her before Levi interrupted us, so how can I not defend her?

"A *respectable* company would allow time to look over the proposal outside of business hours before strong-arming a vendor for an answer."

Levi's Adam's apple bobs up and down before his head joins the bobbing party.

"Perhaps if you hand Ms. Murphy your card, she'll call you once she has examined the offer more thoroughly. Until then, your purchaser must wait. No business matters, whether large or small, happen without legwork. You haven't given Ms. Murphy the chance to stretch her legs, much less her brain."

I inwardly cringe, mindful I disclosed Harlow's surname. I didn't mean to. I was just caught up with formalities, it slipped out before I could reel it back in. Not once, but twice. Mercifully, Harlow is so thrilled by my dressing-down, she fails to notice I used her name.

Pretending he doesn't have sweat beading on his brow, Levi digs into the breast pocket of his jacket, then jots down his cell phone number on a business card before handing it to Harlow.

With the determination of a woman with nothing to lose, Harlow stares into Levi's eyes before ripping the card in half. Not wanting him to misconstrue her silent rejection, she places the two torn strips together before tearing them in half once more. She follows the same routine another two times before releasing the cardboard from her grip.

Levi watches the remains of his business card haphazardly float to the ground before raising his eyes to Harlow. "My number is also on the purchase contract. Call me if you have any questions."

Snubbing her un-choked growl, he spins on his heels and exits the bakery as swiftly as he entered it. He's barely stepped onto the sidewalk when Harlow whines, "Argh. Seriously. The gall of that guy. I don't know how many times I have to spell it out to him. No amount of money will change the fact that my business is not for sale."

She throws her arms into the air before stomping into her kitchen. Forgetting the floor is covered with eggs, she does a weird splits, wild arms flapping thing. Thankfully, my lightning quick reflexes help her regain her footing before she stumbles to the floor.

I wait for the panic to clear from her face before possibly increasing it. "Are you being hassled into selling?" I ask, pretending I don't know the answer to my question.

"'Hassled' is too nice of a word for that guy's tactics." She nudges her head in the direction Levi just went before crouching down to clean up the mess we made.

"What do you mean? What tactics?" The tick of my jaw resonates in my tone.

Harlow dumps a handful of eggshells into a bin under the kitchen counter before raising her eyes to mine. "I really shouldn't say hassle. He just won't get the hint. A change in figures won't alter my mindset."

"Why?" I'm not asking to be nosey. I'm genuinely interested in her reply.

I've seen firsthand the amount properties like hers fetch in Ravenshoe area. Instead of adding to the dark rings circling her eyes, Levi's proposal could have her living on easy street, so why isn't she considering his offer?

"Because money won't make me happy." Harlow's tone indicates she isn't one hundred percent confident with her reply. She wants to believe what she's saying is gospel, but she knows as well as the next person that we live in a money-oriented world.

"Money won't make you happy," I agree, my tone more buoyant than hers. "But a sturdy foundation can."

I bob down to assist her in cleaning up the mess. My suit is already ruined, so what are a few more stains between friends?

"If you're treading in waters out of your depth, is it wrong to accept a lifejacket?"

I expect her to take a moment to deliberate my question, so you can imagine my surprise when she instantly replies, "Yes."

"How?" My tone reveals I think her answer is ludicrous. "If you're drowning, there is no shame in accepting assistance."

"Colt Enterprises isn't offering me a lifejacket; they want me out of the pool altogether."

Now I'm the one sorting the facts. She has a point. A very solid one.

Although I somewhat agree with what she's saying, it doesn't stop me from asking, "So baking cupcakes is more important than living comfortably?"

Harlow's eyes rocket to mine. Her snarl tells me she didn't miss the disbelief my deep tone couldn't stifle.

"You've got to understand my astonishment! You're sitting on a goldmine." I gesture around her bakery that doesn't just need an update—it needs demolishing. The space is spotlessly clean, but it doesn't have the means to cook a Sunday roast, much less the products required to fill its cabinets every day.

"Yes, I am, " Harlow agrees, nodding. "The foundations of my bakery are solid; it just needs some TLC—"

"Or a match and some gasoline. . ."

My reply falls short when the only egg not ruined during our tussle lands on the top of my head. Harlow mushes it in deep, ensuring it will take me at least an hour to remove the shards of shell from my hair, not to mention the ones her pained eyes stabbed my heart with. This isn't just business to her. This is as personal as it gets.

Satisfied I've absorbed the silent warning that our conversation about her selling is over, Harlow rises to her feet. "I'll have your cupcakes ready for pick up at 8 AM."

Her dismissive tone hurts me more than my backside's collision with the ground. Gone is the woman who stole the air from my lungs with one glance of her face, exchanged for one who appears lost and vulnerable.

After clearing away the remaining mess, I join Harlow at the stainless steel counter she's peering at, lost in thought. I want to kiss her until the impish gleam her eyes held earlier returns stronger than ever, but since I'm treading in foreign waters I swore I'd never wade in again, I harness my desire—barely.

Kissing her won't make matters better. If anything, it will make them ten times worse. So, no matter how badly I wish it weren't true, I can't kiss her. Not now. Not ever.

I push down my disappointment with a quick swallow before advising, "I won't have time to pick up my order tomorrow. Can you have them delivered to my office? I'm happy to pay for the courier service you generally use."

While striving to ignore the gnawing sensation deep inside me, I hand my business card to Harlow. Although I'd give anything to experience this crazy, indescribable feeling again, the anxious knot in my gut is warning me to place distance between us before things grow more complicated than they already are.

This is a connection unlike any I've ever had. It's more emotional than impassive—which, if I'm totally honest, scares the shit out of me. I can't remember the last time I've felt this alive, but I'm certain it comes at a cost. One I'm not willing to pay again. So for that alone, I must trust my instincts instead of my heart.

"My business address is on the bottom of the card; anyone can accept delivery, just tell them they're for me."

Although Harlow's lips twist as she takes in my credentials, she remains as quiet as a church mouse. I've never been a fan of noise until now. I'd rather have her girly giggle piercing my eardrums than be bound by her silence. It reminds me of a quote my mom always said, "At the end, you'll not remember the words of your enemies, only the silence of your friends."

"McGregor?" Harlow murmurs a short time later, blessing me with her syrupy sweet voice.

I nod, praying this is one time my infamous surname remains anonymous.

Before I can ask what caused the extra flutter in her thin neck, Harlow asks, "You're a talent scout for Destiny Records?"

The confusion in her tone makes my lips arch. "Not exactly." When she glances at me with her adorable nose screwed up, I explain, "It's a long story. One neither of us have time to tackle right now." Even more so since glimmers of the woman I was interacting with earlier have resurfaced. I'm glad she's back, but I'm also aware it only gives me seconds to flee before I once again become snared by her hunter's trap.

After glancing at the clock displaying it's nearly 10 PM, Harlow nods in agreement. I thought her earlier mention of being awake since 3 AM was an exaggeration; only now am I realizing it wasn't.

"I could arrange to have your order delivered, but I'm not sure I should trust couriers with your shipment. They barely deliver my cake boxes in one piece, and they're empty during transport."

"Then why don't you bring them?"

I mentally slap myself. I'm supposed to be putting distance between us, not encouraging additional visits.

Harlow glides her hand around her scarcely lit bakery. "This doesn't run itself." She swivels on the spot as she silently contemplates. "I could deliver them before I open? It will be early, but your order will arrive safely."

"Alright, that could work. What time?" I try to act as if I didn't hear the hope in her voice. My attempts are half-assed.

She props her hip on the glistening counter before suggesting, "Around seven?"

I cringe. There is only one reason I wake up that early. It isn't for sugary bundles of joy. Although from the way Harlow's teeth rake her bottom lip as her eyes continually scan my body, I begin to wonder if cupcakes will be the only sweet thing on offer tomorrow?

Snubbing my disturbing—*and highly wishful*—inner monologue, I mutter, "I'll make sure someone is at my office then."

"Okay," Harlow agrees again, nodding more assertively this time. "Then it's set. I'll meet *you* at your office at 7 AM tomorrow."

Stealing my chance to reply that from here on out I must avoid her like the plague, she presses her lips to the edge of my mouth. Any hang-ups I'm having vanish in an instant when her sugar-scented breath fans my lips. She smells as scrumptious as I'm sure she tastes.

Pretending I don't have hair full of egg and a heart just as messy, I return her embrace before promptly retreating. With the business side of my brain overruled by its less astute counterpart, faking disinterest seems more of a choice than a requirement. I want to know if she tastes as sweet as she smells. I just wish I could find out without complicating things.

"Until tomorrow?" Harlow's voice is ten decibels lower than mine and one hundred times hotter.

Even though I command my head to shake, it bobbles instead. "Until tomorrow," I parrot, unworthy of the fight.

After a dip of my chin, I make a beeline for my town car idling at the curb. Harlow and I started our night as strangers, but I already know her well enough that I don't need to look at her to know she's eyeballing my backside for the umpteenth time this evening. Her heated gaze is felt from my egg-covered scalp to my sock-enclosed feet.

When I hit the sidewalk outside her bakery, I keep my eyes locked on my driver, praying his leering expression will stop me spinning on my heels and finishing what I started. I asked to kiss Harlow. She gave me permission without any hesitation, so why the fuck am I parading around town with an egg-smeared face and an erection?

The solution for my predicament is a more-than-willing participant, yet I'm walking away from what could potentially be something great because I've either become more like my father than I'd care to admit, or I'm even more spineless than I was when he was alive.

My driver's smile grows the closer I get to him. My staff have never seen me like this—wild and carefree. They see the man I had intended to show Harlow tonight. I'm not stern. I'm just smart. Well, I was until a woman who is as beautiful as she is mischievous blindsided me.

When I enter the warm cab of my Bentley, my driver's eyes stray to the rearview mirror. The halfhearted grin on Augustus' face turns smug when he observes my disheveled appearance in closeup detail. I glower at him, warning him I'm two seconds from blowing my top. I'm not. I just don't have a better defense, so I use the easy, more anticipated response.

After a quick swallow to relieve his throat of the rock my rueful glare lodged in there, Augustus pulls my car away from the curb. I wait for the lights of Harlow's bakery to shine like a star in the sky before shifting my gaze sideways.

"Sorry," Levi apologizes, his tone sincerer than his facial

expression. "If you had forewarned me of your plan of attack, I wouldn't have shown up tonight. I know you like getting your hands dirty, Cormack, but you left me flying blind."

His eyes scan my egg-smeared hair and ruined suit. "Although some may say my arrival was a godsend. I've had a door slammed in my face numerous times the past twelve months, but this is the first time Ms. Murphy has resorted to wasting food. With how deep her books are in the red, I'm surprised she can afford the loss."

He stops talking as his face lights up like a Christmas tree. "Ah, you've always been as clever as you are smart. Why didn't I think of this earlier? Don't negotiate with terrorists. Run them out of town. Her sales have already fallen from the makeshift bakeries we placed within a mile radius of her shop. Now we've got her wasting ingredients she can't afford to replace. Sheer brilliance. That's why you're the boss and I'm merely your pawn."

Before I can respond to his inaccurate statement—the part about me arriving at Harlow's bakery to purposely waste her products, not that we placed bakeries in her direct competition —Levi signals for Augustus to stop.

"Seriously, Levi? Again?" I ask when we come to a stop at the front of a Chinese restaurant on the outskirts of town. Although Levi's obsession with a pretty Asian woman is well known amongst our colleagues, I pretend it isn't, preferring to shift the focus away from me and my eggy night.

"This place serves the best dumplings in town." Levi throws a bundle of bills to Augustus, treating him like a taxi driver instead of a chauffeur/security detail. "Drop back in around an hour. I should be done with my meal by then."

"We all know you're not here for the dumplings," I grumble under my breath.

Levi shoots me a vicious sideways glare, revealing he heard my mumbled comment. "Just like I know you didn't pretend we didn't know each other for no reason."

I keep my mouth shut, once again having no plausible defense. I did go into Harlow's bakery with the intention of disclosing I'm a co-owner of the corporation attempting to buy her out. I left wondering who I am.

Harlow's bakery sits on a parcel of land I need to extend my record label from a thriving mid-sector business to a global entity. My company has been based in Hopeton the past two years, but my wish to relocate it to Ravenshoe are well known amongst community members. My investment in this region is as vigorous as my college friend and business partner, Isaac's. Our corporation, Colt Enterprises, is responsible for the massive increase in development and infrastructure in Ravenshoe the past four years.

Although I could live off my investments until my demise, financial stratagems and real estate takeovers are Isaac's babies. My passion has always resided in music production. I'm the sole owner of my record company, Destiny Records. I'm also its only talent scout. I'm so determined to see the little guy succeed, I dig through the trenches myself to find the next musical prodigy.

My methods are unheard of, but highly effective. Rise Up's skyrocketing success will be proof of that. It will reveal that I am not my father's son. I worked for every penny I have. I tunneled through the shit and built an empire worthy of its soon-to-be *Fortune 500* listing. Despite the words my father whispered on his death bed, I'm not a failure.

That's why I'll secure Harlow's bakery. Relocating Destiny Records to Ravenshoe has been in motion for years. I can't let anything or anyone get in the way of that. To restructure my plans to exclude Harlow's bakery would cost millions. I'd rather buy her out than hand more of my hard-earned money to the pessimists who constantly tell the optimists they can't do something.

With my family's name granting me access to over six billion dollars in assets and funds, I could forgo the dream I've been inching toward since my college days, but with the blood of a fox and the determination of a hound, I refuse to back down. I don't want my dad's money. I don't even want his last name, but I do want Harlow's bakery, and I'm willing to do anything to get it.

I'll even woo it away from her if I must.

Bound Series - Steamy Romance & BDSM

Chains (Marcus and Cleo)

Links (Marcus and Cleo)

Bound (Marcus and Cleo)

Restrained (Marcus and Cleo)

Psycho (Dexter)

Russian Mob Chronicles

Nikolai: A Mafia Prince Romance

Nikolai: Taking Back What's Mine

Nikolai: What's Left of Me

Nikolai: Mine to Protect

Asher: My Russian Revenge

Infinite Time Trilogy

Lady In Waiting (Regan)

Man in Queue (Regan)

Couple on Hold (Regan)

Standalones

Just Playin' (Presley and Willow)

COMING SOON:

Skitzo

Colby

Made in the USA
Coppell, TX
10 September 2020